* * *

Battle of Shadows

Book Three of the Battles of the Republic

* * *

By James Rosone
and
Brandon Ellis

* * *

Illustration © Tom Edwards
Tom EdwardsDesign.com

* * *

Published in conjunction with Front Line Publishing, Inc.

ISBN: 978-1-967436-28-6
Sun City Center, Florida, United States of America
Library of Congress Control Number: 2025918327

Table of Contents

Chapter 1:
Angels Hundred

Year 2098
RNS *Gallipoli*
Intus Orbit

Blake "Coop" Cooper lay on his bunk in the pilot quarters, staring at the ceiling and trying to decompress from another long day of flight ops. The bulkheads whirred with the constant vibration of the ship's engines—a sound now just as familiar as his own damn heartbeat after so long aboard the *Izumo*-class heavy orbital assault ship.

On his pillow and next to his ear, his Qpad chimed with an incoming message. He turned to face it, eyes wide. The screen showed, "FLEET PERSONNEL COMMAND — IMMEDIATE ATTENTION REQUIRED." He sat up quickly, heart skipping a beat.

Is this it? he wondered. *Lord, it just might be.*

The cramped quarters housed several pilots, their bunks stacked two high against opposite bulkheads. Personal belongings were crammed into small lockers. The overhead lighting always bugged him, and he simply hadn't gotten used to it. Regardless, Coop looked around. Had anyone else gotten the same alert? He looked at his bunkmates—several were asleep, but the ones on their own devices showed no recognition of receiving any important messages, which meant at that moment, they were oblivious to this notification that might change everything in Coop's life.

When he opened the message and read the words, a cold shock ran through him.

"Your application to join the 1st Special Tactics Wing has been ACCEPTED."

Accepted—the word reverberated in his mind.

What? No way!

He looked at the words a second time. To his surprise, he wasn't hallucinating. This was really happening.

"Balls the size of Texas," he whispered, remembering the recruitment ad's ridiculous language.

Closing his eyes, Coop's mind drifted back to about a month ago when he'd been scrolling through routine fleet correspondence during his off-duty hours. The pilot quarters had been quiet that night, just the steady sound of life support systems and the occasional snore from Bear's bunk. Buried among the usual administrative notices and training bulletins, he'd spotted something that stopped him cold. A special request, a recruitment advertisement, from Rear Admiral Dallas Travis, commander of the 1st Special Tactics Wing.

The message had been as blunt as it could possibly be: "Looking for Navy pilots with the right stuff and balls the size of Texas to become Tactical Air and Space Controllers."

Intrigued despite himself, Coop had clicked on the advertisement and discovered these were the shadowy operators he'd heard on the comms in those hair-raising close-air support missions during his brief stint flying AS-90 Reaper drones. Their voices on the comm had always sounded calm. They were professional. And deadly. He'd always wondered who had the nerves to coordinate orbital strikes and artillery support while embedded with Army units on hostile worlds. Turned out, many of them were Navy pilots like himself, wearing the coveted red berets of the Special Tactics Wing and working hand in glove with Republic Army forces.

As he'd read through the requirements that night, doubt began creeping in. Self-doubt clawed its way from the depths. The physical standards were more than brutal, the mental evaluations seemed legendary, and the specialty schools had washout rates that would make most pilots reconsider their career choices. He'd hesitated, finger hovering over the application button. Could he do this? The question had gnawed at him. The job description told of facilitating orbital strikes from Republic vessels, coordinating artillery support, and calling in close-air support from F-97 Orions, B-99 Raiders, and other Fleet assets. All while embedded with ground forces in the thick of combat.

Lieutenant Lincoln "Bear" Bowman was in his bunk across the narrow aisle, reading a worn paperback book almost extinct in this day and age. The muscular brute barely fit in the standard Navy bunk, and his feet hung over the edge.

"Bear," Coop whispered, trying not to wake the others. "I need to talk to you."

Bear looked up from his book. "What's up, Coop?"

"Follow me. Somewhere private."

Bear scrunched up his nose. "What did you do this time, Coop?" he pressed. "I'm not interested in any multilevel marketing program, if that's what this is about."

"A multi…what?" Coop shook his head. His stomach tightened. "Just come on."

Bear marked his page and swung his legs over the side of his bunk. They made their way quietly out of the quarters and down the corridor.

"What's this about?" Bear asked, his voice echoing slightly off the metal walls.

"Keep your voice down," Coop whispered.

"Is this about the TASC thing?" Bear pressed. "You know those guys are crazy, right?"

Coop's stomach tightened. *How did Bear know?* He sighed and pulled out his datapad, showing him the message. "Well…" he said.

Bear's eyes narrowed as he read. He shook his head. "Coop, the skipper is going to kill you if you somehow get accepted. You better hope they send you a denial and no one finds out." He paused, looking at the screen again. "Wait. This says accepted."

"Yeah."

"And you just got made squadron cyber expert. That's one of your new extra duties. Why the hell would you—"

"I know."

Bear ran a hand through his hair. "Man, Strike is going to lose his mind. You know how he feels about pilots trying to transfer out of his squadron."

They walked back to the quarters in silence, Coop's head down in thought, Bear crossing his arms, scratching at his chin. Coop climbed back into his bunk, pushing his great-great-grandfather's diary aside. The leather-bound journal had been his constant companion during difficult moments. Right now, however, he needed to focus on the present.

Bear got back up. "Be back. See you in a bit."

"All right."

Where the hell is he going?

Coop opened his Qpad again. There was the message. He stared at the acceptance notification. Kept his eyes on it. Wouldn't blink. A mixture of excitement and terror coursed through his very cells. This was really happening. He was going to become a TASC, a Tactical Air and Space Controller, one of the elite controllers who bridged the gap between Navy firepower and Army operations.

The red beret. The specialized training. The chance to prove himself in ways that went beyond flying drones from the safety of the *Gallipoli*. It was everything he'd wanted and everything he'd feared.

Before he could fully process what his acceptance meant, another message appeared on his Qpad: "Report to Squadron Commander immediately."

The air in his lungs seemed to freeze. Somehow, word had already gotten out.

Ten minutes later, Coop stood at attention outside the squadron commander's office. He straightened his posture, set his jaw, and prepared to meet whatever came next, even as panic burned at his gut. His mind spun with possible explanations. None of them sounded good.

The hatch slid open with a soft hiss.

"Enter," came the crisp command from inside.

Coop stepped through and froze. Bear was already there, standing rigid beside Commander Spencer O'Connell and Commander Lance Danning, call sign "Strike." Strike looked like he'd swallowed a plasma torpedo.

The tension in the room was thick.

"Report," O'Connell ordered.

His expression was unreadable. Coop snapped to attention and delivered his standard greeting. O'Connell let him stand there. The silence stretched. His eyes bored into Coop like Zodark Vulture starfighters ready to kill.

The commander seemed to be deciding how to proceed. Whatever bombshell he was about to drop, it wasn't going to be pleasant.

"Are you two unhappy with me?" O'Connell began.

His voice was deceptively calm. He looked between Coop and Bear like a predator sizing up prey.

"Are you dissatisfied with your jobs as pilots? Because I'm trying to understand why two of my supposedly reliable officers would go behind my back and apply for transfers without so much as a word to their commanding officer."

His gaze fixed on Coop. "Did I make a mistake trusting you with that extra duty as squadron cyber instructor? Because that's what I'm starting to think. That I made a bonehead move. Did something you couldn't handle. Too much stress, was it?"

Coop opened his mouth to respond. No words came out.

How could he explain himself? Should he say that he hadn't expected to be accepted? That it had been more impulse than calculation? The weight of his commander's disappointment was crushing, he thought as Bear shifted uncomfortably beside him.

They'd both stepped in it now. No backing out.

"Sir, I—"

"I wasn't finished, Cooper."

O'Connell's voice cut through the air like a blade. Coop's mouth snapped shut.

Strike hadn't said a word yet. His jaw was clenched so tight Coop thought it might crack. The squadron leader's reputation for being a hardass was well earned, and this situation was about to make it worse.

"For reasons that escape my understanding," O'Connell continued, "and perhaps because the Fleet has run out of more highly qualified candidates, both of these officers have been selected to attend training for the 9th Special Tactics Squadron."

Coop's jaw nearly hit the deck. He turned to stare at Bear in shock.

Bear? Bear filled out the application too?

"Bear…" Coop's voice trailed off as the realization hit him. "Don't tell me…"

Bear just gave him a look that said "obviously."

Coop felt a mix of relief and terror. Relief that he wouldn't be going through this alone. Terror at what they'd both gotten themselves into. That Bear had applied without telling him was almost as surprising as his own acceptance.

"You think this is going to be fun?" O'Connell's voice cut through their moment.

The temperature in the room seemed to drop ten degrees.

"Clearly, neither of you did any research about what you've volunteered for. The training has a seventy percent washout rate, and should you somehow survive that nightmare, the two-year survival rate for TASCs is just thirty-four percent."

He paused. Let that sink in.

"That's right. Only thirty-four out of a hundred volunteers are still breathing at the end of their first tour."

The blood drained from Coop's face. The reality of what he'd signed up for hit him like a meteor strike. Beside him, Bear's confident expression crumbled. The same terrible mathematics sank in.

Seventy percent washout rate. Thirty-four percent survival rate.

Those weren't odds. They were a death sentence with paperwork.

But even as fear clawed at his gut, Coop felt something else stirring. Determination. The damn opposite of doubt. His dad hadn't raised a quitter. At least that was one thing he did well. He'd be damned if he'd let statistics scare him away from this chance.

Strike finally spoke up. "Sir, if I may. These are two of my best pilots. Cooper especially has shown exceptional skill in drone operations. Losing them both—"

"Is exactly what's going to happen," O'Connell finished. "Because they've already made their choice. Without consulting their chain of command. Without considering the impact on squadron readiness. Without thinking at all, apparently."

The commander's gaze swept between them again. "You have twenty-four hours to pack your gear. The next rotator shuttle to Earth leaves tomorrow, and you'll be on it."

He stood up from behind his desk. "Dismissed."

Chapter 2:
Acceptable Risk

Year 2098
RNS *Gallipoli*
Intus Orbit

Coop walked into the squad bay to find the usual evening routines disrupted by hushed conversations and sidelong glances. All aimed at him. The cramped space, lined with personal lockers and featuring a few worn chairs arranged around a small table, had always been their sanctuary. A place where the squadron gathered to decompress and maintain the bonds that kept them functioning as a unit.

Did I step in some cow manure on the way here or something? What's going on? Coop thought.

Lucky sat cross-legged on one of the chairs while Ninja leaned against his locker with arms crossed. Raven, Phantom, and Ajax had formed a loose semicircle, their expressions ranging from confusion to barely concealed hurt. Other pilots meandered around, some sitting as if waiting for an explanation.

Bear strode into the bay behind him, getting the same looks. Then it hit Coop. Word had most likely spread through the squadron's informal networks, and fast. Now they both faced the collective stare.

Great... just... great...

"So," Lucky said. "Special Tactics Wing, huh?"

The words floated, slowly descending in anticipation of a response. Coop worked his jaw, trying to find the right reply. Why did he feel like he'd been caught stealing squadron funds?

"Who told you?" Bear asked, leaning against the nearest bulkhead.

"Does it matter?" Phantom replied. "The question is why we had to hear it from someone else."

Bear chuckled. "You sound like my ex-girlfriend."

Nobody laughed.

Ajax shifted in his chair. "I thought we were tight, you know? All of us."

"We are tight," Coop said.

"Bullcrap." Raven shook his head. "You don't apply for suicide missions without telling your wingman. Not if you're tight."

The words hit hard. Raven had been his wingman on thirty-seven missions. Thirty-seven times they'd watched each other's backs, coordinated strikes, pulled each other out of the fire.

"Did we screw something up?" Lucky asked, and Coop caught the tremor in her voice she was trying to hide. "Because if we did something—"

"No." Coop's voice came out sharper than intended. "This isn't about you guys."

"Then what's it about?" Phantom rose from his chair. "Because from where I'm sitting, it looks like you're abandoning ship for some glory-seeking…"

"Glory?" Bear stepped forward, folding his arms across his chest. "You think a seventy percent washout rate is glory?"

"I think leaving without a word to your squadronmates is some chicken stuff if I've ever seen it," Ninja said. "And I think applying behind our backs means you never trusted us enough to talk it through."

"Talk what through?" Ajax demanded. "The part where they decided we weren't worth staying for? Or the part where they figured ground-pounding was more important than flying with us?"

Lucky uncrossed her legs and leaned forward. "Right now, it feels like all this time having your back meant jack to you."

The accusation landed like a swift jab to the nose. These weren't just fellow pilots. They were his chosen family. The people who'd pulled him through his worst missions, who'd celebrated when he finally got his act together, who'd covered for him when Strike was ready to write him off as a screw-up.

Raven stood up slowly. "Thirty-seven missions, Coop. Thirty-seven times I've been your wingman. How many times did I save your ass when you got too aggressive on target runs?"

"Raven—"

"How many times did you save mine? Because I remember every single one. And you couldn't be bothered to mention you were thinking about bailing? Not once?"

The hurt in Raven's eyes…

This was the guy who knew his flying style better than anyone, who could anticipate his moves before he made them, who'd trusted him dozens of times over.

"Listen"—Coop rubbed the back of his neck, eyes on the floor—"I know how this looks."

Ajax leaned back in his chair. "Who's going to cover our shifts while you're off playing soldier? The squadron's already running thin, and now we lose two experienced pilots for what? So you can call in air strikes from a foxhole?"

"It's about… finding out what I'm made of, on my own," Coop said, finding the words coming slowly as he tried to articulate the restless energy that'd been building for months.

The whole room shifted. At that moment, Coop realized he'd chosen the wrong words.

"So we're not good enough for you anymore?" Ninja said.

"That's not what I meant."

"Then what did you mean?" Raven stepped closer. "Because it sure as hell sounds like you're saying years of combat missions with us was just marking time… that we're just enjoying ourselves, that this is just a walk in the park."

Coop met his wingman's eyes. "My great-great-grandfather flew P-51s in World War Two. My grandfather, my father… they all served with distinction. They all answered the call when they felt they needed to answer it."

After letting out a sigh, Coop continued, "I screwed up when I first got to the Navy." He met each of their eyes in turn. "Made some bad calls, questioned orders I should have followed. The Cooper name used to mean something in military circles, and I tarnished it. This is my chance to fix it."

"And you're taking Bear with you too?" Ninja pressed. "Honestly, this is crap."

Bear cleared his throat. "For me, it's different. I've been flying drones for so many years, I can't even count anymore. Good at it, sure, but I keep thinking about the ground troops who need support up close. Someone willing to get dirty alongside them."

He looked around the room. "I want to be boots on the ground, making a difference face-to-face. Drone work's important, don't get me wrong, but I feel my place is down in the trenches. That may change, because I might get my ass scared out of me…" Bear trailed off, a confused grimace twisting his face. "Well, that came out weirder than I meant." He shook his head. "But what I'm saying is I might be back here sooner than you realize. Sometimes change is a good thing, makes you know where you fit in the most."

Phantom sat back down heavily. "So, what happens to mission tempo when you're gone? Who picks up the slack? Or did you not bother thinking about how this affects squadron readiness?"

"The skipper will figure it out," Bear said.

"The skipper's already pissed about losing two experienced pilots," Ninja pointed out. "And now the rest of us get to fly extra missions to cover for your career moves."

Lucky's expression softened. "You know, I get wanting to prove yourself. I don't like it, but I get it."

Raven looked off in thought. "The survival rate for Special Tactics is what, forty percent over two years?"

"Something like that," Bear admitted.

"And you're both OK with those odds? Because the rest of us aren't OK with watching our friends go get themselves killed for no good reason."

"The odds are what they are," Coop said quietly. "I have to do this, Raven. For me."

He looked around at his friends' faces, seeing the mix of anger, hurt, and grudging respect.

"And if it gets you killed?" Lucky's voice was quiet now, the anger replaced by something rawer.

Phantom shook his head. "You're both insane."

"Probably." Bear grinned, some of his usual humor returning. "Well, not me, but…"

With a bigger smile, Bear jokingly gestured toward Coop.

Everyone chuckled but Raven, who stepped up to Coop, close enough that they were almost nose to nose. "Thirty-seven missions," he said quietly. "Don't make them meaningless by getting yourself killed in some damn foxhole. Understand, Lieutenant?"

Coop smiled. "Understood."

"We ship out tomorrow," Bear said into the silence.

"Tomorrow?" Lucky's voice cracked slightly. "You really weren't going to tell us until you were gone."

The room fell into silence a second time. The anger seemed to have turned into a bit of acceptance. Maybe. Or just exhaustion.

Ninja finally spoke up. "Don't get yourselves killed on purpose, you idiots. We've invested too much time in keeping you alive to have you throw it away."

"We'll try not to disappoint you," Bear said.

"See that you don't," Lucky replied.

Chapter 3:
Lessons in Command

Year 2098
Fort Moore
Columbus, Georgia
Earth

The transport's engines whirred beneath Coop's boots as he stared through the small porthole. After years stationed above Intus, Earth looked impossibly blue. The swirl of white clouds over familiar terrain made his chest tighten in a way he hadn't expected.

Home.

Intus had its beauty. Those mountain ranges and ancient forests full of giant trees stretching for hundreds of kilometers. Earth was different. It was the planet where he'd learned to walk. Where his mother still lived in that small house outside of Charleston, South Carolina. Where his father had taught him how to fly planes while doing nothing else but try to strip Coop of any personality, to kick all ego out, and to chisel his self-worth down to nil.

He should at least call his mom when this training cycle finished. Should, but probably wouldn't. Time had a way of getting away from him.

"Thirty seconds!" Lieutenant Colonel Braggs called from the front of the Osprey's cabin.

Coop checked his gear one final time. Standard atmospheric jump kit, nothing fancy. His first of five qualifying drops for the TASC program. The guy next to him, Ortiz, was running through his checklist. Another trainee, Specialist Sawyer, sat across the aisle, maintaining the thousand-yard stare of someone trying not to think too hard about stepping out of a perfectly good aircraft.

"Ten seconds!"

Bear grinned at him from two seats down, then dipped his head at Coop, and Coop nodded back.

The rear ramp dropped. Georgia's pine forests spread out like a green carpet below. Wind roared through the cabin.

"Go! Go! Go!"

Coop stepped into the void.

The initial rush never got old. That moment when gravity took hold and yanked him earthward, when his brain screamed against what his body was doing. Wind tore at his jumpsuit as he fell, the transport shrinking to a speck above him.

Earth filled his vision. Real Earth, not some holographic display or filtered viewport. The Chattahoochee River curved through the landscape below, its dark water visible as it wound between the tree lines. Interstate highways carved straight lines through the wilderness. Somewhere down there, people were driving to work, drinking coffee, living ordinary lives that didn't involve jumping out of a troop transport.

His altimeter read fifteen thousand feet. Bear was somewhere above him, the brute of the man probably enjoying the free fall. Ortiz and Sawyer were black shadows against the green below, maintaining good separation. Twelve other trainees from their class were scattered across the sky like black specks, along with three instructors keeping overwatch. Twenty jumpers total. All of them falling toward Georgia's pines at terminal velocity.

Six weeks of training at Fort Moore had led to this moment. When Coop had first arrived at the sprawling Georgia base, he'd expected something similar to his initial pilot training—structured but familiar. The difference? This time, he was part of a temporary duty assignment that would fundamentally change how he served.

Twelve thousand feet. Time to get serious.

Coop spread his arms and legs, stabilizing his descent. The wind resistance tugged at his gear, and he made minor adjustments to his body position. The 1st Special Tactics Wing was expanding, creating the new 9th Special Tactics Squadron to meet growing Republic Army demands for close-air support coordination. Coop would remain a Republic Navy pilot, but his new role as a TASC, pronounced "Tassee," would embed him directly with Army ground forces.

Ten thousand feet. Forty-seven hours in the orbital assault simulators had prepared him for this. Learning to coordinate strikes while falling through virtual battlefields. Basic infantry skills he'd never needed as a pilot. Communications protocols for working with Army units.

Eight thousand feet. He reached for his rip cord handle, fingers finding the grip. He'd completed eight practice drops from standard aircraft over the past three weeks, getting comfortable with the gear and procedures. Today marked the beginning of his final qualification phase. Five jumps that would determine whether he earned his TASC rating or washed out back to drone pilot duty.

Six thousand feet. Perfect altitude for deployment.

He pulled.

The drogue chute burst out first, followed immediately by the main canopy. The harness bit into his shoulders as deceleration slammed through his body. Above him, the rectangular chute filled with air, its tug reassuring against the straps.

Something felt off. A slight wobble in his descent, nothing dramatic. His left steering line felt loose in his hand.

Coop looked up at his canopy. One of the steering lines had stretched more than its partner, giving him uneven control. Not dangerous, just sloppy. He compensated by adjusting his body position and using more right-side input.

The position traced its roots to the old United States Air Force, when they were called TACPs, for Tactical Air Control Party. Now they were TASCs, still Navy but working hand in glove with the Republic Army wherever the fight took them.

The ground rushed up to meet him. Coop bent his knees, held his feet together, and prepared for impact. The landing came hard but clean—a textbook parachute landing fall that sent him rolling across the drop zone's sandy soil.

He popped the canopy release and gathered his lines as Bear landed fifty meters away with considerably less grace. The big man hit, rolled, and came up grinning.

"Show-off," Bear called over.

Lieutenant Colonel Braggs approached as Coop finished packing his chute. The colonel's wrinkled face showed years of squinting into too much sunlight and making too many hard decisions.

"How'd that feel, Lieutenant?"

"Good, sir. Slight control issue on the left steering line, but nothing major."

Braggs nodded, examining the line in question. "Stretched toggle. Happens when you don't pay close enough attention during the prejump inspection. That line was probably a centimeter longer than regulation when you geared up."

"Copy that, sir."

"Won't kill you, but it'll make your approach less precise." Braggs handed him the line. "Check everything twice—your gear, your buddy's gear—then check it again. The enemy won't give you points for close enough."

"Understood, sir."

"Good jump otherwise. Clean exit, good body position, textbook landing." Braggs gave him a nod. "Two more familiarization drops, then we start the fun stuff."

As the colonel walked away, Coop looked back up at the Georgia sky. Somewhere above those clouds was the transport heading back to base. Somewhere beyond that was space, and Intus and New Eden and his old Jolly Rogers squadron on the RNS *Gallipoli*, and the war that had brought him here.

For now, he was home. Feet on familiar ground, breathing.

Chapter 4:
Middle Reach

Year 2098
RNS *Poseidon*
Middle Reach
Sector 8

Ripley Willis Lee sat in the command chair, something he'd been doing way too much. One of these days, he'd need to get back to working out as frequently as he used to. The few extra pounds that had expanded his midsection over the past year were evidence he needed more physical activity, and he couldn't continue to ignore it.

He studied the tactical action map. The TAM glowed blue in the dim light of the bridge. The holographic readout showed their current position in Middle Reach, a sector between Rass and Intus, space notorious for its dense fields of cosmic debris. His ship sat anchored in the center, a small green triangle. Friendly vessels blinked in formation around *Poseidon*.

"Sato, status report on our task force," Lee said.

Lieutenant Commander Noriko Sato glared at the small holo screen projecting from her seat's armrest. "All ships maintaining formation, sir. No anomalies detected in their systems, or around them."

"Rhom, bring up the fleet status," Lee asked.

"Aye, sir." Lieutenant Connor Rhom typed on his interface. The tactical display changed, highlighting their small task force.

The Republic ships appeared in green: the frigate RNS *Bolt*; the RNS *Cobalt*, another frigate; and their trio of corvettes—the RNS *Polaris*, the RNS *Scimitar*, and the RNS *Horizon*.

Alongside them, shown in blue, cruised the Primord vessels under Captain Dharek's command. The battleship *Ek* led the formation. The *Kulente* and the *Nyx* flanked their flagship, while the *Simsu*, *Sulvaar*, and *Vora* brought up the rear guard.

It still amazed Lee how completely these ships had recovered from their recent battles—not only the Primord vessels but his own Earther ships as well. The Kita Shipyard's Primord engineers had worked miracles, as always, returning the vessels to service quickly, and in some cases better than they were before they were damaged.

"Remarkable work by the Primord repair crews," Lee said. "Those ships look better than new."

"The Kita yards never cease to amaze," Sato replied. "Their engineering teams could teach our dockyards back home a thing or two."

Lee settled back. Here in this sector, every week brought reports of new Zodark activity—new threats needing to be neutralized before any major offensive at Rass, another Primord planet awaiting liberation, could begin. The mission clock kept ticking backward instead of forward.

Lee thought about the Rass invasion again. It was another Primord world to liberate from Zodark control, another battle where Republic forces would bleed alongside their Primord allies. Three hundred years of Zodark occupation had left deep scars on the Rass star system. The Galactic Empire alliance, notably the Altairians, Primords, and Earthers, wanted it back. Apparently, a critical stargate resided there, and many worlds and moons in the Rass system were rich in minerals needed for shipbuilding and fuel sources. Plus, it would create a buffer zone, protecting other systems. This was, of course, in addition to the moral good of being able to free Primord citizens under Zodark occupation.

With the Rass invasion on the docket soon and new Zodark activity patterns emerging across the sector, they'd have to make do with what they had at the moment.

"Sir," Ensign Mark Baldry said, "long-range sensors are picking up unusual debris patterns at heading three-one mark two."

Lee studied the readout. The Middle Reach was a graveyard of shattered planets from past wars dating back thousands of years, but something about this particular field felt wrong. "Analysis?"

"Configuration suggests recent weapons fire, but the decay patterns don't match known Zodark ordnance."

"Keep monitoring that debris field," Lee ordered. "Reynolds, maintain our current heading but adjust our formation to give that area a wide berth. The last thing we need is to stumble into another Zodark trap."

He'd already done that enough times in the past. Lee's experience had taught him to be more cautious in his approach to patrolling unknown sectors.

"Aye, sir," Lieutenant Lewis James Reynolds replied, patching in the course correction.

Two months, thought Lee. That was what they'd been given—two months to gather intelligence, to run counteroperations, and to watch these anomalies across the sector. The Rass invasion would have to wait while the powers that be made sense of evolving Zodark tactics.

He watched the debris field slowly drift past on the main holo. The Middle Reach had seen more than its share of destruction, and Lee had a feeling they'd be adding to that tally before long.

"Captain Dharek of the *Ek* is hailing us," Lieutenant Lucia Rodriguez said from her communications station.

Lee held back a sigh. Relations with the Primord captain had grown strained over the past weeks, and that was putting it gently. "Patch him through."

In a way, it was Lee's fault. He knew this, but his ego kept holding him back no matter how much he chipped away at it. Dharek was in charge of the entire task force, and Lee was only in charge of his Earther battle group. Dharek outranked Lee, so he'd need to get over it quickly. Thing was, he didn't like the guy. He seemed…pompous, entitled, or whatever. The guy held this aura of being better than everyone else, especially Lee.

Lee stood at his command position, shoulders squared as Dharek's image materialized on the main viewscreen. The Primord captain's eyes stared at Lee with an intense boldness the guy was no doubt born with, while his pointed ears and nose gave him quite a different appearance that Lee still hadn't quite gotten used to.

"Captain Lee, I would like to show you something of importance," Dharek said. There was no warmth in the man's voice. There never was.

"Go ahead, Captain."

A holographic star map appeared on the holo, overlaying the debris field ahead. Glowing lines traced patrol routes through the sector as Dharek gestured with long fingers.

"These debris clusters provide optimal concealment for Zodark scout ships," Dharek said. "We will modify our patrol pattern to incorporate these specific vectors." Red lines slashed across the map, cutting paths through the field. "My tactical analysis suggests focusing our sensor sweeps along these trajectories will maximize our detection probability."

Lee shifted his weight, crossing his arms as he studied the proposed routes. The change in body language no doubt betrayed his growing irritation with Dharek's imperious tone, but Lee didn't care who noticed.

"Your current Republic formations leave significant blind spots," Dharek continued, highlighting gaps in their standard patrol grid. "The spacing between your vessels is inefficient. The response time to potential threats would be delayed by approximately forty-one seconds. Fix that."

"That's an… interesting perspective, Captain," Lee replied, his emphasis carrying a hint of condescension he figured only Sato caught from her position beside him. What he wanted to say was, *However, our current patterns are based on years of tactical experience in similar sectors.* Instead, he replied, "I'll fix it, sir."

"You have a problem with this?"

"Negative, sir."

"As you know, we are here in this sector because of Zodark anomalies we have detected, and we need to investigate. What are your thoughts, Commander?"

The subtle reference to Lee's rank irked him a bit. "Our current spacing allows us to maintain optimal sensor coverage while preserving our ability to rapidly concentrate forces. I'm not open to being ambushed again or walking into a trap, something Space Command, and especially Captain Eamon Roberts at FOB Bulwark and Captain Sornvek or Admiral Velmiran, the head of Primord Intelligence, don't want either."

"Negative, Captain Lee," Dharek chided. "Perhaps it would be considered optimal by Republic standards, passed along to you via their fear." Dharek paused. "The Primord fleet has developed more sophisticated approaches, ones not based in fear and silly ideas about traps. I know you may be unaware of Zodark movements because you do not share our predictive movement analysis, but this recommendation is based on intelligence. Do you have more to explain? If so, please do. I am taking my time to understand you…humans…time I hope is not wasted. Otherwise, I would simply give orders, and you would take them. Does this make sense, Commander?"

"It does, sir. Now, to answer your question, I think your proposed vectors would fragment our formation and leave us vulnerable to divide-and-conquer tactics."

Sato gave Lee a look, and he could tell she bit her tongue, and hard.

"You assume the Zodarks would recognize the opportunity," Dharek said. "Their tactical doctrine has grown… predictable. And bad."

"Understood."

"I do not think you do, so I would like you to share with us— why?" Dharek replied.

"First, Captain, can you explain the anomalies we've been tracking? The dark settlements, the overrun colonies—their behavior is anything *but* predictable lately."

It was rare that a lower rank would speak with a higher rank in such a manner, but Dharek had asked for it, so Lee gladly delivered.

"Which is precisely why we must adapt our methods," Dharek insisted. "This task force will change its current formation and patrol routes. Clear? I will be sending you the updates shortly, and you will follow orders."

"Understood."

"Good. Dharek out."

Why's he being a pain? There's no need. What would Captain Oldendorf do? Lee wondered. *Eh, he'd probably be perfectly fine. Like water off a duck's back.*

Nonetheless, it was just a month ago when his task force had faced down a Zodark battle group in Sectors 2 and 3. Lee thought Dharek needed to get a clue or get off his back. They needed to work as one, not against one another.

During the last campaign, they'd not only survived but prevailed, securing their primary objective despite heavy opposition. The memory of that victory made Dharek's current attitude all the more grating. Lee had made the difficult call to maintain focus on destroying the Zodark outpost when Dharek had flagged them for support, requesting they shift fire to screen a Primord battleship, the *Vrallin's*

Spear. Lee had ordered Rhom to engage with Havoc missiles but refused to split their guns or alter their assault vector. His decision had been tactically sound. The outpost was their objective, and the Primords were there to keep Zodarks off their backs. The thing was, because of that decision, some of the Primord ships hadn't made it. Even though both Republic and Primord military analysis had validated Lee's decision as strategically correct, the personal cost to Dharek—the loss of several ships and crews—had created a rift between the commanders that tactical justifications couldn't bridge.

Lee gritted his teeth and clenched his fist before relaxing, taking a deep, long breath. He looked at Sato. "Thoughts?"

"Sir, the Primords approach command dynamics… differently," Sato replied. "Their directness isn't meant as disrespect, sir. It's deeply cultural. It's their way of educating, even if they're wrong, and it's rare they believe they're incorrect, especially with other species. Let them teach. Take what you will. They value absolute candor over diplomatic phrasing. Captain Dharek likely believes he's showing respect by asking for your tactical assessment so openly, and he might be getting irritated you're not taking it in with a smile. Also, understanding their perspective might help us collaborate more effectively. The Primords' analytical capabilities have proven valuable before."

Lee acknowledged her point with a nod, though he viewed it as more than mere cultural differences. There was something his guy didn't like about Lee's style—or it could be deeper than that. And it probably was.

Lee's shoulders dropped a tinge. The constant friction with Dharek drained him more than he wanted, as if the guy was purposely finding ways to annoy Lee.

Perhaps I'm tired. I've gotta get over it, he told himself.

"Lieutenant Rhom, you have the conn," Lee said, rising from his chair. "Commander Sato, join me for lunch? We should discuss these patrol strategies."

"Aye, sir," Rhom acknowledged, moving to take command.

As they walked off the bridge, Lee's mind burned over Dharek's orders. To Lee, their current tactics were sound. There was no need to change unless necessary, and nothing was presenting itself as necessary. He'd led successful operations across multiple sectors, earned commendations for his strategic innovations. Yet here was

Dharek, presenting his commands as if they were obvious improvements any competent captain would have already implemented.

"The arboretum should be relatively quiet this time of day," Sato observed as they entered the corridor. "Lunch there?"

"Always. Favorite place, as you know," Lee said, striding down the corridor.

"Mine too."

Lee barely heard her, still fuming over Dharek's attitude. The Primord captain's words echoed in his mind. Sato and Lee would discuss it over lunch. Lee knew one thing for certain—he wouldn't let Dharek's arrogance compromise the safety of his battle group.

Before they could reach the arboretum, Rodriguez's voice came through Lee's personal comm device.

"Captain, priority communication from FOB Bulwark. Captain Roberts has sent you a recording."

Lee stopped midstride. "Route it to my ready room," he replied. "Sato will join me."

When they entered, Lee activated the viewscreen. Commander Eamon Roberts's face appeared, the RNS *Australia*'s command center visible behind him. Roberts's stern expression looked even more severe than usual.

"This message is being sent to Captain Lee and Captain Dharek," Roberts said with a crisp professional tone.

Lee unconsciously straightened his posture.

Roberts leaned forward slightly. "I've been reviewing the intelligence from your sector sweeps. The anomalies you've been tracking are consistent with what we're seeing in three other sectors. Space Command believes these are preparatory moves for something significant."

Roberts nodded. "As Captain Dharek has surmised, we believe the Zodarks are positioning assets. What you're doing out there is critical to the Rass campaign. If we launch without understanding these anomalies, or if there are hidden Zodark outposts we haven't identified, we could be walking into a strategic catastrophe. Based on our intelligence analysis and the limited sensor data acquired from that sector, we assess with high confidence the presence of a Zodark forward operating base. Multiple indicators and warning signs are consistent with established Zodark deployment patterns. While we cannot guarantee with absolute certainty without visual confirmation, all available intelligence points to an active installation that meets our targeting criteria. We are proceeding with operational planning accordingly.

"Your task force is our eyes and ears, gentlemen, so remember this," Roberts continued. "The Rass invasion planning is complete, but we can't execute until we understand what we're seeing in Middle Reach. The disappearance of vessels and drones last month wasn't random.

"Now, upon positively identifying the outpost, you'll conduct a thorough tactical assessment. If circumstances permit, your primary objective is to neutralize the installation while gathering all available intelligence. However, if you encounter defenses beyond your combat capability or face unacceptable risk to your task force, you're authorized to withdraw and return with collected reconnaissance data. The preservation of your force takes precedence over the destruction of the target. Exercise your judgment as task force commander, Captain Dharek. I expect your thorough assessment before commitment to decisive engagement.

"Captain Lee, I understand you're expanding our search patterns," Roberts continued. "And Captain Dharek has given some tactical adjustments based on Primord sensor capabilities. The Primords' predictive analytics have proven valuable."

Roberts's eyes narrowed slightly. "The success of this campaign depends on seamless coordination between Republic and Primord forces," he said pointedly. "If you two can't figure out how to integrate your tactical approaches now, we're going to have a serious problem."

Lee almost found himself defending himself against the recording but realized quickly enough that Roberts wouldn't be able to hear or respond to him.

"I don't need the details of whatever's causing friction," Roberts said, as if anticipating an interruption. "What I need is for both of you to sort it out. Captain Lee, you've proven yourself a capable tactician. Captain Dharek, your record speaks for itself. Together, you represent the future of this alliance's military operations."

Roberts leaned back slightly and cleared his throat. "Let me be clear. I'm not here to hold hands or mediate personality conflicts.

You're officers of your respective groups. Act like it. Figure out how to leverage each other's strengths or I'll find commanders who can.

"The intelligence you gather in the next weeks will determine whether we move forward with Rass sooner rather than later," Roberts said. "Those anomalies could be anything from sensor ghosts to a full Zodark battle group preparing to hit our flank. Find out what we're dealing with. Do it together."

Roberts checked something offscreen. "I've authorized additional reconnaissance drones for your task force. They'll arrive within thirty-six hours. Use them to expand your search capacity. We're reaching beyond communication range, so you two will be on your own soon. Work together.

"Roberts out."

The transmission ended and Roberts vanished, leaving Lee and Sato staring at the empty viewscreen.

"Well," Sato said after a moment, "that was unexpected."

"He's right," Lee admitted. "If we can't work with Dharek now, how the hell are we supposed to coordinate when we engage the enemy?"

"Roberts has changed," Sato observed. "Three or four months ago, he would've just dictated tactics and questioned your command decisions."

Lee nodded slowly. "Maybe we all need to change a little." He tapped his comm. "Bridge, contact the *Ek*. I'd like to arrange a meeting with Captain Dharek. In person this time."

Chapter 5:
Standing Orders

Year 2098
RNS *Poseidon*
Middle Reach
Sector 8

The main viewscreen stretched across the bridge's forward bulkhead. Earlier, Lee had had a one-on-one conversation with Dharek, and matters seemed… the same. Not much had changed.

In time, things will improve, Lee believed.

On the display, a field of artificial gravity wells littered Sector 8. These spatial distortions were the result of failed terraforming projects, abandoned colonies where massive gravity generators still whirred away, their degrading systems warping the fabric of space-time. Some were ancient, dating back to the first wave of colonization attempts from species known and unknown, while others bore the scars of recent evacuations during Zodark incursions.

The thing was, what stood on the holodisplay before Lee was only a training exercise. Those gravity wells indeed existed across space, however, not in this sector… not yet. Not that they'd seen. They were out there, though, some detected in Sectors 5 and 13. Practicing ways around and through them and using them to tactical advantage had become standard training for Republic Fleet crews.

From his command chair, Lee watched the tactical display track each gravity signature. Every well told a story: a moon colony's atmosphere generators running wild decades after its inhabitants had fled, a planetary engineering project's gravity anchors creating dangerous eddies in space, or asteroid mining operations where stabilization fields had collapsed into a myriad of vortices. They were beautiful and deadly at the same time.

The last three hours of training focused on drilling his crew and his battle group on gravity well navigation, teaching them to read the subtle signs of gravitational shifts and how to use the distortions to mask their movements or amplify their weapons' effectiveness. What had once been seen as obstacles were now opportunities waiting to be exploited—something Lee relished doing.

Lee's love for the military had started in his childhood, when he'd crouched in the Wyoming woods with his grandfather's old rifle, lining up shots on tin cans and tree knots. Even then, something had clicked. He had an inner knowing, an inner feeling. He knew how a shot would travel, where it needed to go. Heck, he'd become an Olympic gold medalist because of his instinct for the perfect shot. That instinct had grown into something bigger now, yet the core feeling hadn't changed. He just knew where things would end up; he could see flight paths and angles, leaving others scratching their heads. He often predicted enemy movement before it happened. It was a gift that had turned him from a kid with a rifle into one of the Fleet's most feared tacticians. It didn't matter if it was a bullet or a battleship's mass driver—to Lee, they were all just objects in motion.

These days, other than rare sessions at the range, he channeled his gift into fleet coordination and weapons placement. The bridge was his shooting perch now. The tactical display was his scope, and the entire group of ships was his ammunition. There was an art to it. It gave him the same satisfaction he'd felt as a boy leading a target, only now it had multiplied across three dimensions of space and dozens of vessels moving in concert.

"Helm, maintain course through the wells. Tactical, continue tracking gravitational distortion levels," Lee said.

Reynolds punched in commands across his nav console. "Gravitational distortion increasing to twenty percent, sir. Adjusting engine output to compensate."

Rhom's voice cut through. "Sir… new contacts." There was something in his tone that made Lee's hand freeze over his chair's holo.

"Verify those signatures, Lieutenant," Lee said.

"Confirmed, sir. Two Zodark battleships, bearing zero-four-niner. Definitely not part of the simulation."

Lee frowned, studying the tactical display. He saw the signatures of two battleships…just two. His mind spun. Zodarks rarely ever deployed in such small numbers, especially not against a larger force. Even with the Zodark vessels' large tonnage, it was tactically unsound. The Zodarks were aggressive, but they weren't stupid.

"Open group-wide channel," Lee began, but Rodriguez cut him off.

"Sir, incoming transmission from Captain Dharek on the *Ek*."

"Put him through."

Dharek's face filled the viewscreen. "Captain Lee, we have detected Zodark vessels. Your Republic ships will maintain position. Primord vessels will engage."

"Captain, with all due respect—"

"This is not a request, Captain Lee," Dharek interrupted. "This is a tactical order. The Primord battle group possesses superior firepower and defensive capabilities for this engagement. You'll stand by and wait to see *if* we need you."

Lee's fingers tightened on his armrest. "And if you're walking into a trap, sir?"

"We are not," Dharek replied with characteristic Primord confidence. "Your vessels will stand by as tactical reserve. Maintain combat readiness, but do not engage unless explicitly ordered. Dharek out."

The transmission ended before Lee could respond. He exhaled slowly, controlling the flare of frustration.

"Captain?" Sato asked quietly from beside him.

"All ships, battle stations," Lee ordered. "Maintain formation and hold position. This is not a drill."

Klaxons sounded throughout *Poseidon* as crew members rushed to combat positions. Lee forced his voice to remain calm when he spoke again. "Reynolds, maintain current coordinates but reorient for optimal observation of the engagement zone. Rhom, full sensor sweep. I want continuous tracking of all vessels and weapons fire. Rodriguez, open a secure tactical observation channel to all Republic captains."

Deep down, Lee figured this had something to do with their last mission. Perhaps Dharek was still punishing him for the Primords' lost battleship. Perhaps not. Although it could be argued that Dharek was using his command of the entire task fleet as leverage to force Lee to bend to the Primord captain's will, and to his anger.

"Aye, Captain," his officers acknowledged in sequence.

On the main viewscreen, the Primord vessels moved. The battleship *Ek* led their formation, with *Kulente* and *Nyx* spreading outward in a pincer-type approach. The other Primord vessels, *Simsu*, *Sulvaar*, and *Vora*, accelerated ahead as screening elements.

Lee studied their movements. "Reynolds, log their tactical approach. Note those formation gaps. They're deliberately creating targeting channels."

"Logging, sir."

Sato leaned closer to Lee's chair. "Primord naval doctrine emphasizes concentrated fire corridors. They're setting up a cross fire."

"And exposing their flanks in the process," Lee muttered. He raised his voice. "Rhom, maintain continuous sensor sweeps beyond the visible engagement zone. Six-hundred-thousand-kilometer radius."

"Yes, sir."

The Zodark battleships adjusted course, strangely unperturbed by the approaching Primord battle group.

How is Dharek not seeing this? Lee wondered. *Suspicious as hell.*

"Two Zodark battleships don't stand and fight against Primord battleships that vastly outnumber them," Lee said quietly. "Not unless they have a significant tactical advantage we can't see."

"The debris field provides considerable cover," Sato replied.

"Too convenient." Lee kept watching. "Reynolds, prepare phased withdrawal coordinates for all Republic vessels. Don't transmit, just have them ready."

"Aye, sir."

On the tactical display, the engagement unfolded with the Primord vessels moving to envelope the Zodark battleships. The first exchange of fire lit up the void. Energy beams from the Primord cruisers met the battleships' defensive countermeasures.

"Primord targeting systems operating at ninety-seven percent efficiency," Rhom reported. "First volley scored multiple hits on the lead Zodark vessel."

Lee nodded but remained focused on the TAM. Something wasn't right. The Zodarks were too relaxed, too accepting of the engagement despite being outgunned.

"Rodriguez, open channel to all Republic captains," Lee ordered. "Visual confirmation of tactical readiness."

One by one, the faces of his ship captains appeared on a secondary display. All looked ready, alert, but equally frustrated at being sidelined.

"All vessels, maintain combat readiness," Lee told them. "I believe we're observing a trap. Captain Bayes, move *Polaris* to these coordinates." He transmitted the position data. "It provides optimal sensor coverage of the debris field's eastern quadrant."

"Understood, Commander," Bayes acknowledged.

"What are you thinking, sir?" Sato asked.

"I'm thinking the Zodarks want the Primords committed to this engagement," Lee replied. "And I'm wondering what we're not seeing."

On the main screen, the battle intensified. The Primord ships executed a textbook envelopment maneuver, their combined firepower hammering at the Zodark battleships. The enemy vessels returned fire, their weapons striking against the *Ek*.

"Primord battleship taking minimal damage," Rhom said. "Zodark battleships showing signs of major armor degradation."

Lee wrinkled his brow. "They're not retreating. They should be attempting to withdraw, but they're holding position."

"Sir," Rodriguez chimed in, "Captain Dharek is signaling the *Simsu* and *Vora* to close range with the enemy vessels."

Lee frowned. *They're committing too close. Why press the advantage when you're already winning from a distance?*

The smaller Primord vessels accelerated toward the Zodark vessels, weapons blazing. The Zodarks immediately adjusted tactics, concentrating fire on the approaching ships.

"*Simsu* taking heavy fire," Rhom said.

"Still no additional contacts?" Lee asked.

"None, sir, but…" Baldry at the sensor station paused, adjusting his readings. "Sir, I'm detecting unusual mass readings from within the largest debris cluster. Could be sensor ghosts from the gravity wells, but…"

"But your instincts say otherwise," Lee finished.

"Yes, sir."

Lee nodded. "Rodriguez, open channel to Captain Dharek."

"Channel open, sir."

"Captain Dharek, this is Lee. We're detecting anomalous mass readings within the central debris field. Recommend immediate withdrawal of *Simsu* and *Vora*."

Dharek's response was delayed by several seconds. "Your sensor readings are noted, Captain Lee. We have the situation well in hand."

"Sir, with respect, I believe—"

"Maintain your position, Captain," Dharek interrupted. "Primord vessels will continue engagement as planned."

The communication cut off.

"Hardheaded son of a—" Lee caught himself. "Reynolds, move us three thousand kilometers to heading one-four-seven. Keep us outside the engagement zone, but position for optimal sensor coverage of that debris cluster."

"Aye, sir."

As the *Poseidon* adjusted position, Lee studied the tactical display with growing concern. The Primord *Simsu* and *Vora* were now fully committed to the engagement, exchanging heavy fire with the Zodark battleships at close range. The battleship *Ek* maintained its position, providing covering fire while the other Primord battleships moved to support *Vora* and *Simsu*.

"Sir," Rhom called out, "mass readings spiking in the debris field. Metallic signature consistent with a Zodark battleship."

"Full alert," Lee said. "Rodriguez, emergency channel to Dharek, now!"

Before Rodriguez could comply, the debris field erupted with weapons fire. A huge Zodark battleship emerged from the floating wreckage. Its first salvo caught the *Simsu* broadside.

"*Simsu* taking hits," Rhom said. "It's battered but pulling through. Not much damage…"

"Rodriguez, group-wide channel. All Republic vessels, combat formation Gamma. Prepare to engage on my mark. Reynolds, plot intercept course to support the Primord destroyers."

"Sir," Sato cautioned, "Captain Dharek ordered us to hold position."

Lee met her gaze. "And Captain Roberts ordered us to work together. If we sit here and watch a Primord ship get torn apart, we'll be in the center of a beaten-down joint task force."

He turned to face the viewscreen, where the hidden Zodark battleship was now fully revealed. Its colossal weapons batteries were targeting the exposed Primord vessels.

"Rodriguez, signal Dharek," Lee ordered. "Tell him the Republic forces are moving to support. Not asking permission. Informing him of our intentions."

"Aye, sir."

"Reynolds," Lee said, "bring us in. Rhom, targeting solutions on the Zodark battleship's weapon emplacements. Let's show our Primord allies what Republic ships can do."

While the *Poseidon* and its escorts accelerated toward the engagement, a grim satisfaction washed over Lee. Being right about the trap was small comfort with Primord lives at stake. But perhaps, just perhaps, this was the moment that would forge something stronger between the two commands than diplomatic necessity ever could.

And Lee was right. Dharek was wrong. This would give Lee some leeway when it came to strategies and suggestions, he mused.

The real test of the alliance was here, and right in the fire and fury of combat—where the only thing that mattered was who stood with you when the shooting started.

Chapter 6:
Communication Dark

Year 2098
Primord Battleship *Ek*
Middle Reach
Sector 8

Is Lee disobeying my orders? Captain Dharek thought. Too much was happening across the entire fleet for him to micromanage every captain's decisions, but as fleet commander, he had to monitor all vessel positions and tactical choices—especially those of an underexperienced and overconfident Earther who might jeopardize the coordinated defense against these attacking Zodarks.

The Primord sat rigid at the forward command deck, his jaw set like carved stone. *Ek*'s bridge was a bedlam of real-time tactical overlays projecting from the ceiling and floor alike. All cast violet and indigo reflections across the obsidian plating and matte white walls.

Warning indicators flashed across every console as dormant mining platforms activated across this sector of space, their ancient comm arrays alive with interference patterns. Dharek's expression remained unchanged, though his eyes narrowed fractionally. The Zodarks had concealed their signatures remarkably well. He'd seen it before.

He'd seen it *all* before.

The Zodarks were a taking and grabbing species. They rarely came up with their own innovations, instead stealing from what they blew up and reverse engineering what they witnessed from the opposing army on the battlefield or starfield. This meant that the Zodarks were master observers and did a great job of mimicking their enemy, even improving on their enemy's technology.

Dharek knew the humans were becoming aware of all this, but they didn't *know* and *understand* the Zodarks the way the Primords did. Dharek's species had battled these four-armed blue beasts for all too long. They understood this enemy like they understood mathematics— very well. For this reason, in Dharek's mind, no space task force or fleet should be commanded by any Earthers.

At the moment, the Zodarks' advanced comm scramblers operated on frequencies beyond the task force's detection capabilities. After they survived this encounter, Dharek would ensure that Primord intelligence thoroughly investigated the technology that had allowed these vermin to remain invisible for such an extended duration.

"Communications are failing across all frequencies," Commander Saelith reported, her focus dead set on her console. "We maintain internal ship communications, but all external channels are inoperative. The Zodark battleships appear to be utilizing the platforms to generate a signal disruption matrix."

"Confirm status of target acquisition systems," Dharek said.

Tactical Officer Vrenn's hands moved across his station. "Target acquisition systems are nonfunctional, Captain. Combat artificial intelligence cannot establish weapons lock. Their jamming affects all smart-target systems."

"Implement manual targeting protocols," Dharek ordered as the *Ek*'s systems fluctuated between static and erratic displays. "Focus beam-laced plasma batteries on their command tower. Distance?"

"Six thousand kilometers and closing," Vrenn reported. "Firing solution prepared, but accuracy probability is minimal at current range."

"Acceptable. Execute firing sequence," Dharek replied.

The *Ek*'s plasma batteries discharged, sending streams of energy across the starlit darkness. The majority missed their intended target, impacting debris and vaporizing fragments into clouds of hot particles.

The newest enemy vessel advanced. Its support battleships spread out, seeking multiple attack vectors. The Republic vessel *Poseidon*, positioned near the outer defense perimeter, continued to move toward Dharek's group. If he could communicate with the Earther, he'd tell the man to hold their pattern. As it was, he couldn't.

The remaining Primord vessels accelerated into combat formation—the *Vora*, *Simsu*, and *Sulvaar* taking forward positions while *Kulente* and *Nyx* moved to support the flanks. The Republic ships—*Poseidon*, *Horizon*, *Scimitar*, *Polaris*, *Bolt* and *Cobalt*—appeared to struggle with coordination in the absence of proper communications.

"Communications status?" Dharek asked, his gaze never leaving the tactical display.

"Unchanged, Captain," Saelith replied. "Attempts to penetrate interference continue without success."

"Maintain efforts and stay calm," Dharek said. "Our priority remains the reestablishment of fleet coordination."

A curious movement on the main holographic display caught Dharek's attention. The *Poseidon* pulled back and, instead of joining the fight, which Dharek did not want at the moment, appeared to be… repositioning its auxiliary laser arrays? Focused beams of coherent light pulsed from multiple points along its hull in distinctive patterns.

"Captain, observe this anomaly." Saelith enhanced the image. "The Republic vessel appears to be utilizing focused laser beams and bouncing them off debris fragments. The metal surfaces are acting as mirrors, creating a communication relay network throughout the field."

In a way, that was brilliant. These Earthers were formidable fighters in land, sea, air, and space, but Dharek hadn't pegged them as the quickest thinkers. Not like this. He'd add that to his list of interesting anomalies this species possessed.

Dharek's interest sharpened. Like the Primord vessels, the Republic ships had lost standard communication capabilities. He leaned forward, studying the phenomenon for a moment. Captain Lee's vessel continued its precise laser targeting, the coherent-light beams reflecting off metal debris in expanding geometric patterns.

"The patterns demonstrate systematic structure," Saelith noted. "Different metallic surfaces provide varying reflectivity coefficients. The laser pulses are being modulated in frequency and duration. With sufficient analysis, construction of a translation matrix appears feasible."

"Proceed with analysis," Dharek commanded as another volley struck the Republic vessel *Polaris*. "We require coordinated defense before—"

The deck trembled as a direct hit impacted the *Ek*. Warning indicators activated as damage reports populated the displays. Throughout the disruption, Saelith continued decoding the Republic transmission method. She mapped laser-pulse sequences to comprehensible meaning.

"The optical structure demonstrates remarkable elegance," she observed. "Each frequency and pulse duration combination corresponds to specific tactical concepts. The methodology resembles traditional Primord coherent-light communication protocols."

Whoever their communication officer is… I am impressed. Rodriguez, I believe.

Dharek divided his attention between the tactical display showing his scattered forces and Saelith's efforts to establish communication. The new Zodark battleship, designated battleship-keta, loomed increasingly dominant on the telescopic display. Its battleship escorts—battleship-vorth and battleship-jelik, according to Primord tactical classification protocols—pressed their advantage while task force vessels fought in isolation. The combat AI automatically assigned threat designations based on vessel mass, weapons signatures, and formation positioning.

Four thousand and five hundred kilometers and closing. A little closer, and they'd punch these Zodarks out of existence. There were no doubts in Dharek's mind. *An ambush? No.* And he believed Lee would think such a thought, but Dharek's team detected nothing of the sort. These Zodarks were simply in the wrong place, at exactly the wrong time.

Right now, Dharek's task force's most promising strategy lay in understanding the Republic's method of communication. If Dharek's crew could decipher it promptly and transmit the information throughout the Primord fleet and the Earther fleet, it would facilitate coordinated action. The combined Primord-Republic force possessed numerical superiority against the Zodarks, but without proper command channels, the engagement teetered out of balance.

Another pattern reflected through the debris field. It carried unknown critical information between Republic vessels until Saelith's posture straightened. "Captain, I am constructing a framework to translate these laser-pulse sequences into comprehensible tactical language."

"You have decoded their method?" Dharek asked. The *Ek* shuddered as another impact transferred through the command deck.

"Affirmative, Captain."

"Modify our auxiliary laser arrays to replicate these frequencies and pulse patterns," Dharek said, his decision immediate, as always.

"Implementation already initiated, Captain. Our laser communication systems are more sophisticated than theirs. We can achieve greater precision in the reflection angles and use multiple wavelengths simultaneously."

A torpedo barely scraped the Republic vessel *Polaris*. If it had hit head-on, it would have had a devastating effect. The captain of that particular ship impressed Dharek.

Bayes—yes, Captain Bayes.

"Transmit to all Primord vessels: 'Adjust resonator frequency to match Republic pattern. Execute coordinated response.' Include technical specifications for implementation," Dharek instructed.

The bridge lighting blinked off and on as another blast reverberated through the *Ek*. On the viewport, the Zodark battleship-keta advanced while battleship-vorth and battleship-jelik deployed into an even wider formation, absorbing scattered fire from Primord vessels, most shots failing to find their marks.

"Republic vessels approaching optimal firing position," Tactical Officer Vrenn reported. "Estimated time to engagement: sixty seconds. What shall we do, Captain?"

Dharek acknowledged with a slight nod. "Nothing at the moment. Tell them to hold." He turned to Vrenn. "Target plasma cannons on enemy battleship at bearing three-two-zero mark four, range three thousand seven hundred kilometers, decreasing rapidly." He shifted focus to Navigation Officer Mekari. "Navigation, execute full reverse thrust on stern propulsion, then initiate roll to port, forty-four degrees. Implement two-second burst on ventral stabilizers upon achieving position. I require their vulnerable sections exposed to our broadside."

Mekari executed the maneuvers. The *Ek*'s stern thrusters fired, creating backward momentum as the vessel rolled to port, inertial compensators maintaining internal gravity despite the difficult movement. The stars changed perspective until the massive ventral structure of the Zodark battleship dominated their view. Its dark green hull came into visual range, studded with weapon emplacements and torpedo tubes. As the tactical display enhanced magnification, Dharek identified the profile of the Zodark ship's primary reactor housing—an ideal target for the plasma batteries.

The concentrated energy beams cut through space. Several missed their mark, disappearing into the expanse. One concentration struck the enemy battleship. The impact vaporized sensor arrays and communication apparatuses. It sent debris spinning into the vacuum. The battleship shifted starboard upon impact.

"Incoming torpedoes!" Vrenn yelled. "Five… correction, six projectiles detected!"

"Activate point-defense grid, prioritize nearest threats," Dharek ordered. The defensive laser grid engaged. The high-energy point-defense system intercepted three torpedoes in rapid sequence. They detonated in blue-white expansions. A fourth penetrated defenses and struck the *Ek*'s forward armor plating. The impact transferred throughout the hull structure but did little damage, according to the reports scrolling on the screens. Forward armor integrity was reduced to eighty-nine percent. Structural compromise was minimal. Secondary defensive systems remained operational.

Dharek almost smiled, something rare for his species and rarer for him. "Dispatch technical units to reinforce affected sections. Prioritize structural integrity."

Vrenn confirmed and transmitted orders to repair teams. "Technical units deploying now, Captain."

"Prepare torpedoes for launch. I require armor-penetrating warheads in position."

"Torpedo tubes one through four loaded and prepared, Captain."

"Adjust our heading three-six-one mark three. Should we fail to eliminate battleship-keta, we require a clean targeting solution on the escorts positioned at its starboard flank."

The torpedoes launched from tubes, their propulsion systems creating luminous trails across space. The Zodark battleship's point-defense intercepted two. But one pushed through, detonating against the Zodark battleship's outer armor plating. The remaining projectile diverted from its initial trajectory, acquiring battleship-vorth instead. The big vessel's structural integrity failed, its reactor housing visibly compromised.

"Initial laser communication network established," Saelith reported from her station. "The debris field provides excellent reflective surfaces. Significantly more efficient than direct line-of-sight signaling. Confirming fleet response… all communication officers report successful optical link establishment and confirm signal comprehension."

"Excellent. Order *Vora, Simsu,* and *Sulvaar* to form on our starboard position. *Kulente* and *Nyx* to port," Dharek directed, and the commands propagated through the improvised network. "Republic vessels are adjusting position to match formation."

The enemy undoubtedly perceived the shift in tactical positioning. The Zodark battleships' weapons discharged, attempting to disrupt their reformation. The task force vessels navigated through the debris field. Metal fragments resonated with transmitted commands.

"They are targeting our flanks," Dharek said. "Saelith, transmit laser-pulse sequence to the fleet to divide into tactical groups. *Kulente* and *Nyx* will engage battleship-vorth at bearing zero-four-one. *Ek* and Republic vessel *Poseidon* will neutralize battleship-keta. *Simsu* and *Vora*, concentrate firepower on battleship-jelik at three-three-five. *Sulvaar* and Republic vessel *Horizon*, provide covering fire for slightly compromised vessel *Polaris*. Extract it from the combat zone. Republic vessel *Scimitar*, escort *Polaris* to safe coordinates at two-one-zero once disengagement completes."

Saelith adjusted the laser array controls, sending precisely timed light pulses that bounced off strategically positioned debris fragments. The response manifested immediately. Primord and Republic ships moved as a unified force.

"Captain, I am achieving improved resolution on the laser communication protocols," Saelith reported. "I can now transmit complex tactical data through multiwavelength burst patterns."

"Excellent. Signal all vessels to execute Combat Spear Vonlan Five on my command." Dharek observed the enemy formation, calculating the precise moment. "Execute."

The task force vessels advanced. Plasma batteries and magrail weapons discharged as ships separated into assigned groups, trapping the Zodarks in devastating cross fire. The enemy ship at zero-four-one attempted evasive maneuvers but found itself caught between the combined firepower of his Primord vessels and their Republic escorts. It disintegrated under the sustained barrage. Secondary detonations chained through its hull structure before it separated into fragments in massive explosions.

Shortly thereafter, the remaining battleship escort shifted position. Its green hull placed itself between the task force and the now damaged battleship-keta, which had sustained multiple direct impacts from both *Ek* and *Poseidon*. Debris from destroyed and the remaining damaged Zodark escort created a rotating field of wreckage.

"Saelith, signal all vessels. Execute Pattern Yaelil Three. We shall utilize this debris field to tactical advantage."

She manipulated the laser array controls, sending coordinated light bursts throughout the reflective debris field. The task force vessels responded, breaking formation to navigate through the wreckage. Each vessel utilized larger fragments as concealment, masking their positions.

"Saelith, transmit laser coordinates to Republic vessel *Polaris* to withdraw from the engagement zone. Further damage to that vessel is unacceptable." Dharek studied the tactical display as *Polaris* retreated from the combat area. "All vessels, prepare to engage on my command. Saelith, coordinate timing through the optical network."

The Zodark battleship's weapons discharged, attempting to track targets through debris. The command deck's auxiliary systems hummed as Saelith transmitted the attack signal through precisely angled laser reflections.

"Engage!"

Weapons fire erupted from multiple concealed positions. The last Zodark escort's defensive systems failed under the concentrated barrage, its hull structure compromised as salvos penetrated armor plating. External illumination systems deactivated progressively until darkness enveloped the hostile vessel. The task force had achieved encirclement.

"Vrenn, load six antimatter torpedoes. Implement manual targeting with plasma batteries and laser beams," Dharek commanded. "Saelith, signal the battle group and transmit engagement authorization. Unrestricted weapons release."

Status reports were transferred between stations as targeting solutions were finalized. The command deck resonated with energy as *Ek*'s weapon systems activated to full capacity. The harmonic signature of laser cannons charging permeated the atmosphere.

"All weapons systems operational, Captain!" Vrenn positioned his hands above the control interface. "Targeting solutions confirmed!"

"Commence firing."

Torpedoes launched from tubes. Cannons discharged; concentrated energy beams cut through darkness toward their targets. Death to the Zodarks had been delivered.

The command deck illumination diminished momentarily as *Ek*'s weapons drew maximum power allocation. The hull structure vibrated with each shot from the cannons, while the continuous reverberation of torpedo launches transferred throughout the vessel. Status displays presented weapon telemetry data, monitoring the destruction they had initiated.

Throughout the battlefield, Primord and Republic vessels discharged all available weapons systems. The debris field illuminated with intensity comparable to stellar phenomena as energy weapons, magrails, missiles, and torpedoes converged upon the enemy. The Zodark battleships disappeared behind a downpour of detonations and weapons impacts. Their retaliatory fire… insignificant.

"Battleship-keta's reactor exhibits critical destabilization," Saelith said. "Sensors detect huge power fluctuations throughout enemy vessel."

"All vessels, evacuate detonation radius," Dharek ordered. The laser-pulse signals transmitted his command throughout the debris field. Task force vessels withdrew as battleship-keta's structural integrity failed completely. The massive detonation's shock wave tore through nearby battleship-jelik, which had moved too close in a desperate attempt to shield the flagship, secondary explosions rippling through its hull as the chain reaction consumed both vessels. The resulting detonation illuminated the surrounding space momentarily. Metallic fragments flew across the void as Dharek exhaled.

"Enemy vessels neutralized," Saelith confirmed. "Republic vessel *Polaris* reports achievement of safe distance. Damage control units are responding."

Dharek permitted himself a brief moment of satisfaction. *Victory.* As the final Zodark vessel blasted into bits in the expanse, external communications and targeting systems reactivated automatically.

He turned to Saelith. "Your analytical efficiency proved instrumental today. Your performance will be documented in official records."

Before she acknowledged, the main viewscreen activated with an incoming transmission request. Captain Lee's face appeared. Dharek noted the Republic officer's satisfaction at their victory but detected underlying concern as well.

"Captain Dharek," Lee began, "I commend your tactical leadership."

"Your adaptation to circumstances demonstrated commendable ingenuity, Captain Lee," Dharek replied. "However, I have observed your vessels exceeded tactical boundaries established in our engagement protocols. The Republic vessel *Poseidon* almost engaged the Zodark battleships despite my explicit orders regarding formation assignments before we went communication dark."

Tension crossed Lee's features. "Captain, with respect, the dynamic nature of the engagement required immediate tactical adaptation. Look, the *Poseidon*'s weapons systems complemented *Ek*'s attack vectors, and we would have helped you win this victory at a much faster pace."

"Noted," Dharek said. "We will discuss proper command hierarchy at greater length in private communication. This topic is not appropriate for open-channel discussion."

It looked as if Lee withheld a grimace, his face tightening just a little. "Of course, Captain. I remain available at your convenience."

"Excellent. Transmission concluded." Dharek terminated the connection before Lee could respond.

Saelith approached his command position once the screen deactivated. "Captain, the Republic vessels performed admirably under combat conditions. Their initiative proved advantageous to our tactical position."

"Their performance is not in question, Commander. The Republic ships possess considerable combat effectiveness. However, command structure must remain inviolate, particularly during hostile engagement. Captain Lee possesses admirable tactical instinct but requires an improved understanding of Primord operational doctrine."

He returned his attention to the tactical display, where the Republic vessel *Polaris*'s damage appeared prominent in holographic representation. His expression hardened. "The Republic vessels sustained disproportionate damage during this engagement. What looked like a slight hit was bigger than expected. I made a much-needed call to move that vessel out of the fight as soon as I could."

"*Polaris* positioned itself in a vulnerable tactical position," Saelith replied. "Their maneuver lacked proper defensive consideration."

"An observation Captain Lee should have made before I was required to intervene," Dharek responded. "Initiate comprehensive battle analysis. I require a detailed assessment of Republic vessels' performance relative to established engagement parameters."

"As commanded, Captain."

Dharek studied the tactical display showing debris from destroyed Zodark vessels scattered across space. Their victory remained undisputed, yet the manner of its achievement left him dissatisfied. The Republic vessels demonstrated commendable combat capability, but their command structure required refinement.

He recalled Lee's initiative during the height of battle. The human captain had adapted remarkably to circumstances, implementing the laser communication network with impressive efficiency. Such ingenuity deserved recognition. Yet Lee's disregard for established command protocols remained problematic.

Dharek had expected the taciturn Earther to resist Primord tactical doctrine. What he had not anticipated was Lee's remarkable effectiveness despite such resistance. The contradiction warranted further consideration.

Chapter 7:
Milk Run

Year 2098
FOB Oteren
Planet Intus

Granger's assistant knocked on the door three times, sharp and precise.

He always knocks in the exact same way, noted Lieutenant Naomi Love.

"Enter." Commander Rhett Granger's voice carried through the reinforced door.

Love stepped into the climate-controlled office, grateful for the reprieve from Intus's oppressive humidity. Sweat had already soaked through her flight suit during the brief walk across the compound. The commander sat behind his desk, studying a holographic display that cast blue light across his weathered features.

"Lieutenant Love reporting as ordered, sir."

Granger gestured to the chair across from him without looking up. "Sit. This won't take long."

Love settled into the seat, back straight, hands resting on her thighs. Through the office's small window, she could see maintenance crews servicing a row of Ospreys on the flight line. The afternoon sun blazed overhead, creating shimmering heat waves above the tarmac.

"I need you and your crew for a transport run," Granger said, finally meeting her eyes. He swiped the hologram, bringing up a topographical map of the region. "Primord Ambassador Nyranor Taevlix and his family need extraction from a diplomatic compound outside Hatteng City. They're rotating back to the capital for security consultations."

Love leaned forward, studying the route. "Threat assessment?" she asked.

"Minimal." Granger highlighted several areas on the map with red markers. "We've had reports of small Zodark cells—stragglers mostly, groups of five or six hiding in the jungle. Nothing organized. I know I thought the liberation was thorough enough, but you know how it is. Some refuse to accept defeat."

"Understood, sir," said Love. "Timeline?"

"Wheels up in two hours. It's a twenty-minute flight to the pickup coordinates, and another seventeen to Hatteng City. We should have you back before evening chow." Granger pulled up another screen. "There's a secondary objective. You'll rendezvous with one of our intel contacts in Hatteng—quick handoff of some operational plans we've been developing with the Primords. Location and recognition protocols are in your mission packet."

Love nodded. *Simple enough*, she thought. She'd flown dozens of similar missions since arriving on Intus.

"Passenger manifest?" she asked.

"The ambassador, his wife, and his daughter. Plus his security detail—two plainclothes bodyguards and six Primord Special Forces soldiers." Granger's fingers moved across the display, bringing up the numbers. "Total of eleven personnel. Well within your capacity."

"The Special Forces troops—full combat gear?"

"Affirmative, but they'll be under diplomatic protocols. They're there as a precaution, not expecting trouble." Granger's expression remained neutral. "The ambassador insists on his full detail. Primord politics."

"Standard loadout for us?"

"Diplomatic protocols apply. Keep the weapons powered but not hot. We want to project security without aggression." Granger's expression softened slightly. "How's your crew?"

"Solid, sir. Ford's been running extra maintenance cycles on the *Jack*. Says he wants everything perfect."

"That sounds like Ford." Granger deactivated the hologram. "This should be straightforward, Lieutenant. In and out, nice and clean. The ambassador specifically requested Republic transport—apparently his daughter is fascinated by our Ospreys, and I guess they saw some action recently."

Love stood, sensing the dismissal. "We'll take good care of them, sir."

"I know you will. Mission packet's already uploaded to your datapad. Dismissed."

Love snapped a salute and exited the office. The wall of heat hit her immediately as she stepped outside. The afternoon air hung thick and heavy, carrying a faint scent of burnt metal from all the different welding repairs. She quickened her pace toward Hangar Seven.

Inside the hangar, the temperature dropped by several degrees. Love found her crew exactly where she expected—clustered around their Osprey AT-70C, call sign *Jack*.

Chief Brian Ford lay on a mechanic's creeper beneath the starboard engine, only his legs visible. The metallic clink of tools echoed in the space. Green sat in the cockpit, running through system diagnostics. Williams performed checks on the port-side gun mount, his movements methodical and precise.

"Mission brief in five," Love called out.

Ford acknowledged that he'd heard her and finished what he was working on before he slid out from under the Osprey, wiping his hands on a rag. Oil streaked his cheek. "So, what've we got, Lieutenant?"

"Diplomatic transport. Real simple stuff." Love pulled up the mission data on her datapad, projecting it for all to see. "Ambassador Nyranor Taevlix and family, pickup at these coordinates, delivery to Hatteng City."

Williams descended from his gun position. "Primord VIP, huh?" he said.

"Yep, but we aren't expecting any trouble. We'll keep the weapons ready, though, of course." Love highlighted the route. "Twenty minutes out, seventeen back to Hatteng City, quick stop to pick up some intel, then home. Should be a milk run."

Green emerged from the cockpit, his flight suit still crisp despite the heat. "Weather's looking clear. There's some cloud buildup to the west, but nothing that should affect our flight path."

"Zodark activity?" Ford asked.

"Minimal," said Love. "There are still a few small cells in the jungle, but nothing organized at this point." Love closed the projection. "We launch in two hours. I want full preflight complete in ninety minutes."

"On it," Ford said, already turning back to the Osprey. "I'll double-check the inertial dampeners. Don't want to jostle diplomatic passengers."

Williams headed for the weapons locker. "I'll pull standard loads. Better to have and not need."

"Green, file our flight plan and get updated intel on those Zodark positions," Love ordered. "I want to know exactly where every reported sighting has been in the last seventy-two hours."

"Copy that, Lieutenant."

Love watched her crew disperse to their tasks. The hangar filled with the sounds of preparation—the hum of diagnostic equipment, the click of ammunition being loaded, the steady rhythm of Ford's tools. This was their element, where everything made sense.

She walked to the nose of the Osprey, placing her palm against the hull. The metal felt cool under her touch. Inside the cockpit, the small photo of Jack was still taped to the instrument panel, right where she'd left it.

"Just another milk run," she whispered to herself, though something in her gut stirred with unease. After all these missions, she'd learned to trust that feeling.

But orders were orders. In two hours, they'd be airborne.

****

Two Hours Later

The Osprey's engines hummed to life, their pitch rising from a low growl to the familiar whine that meant it was ready for flight. Love's hands moved across the controls with practiced ease, each switch and dial exactly where her muscle memory expected.

"Tower, this is *Jack* requesting departure clearance, diplomatic priority transit."

"*Jack*, you're cleared for vertical on pad seven. Winds two-seven-zero at eight knots. Safe travels."

Love eased the controls back, feeling the Osprey respond instantly. The landing struts compressed, then released as twenty-eight tons of aircraft lifted smoothly into Intus's thick air. Below, the tarmac fell away, heat shimmer distorting the rows of parked vehicles.

"Gear up," Green announced from the copilot's seat. "Transitioning to forward flight."

The *Jack* tilted forward with mechanical precision. Love felt the subtle shift in the controls as the Osprey transformed from helicopter to airplane, accelerating smoothly to cruising speed. The base perimeter swept past them down below: defensive turrets, patrol roads, the occasional Synth maintenance crew, working without stopping.

"First waypoint in three minutes," Green reported. "Navigation locked, all systems nominal."

Ford's voice crackled through the intercom from the crew compartment. "Port engine's purring like a kitten. That new coolant flush did the trick."

"Told you it would," Williams chimed in from his gun position. "Though I still say we should've replaced the whole assembly."

"Why replace what isn't broken?" Ford shot back. "That's wasteful thinking."

Love smiled behind her visor. The familiar banter meant her crew was relaxed, focused. "Cut the chatter and keep eyes on sectors," she ordered, her voice not carrying sufficient sternness to be taken seriously.

"Copy that, Lieutenant," Williams replied, though she could hear the grin in his voice. "Sector clear. Nothing but jungle and those weird purple birds."

Below them, Intus spread out in all its alien beauty. The jungle canopy formed an unbroken sea of blue-green, punctuated by towering emergent trees whose crowns spread like umbrellas hundreds of feet above their neighbors. Flocks of native birds—the purple ones Williams had mentioned—maneuvered together in formation, their metallic feathers catching the afternoon sun.

"Coming up on the ruins," Green announced.

Love banked slightly to follow the navigation track. Ahead, ancient Primord structures jutted from the jungle like broken teeth. These artifices predated the occupation, their crystalline spires now cracked and overgrown but still magnificent. Vines with bioluminescent flowers had colonized the lower levels, creating a patchwork of natural and artificial beauty.

"Every time I see those, I wonder what they were," Ford mused.

"Research stations, according to the briefing," Green supplied. "Before the Zodarks came."

They passed over a cleared area where new construction had begun; the Primords were reclaiming their world one building at a time. Automated constructors moved in precise patterns, extruding walls and supports from programmable matter. The contrast between old and new was stark.

"Waypoint two achieved," Green called out. "Adjusting heading two degrees south."

Love made the correction, noting how the atmospheric pressure had shifted slightly. Intus's weather could change rapidly, but today, it seemed pretty stable. Thin, wispy clouds streaked the sky above them, and to the west, larger formations built along the horizon. Love did not register those clouds as threatening; she'd come to learn that this was a part of the planet's normal afternoon convection cycle.

"Got some smoke columns about ten klicks north," Williams reported. "Looks old, though. Probably just our maintenance crews."

Love glanced in that direction. Three thin wisps of gray rose from the jungle, already dissipating in the upper atmosphere. Battlefield cleanup was ongoing across the continent—burned-out Zodark positions and destroyed equipment had to be managed somehow. The liberation had been successful, but its scars remained.

"Five minutes to destination," Green announced. "Diplomatic compound should be visible soon."

"Running final approach checklist," Love responded. She pulled up the compound's landing protocols on her display. Diplomatic sites had specific requirements—slower approach speeds, broadcast of identification codes, predetermined landing vectors to avoid defensive systems.

The jungle thinned ahead, and through gaps in the canopy, she caught glimpses of manicured grounds, geometric gardens laid out in traditional Primord patterns. Then the compound itself came into view.

"That used to be something," Ford observed.

He wasn't wrong. The diplomatic compound retained hints of its former elegance, with its sweeping arches of white stone, graceful towers with faceted windows, and landing pads that seemed to float above reflecting pools. But abandonment had taken its toll. Several windows were shattered. Vegetation encroached on the formal gardens. One of the secondary buildings showed fire damage along its eastern wall.

"Initiating landing sequence," Love announced. "Green, broadcast our codes."

"Transmitting now. No response from compound control, but that's as expected, since it's unmanned."

Love circled once, performing a visual inspection. The main landing pad appeared intact, though debris littered its edges. She noted the windsock there hung limp.

Good, she thought. *No gusts to complicate the approach.*

"Sector's clear," Williams reported. "Nice and quiet down there."

"Too quiet," Ford muttered, then louder, he said, "Landing struts deployed and locked."

Love brought them in slowly, precisely. The Osprey descended through its own rotor wash, dust and loose vegetation swirling away from the pad. She felt the subtle changes in control responsiveness as ground effect took hold, cushioning their descent.

The landing struts touched down with barely a bump. Love held the controls steady as the Osprey settled, then began reducing power.

"Contact light," Green confirmed. "We're down. Textbook approach, Lieutenant."

"Maintain engine idle," Love ordered. "Ford, lower the ramp. I'm going to meet our passengers. Green, you have the aircraft."

"Roger that," Green confirmed.

Love unbuckled and made her way back through the crew compartment. Ford had the ramp down, and the afternoon heat rushed in to mix with the cooler air inside. Williams maintained his position at the gun, eyes scanning the perimeter.

"I'll be quick," Love told them, stepping down onto the pad.

The heat hit her like a physical wall, and the humidity made breathing feel like drowning. She strode toward the main building, noting how her boots left prints in the thin layer of dust and pollen covering the pad.

The main entrance doors were tall, having been designed for Primords, and stood partially open. Love paused at the threshold, letting her eyes adjust to the dimmer interior.

"Ambassador Taevlix?" she called out. "Lieutenant Naomi Love, Republic Navy. We're here for your transport."

Movement in the shadows resolved into figures approaching. Ambassador Nyranor Taevlix stood nearly seven feet tall, his elongated frame moving with practiced dignity. His formal robes, deep purple

with silver threading, seemed untouched by the compound's decay.
Beside him, his wife, Keirzi, matched his grace, though Love noticed
the subtle tension in her posture. Her hands were clasped too tightly,
and her eyes darted to the windows.

Between them walked a young Primord girl, who was obviously
their daughter. In contrast to her parents' dignified restraint, she
practically vibrated with excitement, large eyes fixed on the Osprey
visible through the doorway.

Behind the family, Love counted the security detail exactly as
briefed—two plainclothes bodyguards flanking the family, their
movements screaming professional protection despite civilian attire.
Six Primord Special Forces soldiers in full combat gear brought up the
rear, weapons held with casual competence.

"Lieutenant Love," said the ambassador, "we are grateful for
your punctuality. May I present my wife, Keirzi, and our daughter,
Merina."

"Ma'am. Miss." Love nodded to each. "We'll have you safely to
Hatteng City within the hour."

"Is that really an Earth flying machine?" Merina burst out, her
voice carrying a hint of the melodic Primord language. "Does it truly
transform? Can it fly to space?"

"Merina," Keirzi said softly. "Please excuse her, Lieutenant.
She has been quite excited about riding in a Republic Osprey."

"No need to apologize," Love said, finding herself smiling at the
girl's enthusiasm. "Yes, it transforms from vertical to horizontal flight.
And, yes, it can fly in space—these Ospreys are designed to operate
from ship hangars to planetary surfaces. We use different propulsion
systems for vacuum operations."

"That's amazing!" Merina's eyes grew even wider. "So you
could fly all the way back to your ship? Right now?"

"Theoretically, yes. Although we'd need to switch to sealed
operations and engage the ion drives. Today we're staying in
atmosphere." A part of Love that she hadn't realized was there began to
hurt as she spoke to the little girl. This rubbed salt into the wound that
she'd never had a child of her own with Jack.

Love glanced at the time. "Ambassador, we should board. The
weather's good now, but afternoon storms can develop quickly here."

"Of course." Ambassador Taevlix gestured to his security detail. The Special Forces soldiers moved with smooth efficiency, two taking point while the others formed a protective formation around the family.

As they walked toward the Osprey, the lead bodyguard—a compact Primord with scarred hands—stepped closer to Love. "Lieutenant, I am Korvash, head of security. My team will need to inspect your aircraft before the ambassador boards."

Love had expected this. "Of course. My crew chief will assist you. We're on a diplomatic timeline, so please be efficient."

They reached the Osprey, where Ford waited at the ramp. Love made quick introductions, and Korvash's team swept through the crew compartment with practiced eyes, checking sight lines and exits.

"Acceptable," Korvash announced after barely two minutes. "My team will take defensive positions. The ambassador and family will sit center, protected on all sides."

The Primord security detail was sharp, meticulous, and watchful of their surroundings. "Impressive," she muttered to Ford, nodding toward the soldiers.

Ford smiled knowingly. He also appreciated professionalism and efficiency.

As the security team boarded and arranged themselves, Merina tugged on Love's sleeve. "Lieutenant, will we see clouds from above? My teacher says Earth people fly above clouds all the time."

"We'll be flying at about three thousand meters today," Love told her. "Perfect height for cloud watching."

The girl beamed, and even Keirzi's tension seemed to ease slightly.

"All secure," Ford reported as the last soldier took position. "Eleven souls on board, cargo secured."

"Thank you, Chief." Love turned to the ambassador. "We'll have you in Hatteng City shortly. Please keep your restraints fastened during flight. It should be smooth, but we always prepare for turbulence."

"We place ourselves in your capable hands, Lieutenant," Nyranor said formally.

Love made her way back to the cockpit, settling into her seat. "I have the aircraft," she told Green.

"You have the aircraft," he confirmed.

Something about the girl's excitement, the mother's tension, and those battle-hardened soldiers made her gut stir with a certain sense of unease she couldn't explain.

Twenty minutes to Hatteng City, she reminded herself. *We'll keep them safe for twenty minutes.*

****

Chief Brian Ford overheard the young Primord girl ask her mother, "Mama, why do they call this ship the *Jack*?"

"Merina," her mother said softly, but Ford smiled.

"That's all right," said Ford. "Actually, our pilot, Lieutenant Love, was married to a man named Jack. He passed away in an unexpected battle. He was brave and strong, and she likes to think that he watches over us as we fly."

"Oh…" said Merina, her bubbly personality softening just a bit. "I think that was a good choice for a ship name," she declared after reflection.

Ford smiled. "I hear you are very interested in Ospreys. You've really got to watch the nacelles—those big engines on the wings—when we take off. They'll tilt forward once we're airborne."

Merina smiled with genuine interest and asked several more questions before Williams's voice over the intercom brought Ford back to the seriousness of his duties.

"Lieutenant, I just spotted some movement to our rear," said Williams from his gunner's station. "It's in the tree line, bearing two-seven-zero. Multiple signatures."

Ford felt his heart quicken, and he turned to look in the direction Williams had called out. Through the open ramp, he squinted at the jungle edge. *There*, he thought. Shadows moved against shadows, barely visible at three hundred meters.

"Talk to me, Williams. What do you see?" Love's voice came through, calm but alert.

"Four, maybe five contacts. Moving through the underbrush. Blue skin visible… ah, hell. Zodarks. Three hundred meters and closing."

Korvash was already moving, speaking rapid Primord to his team. The Special Forces soldiers checked their weapons, ready to deploy. One of the plainclothes bodyguards, whose name Ford unfortunately hadn't learned, leaned forward urgently.

"Our transportation is compromised," the bodyguard asserted. "The ambassador's movement schedule—someone must have leaked it. We should abort, move to a safe house, reassess—"

"Chief, what's happening?" asked Ambassador Taevlix, maintaining his calm despite the sudden tension.

Ford keyed his comm. "LT, security's concerned about compromise. They're suggesting we abort to a safe location."

"Negative." Love's response was immediate. "We can be airborne in thirty seconds. Tell them it's just a patrol—probably stragglers who stumbled onto us. We leave now, no engagement, no confirmation of VIP presence."

Ford relayed the message, but Korvash looked skeptical. "If they've tracked us here—"

"Then staying gives them time to call friends," Ford interrupted. "The lieutenant's right. We dust off now, they've got nothing but an Osprey sighting."

Through the ramp, he could see the Zodarks had stopped, perhaps assessing. They hadn't opened fire—might not have even identified the Osprey's passengers yet.

"All hands, prepare for immediate departure." Love's voice carried crisp authority. "Ford, button her up. Now."

"Copy. Twenty seconds!" Ford hit the ramp controls, turning to the passengers. "Everyone hold tight. This might get bumpy."

The hydraulics whined as the ramp began rising. In the narrowing gap, Ford saw the lead Zodark raise what looked like a comm device.

Did he see the ambassador? he wondered. *Maybe they're calling for backup.*

"Mama?" Merina's voice quivered slightly.

Keirzi pulled her daughter close, whispering something in the Primord language. Nyranor's hand found his wife's, a gesture of comfort that still maintained his dignity.

The engines' pitch climbed from idle to urgent roar. Ford felt the deck plates vibrate as Love poured power to the systems. Through the closing ramp, he glimpsed the Zodarks breaking into a run—four arms pumping, weapons rising.

"Williams, if you get a shot, take it," Love commanded.

"Copy," said Williams. "I'm trying to get an angle… almost…"

"Ramp sealed!" Ford exclaimed

Ford grabbed a handhold as Love pulled them off the ground without ceremony. The Osprey leaped skyward, pressing everyone into their seats. Merina let out a small shriek that might have been fear or excitement. The deck tilted as Love kicked the rudder, spinning them away from the potential threat.

"Contacts breaking into the open," Williams reported. "No weapons discharge. They're… they're just watching us go."

Ford felt the subtle shift as the nacelles began rotating, transitioning to forward flight. Through a window, he watched the compound shrink rapidly; the Zodark patrol was now just a group of blue specks against the landing pad.

"Clear of immediate threat," Williams confirmed. "Lost visual on the patrol."

Ford checked his passengers. The Special Forces soldiers were already relaxing slightly. They were professionals and they recognized the danger had passed. The bodyguards maintained their vigilance but seemed satisfied with Love's response.

"That was exciting!" Merina said, fear transformed to wonder. "We flew straight up! Like a rocket!"

"Just like a rocket," Ford agreed, relieved to see her smile return. He keyed his comm. "All secure back here, Lieutenant. Passengers safe, no injuries."

"Copy that. Seventeen minutes to Hatteng City. Let our guests know the rest should be much smoother."

Ford turned to the ambassador. "Sir, the lieutenant apologizes for the rapid departure. We should have clear flying from here."

Ambassador Taevlix inclined his head graciously. "Your pilot made the correct decision. Quick thinking, decisive action. Please convey our gratitude."

Korvash leaned over from his position. "Chief Ford, that patrol—they had communication equipment. If they report our direction…"

"Then they report an Osprey heading toward Hatteng City, where dozens of flights go daily," Ford reasoned. "Could be cargo, could be patrol, could be diplomatic—they've got nothing specific."

The security leader considered this, then nodded slowly. "Your lieutenant thinks tactically. Good."

Ford settled back into his position, one hand still on his sidearm out of habit. Through the windows, Intus's jungle canopy blurred past beneath them.

Seventeen minutes to Hatteng City, he thought. But something nagged at him. The way those Zodarks had appeared, their positioning, that comm device—something about it was odd. Zodarks didn't usually observe and report.

He caught Korvash's eye and saw the same thought there.

This might not be over.

But for now, they flew on, five hundred meters up and climbing, leaving questions and concerns behind with the abandoned compound. Ford's job was here, keeping these people safe for seventeen more minutes.

He could do that. They all could.

Chapter 8:
Ambush

Year 2098
En Route to Hatteng City
Planet Intus

Lieutenant Naomi Love kept the Osprey steady at three thousand meters, the jungle canopy flowing beneath them like a green ocean. Five minutes had passed since they'd left the compound, and everything felt routine…too routine.

"Sector scan complete," Williams reported from his gun position. "All clear."

In the crew compartment behind her, she could almost overhear Ford explaining something else technical about the Osprey to the ambassador's daughter. In the monitor, Love saw the Special Forces soldiers sitting there, silent and professional.

"Lieutenant." Green's voice carried a sharp edge. "I'm getting anomalous heat signatures. Bearing one-seven-five, about two hundred meters below our altitude."

Love's hands instinctively tightened on the controls. "Define anomalous."

"Multiple signatures, stationary but—" Green's voice cut off as his console lit up. "They're moving! Eight contacts, dispersing from concealed positions—"

The first plasma bolt slammed into their starboard hull with a sound like a sledgehammer on steel. Then another. And another. The cockpit erupted in warning lights as superheated energy splashed across their armor.

"Contact! Contact!" Williams roared, his gun already traversing. "Ground fire from multiple positions!"

Love didn't think—all her training and experience took over. She threw the Osprey into a hard bank left, diving toward the deck. G-forces crushed everyone into their seats as she traded altitude for speed and angle.

"Missile launch!" Green's voice spiked. "MANPAD, four o'clock low!"

Love saw a bright streak climbing from the jungle canopy, headed right for them. "Countermeasures, now!"

The Osprey's defensive suite activated automatically. Flares burst from the tail in brilliant cascades while electronic jammers screamed across all frequencies. Love rolled right, pulling hard, feeling the airframe protest.

The missile wavered, confused by the flares, then corrected. It was too smart for basic countermeasures.

"Brace!" Love yanked the controls, pulling the Osprey into a climbing spiral that pushed the aircraft to its limits. The missile tried to follow, but the combination of flares, jamming, and violent maneuvering finally broke its lock. It detonated harmlessly fifty meters behind them, the blast wave barely rocking their tail.

Williams's gun hammered out its rhythm, walking fire across the jungle below. "Suppressing grid three-seven! They're dug in deep!"

More plasma bolts streaked past, several finding their mark. Love felt each impact through the controls—vibrations that shouldn't be there, subtle changes in response. In the crew compartment, someone screamed—Love realized it was little Merina, terrified by the violence.

"Port engine four is hit!" Green's fingers flew across his console. "Temperature spiking, oil pressure dropping fast!"

Love checked her displays. Engine four was redlining, threatening to tear itself apart. "Shutting down four. Redistributing power to remaining engines."

The Osprey lurched as she killed the damaged engine, automatically compensating with the other three. They could fly on three—she'd trained for it—but maneuverability suffered.

"Can we maintain altitude?" she asked, jinking left to avoid another stream of plasma fire from the Zodark rifles.

"Affirmative, but we're sluggish," Green reported. "Recommend we—incoming, nine o'clock!"

Love rolled right, diving toward the jungle canopy. At this altitude, the Zodarks had cleaner shots, but she could use terrain. A ridgeline loomed ahead—she pulled up at the last second, using the hill to mask their escape.

Williams kept firing. "Think I tagged one! They're falling back!"

In her peripheral vision, Love caught the crew compartment on her monitor. The Primord bodyguards had positioned themselves around the ambassador's family, speaking calmly in their language despite the chaos. One held Merina's hand while the other shielded them with his body—professional protection under fire.

"Clear of effective range!" Williams announced. "No pursuit visible. They're breaking contact."

Love leveled off at four thousand meters, finally able to assess their situation. Three engines were running smoothly, and one was dead. They had multiple hull impacts, but no breaches. Systems were nominal except—

"We've got hydraulic warnings on the port control surfaces," Green reported. "Nothing critical, but she's going to handle like a drunk Synth."

"Copy." Love adjusted their heading for Hatteng City. "Time to destination?"

"Twelve minutes at current speed. We can push it, but—"

"No." Love kept her voice steady despite the adrenaline flooding her system. "We maintain standard cruise. No need to stress damaged systems." She keyed the intercom. "Ford, casualty report."

"No injuries," Ford replied. "Passengers are shaken but secure. The ambassador's asking about our status."

"Tell him we took some hits but we're fully operational. ETA to Hatteng unchanged."

Love felt the Osprey responding differently now—heavier on the port side, requiring constant minor corrections. Flying on three engines wasn't dangerous, just different.

How the hell did they get their hands on a MANPAD system? Love wondered. For a small insurgent pocket, those Zodarks had really caused some damage.

She keyed her radio. "Oteren Control, *Jack* took ground fire from eight-person Zodark cell. Minor damage sustained, one engine offline, no casualties. Continuing to Hatteng City."

"Copy, *Jack*. Be advised, we're tracking additional increased insurgent activity across the sector. Proceed with extreme caution."

"Understood, Oteren. Jack out."

Love glanced at her copilot. Green was already running calculations for their approach on three engines, adjusting for the hydraulic issues. He was professional and calm—exactly what she needed.

Behind them, Williams remained at his gun, scanning for threats. The adrenaline would be hitting him now—the postcombat high that made gunners love their work.

"Nice flying, Lieutenant," Green said quietly.

Love nodded, hands steady on the controls despite everything. Only twelve minutes remained on their journey to Hatteng City. But that was twelve minutes on three engines with a hull full of VIPs and insurgents armed with more than rifles somewhere behind them.

The milk run had officially gone sour. But they were still flying, still fighting, still completing the mission. That was what mattered. That was what always mattered.

****

The vibration started as a subtle tremor through the control stick. Within thirty seconds, it had become a pronounced shudder that Love felt in her teeth.

"Port engine temperature climbing," Green announced, his calm tone belying the urgency. "Tree-niner-five degrees and rising. Pressure dropping in the coolant system."

Love's eyes flicked between her instruments and the horizon. *Eight minutes to Hatteng City.* They could push it, maybe. But if the engine seized at altitude…

Another warning light flashed amber. The vibration intensified, accompanied by a grinding harmonic that made her stomach clench.

"Four-one-zero degrees," Green continued. "Recommend immediate—"

"I see it." Love scanned the terrain below. Jungle gave way to patches of cleared land—old agricultural zones from before the occupation. "Find me somewhere flat."

Green's fingers flew across his display. "We've got an abandoned field, bearing zero-niner-five, approximately five klicks from city limits. Looks like old grain cultivation."

"That'll do." Love keyed the comm. "All hands, prepare for emergency landing. Ford, secure the passengers."

"Copy that," Ford's voice came back steady. "Already on it."

She keyed her radio again. "Oteren Control, the *Jack* sprang a coolant leak as well, and we're going to have to make an emergency landing. Requesting immediate QRF evac."

"*Jack*, Oteren Control. Copy that. Scrambling QRF. Stand by."

Love began their descent, fighting the increasingly sluggish controls. The port stabilizer's damage was complicating everything—each adjustment required double the input, and the Osprey wanted to roll left constantly.

"Four-two-five degrees," Green reported. "Vibration approaching critical threshold."

The field rushed up to meet them. Overgrown purple-black crops swayed in neat rows, broken by ancient irrigation channels that carved geometric patterns across the landscape. Love flared the Osprey, nacelles rotating to vertical as she bled off speed.

"Fifty meters," Green called out. "Forty…thirty. Brace for landing."

The port engine coughed and stuttered. Love compensated with starboard thrust, wrestling the Osprey level as the landing struts touched down harder than she'd intended. The impact jarred everyone, but they were down.

"Shut down port engine," Love ordered, fingers already moving across the emergency controls. "Williams, Ford—defensive positions. Now."

The rear ramp dropped before the engines had fully spooled down. Williams was out first, weapon ready, scanning the tree line that bordered the field. Ford followed, directing the ambassador to keep his family low and centered in the Osprey.

"Perimeter secure," Williams reported, taking position behind a raised irrigation berm. "No immediate contacts, but we're exposed out here."

Love killed the remaining engine and unbuckled. The sudden silence felt oppressive after the constant engine noise. In the distance, she could hear the urban hum of Hatteng City—aerial traffic, industrial noise, life continuing unaware of their predicament.

"Ford, what's our damage?"

Her crew chief had already grabbed the maintenance kit and ducked under the port nacelle. "Coolant line ruptured—looks like shrapnel from the ambush. Hydraulic pressure's low on the stabilizer actuator too." He emerged, wiping his hands. "Twenty minutes, maybe fifteen if you help."

"Do it." Love turned to the crew compartment, where Ambassador Nyranor stood. "Ambassador, I need you and your family to remain in the Osprey. We'll be airborne shortly."

"Lieutenant," Ambassador Taevlix said, his dignified voice carrying quiet concern, "is there anything I can do to assist? I have some technical training."

"Appreciate the offer, but we've got it handled," she replied.

She walked around to see if she could provide any help herself. "How we doing, Ford?"

"Coolant bypass is holding," he called from under the nacelle. "Working on the hydraulic adjustment. Ten more minutes."

From the Osprey's interior came a soft melody. Keirzi was singing to her daughter in the flowing tones of the Primord language. The lullaby was hauntingly beautiful, its alien harmonics somehow soothing despite the circumstances.

"Movement," Williams announced, his voice sharp. "Southeast tree line. Local wildlife, looks like. Those six-legged deer things."

Love watched the creatures bound away from the field, startled by their presence. But what had caused them to travel into the open in the first place? She strained her ears, catching something beneath the city sounds and Ford's work.

She heard…*engines*. And they were growing closer.

Love popped her head back into the Osprey and made eye contact with Korvash. "I think I hear movement incoming. Do you hear engines too?" she asked.

The Primord security chief perked up, and several of the soldiers instinctively took positions just outside the ramp.

"Seven minutes," Ford announced, sweat dripping despite the cooling afternoon air. The sun hung low, casting long shadows across the crops. Each shadow could hide a threat.

The noise of engines was definitely closer now. Love realized they were ground vehicles, and they were moving fast. She made a quick calculation—if they maintained speed on the access roads she'd seen from altitude…

"Ford, you've got five minutes."

"That's not—"

"Five minutes." Love raced to the cockpit, beginning the start-up sequence. They'd have to launch with whatever repairs were complete.

The late-afternoon sun painted the field in deep purples and golds. It was a beautiful sight, if they'd had time to appreciate it. Instead, Love found herself counting seconds, watching shadows lengthen, and listening to those engines grow ever closer.

In the crew compartment, Merina had stopped crying. She watched with wide eyes as her mother continued the lullaby, while her father sat with the rigid posture of someone prepared for whatever came next.

"Four minutes," Love announced. "All hands, prepare for hot departure."

The smell of leaking coolant mixed with the alien sweetness of the crops. Somewhere in the tree line, more wildlife fled from whatever approached. And beneath it all, those engines grew louder, closer, carrying an unknown threat toward their exposed position in the abandoned field.

****

Dust plumes rose from the access road like brown phantoms against the afternoon sky. Three vehicles were rapidly closing the distance to their position.

"Contact!" Williams called out, his voice sharp over the comm. "Three vehicles inbound. Estimate eight hundred meters and closing!"

Love's hands flew across the start-up sequence. "Ford, talk to me!"

"Three minutes!" Her crew chief's voice came strained from beneath the nacelle. "The hydraulic seal won't—"

"Make it work!"

Through her optics, Love watched the lead vehicle slide to a stop in a cloud of dust. Doors flew open. Blue-skinned figures poured out—four from the first vehicle, moving with the coordinated precision of trained soldiers. The other two vehicles flanked wide, creating a cross-fire position.

Williams's gun spoke first. The heavy crack of the magrail cannon split the air. His first burst caught a Zodark fighter in the open, spinning the four-armed soldier into the dirt. The others dove for cover.

"Good hit!" Korvash called out, repositioning to cover the opposite approach. "Count twelve hostiles. Spreading out!"

The Zodarks returned fire. Plasma bolts sizzled through the air, impacting the earth around Williams's position. One struck the irrigation berm, singeing the air near Williams and throwing a cloud of vaporized soil in a chaotic spray.

"They're using the channels!" Williams reported, walking his fire along the geometric depressions. "Smart bastards!"

Love continued the start-up sequence, each second stretching like an eternity. The port engine coughed to life, then steadied. Love began the starboard sequence.

"Two minutes!" Ford shouted, tools clattering. "Almost there!"

Four hundred meters now. The Zodarks advanced in pairs, one team laying down suppressing fire while another rushed forward through the irrigation channels. They were professional and disciplined.

They aren't acting like random insurgents, Love thought.

Williams tracked the lead element, his rounds forcing them down, buying precious seconds. But there were too many, and they were too spread out. A plasma bolt scorched close to his position.

"Korvash, left side!" Williams called.

The Primord security chief swung his weapon, catching a flanking team trying to use a drainage culvert. His burst sent them scrambling back, one fighter dragging a wounded companion.

"Engines hot!" Love announced. "Ford, Williams—I need you both aboard in sixty seconds!"

"Copy!" they replied in unison

The Zodarks were three hundred meters out now. The firefight intensified. Plasma bolts and conventional rounds crisscrossed the field, turning the purple crops into smoking craters. A burst hammered into the Osprey's hull, leaving a glowing scar on the armor.

"They're getting close!" Ford warned.

Williams shifted position, trying to cover multiple advancing teams. His accuracy was impressive—another Zodark went down—but they kept coming.

"Done!" Ford announced as he rolled out from under the nacelle, grabbing his tools. "It'll hold, but don't push—"

"Get aboard!" Love commanded. "All hands, prepare for immediate dust-off!"

Ford sprinted for the ramp. Korvash began backing toward the Osprey, laying down covering fire. But Williams held his position, trying to keep the Zodarks' heads down during the vulnerable boarding process.

"Williams, displace!" Love ordered.

"Ten more seconds!" He fired another burst, forcing a Zodark team back into cover. "Almost—"

The Osprey's engines reached takeoff power, drowning out his words. They were only two hundred meters away now. The Zodarks were close enough that Love could see their facial expressions.

"Now, Williams!"

He rose from cover, weapon still firing, backing toward the ramp. Ford reached out, ready to pull him aboard. The Osprey began to lift, Love fighting to keep it steady as the damaged stabilizer protested.

Love watched the rear camera feed in horror as a plasma bolt struck Williams in the leg, which instantly buckled beneath him. His weapon dropped from nerveless fingers.

"No!" Ford didn't hesitate. He lunged from the rising ramp, catching Williams before he hit the ground. Plasma fire erupted around them, superheating the air, scorching the Osprey's hull.

"Get them in!" Love roared, holding the Osprey in a hover three feet off the ground.

Ford dragged Williams backward, his own weapon forgotten, focused only on getting his wounded comrade aboard. Korvash appeared at the ramp, grabbing Williams's other arm. Together they hauled him up as Love poured power to the engines.

The Osprey clawed for altitude. Plasma bolts chased them skyward, several finding their mark. Warning lights flashed as minor systems took damage. But they were rising, accelerating, leaving the Zodarks and their vehicles shrinking below.

"Clear!" Green shouted. "We're clear!"

But the celebration died as Ford's voice cut through: "Medic! I need—Williams is hit bad!"

Love looked back at the rear camera again. Williams lay on the deck, and Ford applied pressure to a horrific burn on his left thigh. The plasma bolt had carved through muscle, cauterizing as it went. Blood seeped around the edges of the wound.

"How bad?" Love demanded, banking toward Hatteng City.

"Bad," Ford replied tersely. "But he'll make it. You hear me, Williams? You're going to make it!"

Williams's response was a pained groan, but he was conscious and alive.

Love pushed the throttles forward, ignoring the temperature warnings from the port engine. There were only four kilometers left to Hatteng City. They'd make it. They had to.

Behind them, the agricultural field receded into memory, marked by smoke and scattered Zodark bodies. Their simple taxi run had become a running gunfight, and now they had a casualty. But they were airborne, alive, and headed for help.

"Hatteng Control," Love transmitted, her voice steady despite everything. "This is *Jack* declaring a medical emergency. We met with more Zodark engagement and had to take off again. We have one wounded, requesting immediate medical support on landing."

"Copy, *Jack*. Medical teams standing by. You're cleared for emergency approach, pad seven."

Love flew on, the damaged Osprey responding to her touch, carrying them toward safety and whatever came next.

Chapter 9:
Running Battle

Year 2098
En Route to Hatteng City
Planet Intus

Williams watched as Ford's hands worked with practiced efficiency, cutting away the melted fabric around his thigh. The plasma burn was ugly—a hand-sized crater of charred flesh that wept blood at the edges where the cauterization hadn't sealed the wound completely.

"This is going to hurt," Ford warned, spraying a nanite gel into the wound.

Williams's teeth clenched, a strangled grunt escaping as the gel foamed and expanded. A chemical smell mixed with the stench of burnt flesh. and made Ford's stomach turn, but he kept working, wrapping the field dressing tight.

"Speeders!" Green's voice cut sharp from the cockpit. "Two Zodark speeders lifting off from the field. They're pursuing!"

Williams's eyes snapped open. "How far?"

"Don't even think about it," Ford said, pressing him back down. "You're in shock. That leg—"

"How far?" Williams repeated, already trying to push himself up.

"Eight hundred meters and closing fast," Green replied. "Lieutenant, they're gaining on us."

Love's response was to bank hard right, throwing everyone against their restraints. The damaged stabilizer made the maneuver sluggish, and she could feel the port engine temperature climbing past safe limits.

"I need to get to my gun." Williams grabbed Ford's arm, his grip surprisingly strong. "Help me up."

"You can barely stand!"

"Then I'll sit." Williams's face was pale, sweat beading on his forehead, but his eyes burned with determination. "They catch us, we're all dead. Help me, or get out of my way."

Ford wanted to argue, but plasma bolts screamed past the Osprey's tail. The speeders were closing. He made his decision.

"Lean on me," Ford growled, slipping his shoulder under Williams's arm. "You pass out up there, I'm dragging you back."

Together they struggled toward the rear gun mount. Williams's left leg dragged, useless, and blood was already seeping through the dressing. Each step drew a pained breath, but he kept moving.

"Six hundred meters," Green called out. "They're splitting up!"

Love threw the Osprey into a diving turn, using a ridgeline to break line of sight. The maneuver bought seconds, nothing more. The speeders were faster, more agile. It was only a matter of time.

Williams collapsed into the gunner's seat, hands finding the controls by instinct. The gun mount hummed to life, tracking smoothly despite the Osprey's damaged flight. He blinked sweat from his eyes, fighting the gray creeping into his peripheral vision.

"Contact, five o'clock high!" Green shouted.

The lead speeder came in fast, its sleek form knifing through the air. Plasma cannons mounted on its nose sparked to life. Williams swung the gun, leading the target, but his hands shook. The first burst went wide.

Love rolled left, presenting a harder target. The speeder's plasma bolts seared past, one clipping the starboard engine cowling. More warning lights flashed in the cockpit.

"Come on," Williams muttered, forcing his breathing to steady. The pain was a living thing, trying to drag him under, but he pushed it down. *Focus. Lead the target.* He fired again.

This time his rounds found their mark. Sparks flew from the speeder's nose as bullets tore through its light armor. It veered off, trailing smoke.

"Second speeder, nine o'clock!" Green's voice was tight with strain. "Port engine temperature critical!"

The Zodark pilots were coordinating now, trying to bracket them. They had few options—the damaged stabilizer limited their evasive capabilities, and the overheating engine meant Love couldn't maintain maximum power much longer.

Williams swung the gun to track the second speeder, but the first was coming around again, smoke still streaming from its damaged nose. He made a choice, staying on the wounded one.

"Ford, starboard side!" Love ordered.

Ford had already been on his way to the second gun position. "I'm there, LT," he answered. He fired his magrail projectiles, forcing the second speeder to adjust its attack run.

The wounded speeder came in for another pass. Williams could see the pilot through the canopy—four arms working the controls, blue face set in concentration. He led the target, compensating for the Osprey's movement, ignoring the fire racing up his leg.

The gun mount vibrated as he squeezed the trigger. Rounds walked across the speeder's fuselage and found the engine compartment. Something critical gave way. The speeder's engine exploded in a ball of orange flame. It nosed over, spinning wildly before slamming into the jungle below. Black smoke marked its grave.

"Splash one!" Williams called, his voice rough with pain.

But the second speeder was lining up for a perfect shot, and they had nowhere to go—there were mountains to the right, the damaged engine prevented a climb, and the stabilizer made sharp turns difficult.

Williams traversed the gun, knowing he might not make it in time. His vision blurred. Blood ran down his leg, pooling in his boot. But his hands stayed steady on the controls.

The speeder fired. Plasma bolts streaked toward them. Love threw the Osprey into a desperate sideslip, using the sun behind them to blind the pilot. Most shots went wide, but one found its mark, punching through the cargo compartment's roof.

Merina screamed. Ambassador Nyranor pulled his family flat as superheated air rushed through the hole.

Williams fired everything he had. The gun mount shrieked as he held the trigger down, walking fire across the speeder's path. Rounds sparked off its armor and shattered the forward viewport before they found something vital.

The speeder lurched, banking hard away. Smoke poured from multiple holes in its fuselage. The pilot had had enough—the Zodark turned back toward the field, abandoning the chase.

"Clear!" Green announced. "They're breaking off!"

Williams slumped in the gunner's seat, the weapon falling silent. His hands dropped from the controls, shaking uncontrollably now. The adrenaline that had sustained him was fading, leaving only pain and exhaustion.

"Williams?" Ford was there, checking his pulse. "Talk to me!"

"Did we…?" Williams's voice was barely a whisper. "Did we make it?"

"Yeah, buddy. We made it. You got 'em."

Williams managed a weak smile before his eyes rolled back. Ford caught him as he slumped forward, carefully lowering him to the deck.

"He's out," Ford reported, checking the field dressing. Fresh blood soaked through. "But alive. Pulse is thready. We need to get him help fast."

"Three minutes to Hatteng City," Love replied, pushing the damaged Osprey as hard as she dared. "He'll make it. He has to."

The crew fell silent except for Green's periodic system reports and Ford's quiet reassurances to the unconscious Williams. Behind them, smoke columns rose from the crashed speeder. Ahead, the towers of Hatteng City grew larger, promising help for their wounded warrior who'd saved them all.

****

The skyline of Hatteng City rose before them, a welcome sight after their running battle. Love keyed the comm, relief flooding through her as modern buildings and defensive towers came into view.

"Hatteng Control, this is *Jack* on emergency approach. We have one critical casualty requiring immediate medical assistance."

"*Jack*, Hatteng Control. You're cleared for pad seven, diplomatic district. Medical team standing—wait one." The controller's voice turned sharp. "Break, break, break! *Jack*, abort approach to pad seven. We have active hostile contact in the diplomatic quarter."

Love's hands tightened on the controls. "Say again, Control?"

"Insurgent activity confirmed in sectors twelve through fourteen. Estimate twenty to thirty hostiles. Do not—repeat—*do not* approach diplomatic district."

Through the cockpit glass, Love could see smoke rising from the eastern section of the city. Not the widespread devastation of a major assault, but three distinct columns of black smoke marking burning buildings. As they flew closer, plasma fire erupted from street level—brief exchanges between unseen combatants.

"We need that medical team," Love said, fighting to keep frustration from her voice. Williams didn't have time for delays.

The comm channels erupted with overlapping traffic: "—hostile contact, grid reference—" "—need backup at the municipal—" "—confirmed Zodark fighters moving west on—"

"Green, find us another landing zone," Love ordered, banking away from the smoke.

Her copilot was already working. "Commercial district, bearing two-seven-zero. Approximately two kilometers from our original LZ. Pad looks… mostly clear."

"Mostly?"

"Abandoned ground vehicles, some debris. It's workable."

The port engine chose that moment to hiccup, causing the temperature to spike past redline. Love reduced power, feeling the Osprey wallow in response. The damaged stabilizer made every adjustment a fight.

Below them, the city showed a schizophrenic mix of normalcy and chaos. Most streets hummed with regular traffic, civilians going about their business. But in the affected district, emergency vehicles raced toward the smoke while others fled. Love caught glimpses of firefights—Primord security forces engaging Zodark positions.

"Plasma fire, two o'clock!" Green called out.

Blue-white bolts lanced up from a rooftop. Love jinked left, the Osprey responding sluggishly. The shots went wide, but close enough to feel the heat through the cockpit glass.

"What's the situation down there?" Ford demanded from the cargo bay. "Williams needs help now!"

"Working on it," Love replied through gritted teeth.

More comm traffic flooded the channels. The picture became clearer through the chaos—a Zodark cell had infiltrated the city, hitting multiple targets simultaneously. Hit and run, not trying to hold territory. But the Primord response was swift. She could see security speeders converging, automated defense turrets coming online.

"That was coordinated," Ambassador Nyranor said quietly, his voice carrying forward. "They knew we were coming."

Love didn't respond, focused on nursing the failing Osprey toward their alternate landing zone. The commercial district looked abandoned—shop fronts sealed, pedestrian areas empty. The hasty evacuation was evident in overturned carts and scattered belongings.

"Landing pad in sight," Green announced. "Confirming… yeah, there's debris. Couple of crashed cargo lifters, but we can fit."

The Osprey descended through the urban canyon, buildings rising on either side. Late afternoon shadows made every window a potential threat, every alley a hiding spot. Love's eyes constantly scanned for movement.

"Port engine's finished," Green reported as another alarm joined the ruckus. "We're on starboard only."

"Just need another thirty seconds," Love muttered, fighting the controls as the Osprey wanted to spin with uneven thrust.

The landing pad rushed up—scarred concrete littered with twisted metal from what looked like a cargo accident. Love picked her spot carefully, mindful of the Osprey's damaged undercarriage.

They touched down harder than she would have liked, the impact jarring everyone. But they were down.

"Ford, status on Williams?"

"Pulse is weak but steady. He's lost too much blood. We need to move him now."

Love killed the engines, the sudden silence oppressive. Through the cockpit, she could see the empty commercial district stretching around them. Storefronts stared back with dark windows. In the distance, plasma fire flickered between buildings, and the sound of explosions echoed off glass and steel.

"We're two kilometers from any medical facility," Green said quietly, pulling up area maps. "And between us and them…"

He didn't need to finish. The contested zone lay directly in their path.

"This isn't over," Love said, unbuckling her harness. "Ford, prepare Williams for transport. Green, see if you can raise any friendlies on local channels. We need options."

"What about city emergency services?" Ford asked.

Love gestured toward the distant smoke. "They're busy. We're on our own."

Ambassador Nyranor stood carefully, helping his family. "Lieutenant, I know this city. There are other ways to reach help."

"I'm listening."

"Service tunnels run beneath the commercial district. They connect to the government quarter. If we can access them…"

Another explosion echoed across the city, closer this time. Love made her decision.

"We move in five minutes. Green, strip the emergency medical kit. Ford, rig a carry system for Williams. We're not waiting for the fight to come to us."

Through the Osprey's hull, they could hear sirens, distant gunfire, the sounds of a city under siege. They just had to stay ahead of the chaos long enough to save Williams's life.

The commercial district waited, empty and foreboding, as shadows lengthened toward evening.

"Engines need five minutes to cool," Love announced, killing the power. "We move now. Ford, Green—get Williams mobile."

The rear ramp dropped, revealing the empty commercial plaza bathed in failing emergency lights. Abandoned ground cars sat at odd angles where their owners had fled. Shop windows stared back like dead eyes.

"I can walk," Williams insisted through gritted teeth, pushing himself up from the deck. His left leg buckled immediately.

"Like hell." Ford caught him, slipping under his shoulder. "Green, take his other side."

Together they maneuvered Williams down the ramp. Fresh blood seeped through the field dressing with each step, leaving dark spots on the metal. Love tried not to count them.

"Ambassador, keep your family between us," Love ordered, weapon up and scanning. "Single file, close interval."

They formed up quickly—Love on point, the Taevlix family in the center with their Primord security contingent, Ford and Green supporting Williams, and Williams somehow still managing to cover their six despite everything.

"Checkpoint's that way," Green said, nodding toward a main avenue lined with shuttered shops. "Six hundred meters, straight shot."

"Too exposed," Williams gasped. "Need cover."

He was right. The avenue stretched wide and empty, perfect for ambush. But the alternatives meant longer routes through unfamiliar terrain.

"We go fast," Love decided. "Speed over stealth."

They moved out, footsteps echoing off empty buildings. Every doorway could hide a threat. Every window could frame a shooter. The emergency lighting created pools of shadow between harsh illumination.

They'd covered maybe one hundred fifty meters when Love noticed a fuel canister tucked against a support pillar. There were....*wires* coming out of it.

"IED!" she yelled. "Move, move, mo—"

The explosion wasn't massive, but in the confined urban space it hit like a giant's fist. The pillar disintegrated, bringing down a decorative archway and part of a shop facade. Rubble cascaded across the avenue in a cloud of dust and debris.

Love's ears rang. Through the haze, she saw their route blocked by twisted metal and broken concrete. It wasn't impassable, but it would take time they didn't have.

"Everyone OK?" she called out.

"We're good," Ford replied, though Williams sagged heavier between him and Green.

Merina was crying, her face pressed into her mother's robes. Ambassador Taevlix sheltered them both, dust turning his purple garments gray.

"Service alley," Green said, pointing to their left. "Should parallel the main route."

Love didn't like it—alleys meant confined spaces, limited options—but the explosion would draw attention. They needed to move.

"Go," she ordered.

The service area was all industrial functionality. Loading docks gaped empty. Dumpsters overflowed with rotting produce from abandoned restaurants. The smell mixed with cordite from the explosion, creating a nauseating cocktail.

They'd made it halfway down the alley when shadows moved ahead.

"Contact front!" Love hissed.

Four Zodarks emerged from a loading dock, weapons rising. But their body language showed surprise—they'd been investigating the explosion, not waiting in ambush.

The alley erupted in violence. Love's first burst caught the lead Zodark center mass. He spun and fell, four arms flailing. Ford shoved

Williams behind a dumpster and returned fire, his shots sparking off metal doors.

"Keep the family down!" Love shouted, advancing to better cover.

Williams tried to raise his weapon, but his hands shook. The rifle wavered as he fought to acquire targets. Green fired over his head, dropping a Zodark who'd tried to flank them.

The confined space amplified everything—muzzle flashes strobing like lightning, gunfire echoing off walls, and Merina's terrified screams cutting through it all.

A plasma bolt seared past Love's head, close enough to smell her singed hair. She pivoted and double-tapped the shooter. *Three down.*

The last Zodark dove behind a loading platform, firing wildly. His shots went high, panicked. Williams finally steadied his weapon, waited for the fighter to expose himself, and put a round through his skull.

"Clear," Williams wheezed, then collapsed against the dumpster.

Ford was beside him instantly. "The dressing's soaked through. He's losing too much—"

"I'm fine," Williams interrupted, though his skin had gone ashen. "Just need…a minute."

Love quickly assessed. Four dead Zodarks meant others would come investigating. The explosion would have been heard across the district. And Williams…blood pooled beneath him despite Ford's efforts. His breathing came in short gasps. When he tried to stand, his leg wouldn't support any weight at all.

"New plan," Williams said, voice steadier than his body. "You leave me here with ammo. I'll—"

"We're not having this discussion," Love cut him off. "Ford, Green—carry him if you have to."

"Lieutenant." Williams met her eyes. "Look at me. Really look."

She did. Saw the gray pallor, the unfocused gaze fighting to stay sharp, the blood that wouldn't stop flowing. Saw a warrior running on pure will with nothing left in the tank.

"Not yet," she said firmly. "Green, how far to the checkpoint?"

"Four hundred meters, maybe less." He studied his datapad. "But this alley ends in fifty meters. We'll have to cross open ground."

Williams laughed, a wet sound. "Four hundred meters. Might as well be four kilometers."

"We'll make it," Love insisted.

But looking at the blood trail leading back toward the dumpster, at Williams's trembling hands, at the long path still ahead, she wondered if she was lying.

In the distance, she heard engines—ground vehicles moving fast. Zodarks or Primords? No way to tell.

"On your feet," she ordered. "We move now."

They hauled Williams upright, his strangled grunt cutting deep. More blood…more precious seconds ticking away. But they moved, because staying meant dying, and Love wasn't ready to lose anyone else.

Not yet.

The alley stretched ahead, industrial and unforgiving, while behind them four blue bodies cooled in spreading pools of their own blood. The checkpoint waited somewhere beyond the shadows.

They just had to make it that far.

Chapter 10
Blindside

Year 2098
Fort Moore
Columbus, Georgia
Earth

Coop stood at the edge of the parade ground, the afternoon air biting at his skin. Six months of difficult-as-hell training had come to an end. He glanced over at Bear, who was yanking at the cuffs of his pressed uniform.

"Feels good to be done with all that, doesn't it?" Coop said.

Bear's massive shoulders relaxed for the first time in months. "They weren't kidding when they said this school separates the men from the boys. Even us old dogs learned some new tricks."

Ava Sawyer headed in their direction. Beneath her cap, she'd tucked in her hair. She held herself with the confidence of someone who'd lived to tell about Hell Week and come out stronger because of it. Coop could practically count on both hands how many people stayed with the training until the end—now only twelve.

"Looks like we're not the only ones enjoying a moment of peace." Sawyer nodded toward the small cluster of soldiers milling about. Ortiz was amongst them.

There was a sense of accomplishment in knowing they'd made it through one of the most grueling qualification courses the Republic Navy had to offer. Their graduation into the 9th Special Tactics Squadron showed their skill and perseverance as they prepared to work closely with the Republic Army in their new roles as TASCs.

"Hard to believe we're here," Coop said. "Feels like yesterday I was trying to make it through the Academy."

"This was pure hell, but we earned these tabs," Bear replied, adjusting the Special Tactics insignia on his uniform.

"Worth every second," Sawyer crossed her arms. "Now comes the real work."

"You can say that again," Bear said.

"She definitely outperformed both of us," Coop said.

"At least someone was keeping score," Sawyer replied, a hint of a smile trying to creep onto her face.

A whistle burst through the air. An officer beckoned them toward a nondescript building on the far side of the camp.

"First mission briefing," Coop noted. "Let's go."

They joined the procession into the secure facility. Inside, the briefing room was boring, simple. All gray walls devoid of any decoration with rows of metal chairs facing a long table equipped with holo-projectors.

Coop took a seat between Bear and Sawyer. Accompanying them were soldiers they'd trained alongside during the qualification course. As they sat, the atmosphere was tense with anticipation. This was it… their first assignment as members of the 9th.

When he'd first volunteered for the temporary duty assignment to Special Tactics training with the 1st Special Tactics Wing, they'd made it sound challenging as hell but straightforward. Just survive the course, follow protocols, meet the standards. After many, many horrendous months of being pushed beyond his limits, Coop understood something important. The instructors weren't just testing physical ability or tactical knowledge—they were forging operators who could think independently while functioning seamlessly as a team. Raw talent simply wasn't enough. Neither was experience. They wanted the complete package.

A door at the front slid open. Lieutenant Colonel Waylon Braggs strode in and stood at parade rest behind the podium, looking over the room. The silence was thick.

"At ease," he commanded. "Congratulations to all of you who earned your place in the 9th Special Tactics Squadron. The training you've completed represents one of the most rigorous qualification courses the Republic Navy offers for those who will work directly with the Army."

He paused, scanning the room, no expression on his face whatsoever.

"Today marks your official integration into your operational teams." Braggs lifted a datapad. "Of the twelve graduates from this Special Tactics Assessment and Selection Course, I'm assigning the following primary TASC elements: Lieutenant Bradley 'Coop' Cooper, Lieutenant Lincoln 'Bear' Bowman, Staff Sergeant Diego Ortiz, and

Technical Sergeant Ava Sawyer—you four will deploy as our lead TASC officers, supporting Alpha, Bravo, Charlie, and Delta Companies of 1st Battalion, 504th Infantry Regiment, 'Red Devils,' respectively. You'll each be responsible for coordinating all orbital strikes, artillery support, and close-air support for your entire assigned company."

The room remained silent as Braggs continued assigning the other graduates to their respective teams.

"Now that team assignments are complete," Braggs continued, "we can proceed to your first operational briefing." He straightened. "This mission is classified at the highest level."

Without skipping a beat, a large screen flickered to life behind Braggs. It displayed a rotating holographic image of a moon labeled PTX-419.

"Let's get started," Braggs began. "Those who made it, congratulations on completing your training. As of today, you're operatives of the 9th Special Tactics Squadron. You'll be supporting the 3rd Brigade Combat Team of the 82nd Orbital Assault Division in Operation Blindside. This is part of a division-wide assault targeting five critical Zodark facilities across Nightfall, the farthest moon in the Rass system. This mission is classified at the highest level. What you hear in this room does not leave it. Understood?"

"Yes, sir," everyone replied at the same time.

Braggs tapped a control panel. The holographic image zoomed in on PTX-419. "This is Nightfall. It houses a critical Zodark communication relay station that serves as a primary node in their network, coordinating all military traffic throughout the Rass sector."

Detailed terrain models displayed on the holo. Coop's initial excitement at making it onto the 9th, and in one piece, had quickly subsided. On the holographic display, rugged mountains interlaced with deep canyons, and all around, a forested landscape spread far and wide.

"This comm station sits directly in our planned invasion corridor to Rass," Braggs continued, tracing a path on the tactical display. "Left operational, it would provide the Zodarks with real-time intelligence on our fleet movements and allow them to coordinate a devastating counterattack. Taking it out is essential for the success of our imminent Rass invasion. It'll be like cutting two of their three eyes out."

He highlighted several communication pathways flowing from the station. "Beyond neutralizing it, we need the intelligence stored there to finalize our invasion plans. Most critically, this operation includes uploading our specialized 'Blackout' malware package."

Braggs switched to a simulation showing digital pathways. "Once introduced at Nightfall, this malware will silently replicate across their entire Rass communication grid over approximately twelve hours. When activated, it will simultaneously disrupt their defensive coordination capabilities across the sector."

"Sir, why not just destroy the station from orbit?" Sawyer asked.

Braggs nodded. "Excellent question. A direct attack would alert their entire network and trigger immediate security protocols. They'd isolate systems, reconfigure frequencies, and our malware would be useless. This has to be a covert insertion. Upload the malware, extract the intelligence, then withdraw within our twelve-hour window. Once the malware has fully propagated throughout the Rass system, we'll remotely neutralize the outpost to cover our tracks. The success of the entire Rass campaign hinges on this operation."

Braggs paused, his gaze sweeping across the room. "The 9th's specific role will be providing tactical air and space control expertise for the Republic Army's 82nd Orbital Assault Division. Lieutenant Colonel Harkins, the brigade commander, has specifically requested our unit's support given the critical nature of the operation. Operation Blindside represents the brigade's most critical mission since its formation. You'll be coordinating orbital strikes and facilitating extraction if things get hot."

Coop felt a rush of relief. This was his wheelhouse—utilizing his piloting knowledge in a tactical support capacity.

"And, due to the sensitive nature of this operation," Braggs continued, "we'll be utilizing experimental units. Advanced Combat Synthetic Soldiers, ACSS1s, or C100 combat synthetics." He turned to his right. "You may enter."

At this, a side door opened. Two figures walked into the room. At first glance, they looked nothing like soldiers. Coop immediately recognized them as C100s. They stood eight feet tall with broad shoulders.

Unlike standard Synths with their humanoid appearance, these C100s had no synthetic skin covering their frames. Their exoskeletons were mostly exposed metal or covered with tactical armor plating. From what little he understood about them, Coop knew that their metallic skin contained advanced adaptive camouflage technology. They were able to morph and mimic surroundings, whether in woodland, urban, or arctic environments.

Their faces bore only a passing resemblance to anything human. Instead of eyes, each had a one-inch-wide horizontal band wrapping around from ear to ear—a sensor array providing them with 180-degree vision. A single blue light tracked slowly from right to left across this band, indicating that they were active rather than in standby mode.

They moved oddly, each step perfect. On one arm, each bore an integrated weapons system; the other ended in an articulated hand capable of both delicate manipulation and crushing force.

A chill ran down Coop's spine. He'd heard stories about Synths—synthetic humanoids engineered for combat. History lessons came to mind about the Great War. There were tales of machines turning on their creators and causing devastation too terrible to recite out loud, even in campfire stories.

"These are the C100s," Braggs said. "Advanced combat Synths designed to support our operations. They possess enhanced strength, reflexes, and tactical processing capabilities. They'll be integrated into each company of the 1-504th for the initial breach."

Sawyer folded her arms, skepticism evident on her face. Bear's entire body went rigid.

Coop couldn't hold back any longer. "Sir, with all due respect," he said, "are we confident these units won't pose a risk to the mission? History hasn't been kind regarding synthetics in warfare."

Braggs gave him a stern look. "The C100s are fully under our control. Latest safeguards are in place to prevent any malfunctions or unauthorized actions. They're an asset, not a liability."

Coop nodded, although unease lingered in him. Vids of cities razed to the ground by rogue machines filled his head, the human cost of technological experimentation and tech wizardry gone awry.

"The success of this mission depends on seamless integration between all units," Braggs said. "That includes the Synths." He returned his attention to the holographic display. "Now, the approach. We'll insert under the cover of Nightfall's orbital characteristics. The moon's rotation and irregular magnetic field will mask our ships from

Zodark sensors. We'll have a contingency of EW frigates also masking the fleet from approach."

Coop studied the projected flight paths. There was something off. Why would they go in that way? After he'd studied it for less than a minute, a solution came to him quickly. "Sir, I recommend we modify our insertion corridor to heading two-one-four. We can use that crater wall's gravity well for a low-energy approach. Cuts our exposure time in half and keeps us below their sensor threshold."

The room fell silent. All eyes turned to Coop as Braggs's expression hardened. "Lieutenant Cooper, are you questioning the mission plan that was devised by Space Command?"

Coop hesitated. "Not questioning, sir. Offering a suggestion to enhance our success."

A muscle twitched in Braggs's jaw. "Your approach vector would indeed reduce exposure time. However, it places our insertion ships dangerously close to the moon's automated defense grid. The current flight path maintains optimal distance from known Zodark sensor arrays."

Coop studied the plan again, understanding what Braggs was pointing out. "I see the issue now, sir. You're right. The defense grid would pose a greater risk than the longer approach."

Braggs seemed surprised by Coop's quick acknowledgment. "Good assessment, though, Lieutenant. That kind of tactical thinking is why you're in the 9th. Keep offering input, but always be ready to integrate new information."

"Yes, sir," Coop replied.

"As I was saying," Braggs continued, "timing is critical. The 3rd Brigade Combat Team of the 82nd Orbital Assault Division has been training specifically for Operation Blindside for months. Within the 3rd Brigade's area of operations, the 1-504th Infantry Regiment will spearhead the communications relay assault, with your TASC teams embedded with each company. The other battalions in the 3rd Brigade will provide security and support elements. Your Army teams will conduct a precision infiltration of the communication relay. The facility is heavily fortified with Zodark security forces. Extracting whatever intelligence we can will provide invaluable data for our entire campaign strategy."

Detailed schematics of the station appeared on the screen. A central command hub stood surrounded by enormous transmission arrays, all interconnected by power conduits and subterranean access tunnels. Relay dishes pointed skyward, forming a sophisticated communications web across the moon's surface.

"The station operates as a primary hub in their network," Braggs explained. "Intelligence estimates twelve to fifteen thousand Zodark forces across Nightfall, with two thousand defending this primary communications relay. The remaining forces are distributed among the other four facilities and their mobile reserves. These relays coordinate all Zodark military movements in the sector using encrypted communications. If we simply destroy it, they'll activate redundancy protocols. The C100 units will support the infiltration teams by providing perimeter security."

Coop glanced at the Synths. They stood motionless, their tin can faces unreadable. Some called them Terminators. Coop preferred toasters. The thought of coordinating a stealth operation with machines made his skin crawl until he pushed the negative sensation aside.

"Once inside," Braggs continued, "your specialists will access their central database, extract critical intelligence, and upload our 'Blackout' malware into their systems. This custom virus will propagate throughout their network over twelve hours, creating backdoor access to their entire communication infrastructure. When activated during our main assault, it will cripple their ability to coordinate defensive operations across the Rass system. Your job will be to maintain operational security and provide tactical guidance while attached to the infiltration elements. Questions?"

Sawyer raised a hand. "Sir, what's the extraction plan?"

"A window of thirty minutes after mission completion. Extraction points will be relayed once on the ground. Forward Operating Base Farside will be established at the division's primary landing zone. While the 3rd Brigade targets the primary communications relay, the 1st, 2nd, and 4th Brigades will each assault one of the remaining major facilities. The fifth objective—the smaller defense monitoring outpost—will be neutralized by Task Force Scalpel, a composite battalion-sized element drawn from the division's QRF and special operations assets. You'll need to be off-station before the twelve-hour propagation period completes, after which we'll remotely trigger the malware's secondary protocol to neutralize the facility. They'll automatically trigger the charges set by your teams."

Coop swallowed. In and out in twelve hours. Sounded simple enough on paper, but he knew better. Apparently, the impossible was what these spec ops teams did.

"What about emergency extraction if we're compromised?" Ortiz asked.

"Limited options," Braggs replied. "We need this operation to remain completely covert until the malware fully propagates. The division's coordinated assault on all five facilities will commence simultaneously. While your brigade handles the communications relay, the remaining three brigades will target the weapons development facility, command headquarters, logistics hub, and defense control center. All five operations must succeed for our overall mission objectives to be met. Any indication of our presence could trigger system-wide alerts and compromise the entire Rass invasion. Your teams will have emergency extraction protocols, but understand that premature extraction risks the entire operation and potentially thousands of lives in the main invasion force."

"And our available air assets, sir?" Sawyer inquired.

"The 82nd's fleet will consist of four orbital assault carriers to transport our division's troops, along with five support vessels for equipment and vehicles. The battle group includes two battleships, four heavy cruisers, and eight frigates providing orbital fire support and electronic warfare capabilities. Your specific team will deploy from the RNS *Leahy* with a full complement of Orions, Raiders, and Reapers, plus two stealth gunships for close fire support. The 82nd's assault shuttles will deploy under your tactical guidance." Braggs's expression hardened. "Your targeting data will need to be flawless." He tapped his datapad. "Final mission details will be distributed to your personal devices. Study them thoroughly. Dismissed."

As the room cleared, the C100s moved past Coop. They were too mechanical for him, even with their smooth movements. Yes, they walked amazingly, but it was just odd to watch. Still, their heavy frames somehow made less noise than a whisper despite their size.

Bear hung back as the others filed out. "Watch yourself, Coop," he muttered under his breath. "Some things are better left unsaid." Before Coop could respond, Bear was gone.

"Lieutenant Cooper." Braggs's tone boomed through the emptying room. "A moment."

Coop's stomach tightened as he made his way to the podium. The last few stragglers disappeared through the door, leaving him alone with the colonel.

Braggs studied him for several beats. "I couldn't help but notice your reaction to the C100s."

"Sir, I—"

"Save it," Braggs interrupted. "I've read your file. Your father was a pilot in the Great War. Lost his entire squadron to rogue synthetic humanoid-controlled drones during the Gulf Coast Slaughter. Watched eleven good pilots get shot out of the sky in less than ten minutes."

"That has nothing to do with—"

"It has everything to do with it," Braggs said. "The 9th operates alongside whatever assets Command deems necessary. If you can't handle that, you're in the wrong outfit."

"I don't have a problem with synthetic humanoids, sir," Coop lied.

Braggs held his gaze for what felt like forever. "Good," he finally said. "Because where we're going, your life might depend on them. Dismissed."

Coop turned and walked out. The growing anxiety in his gut was impossible to ignore. The Great War had taught humanity many difficult lessons about trusting machines. Now here they were, putting their lives in combat synthetic hands again. Synths were fine as helpers, but wielding a gun? That was a different story altogether.

Chapter 11
Launch Day

Year 2098
Cape Canaveral, Florida
Earth

In Florida, sweat constantly accumulated on Coop's face. He wiped the perspiration off his brow as he stood on the launch pad at Cape Canaveral Space Force Station. Florida's humidity reminded him of the few planetside visits he'd paid to Intus. It was almost too much.

At the moment, and all around him, the Republic battle group busied with predeployment activity—personnel moving equipment, running final checks, and preparing for the journey to Nightfall.

"Two hours until launch," Bear said.

Coop nodded, watching as soldiers from 1st Battalion, 504th Infantry Regiment—the storied Red Devils of the 3rd Brigade, Republic Army's 82nd Orbital Assault Division—moved in formation toward their designated shuttles. The Red Devils' unit patches had evolved since their World War II days dropping into Sicily, but the fierce reputation remained intact as they transformed from paratroopers to orbital assault specialists. The entire division was deploying for this operation across five critical Zodark facilities on Nightfall. The 3rd Brigade, with the 504th leading the assault element, would target the primary communications relay, while the 1st, 2nd, and 4th Brigades would assault the other major facilities. Task Force Scalpel, a specialized battalion-sized element drawn from the division's QRF, would neutralize the fifth objective—a smaller defense monitoring outpost.

Their standard Army gear made them look bulkier than they already were. Somewhere in that group was Alpha Company, the two hundred and sixty soldiers Coop would be supporting during the operation. As part of the 1-504th's enhanced company structure, Alpha Company had been augmented with additional combat support elements for this mission. While his responsibility would encompass the entire company, he wouldn't physically stay with all of them during the mission. Instead, he'd either move with the company commander's tactical element or attach to a specific platoon of fifty soldiers conducting the main effort or positioned where air support would be most critical.

"We should get to Hangar C," Sawyer said, adjusting the pack on her shoulder. "Final equipment verification before boarding."

Hangar C was a flurry of personnel moving and packing and lifting items, crates, and bags when they arrived. The TASC team had established their temporary operations area amid rows of equipment cases, each marked with serial numbers and color-coded tags. The 3rd Brigade commander stood with his staff reviewing holographic terrain maps of Nightfall while the Major of the 1-504th Infantry Battalion briefed his company commanders nearby.

"Cooper, Bowman, Sawyer," a squadron commander called out. "Your station is in section four. Padilla wants all communications equipment verified before 1400 hours."

Coop made his way to their assigned area, where several C100 synthetics were already running diagnostic protocols on the battalion's integrated battle network systems. He frowned slightly at the machines.

"Let's run manual checks on all the comms gear," Coop said, bypassing the nearest C100. "I want to physically inspect every transmitter and receiver circuit."

Bear shrugged. "You sure? The diagnostics are already running automatically. The C100s can complete full system checks in minutes. I say go with them."

"And miss something critical?" Coop replied, pulling open an equipment case. "I'd rather know for certain. Besides, when we're in the field with Alpha Company, we need to be able to troubleshoot without relying on synthetics."

"You forget," Sawyer reminded him, "I'm not in Alpha Company, and neither is Bear."

For an instant, Coop almost lowered his shoulders in dismay. He'd come to like Sawyer, and Bear had become his right-hand man back on RNS *Gallipoli*, in the Jolly Rogers squadron. Yet it was the military. People came and went as missions and operations changed. You either dealt with it, or… dealt with it. You really had no choice.

They spent the next hour testing each piece of communications equipment, from tactical headsets to long-range battlefield coordination systems.

"Frequency band check on the squad-level tactical net," Coop said. "Sawyer, can you verify signal clarity on channels one through eight?"

As they worked, Coop became increasingly aware of a presence behind him. Turning, he found Captain Dean Padilla, the TASC detachment commander, observing their progress, arms crossed and expression neutral. As the officer responsible for all tactical air and space control specialists supporting the 1-504th Infantry, Padilla would be coordinating their activities throughout the operation.

"Lieutenant Cooper," Padilla said, "what's your current status?"

"Almost complete with manual verification of all comms systems, sir," Coop reported. "Just finishing the tactical net checks now."

Padilla's eyes moved from the equipment spread across their workstation to the idle C100s nearby, then back to Coop.

"Lieutenant, are you aware that the standard protocol for predeployment verification utilizes C100 synthetic diagnostic systems?" the captain asked.

Coop straightened. "Yes, sir. I preferred to conduct manual checks for additional certainty."

To his side, Bear and Sawyer also stood erect, but out of the corner of his eye, Coop caught a glimpse of Sawyer going a bit too rigid, no doubt a little miffed that Coop insisted on manual checks instead of using the C100s.

"I see." Padilla stepped closer, his voice low enough that only their immediate team could hear. "Your manual verification process has taken approximately fifty-eight minutes longer than the synthetic diagnostic would have. Analysis shows that manual communications setup reduces battlefield effectiveness by forty percent and creates unnecessary delays during critical deployment phases."

Coop felt heat rise to his face, but unlike in training, when he might have become defensive, he caught himself. This wasn't about his pride. It was about mission effectiveness.

"You're right, sir," Coop said. "I've been operating under outdated assumptions."

Padilla's expression softened a little. "Your attention to detail is commendable, Cooper. But part of being an effective TASC is utilizing every resource available. Including synthetic support systems. Save your manual skills for when equipment fails in the field.”

“Understood, sir. I’ll utilize the integrated systems during deployment.”

After the captain moved on, Bear nodded at Coop. “That’s growth, my boy. The old Coop would’ve dug in his little, tiny, teeny-weeny heels in the dirt. Sometimes you just gotta listen to the genius in the group, eh?”

“You?”

“Yep.”

“What did you say to make you this incredible genius all of a sudden?”

“All of a sudden? Try *always*. Anyway, I questioned your—”

“Yeah, well,” Coop said with a half-smile, shaking his head, “I didn’t listen, but I should have. That ‘old dog new tricks’ thing comes to mind, meaning I can learn. Anyway, let’s finish up here and get ready to board.”

An hour before shuttle launch, Captain Padilla introduced Coop to Alpha Company’s command element. Captain Saho Nobunaga, Alpha Company commander of the 1-504th “Red Devils,” gave Coop a firm nod. Beside him stood the senior NCO, a barrel-chested master sergeant. The radio operator, intelligence officer, and a few medics rounded out the small tactical team—the people Coop would work most closely with during ground operations. Captain Padilla explained that Coop would either move with this command element or attach to whichever platoon was designated as the main effort, depending on the mission’s needs.

When the time came, Coop strapped himself into one of the orbital shuttles alongside sixty-odd soldiers from Alpha Company’s second platoon. Nobunaga had specifically requested Coop ride with this platoon as they’d be taking point once moonside.

The shuttle shuddered as its engines ignited, pressing them back into their seats as it climbed through the atmosphere. Coop’s stomach lurched as they accelerated, Earth’s blue horizon gradually curving beneath them until it gave way to the blackness of space.

“First time off-world?” asked the soldier next to him, a staff sergeant with “Vega” stenciled on her fatigues.

"No, but first time as TASC," Coop replied. "Been a Fleet pilot since the war started."

Vega nodded. "Good to have you with us. We're gonna need that orbital support once we hit dirt. The Red Devils always lead the way."

As the shuttle continued its ascent, the stars became clearer, sharper without atmosphere to dim them. As always out in space, the stars didn't flicker—just a forever shine. After nearly forty minutes of flight, the orbital docks finally came into view—massive structures hanging in the void where the battle group waited.

Here, the Republic had assembled an impressive force for the Nightfall operation. Two *Ryan*-class battleships dominated the formation—the RNS *Brewster* and RNS *Wilson*, their long hulls covered with weapon systems. Nearby floated four heavy cruisers, including the *Marathon* and *Thermopylae*, built for sustained combat operations. Surrounding them were eight frigates, four loaded with electronic warfare capabilities, and four corvettes for close support. The division's four orbital assault carriers formed the core of the transport fleet, with five additional support vessels carrying vehicles and heavy equipment. It was a small armada capable of deploying all the troops of the 82nd Orbital Assault Division.

Near the center of the formation waited their destination—the RNS *Leahy*, an orbital assault carrier that would transport Coop's unit to Nightfall. It showed broad landing bays and dropship launch tubes along its flanks. Completing the battle group were two medical vessels, four supply freighters, and two fuel tankers. Everything needed for a prolonged operation far from Republic space.

The shuttle docked with a slight vibration, and the personnel began disembarking. Coop followed his big team through the connecting tube and into the RNS *Leahy*'s main receiving bay, where a ship's officer was directing troops to their assigned sections.

"TASC specialists, deck four, section twelve," the officer announced as they approached. "You'll be situated adjacent to the 1-504th's command staff for integrated operations planning."

Coop turned to Lieutenant Spike Gill, a platoon leader that Captain Saho Nobunaga said he'd be working with. "I'll find you after I get settled, sir."

"You do that," Gill replied. "We're running a tactical simulation at 1900 hours. We could use your input on the fire support plan."

As Coop made his way through the carrier's corridors, he found Bear and Sawyer already at their assigned quarters.

"Where's Ortiz?" Coop asked.

"Saw him with Delta Company. He's on his way," Sawyer added. "Captain Padilla wants us in the tactical operations center in thirty minutes to review initial support assignments."

Coop checked his equipment one more time—this would be his lifeline once they hit the ground on Nightfall. His comms gear would connect thirty-five lives to the massive firepower orbiting above them. No room for error. It'd take some time to get there, but that didn't stop him from making sure everything was where he needed it.

"Never thought I'd be the one on the ground," Coop admitted. "Always figured I'd stay in the cockpit. But, you volunteer for something big, you get something big."

"Yep, my man. Times change," Bear replied. "So do we."

By the time they reached the tactical operations center, the battle group was preparing for departure. Through a viewport, Coop watched as the immense ships began to move in perfect formation, breaking orbit around Earth.

The vessels accelerated, their drives glowing as they aligned for the jump to FTL. The revolutionary Ark-Fold drives would compress what would have been a five-month journey into a mere five days, collapsing space-time to achieve one light-year per day instead of the previous two light-years per month.

During the transit, Coop reviewed the intelligence briefing on opposition forces. As many as fifteen thousand Zodark troops were distributed across Nightfall's five facilities, with roughly two thousand of them defending the communications relay that Alpha Company would help assault. Knowing they'd be facing seasoned Zodark soldiers in well-fortified positions made the mission preparation all the more critical.

When the dimensional translation began, Coop felt the familiar pressure against his chest, a small price to pay for technology that had transformed humanity's reach among the stars, thanks to the Altairians. For a moment, reality seemed to bend around them. Coop's stomach twisted and turned. His inner ear rebelled as physics took a day off. As always, colors he couldn't name streaked past the viewports.

In the next instant, everything calmed. The stars around them turned into brilliant streams of light across the darkness.

The mission plan highlighted that Forward Operating Base Farside would be established during their primary assault, serving as the division's landing zone and staging area. The brigades would deploy to their respective objectives, with Alpha Company's assault on the communications relay coordinated with simultaneous attacks on the other four Zodark facilities.

They were underway, days and days of travel ahead before they'd face whatever waited for them on the moon, Nightfall. Combat was coming, and Coop hoped, for the Republic's sake, that he was ready for it.

Chapter 12:
Fight to the Death

Year 2098
Hatteng City
Planet Intus

The alley ended at a wide boulevard. Four hundred meters of open ground stretched before them, broken only by decorative planters and abandoned vehicles. In the distance, the checkpoint's lights beckoned—so close, but impossibly far.

Engine sounds grew louder. Multiple vehicles seemed to be converging from different directions.

"We're trapped," Green said, stating the obvious. He was still supporting Williams's dead weight.

Love's mind raced through options. *Should we sprint across?* she asked herself. But she knew they'd be cut down. *Hold position?* If they did that, the vehicles would box them in. Williams couldn't move fast enough for either choice.

"Lieutenant," Ambassador Taevlix said with a note of urgency. "There are maintenance tunnels. My people's infrastructure runs beneath the entire district."

Love turned sharply. She'd forgotten all about the plan they'd been carrying out earlier. "Where?" she asked.

"The tunnels…are not designed for humans," he answered, his voice cracking. "I was hoping we wouldn't need them. But there's an access point in that loading dock."

Vehicles approached from two directions now. There was no time for hesitation.

"Show us," Love directed.

They backtracked twenty meters to the loading dock Ambassador Taevlix had shown her, and he ran his hand along the floor until he found what he sought—a sealed hatch marked with Primord script.

"Emergency maintenance access," he explained, working the release. "It will be cramped."

The hatch opened to reveal a narrow shaft with ladder rungs. Bioluminescent strips cast pale green light into the depths.

"Ford, lower Williams down. I'll catch him," Love said, already descending.

The temperature dropped immediately. The shaft opened into a tunnel that forced Love to hunch. Organic curves met utilitarian purpose in the architecture, like being inside a living machine.

Williams barely responded as Ford lowered him down. Love caught his weight, staggering as his blood smeared across her uniform. His skin felt cold, clammy.

"Sorry," Williams mumbled. "Making a mess."

"Save your strength," Love told him.

The others descended quickly. Merina whimpered at the alien space, but Keirzi whispered soothing words. Green came last, sealing the hatch above.

"Which way?" Love asked.

Nyranor studied markings on the curved walls—flowing script that seemed to shift in the bioluminescent light. "This way. Two hundred meters to a junction; then we can access the government district."

They moved in a cramped single-file line. Ford and Green dragged Williams between them, his boots scraping along the pale floor. The blood trail was vivid against the tunnel's organic surfaces, impossible to miss.

Pipes and conduits ran along the walls, carrying utilities Love couldn't identify. The air tasted stale, metallic. Every sound echoed strangely in the confined space—their breathing, Williams's pained gasps, water dripping somewhere ahead.

"Stay with us," Ford urged Williams. "Talk to me."

"Did I… did I tell you about Rebecca's birthday?" Williams's voice drifted. "I sent her… something nice. A music box. She likes…"

"You told me," Ford lied. "She'll love it."

Taevlix led them through a junction where three maintenance tunnels met. He chose without hesitation, reading markers Love couldn't decipher. The bio-strips grew dimmer here, leading Love to believe this was an older section of the tunnels.

They'd gone maybe fifty meters when Love heard a noise that didn't belong. It sounded like scraping…metal on stone.

"Down!" she yelled.

The explosion hit like a hammer in the confined space. It hadn't been massive—probably a pipe bomb and crudely placed—but the tunnel had focused the blast. The ceiling ahead cracked, and organic material and concrete rained down. Dust filled the air.

"Everyone OK?" Love called out. Her ears were ringing.

She was answered by coughs and groans that confirmed her group were all still alive, if a bit shocked and temporarily suffering some hearing loss. But their path was blocked by rubble.

"Detour," Ambassador Taevlix directed, voice shaken. "Older tunnels. This way."

The alternate route descended sharply. The bio-strips were failing here, flickering like dying fireflies. Liquid appeared on the floor—ankle-deep, then knee-deep. It was either coolant or condensation from damaged systems above.

Williams had gone quiet. Ford checked his pulse with increasing desperation. "He's going into shock," Ford reported. "He's starting to feel cold. We need—"

"I know what we need," Love snapped, then caught herself. "How much farther?"

"Not far," Nyranor promised, though uncertainty colored his tone.

The fluid beneath them was ice cold, stealing what little warmth Williams had left. Green had given up marking their path—there was no point in planning a retreat when forward was the only option.

"Hey." Williams spoke suddenly, clearly. "Tell my sister… tell her I wasn't scared."

"Tell her yourself," Ford growled.

Williams smiled weakly. "We both know… that's not happening." His hand found Ford's arm. "It's OK. Did my job. Got you this far."

They reached a shaft leading up. It was newer construction and dry. Nyranor checked the markings and nodded. "Government building," he confirmed. "Basement access. We're close."

Love climbed first, pushing open another hatch. She emerged into a mechanical room, which held boilers and ventilation systems. The tech was of Primord origin but recognizable. Through the door, she heard nothing. It meant either safety or an ambush.

"Clear," she called down.

Getting Williams up proved nearly impossible. He was barely conscious, all dead weight. Ford climbed the ladder backward, with Green and Love pulling from above. The Primords gave a hand as well. Williams's head lolled, his eyes unfocused.

"Two hundred meters to the district perimeter," Taevlix said once they'd all emerged. "There will be patrols, security."

Love looked at Williams—pale, blood-soaked, breathing in shallow gasps. Two hundred meters might as well be two hundred kilometers. But they'd come too far to quit.

"Ford, Green—carry position. I'll take point."

They lifted Williams between them, his arms draped over their shoulders. He murmured something—might have been "sorry" or might have been nothing at all.

Love checked her weapon, then the door. The hallway beyond was empty, just the way a government building would normally appear after hours. Emergency lighting showed their path.

Two hundred meters, she reminded herself. *We can make that. We have to.*

"Move out," Love ordered, leading them from the tunnels' dubious safety into whatever waited above.

Behind them, water dripped in dark tunnels, mixing with the blood they'd left behind. Ahead, the government district promised safety…as long as Williams lasted that long. If *any* of them did.

****

The moment they exited, Love heard the sharp crack of plasma fire, the deeper thump of projectile weapons, and orders shouted in Primord. It wasn't right next to them, but it was close. Too close.

Love pressed against the building's wall, scanning the street. Smoke drifted from burning vehicles fifty meters away. Through the haze, she caught muzzle flashes between government buildings. There was a major firefight, and they were about to walk into the middle of it.

"Republic emergency channel," she ordered Green, who still had the long-range comm.

Static filled her earpiece before she found the right frequency. "Any Primord military units, this is Lieutenant Love, Republic Navy. I have Ambassador Taevlix and wounded personnel. Request immediate assistance."

More static. Then a gravelly voice responded. "Republic forces? This is Sergeant Varkoni, Third District Guard. What is your position?"

"Government Building Seven, basement exit. We need—"

"Negative! Do not approach our position. We are heavily engaged. Twenty-plus hostiles."

Love peered around the corner. The Primord position was visible now—a defensive line anchored on an overturned transport, maybe eight soldiers firing disciplined bursts at advancing Zodarks. Professional, well trained, and about to be overrun.

"Sergeant, we have wounded in critical condition. Where's your medic?"

A pause filled with weapons fire. "Still breathing. But we cannot—" His transmission cut to static as an explosion rocked the Primord position.

"Varkoni, do you copy?"

"Still here," came the strained reply. "Lost two. They are flanking east. We cannot hold much longer."

Williams stirred between Ford and Green, his eyes focusing with effort. "What's…the tactical situation?"

"Primord squad pinned down," Love told him. "Between us and the checkpoint."

Williams's head lifted, professional instinct overriding his body's failure. Through the smoke, he studied angles, distances, and cover. "They're focused on the Primords. We could make it past."

"Or help them," Ford said.

"With what?" Williams's laugh turned into a cough. "I can't even hold a rifle."

"Sergeant Varkoni," Love transmitted. "Can you make it to Building Seven?"

"Negative. The moment we displace, they willl cut us down. Reinforcements ten minutes out."

Ten minutes. Love looked at Williams and saw Ford's desperate expression. They didn't have ten minutes.

"There." Korvash pointed to a rubble-strewn alley between buildings. "Dead ground. We could reach their position without crossing the main kill zone."

"Linkup requires crossing that intersection," Love noted. Thirty meters of open space under direct fire.

"Lieutenant." Williams spoke with sudden clarity. "Leave me with them."

"No."

"Listen." His grip on Ford's shoulder tightened. "Their medic can stabilize me. Buy time. You get the ambassador through while the Zodarks are engaged."

"Their position's about to be overrun," Ford protested.

"Maybe. Maybe not." Williams managed a ghost of his old grin. "Either way, it gives me better odds than bleeding out while you carry me."

Ambassador Taevlix stepped forward. "The corporal speaks wisdom," he said. "My family's safety—"

"With all due respect to your position, sir, we don't abandon our own," Love cut in.

There was another explosion. Through the smoke, she saw Zodarks advancing in pairs, using rubble for cover. The Primord fire slackened—whether because of casualties or lack of ammunition, it didn't matter.

"Varkoni, what's the status on that checkpoint?" asked Love.

"Still secure," the Primord sergeant replied. "If you can reach it. But the route—"

His transmission ended in screams and plasma fire.

"Varkoni? Sergeant?"

"Still here," came a different voice. "Sergeant's hit. This is Corporal Venar. We have four effectives. Cannot hold."

Williams pushed himself straighter with visible effort. "Love…Naomi," he said, using her first name for the first time since she'd known him. "You know I'm right. Get them out. Let me buy you time."

Ford checked Williams's pulse again, his face telling the story. "He's going into hypovolemic shock. Blood pressure's barely registering."

"The Primord medic—" Williams started.

"May not be able to fix what you've lost," Ford said brutally. "Even in a full hospital…"

Williams nodded slowly. "That's what I thought." He looked at Love. "So let me make it count. Like we always knew one of us would have to."

Love's throat constricted. The math was brutal but clear. Carry Williams and they all died. Leave him with the Primords, and maybe he'd live long enough to help, maybe not. But the ambassador, his family, the intel—they might make it.

"I can't order you to stay," she said quietly.

"Don't have to." Williams looked at each of them. "Ford, remember about Rebecca. Green, thanks for having my six. Lieutenant… it's been an honor."

Through the smoke, plasma fire intensified. The Zodarks were making their final push. Time had run out for decisions.

"We set him with the Primords," Love decided, voice steady despite the burning in her chest. "Then we move fast for the checkpoint."

Merina, silent through all the violence, suddenly spoke. "The soldier is staying again?"

Her mother pulled her close, but the girl's eyes remained on Williams. There was too much understanding in that young gaze.

"Yeah," Williams told her gently. "But this time, I get to help new friends. Pretty good deal."

Love keyed the comm. "Venar, we're coming to you. Have your medic ready. We're leaving one of ours."

"Understood. Approach from the east. We'll cover."

They prepared to move, everyone knowing this was goodbye. In the distance, reinforcement sirens wailed. Love wondered if they would arrive in time for some, or if they would be too late to make a difference.

The intersection awaited—thirty meters of hell between Williams and his last stand. Love checked her weapon and prepared to lead them across.

"Ready?" she asked, though no one could ever be ready for this.

Williams nodded, pain and determination in his eyes. "Always."

"Covering fire!" Corporal Venar shouted.

The Primord squad opened up in disciplined bursts, their plasma rifles lighting the smoke-filled air. Love sprinted first, low and fast across the intersection. Rounds cracked overhead, too close, but the Zodarks were focused on the Primord position.

"Now!" she called back.

Ford and Green lifted Williams between them, stumbling into the open. Williams tried to help, pushing with his good leg, but it was like carrying dead weight. Plasma bolts seared past. One clipped the ground near Ford's feet, spraying molten concrete.

They crashed into cover behind an overturned transport, Williams crying out as they lowered him. The Primord medic, a thin soldier with steady hands, was already moving.

"Human physiology," he muttered, scanner dancing over Williams's wounds. "Blood loss critical. Internal pressure falling." He met Williams's eyes with professional honesty. "I can give you stimulants, seal the external trauma. But the damage…"

"How long?" Williams asked.

"Minutes. Perhaps an hour with aggressive intervention."

Williams actually smiled. "That'll do."

Sergeant Varkoni dragged himself over, his left arm hanging useless. Despite his wound, his eyes remained sharp, tactical. "Corporal tells me you're staying."

"Looks that way." Williams studied the defensive position. Four Primord soldiers were still fighting; bodies remained where others had fallen. Concrete barriers and overturned vehicles created decent cover, but the Zodarks were massing for another push.

"There." Williams pointed with effort. "Between those buildings. They have to funnel through to reach you."

Varkoni followed his gaze. There was a narrow passage, maybe five meters wide. Debris and abandoned equipment created natural barriers. It was a perfect chokepoint.

"One soldier could hold that for… some time," Varkoni acknowledged.

"My thought exactly." Williams looked at Love. "Get me set up there. Leave me ammo and go."

"Williams—"

"Lieutenant." His voice carried command despite everything. "This is the play. You know it. I know it. Let's not waste time."

The medic pressed a stimulant injector against Williams's bicep. The effect was immediate—his eyes sharpened, his hands steadied. It was an artificial clarity bought with his body's last reserves.

They carried him to the chokepoint. Ford propped him behind a concrete barrier that offered cover while allowing clear sight lines. A Primord rifle lay nearby, abandoned by its former owner.

"Full charge," Williams noted, checking the weapon. "Three spare cells. This'll work."

Love knelt beside him. "Petty Officer Tyrell Williams, your service has been exemplary. Your sacrifice will be remembered."

"Just doing my job, ma'am." He managed a crooked grin. "Tell them I died counting. You know how I hate bad numbers."

Ford gripped his shoulder. "Rebecca…I'll tell her."

"Make it sound good." Williams's voice wavered slightly. "She always liked hero stories."

Green set extra ammunition within reach. "It's been an honor."

"Likewise."

Merina broke from her mother's grasp, approaching despite Keirzi's protests. She pulled a crystal pendant from her pocket, pressing it into Williams's palm.

"For the brave soldier," she said solemnly.

Williams closed his fingers around it. "Thank you, little one. Now go. Be safe."

Love stood, the weight of command settling on her shoulders like heavy lead. "Move out," she ordered. "Checkpoint. Don't stop."

They left him there, propped against concrete with a borrowed rifle and fading time. Williams watched them go, then turned his attention to the killing ground before him.
****

The Zodarks were massing. Through the smoke, Williams counted twenty, maybe more. They'd hit hard, expecting to overwhelm the depleted Primord position. They weren't expecting him.

Movement in the rubble caught his eye. There was a fuel canister wired with explosives, partially hidden near the chokepoint's center. It was the Zodarks' own IED, probably meant to breach the Primord defenses.

Williams smiled coldly. *That will do nicely.*

The first Zodark appeared at the passage entrance, weapons raised. Williams's shot took him center mass. The fighter spun and fell. His companions pulled back, reassessing.

They came again, three rushing forward while others provided cover. Williams worked the rifle with mechanical precision. *One down. Two.* The third dove back, wounded.

"Come on," he muttered. "Mass up for me."

The stimulants were burning through his system, providing clarity at a cost. He could feel his heart racing, struggling to pump what blood remained. But his hands stayed steady. His breathing was controlled.

The Zodarks tried flanking movements, but the chokepoint limited options. Williams had chosen his position perfectly. Every angle was covered. Every approach was under his gun.

Then they did what he'd hoped—gathered for a breakthrough assault. Fifteen fighters massed up at the passage entrance, preparing to rush through together.

Williams shifted his aim to the IED.

They charged as one, a wave of blue bodies and flashing weapons. Williams waited until they were committed, bunched up in the narrow space.

He fired.

The explosion was devastating in the confined area. Bodies flew. Concrete shattered. Smoke and dust billowed out. But Williams was ready.

As stunned survivors stumbled from the blast, he picked them off. *One. Two. Three.* His vision was starting to tunnel, but the targets were so close, so clear.

A wounded Zodark tried crawling to cover. Williams's shot was merciful. Another raised a weapon with two of his four arms broken. That one took two shots, as Williams's accuracy finally began degrading.

Behind him, he heard Primord voices shouting. *Has to be the checkpoint*, he realized. Love had made it through. *Good.*

More Zodarks approached, cautious now. Williams fired, forcing them back, but his shots were going wide. His fine motor control was failing. He braced the rifle against the barrier, using it to steady his aim.

In the distance he heard engines—heavy ones. Military vehicles were approaching fast.

"Just a little longer," Williams told himself.

A Zodark made it to the rubble twenty meters away. Williams fired, missed, then fired again. The second shot spun the fighter down. His hands were shaking now. The stimulants were wearing off, leaving only dying flesh.

The pendant caught his eye, the crystal gleaming even in the smoke. Rebecca would have liked the kid who'd given it to him.

Out of the corner of his eye, Williams spotted something moving. He jerked the rifle up and fired without aiming. He was aiming for suppression now, not precision. *Keep their heads down,* he told himself. *Buy seconds.*

The engines were louder. So close.

A Zodark burst from cover, charging. Williams pulled the trigger.

Click.

The power cell was empty. His fumbling fingers found another and slammed it home. But he was moving too slow. The Zodark was almost on him.

Williams heard a shot from behind—a Primord soldier was advancing with reinforcements. The Zodark crumpled three meters from Williams's position.

"Secure the area!" someone shouted. "Check for survivors!"

Williams let the rifle fall. His job was done. They'd held. Everyone got through.

A Primord medic appeared, scanner already out. Williams waved him off weakly.

"Check the others," he managed. "I'm good here."

The medic hesitated, then moved on. There were others who might be saved.

Williams leaned back against the concrete, clutching Merina's pendant. Around him, Primord reinforcements swept through, professional and thorough. The checkpoint would hold. The ambassador was safe. Love and the others would make it home.

"Twenty-three," he whispered, counting the bodies in his field of fire. "Tell Ford… I counted right."

His vision grayed, tunneled, but he heard the vehicles, the shouted orders, the sound of victory. He'd held the line and kept the faith.

Petty Officer Tyrell Williams closed his eyes, still gripping the crystal pendant, and let go.

The Primord commander found him like that five minutes later, surrounded by brass and bodies, having held an impossible position against overwhelming odds. He was still at his post.

"A warrior's death," said the Primord with respect.

Chapter 13:
Internal Wounds

Year 2098
Hatteng City
Planet Intus

As they approached the plaza, they noticed the Primord soldiers in sleek combat armor directed them with crisp efficiency, their movements coordinated through integrated tactical displays.

"Identification," a sergeant requested.

Love handed over their credentials, noting how the soldier's demeanor shifted the moment he scanned them. His eyes widened slightly behind his visor.

"Ambassador Taevlix," he said. "Commander Vor'nash must be informed immediately."

The checkpoint erupted into controlled activity. Soldiers spoke rapid commands into their comms while others maintained security positions. Within seconds, a tall Primord officer emerged from the command post, his armor bearing the intricate patterns of senior rank.

"Ambassador," Commander Vor'nash said, inclining his head precisely. "We were not informed of your presence in this sector."

"The situation developed rapidly," Taevlix replied. "These Republic soldiers saved my family's lives. They require—"

Plasma fire cracked across the plaza. Three Zodark fighters had pursued them, desperation driving them toward the checkpoint. Love instinctively reached for her weapon, but there was no need.

The checkpoint's defenses responded instantly. Automated turrets swiveled with mechanical precision, laying down interlocking fields of fire. Primord soldiers advanced in perfect formation, their shots disciplined and lethal. In less than fifteen seconds, the threat was neutralized.

"Sector clear," a soldier reported calmly, as if this were routine.

Love watched the effortless display of military superiority with mixed emotions. What had nearly killed them was barely an inconvenience for a properly equipped force.

If only we'd had this support earlier… she couldn't help but think.

"Transport requirement, priority one," Commander Vor'nash was already saying into his comm. "Ambassador Taevlix and family, plus their Republic military escort." He paused, listening. "Confirmed. Three minutes."

Ford stood apart from the group, his gaze fixed on the plaza where Williams had made his stand. Primord medical teams were already moving out, efficient and professional.

"Ma'am." Ford's voice was barely audible. "Request permission to—"

"Denied," Love said gently. "They'll take care of him."

"He deserves better than strangers," Ford pushed back.

"He deserves to have his sacrifice mean something," Love insisted. "We stay with the ambassador." Her command mask held, though she felt it cracking at the edges.

A Primord medic approached. "Your soldier fought with honor. We will ensure proper treatment of his remains."

Ford's jaw tightened, but he nodded.

"Why is the soldier not coming?" Merina's small voice cut through the professional atmosphere. She tugged at her mother's hand, pointing toward the plaza. "He is hurt. They should help him."

Keirzi knelt beside her daughter, whispering in Primord. Love caught fragments—words about bravery and sacrifice. Merina's eyes filled with tears she didn't fully understand.

"Your man held them for seven minutes," Commander Vor'nash said quietly to Love. "Seven minutes against more than twenty Zodarks, wounded and alone. That is… exceptional."

"He *was* exceptional," Love replied.

The armored transport arrived exactly on schedule, a substantial vehicle that made their Osprey look fragile by comparison. Reactive armor plates shifted like scales, gun turrets ready to defend at a moment's notice. The rear hatch opened, revealing an interior that could withstand direct artillery strikes.

"Ambassador, if you please." Vor'nash gestured. "Route planning indicates clear passage to Jusvaktare. My forces are securing the district."

Nyranor paused before boarding, turning to Love with formal precision. "Lieutenant, your corporal's sacrifice preserved not just our lives but critical diplomatic continuity between our peoples. This will not be forgotten."

Love accepted the acknowledgment with a nod, not trusting her voice.

They boarded in silence. The transport's interior was austere but functional: crash seats, medical supplies, and communication arrays. Green immediately moved to the comm station, noting their status and position.

Always the job first, Love thought in a moment of levity amidst the seriousness of the day.

As the hatch sealed, she caught one last glimpse of the plaza. Primord forces moved with choreographed precision, establishing perimeter security. Emergency vehicles clustered near the overturned cargo lifter. Somewhere in that activity, they were recovering Williams.

The transport lifted smoothly, inertial dampeners eliminating any sensation of movement. Through small viewports, Love watched the checkpoint shrink below them. The evening sky had darkened to deep purple, city lights beginning to flicker on despite the crisis.

"Ma'am," Ford said quietly. "His sister. What do I tell her?"

Love met his eyes and felt a pit in her stomach. "The truth," she answered, trying hard not to let her voice crack. "That he held the line. That he saved multiple lives, including a child's. That he died as he lived—protecting others, a hero."

Ford nodded slowly, then turned away. She saw his shoulders shake once before military discipline reasserted itself.

In her corner, Merina had buried her face in her mother's robes. Keirzi held her close, humming the same lullaby from earlier. Ambassador Taevlix sat perfectly still, but Love recognized the signs of suppressed emotion in the rigid posture.

They were safe. The immediate threat had passed. Professional soldiers had taken control. But as the transport carried them toward secure territory, Love felt the hollow victory of survival. They'd made it out, but the cost…the cost was still being tallied in the plaza behind them, where Petty Officer Tyrell Williams had bought them precious minutes with his life.

****

The transport's sudden deceleration pulled Love from her thoughts. Through the forward viewport, she saw Primord military vehicles surrounding a government building, its lobby converted into a field medical station.

"Intermediate stop," the driver announced. "Medical evaluation required before proceeding to Jusvaktare."

The rear hatch opened to controlled chaos. Medics moved between rows of wounded laid out on portable beds. Color-coded bands marked priority—red for critical, yellow for urgent, green for walking wounded. The antiseptic smell hit immediately, mixing with the acrid scent of plasma burns.

"This way." A Primord medic gestured, leading them past the worst cases. Love tried not to look, but glimpses registered—she saw missing limbs and severe burns. It was the price of urban combat, paid in flesh.

They were directed to a screening area where the medic, her movements efficient despite obvious exhaustion, assessed each of them. When she examined Ford, she frowned.

"Multiple lacerations, second-degree plasma burns on both hands, embedded debris in left shoulder…" She looked at Ford disapprovingly. "Why was this not treated?"

"I'm fine," Ford said automatically.

"You're injured." The medic was already preparing treatment supplies. "Sit."

"Really, I don't need—"

"Chief Ford," Love said, her voice cutting through his protest. "That's an order."

Ford reluctantly sat on the examination chair. As the medic began cleaning his wounds, Love noticed how he flinched. Adrenaline no longer masked the pain.

"These burns are hours old," the medic observed, applying bio-gel. "You should have sought treatment immediately."

"We were busy," Ford said through gritted teeth as she extracted a metal splinter from his shoulder.

In the corner, Keirzi knelt beside Merina, growing increasingly worried. The girl sat perfectly still, staring at nothing. Her small body trembled despite the warm air.

"Please," Keirzi said to another medic. "My daughter—something's wrong."

The medic approached carefully. "Hello, little one. May I examine you?"

Merina didn't respond. She didn't even blink.

"Psychological shock," the medic said gently after a few moments. "It is common in children exposed to violence. Her body is protecting her mind." He prepared a mild sedative. "This will help her rest. The trembling should stop."

Love turned away, accessing the transport's communication system. She needed to focus on logistics, on things she could control.

"FOB Oteren, this is Lieutenant Love. Requesting status on Osprey recovery."

Static followed, then she heard a familiar voice. "Lieutenant, this is Chief Rawlins. Recovery team launched twenty minutes ago. Your bird took a beating, but we'll get her home."

"Copy that. Any word on…" She paused, steadied her voice. "On our KIA?"

A longer pause followed. "Primord command transferred Petty Officer Williams to their honor guard ten minutes ago. Full military protocols observed. They're treating him as a hero, ma'am. As they should."

Love's throat tightened. "Understood. Thank you, Chief."

"Ma'am? We're all sorry about Williams. He was one of the best."

"Yes. He was."

She closed the channel, turning to find Green at her elbow with a hydration pack. "You need to drink something."

"I'm fine."

"That's what Ford said." Green's voice was gentle but firm. "We've got another twenty minutes to Concordat Hall. Take care of yourself, or you won't be able to take care of anyone else."

Love accepted the pack, drinking deeply. She hadn't realized how thirsty she was.

Across the medical station, Ford sat still as the medic finished bandaging his hands. White gauze replaced bloodstained skin. He stared at the clean bandages with something like disgust.

"I should have been faster," he said quietly. "Getting Williams into cover. If I'd moved quicker—"

"Stop," Love ordered. "Williams made his choice. Honor it by living with it, not drowning in what-ifs."

Ford nodded slowly, but the guilt remained in his eyes.

"Transport departs in five minutes," the driver announced.

The medic treating Merina had given her the sedative. She slept now in her mother's arms, tiny body finally still. Keirzi looked up at Love with tears in her eyes.

"She kept asking about the soldier," Keirzi said softly. "Even when she stopped talking, her lips kept forming the words. 'Where is the brave soldier?'"

Ambassador Taevlix placed a hand on his wife's shoulder. "She will heal. Children are resilient. But she will remember this day. She will remember the cost of our freedom."

"Ambassador," a Primord officer said as he approached. "Command wishes me to inform you that the district is secure. The remaining insurgents have been eliminated. We can proceed to Jusvaktare whenever you are ready."

"Thank you, Commander." Taevlix turned to Love. "Are your people ready?"

Love glanced at her team. Ford had his bandaged hands. Green still had IV fluids dripping into his arm. She knew that she herself was running on fumes and determination. None of them were ready. But they'd go anyway.

"We're ready," she said.

They loaded back into the transport. Merina didn't stir, the sedative granting her temporary peace. Ford flexed his bandaged fingers, testing mobility. Green's IV had been removed, and he held pressure on the gauze where the insertion site had been.

As the transport lifted off, Love caught a final glimpse of the medical station. More wounded were arriving. They were more casualties of a war that seemed to grind on without end. But outside, the city sounds were changing—there were fewer sirens and more normal traffic. Order was returning from chaos.

"Estimated arrival at Jusvaktare, twelve minutes," the driver reported.

Love leaned back in her seat, exhaustion pulling at her. She had twelve minutes to rest—twelve minutes before she had to be Lieutenant Love again, completing the mission, filing reports, pretending the empty seat beside them didn't scream of Williams's absence.

The transport flew on through securing streets, carrying its battered cargo toward journey's end. Outside, Hatteng City began to heal.

Inside, the wounds were just beginning to be counted.

Chapter 14:
Joint Operations

Year 2098
Republic Liaison Wing, Skjarnhold Command
Valdrakar, Primordia
Kita System

Admiral Chester Bailey stared at the Qpad at the center of the meeting table. There, the image of Commander Eamon Roberts's face was cued up, as Bailey prepared to play the recording he'd sent from FOB Bulwark.

Around the table, the assembled leadership of both the Republic and the Primords created a picture of unified command belying the underlying tensions. Admiral Chester Bailey sat, Rear Admiral Fran McKee at his right. Opposite them, Admiral Torsen was flanked by Admiral Dhorsar, the Primord Chief of Naval Operations, and Admiral Velmiran, whose Primord intelligence network spanned dozens of systems.

"With everyone here, I'll go ahead and get us started," announced Admiral Bailey.

Roberts's recording started. "Approximately four hours ago, Captain Dharek's task force encountered a previously undetected Zodark presence while patrolling what intelligence had designated a low-threat sector."

A data packet that Roberts had sent with his recording began to expand into a detailed holographic tactical display above the table. The hologram showed Primord and Republic vessels moving in formation before suddenly engaging with Zodark forces seemingly materializing from the debris field.

"What you're observing is a reconstruction based on combat telemetry and after-action reports," Roberts continued. "Commander Lee deployed additional reconnaissance probes during the engagement, which proved invaluable. These probes captured comprehensive data on previously undocumented Zodark counterdetection measures.

"The Zodarks employed dormant mining platforms to generate a sophisticated communication disruption field," Roberts explained, highlighting specific elements within the tactical display. "This not only blocked standard communication channels but actively interfered with target acquisition systems. However, Commander Lee and Captain Dharek adapted quickly, and well."

The display shifted to show how the Republic and Primord vessels had utilized debris field optic patterns to maintain tactical coordination.

"The improvised system allowed our forces to coordinate despite electronic countermeasures," said Roberts. "The combined task force neutralized all Zodark vessels with acceptable casualties."

Admiral McKee pursed her lips at Roberts's words. "Define 'acceptable casualties,' Captain," she muttered quickly under her breath.

"The Republic corvette *Polaris* sustained moderate structural damage but remained operational. Primord vessels reported minimal impacts," Roberts explained, as if he'd heard McKee. "What concerns me more is the strategic implication of finding this level of Zodark activity in Sector 8. With additional probes sent out, they've detected abnormal frequency bands farther into the sector. They'll be investigating.

"Given this new intelligence, I recommend immediate reinforcement," Roberts asserted. "The Zodarks demonstrated advanced capabilities that warrant additional firepower and specialized electronic warfare support.

"I propose dispatching the RNS *Oceanus*, RNS *Idaho*, RNS *Thunder* and RNS *Argo* with four EW frigates to augment the existing task force," Roberts said.

There was an outpost out there. Call it an admiral's intuition, but Bailey could just feel it. It helped that intel assumed the same, based on the patterns previously observed in that sector. With this new real-time information, Dharek's task force needed a bigger force. They needed a new, more experienced leader, too. And if they *did* find a Zodark FOB, they'd need to infiltrate. Bailey wanted as much information on that sector as possible, and if anyone could extract such data, it would be the Republic.

"Additionally, I believe an Army Special Forces team would provide valuable intelligence-gathering capabilities on site," Roberts continued. "A suspected outpost is in that vicinity, and if they encounter it, we could infiltrate."

The transmission ended. Admiral Torsen exchanged glances with his fellow Primord admirals before speaking. "Such a significant reinforcement would alter the command structure of the task force. Captain Dharek currently holds overall command as designated by our joint operations protocol."

A momentary tension filled the room.

"I respect Captain Dharek's capabilities," Bailey said carefully, "but given the escalating situation in Sector 8, I believe we should consider a more experienced commander to coordinate the expanded task force."

Admiral McKee raised an eyebrow. "Are you suggesting relieving Captain Dharek of command?"

"Not relieving. Restructuring," Bailey clarified. "Captain Dharek has demonstrated excellent tactical acumen. However, the presence of a *Ryan*-class battleship would naturally alter the command hierarchy."

"You're proposing the *Idaho*," McKee stated, making it clear this wasn't a question.

"Yes. Captain Mensah could assume overall command of the task force. Her experience with joint operations would be invaluable, plus her years in combat. They dwarf both Lee's and Dharek's."

Admiral Velmiran's expression hardened slightly. "Captain Dharek was specifically chosen for this assignment based on his exemplary performance during the last campaign. Replacing him could be interpreted as questioning his competence."

"This isn't about competence," Admiral McKee interjected. "It's about providing appropriate leadership for an expanded operation. Captain Mensah has extensive experience coordinating multispecies task forces."

The discussion continued for several minutes, with Primord admirals emphasizing Dharek's capabilities and the importance of maintaining established command structures, while the Republic representatives argued for experienced oversight of the expanded force.

Admiral Bailey finally raised his hand, silencing the debate. "We're all focused on the same objective—neutralizing the Zodark threat and ensuring the security of the Rass invasion corridor. Let's not focus on Republic versus Primord command preferences. We must focus on an optimal tactical configuration."

Admiral Bailey turned to the Primord admirals. "What we're witnessing in Sector 8 may be the prelude to a larger Zodark offensive. If they're developing new counterdetection technologies, our planned Rass invasion could face significant complications. We need our best people coordinating the response."

Admiral Torsen was silent for a long moment before responding. "Captain Dharek is one of our most promising officers. However, I acknowledge that exposure to Captain Mensah's command methodology could provide valuable experience for his continued development."

"Then we are agreed?" Admiral Bailey asked.

"There are conditions," Admiral Velmiran stated in a firm tone. "Captain Dharek remains second-in-command of the task force, with all Primord vessels directly under his authority. Captain Mensah coordinates overall strategy, but tactical implementation within Primord ship groups remains Dharek's responsibility."

Admiral Bailey glanced at McKee, who nodded subtly.

"Those terms are acceptable," Bailey confirmed. "The *Idaho* and accompanying vessels will deploy immediately. Their primary objective is to secure Sector 8 and gather intelligence on Zodark counterdetection technologies.

"Further," Bailey continued, "we will ensure Captain Mensah understands the diplomatic sensitivities involved. This expanded task force represents our most significant joint operation since the alliance formalization."

Admiral Torsen remained impassive. "The information gathered regarding Zodark communication disruption capabilities may prove crucial. Captain Mensah should prioritize intelligence collection alongside security operations."

The Primord admirals didn't exactly seem enthusiastic, but they didn't bring up any objections to the plan. Admiral Bailey took the lack of opposition as an unstated agreement and rose from his seat. Another pressing meeting was scheduled. In fact, he was late for it. But this came first.

"Then we're settled. The reinforced task force under Captain Mensah's command will secure Sector 8 and continue intelligence-gathering operations."

Chapter 15:
Shifting Stars

Year 2098
RNS *Poseidon*
Middle Reach
Sector 8

Lee sat alone in his quarters, reviewing damage reports from the skirmish. *Not much. Good.* The holographic display showed the *Polaris*'s compromised hull plating, but really, it was nothing to write home about. His personal comm chimed with an incoming transmission marked priority.

Captain Roberts appeared on the screen, his expression serious. Yet he was composed. Unlike the earlier communication, this was for Lee's eyes only. Lee wouldn't be surprised if this was the last message from Roberts for quite some time.

"Captain Lee," Roberts began. "Just received the preliminary reports on your engagement. Impressive work neutralizing that Zodark battleship and its escorts.

"That resonance communication network was particularly ingenious," Roberts continued. "Adapting to combat conditions when standard comms failed. Excellent.

"That said, I'm concerned about the damage sustained by *Polaris*. We need to ensure our vessels maintain appropriate tactical positioning in these joint operations."

Lee controlled the urge to explain himself to the recording.

"I understand the situation developed rapidly," Roberts said, as if anticipating Lee's thoughts. "And I recognize that Captain Dharek's battle group integration remains a work in progress. At least, in my eyes. What matters now is how we move forward.

"Command is watching this deployment with particular scrutiny. Rear Admiral Fran McKee and Admiral Chester Bailey are personally involved. Now, our alliance with the Primords remains strategically vital," Roberts continued. "But that doesn't mean Republic vessels should bear disproportionate risk, or be kept out of risk, at the same time. I need you to ensure tactical integration works both ways, Captain."

Roberts's expression softened a tad. "You've earned my trust over these past months. You know that, and I'm glad of it. Your tactical instincts are sound, which is precisely why you're out there and not tucked safely behind defense platforms at Bulwark."

The acknowledgment was unexpected. Roberts had never been one for overt praise.

"This will likely be our last communication for some time," Roberts added. "The relay network needs maintenance, and we're at the edge of transmission range. I'm sending reinforcements to your position—RNS *Oceanus*, RNS *Thunder* and the RNS *Argo* with four EW frigates. They should arrive within twenty-four hours. An Army Special Forces team will be accompanying them on the RNS *Idaho*."

Idaho. The name hung in the air between them. The battleship was captained by Mensah.

"Captain Mensah will be taking overall command of the task force upon arrival," Roberts said, confirming Lee's unspoken realization. "As senior officer, she'll coordinate joint operations moving forward. Captain Dharek will be second-in-command."

That didn't sit well with Lee. Not because he craved command, but because he knew it wouldn't sit well with Captain Dharek. The Primord commander already struggled with Lee. What would it be like when Mensah started with her orders, shoving Dharek to the side? Still, if Dharek was a true officer, he'd understand. Nonetheless, Lee feared the change would strain his relationship with Dharek even more.

"I'm aware of the diplomatic considerations," Roberts asserted. "Captain Mensah has been thoroughly briefed on the situation. She understands the delicate balance required. That said, recent Zodark activity suggests we need additional firepower in your sector. Keep searching for an outpost. We suspect one is out there."

Roberts leaned forward slightly. "You've done good work, Lee. Keep it up. And when Mensah arrives, give her your full support. The integration of our forces with the Primords remains top priority. Roberts out."

The screen went dark. Lee released a slow, measured breath, then took a sip from a half-empty coffee cup.

The situation had just become more complicated. While Lee respected Captain Mensah's capabilities, her arrival with the *Idaho* would fundamentally alter the command dynamic he'd established with

Dharek. The Primord captain already chafed when talking with Lee…
every single time. Having a Republic battleship and its captain assume
overall command would likely be perceived by Dharek as Republic
overreach rather than a tactical reinforcement.

Thing was, the guy needed to learn to work together on joint
missions. This way, the Primord captain could become educated one
way or another. It would be good for Dharek.

He closed the report with a swipe of his hand. FOB Bulwark
housed an impressive array of firepower, so Roberts was fine in his
current sector, Sector 7. There, the RNS *Australia* and RNS *Idaho*, both
Ryan-class battleships, held enough weaponry to level a small moon.
Roberts kept four Primord battleships integrated into defense
operations along with a handful of Republic cruisers, including RNS
Hydra and *Argo*. Eight frigates and four corvettes provided rapid
response capabilities. Eight converted Primord freight carriers and three
heavy tankers covered logistics, and they had a state-of-the-art mobile
repair platform. Finally, twelve defense platforms created an
impenetrable weapons grid around the entire installation.

With some of those ships leaving to support Lee and Dharek's
task force, still, the Bulwark would be fine. Yes, the *Idaho* was coming
here, bringing with it a shift in command that was sure to complicate
his already challenging relationship with Dharek—but no doubt
Captain Mensah would ease Dharek into it, making for a smooth
transition.

Plus, they all had a possible outpost to find and a recon mission
to continue. The rest was just noise.

Chapter 16:
Home but Not Home

Year 2098
Concordant Hall
Planet Intus

Love ran her hands along the *Jack*'s hull, checking the hasty repairs to her Osprey. Plasma scoring had been patched with emergency sealant. The port stabilizer showed fresh welds. It wasn't pretty, but she'd been assured it was functional. The maintenance crew at Concordat Hall had worked miracles in the time they'd had.

"She will hold," said the Primord crew chief. "Your people are sending a full team for proper repairs, but she will get you home."

Home, she thought. FOB Oteren seemed like another lifetime ago.

Love climbed into the cockpit, settling into her seat with a relief that surprised her. Here, surrounded by familiar instruments and controls, the world made sense. Her hands found their positions automatically—throttle, stick, switches all exactly where they should be.

"Preflight checklist," Green said, sliding into the copilot position. The routine of their partnership resumed, like slipping on comfortable boots.

"Fuel cells?" she asked.

"Ninety-two percent."

"Hydraulics?"

"Pressure nominal. That stabilizer patch is reading yellow, but within tolerance."

They worked through the list with practiced efficiency. Behind them, Ford strapped into his crew chief chair, the empty gunner's seat a glaring reminder of his absence.

"Concordat Control, this is *Jack* requesting departure clearance."

"*Jack*, you are cleared for departure. Safe flight."

Love brought the engines online, feeling the Osprey come alive beneath her hands. The vibration was off—she could feel the repairs in the subtle harmonics—but the *Jack* was flying. That was enough.

They lifted off into the night sky, three of Intus's moons casting overlapping shadows across the cityscape. Behind them, the alien sunset painted the horizon in shades of purple and gold that Earth never saw.

"Setting course for FOB Oteren," Green announced. "Twenty-eight minutes flight time."

As they gained altitude, Love could see the full scope of the day's battle. Smoke still rose from the commercial district where they'd made their emergency landing. The government sector showed scattered damage. Emergency lights clustered around various incidents, but already the city was returning to normal. Life was reasserting itself.

The radio filled with routine traffic:

"Sector 7 secure. Final sweep complete."

"Infrastructure reports sixty percent restoration. Full power expected by 0600."

"Casualty count updated: forty-three hostile KIA, twelve Primord military, twenty-seven civilian."

Love reflected how those clinical numbers didn't capture Williams bleeding out in a plaza, or Merina's traumatized silence.

"Those repairs are holding better than I expected," Ford's voice came over the intercom. He was checking systems from the crew compartment, falling into old patterns.

"Primords know their stuff," Green replied. "Remember that time Williams jury-rigged our…"

He stopped, catching himself.

"It's OK," Ford said after a pause. "Remember that time he jury-rigged our environmental system with kitchen equipment? We flew six hours smelling like a restaurant."

"'Better than the usual smell,' he said." Green managed a small laugh. "He wasn't wrong."

Love listened while maintaining her scan of instruments and airspace. This was how soldiers grieved—through stories, through normal conversation that danced around the edges of loss.

They flew over the plaza where Williams had made his first stand. In the darkness, she could barely make out the overturned vehicles and the checkpoint lights beyond. Primord security vehicles surrounded the area. Tomorrow, cleanup crews would remove all traces, as if it had never happened.

"Lieutenant." Ford spoke carefully. "About his position. I know some gunners at Oteren who'd be solid—"

"Later," Love said. "We'll deal with that later."

But they both knew there was no replacing Williams. Someone would fill his seat and operate his gun. They'd be competent and professional. But they wouldn't be *him*.

Love heard more radio chatter: "Republic forces, be advised—normal flight operations resume as of 2200 hours. Emergency protocols lifted."

Just like that, the crisis is over, she thought. *At least for everyone else.*

Love adjusted their heading slightly, compensating for the damaged stabilizer's drift. Each input required a fraction more pressure, a moment more attention. Like everything right then, it was harder than it should be.

She found herself reviewing the day's decisions as they flew. She thought about the initial ambush. Should she have taken a different route? Then she considered the emergency landing, wondering if they could have pushed through to Hatteng. She mulled over the tunnels, the checkpoint, and Williams's last stand—each choice was examined and reexamined.

But Williams had called it right each time. The math was brutal but clear. They'd made the only choices that led to survival. His survival hadn't been part of that equation, and he'd known it.

"Coming up on the agricultural district," Green noted.

Below, the fields where they'd made their emergency landing stretched dark and quiet. There was no sign of the firefight, the desperate repairs. The land had absorbed the violence and moved on.

"Remember Williams trying to teach the new kids about field repairs?" Ford asked. "He had this whole system with colored tape."

"'If you can't remember red means danger, you shouldn't touch tools,'" Green quoted.

"He was a good teacher," Ford said quietly. "Patient. Thorough."

Love remembered Williams working with fresh transfers, never losing his temper despite repeated mistakes. He'd had a gift for breaking complex tasks into simple steps. He'd had skills that would have made him an excellent senior NCO, given time.

But that was time he wouldn't have.

The base appeared ahead, lights familiar and welcoming. But as Love began their descent, she felt the wrongness of it. They were returning to where they'd started…but diminished. It was the arithmetic of survival: four minus one equals a gap that could never be properly filled.

"FOB Oteren, *Jack* on approach."

"Welcome home, *Jack*. You're cleared for pad seven."

Behind them, Intus's strange sunset finished its display, the alien stars emerging in patterns no human child learned. Another day was ending. Their longest day as a team was ending.

Love brought them down with textbook precision, muscle memory guiding her hands. The landing gear touched down gently despite the damaged stabilizer. Systems powered down, engines cooled, and the mission was complete.

But as she sat in the pilot's seat, hands still on the controls, Love knew something fundamental had changed. They were home, but home felt different now. The empty gunner's position behind her would remain empty, no matter who eventually filled it.

"Good flying," Green said softly. "Williams would've barely felt that landing."

He would have complained anyway, Love thought. *Made some joke about Navy pilots*. The absence of his voice was deafening.

She began the shutdown sequence, each action automatic, while her mind processed what came next. *Reports. Debriefs. Letters to write. A sister to notify.*

It was the cost of duty, paid in full.

****

The briefing room's harsh lights made Love squint after the darkness outside. She'd changed into a fresh uniform, but exhaustion clung to her like a second skin. Green and Ford flanked her as they entered, their footsteps echoing on the polished floor.

Commander Granger stood at the head of the table, surrounded by senior staff. The holographic display showed their flight path in glowing lines, each ambush point marked in angry red. Recording equipment hummed softly, capturing everything for the official record.

"Lieutenant Love, Ensign Green, Chief Ford." Granger nodded to each. "Take your seats."

Love recognized the assembled officers. Major Garcia joined them from Intelligence, her sharp eyes already analyzing data streams. Captain Singh was from Operations, his fingers dancing over a tactical pad. Lieutenant Commander Walsh was the necessary paper pusher from Personnel who had Williams's file already open before him. Master Chief Raines sat at the far end, the senior NCO's weathered face revealing nothing.

"Let's begin," Granger said. "Lieutenant, walk us through the mission from departure."

Love straightened, falling back on military precision. "We departed FOB Oteren at 1420 hours. It was a standard diplomatic transport, Ambassador Nyranor Taevlix and family. Flight time to pickup coordinates was twenty minutes…"

She spoke steadily, clinically, watching her words transform into data points on the holo: the routine pickup, the Zodark patrol at the compound, and the first ambush five minutes into return flight.

"Stop there," Major Garcia interrupted. "The timing is significant. Five minutes puts you…" She manipulated the display. "Here. Maximum distance from both pickup and destination. Classic interdiction point."

"They knew our route," Captain Singh added. "Standard diplomatic flight path. Inside information or good reconnaissance?"

"Continue," Granger ordered.

Love detailed the emergency landing, the ground pursuit. On the holo, their path lit up—a desperate zigzag through hostile territory. When she described the IEDs, Garcia leaned forward.

"Placement patterns," she muttered, highlighting locations. "Not random. These were pre-positioned, expecting ground movement." She looked up. "This wasn't opportunistic. They were herding you."

The debrief continued through the aerial chase, the approach to Hatteng City. When Love described finding the city under attack, Singh and Garcia exchanged glances.

"Coordinated timing," Singh said. "Hit the city to draw security forces, then ambush the ambassador in the confusion."

"Williams identified the pattern first," Love said quietly. "He called it at the government building. Said we were being hunted, not just harassed."

Master Chief Raines spoke for the first time. "Smart man. What was his assessment of the underground approach?"

Ford answered, his voice rough. "He was lucid enough to spot the second IED before it blew. He said the placement was wrong for an ambush—more like they were still trying to direct our movement."

"Toward the checkpoint," Garcia concluded. "Where the main force was waiting."

The room fell silent as Love described Williams's last stand and the selfless sacrifice leading to his final moments.

"Seven minutes," Granger said finally. "He held for seven minutes against superior numbers."

"Twenty plus hostiles confirmed KIA at his position," Singh added. "Primord after-action reports can't stop singing his praises."

Lieutenant Commander Walsh cleared his throat. "Regarding Petty Officer Williams, the Primord government has already approved their King's Cross of Valor. It's their second-highest honor after the King's personal honor, the Star of the Crown. They want to send one of their officials to present it personally to his next of kin"—he glanced at his pad—"his sister, Rebecca Williams, in Colorado Springs."

"That's… very gracious of them. Unless there's an objection, I'm recommending the Navy Cross," Granger said. "Possibly higher. His actions not only saved the ambassador but prevented a significant diplomatic crisis."

"The memorial service?" Ford asked, barely audible.

"Day after tomorrow. Full honors." Walsh's expression softened. "You'll be asked to speak, Chief. As his crew chief."

Ford nodded, not trusting his voice.

"Let's discuss the larger implications," Garcia said, pulling up a regional map. "This level of coordination suggests—"

"Suggests the Zodarks aren't as defeated as we thought," Granger finished. "Three ambush points, pre-positioned IEDs, intelligence on diplomatic movements. This was a planned operation."

"Base security will need review," Singh added. "If they knew the ambassador's schedule—"

"Already in progress," Granger assured him. "But that's tomorrow's problem." He looked at Love's team. "You made the right calls out there. Every decision can be justified tactically."

"Williams made the right calls," Love corrected. "We just followed his lead."

A ghost of a smile crossed Raines's face. "Good soldiers know how to make officers look smart."

The formal debrief wound down, the data were collected, and lessons were identified. But Granger wasn't finished.

"One more item." He nodded to Walsh, who produced three forms. "Mandatory psychological evaluation. 0800 tomorrow."

Love stiffened. "Sir, that's not necessary—"

"It's protocol, Lieutenant. Nonnegotiable." Granger's tone brooked no argument. "Combat trauma with KIA requires professional assessment."

"We're fine," Love insisted.

"No," Granger said gently. "You're functional. There's a difference. Lieutenant Green?"

"I'll be there, sir," Green said simply.

"Chief?"

Ford stared at the form. "Yes, sir."

"Lieutenant Love?"

She wanted to argue, to insist she didn't need help processing what had happened. But Granger's expression mixed command authority with something almost paternal.

"The stigma died fifty years ago," Master Chief Raines said quietly. "We've all been there, Lieutenant. It's not weakness. It's maintenance."

Love took the form. "Yes, sir."

"Good." Granger stood, the others following. "You did exceptional work today under impossible circumstances. Williams's sacrifice honored our highest traditions. But survivor's guilt can destroy careers faster than enemy fire. Don't let his gift go to waste."

He paused at the door. "Dismissed. Get some rest. That's an order."

They filed out into the corridor, the weight of the day settling heavier with each step. Tomorrow would bring evaluations, memorials, the slow process of moving forward. But tonight, they were just three survivors missing their fourth.

"Drink?" Ford asked quietly.

"Rain check," Love said. "I need to…"

She didn't finish. She didn't need to. They understood.

Green touched her shoulder briefly, then he and Ford headed toward the barracks. Love turned the opposite direction, not ready for sleep, not ready for the empty routine of quarters without purpose.

She had one more stop to make…one more goodbye to attempt.

The hangar called, and *Jack* waited, and somewhere in between, she might find a way to let Williams go.

****

The barracks hallway stretched quiet and dim, emergency lighting casting long shadows between bunks. Love's footsteps seemed too loud as she approached Williams's room. Through the doorway, she saw Ford sitting on the floor, an empty box beside him, staring at the perfectly made bunk.

"Couldn't start," Ford said without looking up. "I keep thinking he'll walk in and complain about me touching his stuff."

Love sat down beside him, the floor cold through her uniform. Williams's space was exactly as he'd left it—sheets military tight, personal items arranged with obsessive precision on the small shelf.

"He had a system," Ford continued. "Everything in its place. Used to drive the new guys crazy."

Together, they began. Ford reached for the photos first, hands trembling slightly. Rebecca Williams smiled at various ages— graduation, birthday parties, and a beach vacation. In one, Williams stood beside her, both making ridiculous faces at the camera.

"She looks like him," Love observed. "They had the same eyes."

"And the same stubborn streak, according to him." Ford carefully wrapped each photo. "Talked about her constantly. How she was the smart one, the one who'd make something of herself."

Love found a birthday card on the shelf, in an envelope, addressed but unsealed. Inside, they found Williams's careful handwriting:

Hey, Becca,

Another year older and you still haven't figured out I'm the cooler sibling. This year's been crazy, but knowing you're back home doing your teacher thing keeps me grounded. Maybe when I rotate back, we can hit that taco place you keep—

The message ended midsentence.

"When's her birthday?" Love asked softly.

"Next week." Ford took the card with reverent hands. "We'll… we'll make sure she gets it."

They continued through his belongings. Technical manuals sprouted sticky notes from every chapter; the margins were filled with Williams's observations. "This is wrong—field test proves 30-second cycle time minimum" or "See page 47 for why this gets people killed."

"He was writing his own manual," Ford said. "A practical guide for new gunners. All the stuff the official books miss."

Love fingered the pages. "Mind if I keep these? Someone should finish what he started."

"He'd like that," Ford replied.

A deck of cards emerged, edges worn soft from countless games. Ford smiled sadly. "Never could beat him at poker. I'm pretty sure he counted cards, but could never prove it."

"'If you ain't cheating, you ain't trying,'" Love quoted.

"'But if you get caught, you ain't trying hard enough,'" Ford finished.

The small tool kit revealed Williams's meticulous nature—every tool labeled, some with notes: "Don't lend to Morrison—he never returns anything" or "Ford's favorite—hide when he's in a borrowing mood."

Ford actually laughed. "Guilty as charged."

In the back corner, they found his emergency stash—energy bars, instant coffee, and batteries. He was always the pragmatic soldier, preparing for anything.

They packed in silence for a while, dividing items between what would go to Rebecca and what might stay with the unit. Ford pocketed a challenge coin—Williams's lucky piece from basic training. Love took the technical notes and one photo of the whole crew from better days.

When they finished, the bunk looked violated in its emptiness. It was just another bed waiting for another soldier.

"Walk with me?" Love asked.

They carried the box between them through the quiet base. Other soldiers passed with nods of acknowledgment, understanding the significance of the moment. The hangar doors stood open, spilling light into the darkness.

Inside, the *Jack* sat under work lights like a patient in surgery. Chief Rawlins worked alone, welding torch in hand, starting on what could be fixed to give Ford some time to mourn.

"Lieutenant," he acknowledged, killing the torch. "Chief. Sorry about Williams."

"How bad is our bird?" Love asked, gesturing at the Osprey.

Rawlins wiped his hands, considering. "Seen worse. Port stabilizer needs complete replacement. Hull integrity's compromised in six places. Engine mount took more damage than we thought." He paused. "But it'll fly again. It'll take a week, maybe ten days."

"Better than new?" Ford asked, running his hand along a patched hull section.

"That's the plan." Rawlins studied them. "Lost my own gunner—Zodark heavy weapons, similar situation. Kept flying for six months before I could step foot in an Osprey without seeing his ghost."

"How'd you get past it?" Love asked.

"Didn't." Rawlins shrugged. "Just learned to fly with ghosts. They're good company once you stop fighting them." He nodded toward the empty gunner's position. "Williams trained half the new gunners on this base. Kid had a gift. We're putting up a plaque—small thing, his name and dates. That OK with you?"

"He'd complain about the fuss," Ford said. "Then secretly love it."

Rawlins smiled. "That was Williams." He looked at Love. "Want some time with the *Jack*?"

Love nodded. While Ford and Rawlins discussed repairs, she climbed into the cockpit. Everything was as they'd left it—including Jack's photo, still taped to the dash. Her husband's smile was unchanged by another day of loss.

She sat in her seat, hands finding the controls by instinct. Through the cockpit glass, she could see the work lights, the repairs, and the empty gunner's position. There were two ghosts now…two empty spaces that would never properly fill.

"We lost him today," she whispered to Jack's photo. "Williams. Held the line so we could run. You would've liked him. No quit in him."

The photo smiled back, frozen in time.

Love touched the controls, feeling the Osprey's potential even powered down. In a week, maybe ten days, she'd fly again. They'd have a new gunner, and the same route, but different outcomes. The war would continue its grinding arithmetic.

But Love would fly. For Jack, who'd died saving others. For Williams, who had chosen the same. For everyone who climbed aboard, trusting her to bring them home.

"Still flying," she said firmly. "Still fighting."

She climbed down from the cockpit, finding Ford and Rawlins discussing mounting points for the memorial plaque. They were good men, honoring another good man. It was loss balanced by the continuity of service.

"Ready?" Ford asked.

Love nodded. They left Rawlins to his work, carrying Williams's effects into the night. Tomorrow would bring evaluations, memorial plans, and the slow process of moving forward. But tonight, they'd honored their friend with careful hands and shared memories.

At the barracks, they parted ways. Ford headed to his room with the box. Love stood for a moment in the darkness, feeling the weight of command, of survival, of tomorrow's necessity.

Somewhere above, Intus's three moons continued their dance. Somewhere in Colorado, a sister would receive her brother's final effects. Somewhere in the plaza, they'd already cleaned away the blood.

But here, now, Love stood ready to continue. Changed, scarred, but not broken.

She would still fly, still fight…for all of them.

Chapter 17:
Lessons from Toasters

Year 2098
FTL Travel
RNS *Leahy*

For the last few days, all Coop could think about was how he hated synthetic humanoids, and now these C100s they were being forced to work with. It kept him up a few nights, too. Not that there was night during FTL, but sleep came with a lot of tossing and turning.

The RNS *Leahy* whirred along with a low, persistent vibration Coop had finally grown accustomed to. The massive assault carrier flew through space alongside the Republic battle group, its Ark-Fold FTL drives propelling them toward the Rass system. Coop stood at a viewport, watching the distorted starfield streak by in bursts of strange lights. The *Ryan*-class battleship *Wilson* led the formation, though not visible from Coop's position.

"Enjoying the view?" Bear's deep voice broke through Coop's thoughts.

Coop turned. His hulking teammate walked over with two steaming cups. "Just thinking."

"Dangerous pastime." Bear laughed and handed him one of the cups. "Coffee. Real stuff, not the synthetic crap."

"How'd you score this?"

"I know people who know people." Bear shrugged. "Two more days of this transit. Might as well enjoy the little things."

Coop took a sip. It was a bit too hot and stung the tip of his tongue. "Simulation deck in twenty. West's running the show today. C'mon, arrive together?"

"Sure," Bear said, both of them walking into the main corridor. "That man lives to make us suffer."

"Better prepared or we suffer out there."

Bear grinned. "You're sounding like a true soldier now. I like the change."

"It is what it is." Coop blew into his coffee. "You warm this in a volcano?"

Bear winked. "Yep, during our last stop at the volcano in the middle of FTL."

"You couldn't come up with a better joke?"

Bear shook his head. "Caught me on a bad day."

The corridor filled with personnel as they made their way to the simulation deck. Techs and operators rushed past. The *Leahy*'s crew operated almost as one, all trained like the best of them.

The simulation deck doors parted. Inside, techs calibrated equipment and operators prepared their stations. The room was divided into sections, each representing different combat scenarios. At the center stood a raised platform surrounded by holographic displays—command central.

Sawyer spotted them first. "About time you two showed up." She was already suited up in her tactical gear, her hair pulled back in a tight bun.

"We're on time. A little early, actually. Not as fast as you, I suppose," Coop replied, setting his empty cup on a nearby console. Despite the coffee's heat, he'd downed it on the way here. It tasted damn good. Of all things in the galaxy, nothing beat coffee, or even the thought of it.

Ortiz joined them. "Word is West's cooking up something special for today."

"When's he not?" Coop strapped on his tactical vest, checking each pocket.

The 9th Special Tactics Squadron team gathered around the central platform, each member representing their assigned company. Coop stood with the Alpha Company commanders while Sawyer, Bear, and Ortiz positioned themselves with their respective units.

Staff Sergeant Crawford and Technical Sergeant Li, a few other members of Coop's TASC element, stood nearby. Crawford, Alpha Company's communications specialist, was already reviewing atmospheric data while Li, their tactical data specialist, adjusted settings on a portable targeting system.

A handful of others in the 9th Special Tactics Squadron found their places as well. The thing was, Coop was competitive. He wanted to outperform every one of his comrades.

Captain Milton West entered the room, and conversations died.

"Ladies and gentlemen," West said, "today we're simulating tactical air and space control coordination." He activated the central holographic display, showing a holomap of Nightfall's terrain, the moon also known as PTX-419. "The moon's atmosphere is unexpectedly Earthlike despite its position as the farthest satellite in the Rass system. This rare phenomenon is attributed to Nightfall's unique position in a gravitational sweet spot between Rass's primary star and the neighboring dwarf star Calius-B. This binary influence has allowed Nightfall to maintain a higher-than-expected mass and strong magnetic field, preventing atmospheric stripping that would normally occur at such distances. However, the moon's unpredictable wind patterns will all factor into your mission success."

Coop studied the terrain like a biologist with a microscope. Nightfall's surface was a bunch of jagged rock formations and deep ravines. Here and there, pockets of thick forests, giant trees bigger than skyscrapers, and shrubs the size of houses covered the map. Perfect ambush territory.

"Each platoon will be assigned a sector," West continued, highlighting different regions on the map. "Your objective is to secure your area while providing tactical support to adjacent units. Points awarded for efficiency, accuracy, and minimal collateral damage. Who knows, some of your units might be… scattered."

Bear leaned toward Coop. "Sounds like he's throwing a curveball."

"Wait for it," Coop said under his breath. "It'll get worse."

West stopped and stared at Bear and Coop. "You two got something important to say?"

"Negative, sir," both Coop and Bear replied in unison.

"Good." As if on cue, West's expression shifted to something resembling satisfaction. "There's an additional variable today." He tapped his console, and a new element appeared on the display—C100 combat synthetic models. "We'll be simulating C100 malfunctions at random intervals throughout the exercise. When your synthetic fails, you adapt. No warnings, no second chances."

Coop withheld a groan.

"Problem, Cooper?" West asked.

"No, sir," he lied. The unease churned in his gut. The memory of his father's stories about the early combat synthetics during the

Great War flashed through his mind. He didn't want to have anything
to do with them.

"Outstanding." West's gaze lingered on Coop a moment longer.
"Because Alpha Company, second platoon, will be operating with
twice the normal synthetic complement. Consider it an opportunity to
demonstrate your… adaptability."

Sawyer shot Coop a sympathetic glance from across the
platform.

"Stations in five," West announced. "Remember, this is about
how you handle the unexpected."

The teams dispersed to their simulation pods. Coop adjusted his
tactical headset. *Here goes nothing… and… apparently, everything.
Got a ton of Synths? Wonderful.*

"He's targeting you specifically," Ortiz said as they walked.
"What'd you do to piss him off?"

"Existed, probably," Coop replied. "I seem to have that face,
you know, where I piss off everyone."

Bear nodded. "Can't deny an ugly face when I see one. But,
seriously, just do what you do best. Improvise when everything goes to
hell. You got this, Coop."

"That's the plan, and thanks." Coop stepped into his pod and
settled into the control chair. The neural interface activated,
surrounding him with a virtual representation of Nightfall's surface.
Alpha Company's sector materialized around him, which was a rocky
plateau overlooking a deep canyon system.

Through his headset, West's voice boomed with crystal clarity.
"Simulation commencing in three… two… one…"

The virtual world solidified around Coop. So clear. So real.
Nightfall's rocky terrain stretched before him. His tactical vest felt
heavier than usual, the neural interface making every sensation
unnervingly real.

Crawford appeared at his right flank, portable communications
array already deployed. "Uplink established with orbital assets, sir," he
reported. Li was on his left, tactical data screen glowing with targeting
solutions. "Data network online. Tracking systems green across the
board."

Eight C100 combat synthetics stood at attention beside him,
their blank faces emotionless and waiting. His gut tightened at the sight

of them. Glorified toasters with guns, and West had saddled him with eight of the damn things.

"Alpha Company, second platoon, establish perimeter and prepare for movement," Lieutenant Gill ordered through the comms.

Enemy contacts appeared on scanners almost immediately. Red blips closing fast from the north ridge.

"Contact! Multiple hostiles approaching from sector three!" shouted Sergeant Vega.

Explosive fire erupted from their flank. The simulation rocked as virtual blaster rounds hammered their position. Two soldiers went down immediately.

"Cooper! Need orbital fire support, now!" Gill commanded.

Coop jumped into action, tapping across his TASC console. He called in coordinates manually, calculating wind drift and atmospheric interference the way he'd been trained.

"Calculating strike package," he reported, working the numbers. "ETA forty-five seconds."

A C100 stepped beside him. "Lieutenant, try adjusting for the temperature gradient. Your ballistics are off due to density altitude."

"I don't need your help," Coop snapped, continuing his calculations.

More explosions rocked their position. A piece of shrapnel tore through Gill's shoulder, the captain dropping to one knee. "We need that fire support now, Cooper!"

Coop worked faster. Too many variables. The atmosphere was playing hell with his calculations.

A C100 suddenly sparked and collapsed—West's promised malfunctions beginning. The second synthetic froze midstride, its systems flashing red warning signals.

"Two synthetics down!" Coop called.

"We've got more incoming!" Corporal Otis Skinner warned, firing controlled bursts at advancing enemies. "Heavy units on the ridge!"

Coop's display showed a new wave of hostiles. At least thirty of them advancing through the canyon. His strike was still thirty seconds out. Too slow.

The third synthetic dropped, systems failing with a mechanical whine. Only five remained operational.

"Lieutenant Cooper," one of the C100s stated, "your calculations aren't accounting for the pressure differential in this canyon. Adjust your wind calls two quadrants left and add twenty meters to your elevation."

Blaster fire ripped through their position. Three more soldiers went down. The synthetics might be unreliable, but what if the C100 was right about the atmospheric conditions?

Sweat dripped into Coop's eyes. His pride wasn't worth watching his team get slaughtered.

"Sir, Crawford's comms are down," Li reported. "I can route targeting data through my system, but we'll lose redundancy."

"What were those corrections again?" he growled at the synthetic.

"Two quadrants left wind adjustment, plus twenty meters elevation. The canyon's creating a funnel effect."

Coop punched in commands on his targeting system, inputting the adjustments. He'd been trained on wind calls and elevation adjustments since day one, but the complex terrain was creating conditions he hadn't factored in. The targeting solution suddenly aligned, his ballistic calculations showing a much higher probability of success.

"Strike package inbound," he announced. "All units take cover!"

The virtual sky opened up as Republic Reapers screamed overhead, delivering precision strikes that obliterated the enemy advance. The canyon erupted in explosions, turning the attacking force to ash.

The remaining five synthetics suddenly seized up and collapsed. All eight were now disabled as West had promised. But it didn't matter. Coop had already internalized the terrain adjustment.

Enemy reinforcements appeared from the east ravine. Without hesitation, Coop called in another strike, making similar adjustments for the terrain-induced wind patterns. The strike hit thirty seconds later, eliminating the threat before they could reach firing positions.

"Eastern approach clear," Coop announced.

"Western ridge showing movement," reported Vega.

Coop redirected firepower, applying the same principles to the different terrain features. His manual targeting was responding beautifully with the right adjustments. The speed was intoxicating.

"West ridge clear," he called as the dust settled.

When the final enemy wave approached from the south, Coop called in three simultaneous strikes with pinpoint accuracy, all manually calculated with the terrain adjustments. The battle ended in a decisive victory, with minimal Republic casualties after his adaptation.

The simulation dissolved around them. Coop found himself standing in the pod, evaluation data hovering before him. His performance metrics showed an abysmal start but an exceptional finish, with an overall score in the top percentile.

He stepped out of the pod to find West waiting, arms crossed.

"Almost got your entire company killed at first," West said. "Then you adapted."

"The terrain adjustments," Coop admitted. "The C100 had field observations I missed."

"The point of the exercise, Lieutenant. Information is just information. It's how you apply it that matters." West's stern expression eased. "Some lessons need to be learned the hard way." West turned to address the group. "Debriefing in ten!"

Bear appeared beside Coop. "Never thought I'd see the day you'd take advice from a C100."

"Yeah, well." Coop shrugged, feeling strangely conflicted. "Turns out even toasters can spot something useful sometimes."

"Growth, my friend." Bear grinned. "That's what separates the living from the synthetic. We can admit when we're wrong—or at least know when we're wrong. I don't know, maybe the Synths can too."

"Sounded good, though."

"Yeah. I do my best," Bear replied.

Coop glanced back at the simulation pod, thinking about those final moments when everything had clicked. "Gotta use every tool in the kit, I guess."

Chapter 18:
Ego Clash

Year 2098
FOB Oteren
Planet Intus

The hydraulic line hissed as Love disconnected it. She was careful not to spill fluid on the hangar floor. It had been three days since the memorial, and they'd fallen into a rhythm of maintenance that felt both familiar and wrong. The work continued, but the silence was deafening.

"Pressure check's good on the starboard engine," Green reported from his position under the nacelle. His voice echoed in the space where Williams's commentary should have been—except there were no jokes about Ford's tool organization, and no running critique of factory specifications.

Ford worked at the gunner's station, movements careful, almost reverent. He'd spent an hour cleaning equipment that was already spotless, arranging tools exactly as Williams had left them. The new memorial plaque caught the morning light: "Petty Officer First Class Tyrell Williams – Hold the Line."

Love started to call out a request for the torque wrench, then caught herself. That had been Williams's cue to complain about Navy pilots not knowing basic tools. Instead, she retrieved it herself, the simple action somehow exhausting.

"Chief Ford," Green said, then stopped as if recalculating what he was about to say. "Could you verify the ammunition feed on my side?"

They'd been doing this dance for three days. Moving around the absence. Filling time with unnecessary tasks rather than acknowledging the empty position.

No sooner had Love contemplated the thought of Williams's eventual replacement than she heard the sound of footsteps echoing across the hangar. It didn't take her long to recognize Granger's measured stride. But there was a second set of footsteps—quicker, more aggressive.

"Lieutenant Love," Granger called out.

She straightened, wiping her hands on a rag. Beside Granger stood a compact, muscular man in crisp fatigues. Where Williams had been tall and lanky, this soldier was built like a boxer—broad shoulders, thick neck, and movements that suggested coiled energy. His hair was regulation short, his jaw clean-shaven to the point of shine.

"Lieutenant, I'd like you to meet Petty Officer Second Class Marcus Torres. He just arrived from the 14th Assault Squadron," Granger said. "He's going to be your new gunner."

Torres stepped forward, his eyes already scanning the Osprey with an evaluator's gaze. "Good morning, ma'am. I heard you needed someone who knows their way around an Osprey."

Love smiled, noting his confidence that filled the space like an unwelcome presence. Ford's shoulders tensed as he introduced himself. Lieutenant Green heard them speaking and carefully set down his tools to join them.

"Good morning, Petty Officer Torres," Love acknowledged, her tone neutral. "This is the *Jack*. Welcome to—"

But Torres ignored her reply. He walked past her toward the port gunner station. He ran his hand along the exterior mount with proprietary interest.

"Huh. Interesting setup," he said, not quite hiding his dismissive tone. "You guys must've been a busy squadron. You're still using the older Mark-7s. A lot of squadrons have already upgraded to the Mark-9 months ago."

"That's true," Granger acknowledged. "Good eye. We've been a frontline squadron since the invasion." His voice betrayed his annoyance. Love could see he didn't like Torres's implication. She knew he'd been arguing for the squadron to be relieved so their birds could undergo some much-needed depot-level maintenance.

"Ah, that makes sense. I was beginning to wonder why I saw a lot of outdated equipment still being used on the Ospreys here," Torres replied casually, seemingly unaware of the rank of the people he was addressing.

Ford's wrench hit the deck with a clang. "This 'outdated' equipment still works, and it saved lives last week."

Torres glanced over, seeming to realize the rest of the crew was staring at him. "I'm sure it did," he answered. "Just wait until you see how smooth and lethal the newer Mark-9s are, though. They increased

the rate of fire by thirty percent, and accuracy is even better. You'll
love 'em when we can upgrade to what the rest of the Fleet is using."

The temperature in the hangar seemed to drop with each of the
slights and insults Torres seemed to be oblivious about making. Love
saw Ford's fists clench.

"In combat, you make do with what you have," Ford said, each
word precise. "Perhaps your last squadron didn't see much action, but
ours has been in the fight—"

"It's all right, Chief," Love cut him off, though her own jaw was
tight. "Why don't you show Torres around the *Jack* and his station.
And, Torres, once Chief Ford is done, why don't you head over to the
quartermaster and get squared away with a bunk and finish the rest of
your in-processing if you haven't already. Crew briefing is tomorrow at
0700 hours. We'll finish getting you up to speed then."

"Petty Officer Torres," Green said with forced diplomacy, "after
the morning brief, we'll go over the crew protocols and get you familiar
with how we operate."

Torres shrugged. "Sure. I think there's a lot I can do to help
improve our operations. Like they always say, there's plenty of room
for progress if you're willing to keep learning."

As Torres walked toward the rear hatch of the Osprey, his gaze
finally landed on the memorial plaque. Love watched him glance at it
without recognition; he walked past it like it wasn't there.

Love felt disrespected, and her professional mask was
threatening to crack. "Commander, perhaps we should discuss
integration procedures in your office?"

Granger had been watching the exchange with sharp eyes. He
nodded slowly. "Yeah, let's talk. Walk with me."

When Love was out of earshot of the rest of her crew, she said,
"Sir, I appreciate the replacement and all, but is he the only option I've
got?"

Granger didn't respond right away. "Listen, I get it. He's a little
rough around the edges, and maybe he's wound a little tight. But
Fleet's building up for some other big operations right now and
replacements are tight. He was with his last squadron for three years.
He has good fit reports, and he had the highest gunnery scores in his
squadron," Granger said quietly. "He's technically proficient and has
all his advanced certifications."

"He's great on paper, sir. But that attitude… it's like he's ignorant to rank and chain of command," Love said.

"Yeah, I saw," Granger agreed. "He's not Williams. But he's what we've got." He looked at her. "I need you to make it work, Lieutenant. That's an order."

"Roger that, sir," Love replied, sighing. Williams was gone, and his replacement was going to be…well, a challenge.

****

Love arrived at 0700 to find Torres already in the gunner's position, datapad connected to the targeting computer. The screen showed cascading code as he typed rapidly.

"Morning, ma'am," he said without looking up. "Just finishing some efficiency improvements. This latest software patch should increase target acquisition time by point three seconds."

"Morning, Torres. Did you clear that modification with—"

"All done!" Torres disconnected his datapad with satisfaction. "I also recalibrated the gun harmonization. The previous settings were off by two percent. Whoever set it at seven hundred meters was way off target. Optimal convergence is nine hundred."

"Torres, I know you just got here and you want to help. But we have a system in place and a chain of command that needs to be followed," Love explained, though Torres's mind seemed to be elsewhere.

Ford had walked up behind her and now stood frozen in the hatchway, coffee in hand. Love saw his knuckles whiten around the cup. She knew seven hundred meters had been Williams's preference when he'd operated the station. He'd sworn it accounted for real-world conditions better than the factory specs and their nine-hundred-meter recommendation.

"Torres," Love began carefully, "next time you want to make some system modifications, you need to speak to me or Chief Ford before—"

"Oh, and I reorganized the ready ammunition," interrupted Torres, completely ignoring her. He gestured excitedly at the storage compartments. "I took the liberty of color-coding by type instead of that weird number system you guys had. This is much more intuitive. In my last unit, we found it reduced reload time significantly."

Love was speechless. In less than twenty-four hours, he'd completely erased Williams's number system—the one based on firing sequences he'd developed over two years.

Green suddenly emerged from beneath the starboard nacelle. He took in the scene, and seeing that Chief Ford's face had turned a deep red, he immediately moved between Ford and Torres. "Hey, morning briefing still in five, right?" he asked.

"That's right." Love took the opportunity to change the subject and defuse the situation before Ford could lose his temper. "Let's go over mission parameters first. Systems discussion later."

The briefing was painful. Love outlined the routine patrol they were supposed to complete: sensor station checks along the northern valleys, and visual reconnaissance of last month's battle sites, verifying no further Zodark activity. With the endless questions that Torres asked and his constant suggestions for improvements, this four-hour recon flight started to feel like it was going to be an eternity to her.

Hoping to end the brief, she asked, "Any final questions on the route before we get going?"

"Negative, ma'am," Torres replied. "Though I notice we're not using standard brevity codes for waypoint designation. In my last unit—"

"Dude, give it a rest, Torres. This isn't your last unit. We use the codes that work for us," Ford interrupted harshly.

Torres shrugged. "Sure, Chief. Just saying, standardization exists for a reason. Professionalism matters."

Green's diplomatic mask slipped for just a second before he recovered. "And on that note, we should probably start preflight, so we stay on schedule."

They moved through the checklist with mechanical precision. Where Williams would have called out, "Good to go, boss!," Torres responded with a textbook "Check complete, proceeding to next item." Where they expected "All green on my end," they got "Port weapons systems nominal, no discrepancies noted."

Love started the engines, but the familiar vibration somehow felt off. Everything was exactly right, perfectly by the book, and completely wrong.

"*Jack* ready for departure," she announced.

"Roger that," Torres responded.

"We say 'copy,'" Ford muttered.

"Roger means message received and understood," Torres responded patiently. "It's the correct—"

"Let's just fly," Love cut in, lifting off before the argument could escalate.

The patrol route took them over familiar territory. Below, they saw the agricultural fields where they'd made their emergency landing. There were no longer any signs of the violence that had taken place there. The commercial district of Hatteng City bustled with normal activity. Even the plaza where Williams had made his stand was beginning to return to normal.

"Sensor Station Alpha checks normal," Green reported.

"Roger—I mean, copy," Torres corrected himself with audible condescension. "Maintaining visual scan of sector."

They'd been airborne two hours when the hydraulic warning light flickered amber.

"Pressure drop in the port control circuit," Green announced. "Looks like a minor leak."

"I'll check it," Ford said, already unbuckling.

Torres intervened. "Chief, shouldn't we run a diagnostics, then—"

"We have a hydraulic leak. It's the same leak we've had before," Ford explained.

"What?" asked Torres. "If this is a chronic problem, why isn't it being fixed correctly back at the base? Who signs off on this shoddy maintenance?" Torres's voice carried an edge. "In my last unit, we followed maintenance protocols and technical manuals for a reason. Cowboy repairs and lack of maintenance can cause crashes."

Love kept her focus locked on flying, hands steady on the controls despite the urge to intervene. In her peripheral vision, she saw Ford's jaw working.

"OK, Torres," Ford said. "Go ahead and run your diagnostics for the problem I already know."

Oblivious to Ford's sarcasm, Torres pulled up the technical manual on his tablet, following each step methodically. What Williams would have fixed in two minutes with a wrench and electrical tape took Torres fifteen minutes of troubleshooting to diagnose. The result was the same—a loose fitting tightened—but the method felt alien and wasted time.

"Hydraulic pressure restored," Torres announced with satisfaction. "See? If proper maintenance and procedure is followed, it prevents problems."

"Torres, it's not that you're wrong to check the manual and run a diagnostic. But when we're in combat, you don't have the time to check the manual," Ford said, his words cutting like broken glass. "You have to know the manual like the back of your hand. The enemy isn't going to pause trying to kill you while you figure it out. You either know what the problem is and you solve it immediately, or in most cases, you're dead."

Green saw the verbal exchange and tried to intervene. "Thankfully, we're not in combat," he said. "We have the time to check the manual, and that's good, right?"

"If you say so, sir," Torres replied. "I know when you're in combat, you have to make quick decisions and fixes. As the lieutenant said, we're not in combat. When I was checking the maintenance logs, I noticed a lot of these 'quick fixes.' In my last unit, we'd have flagged this bird for depot-level maintenance. Standards matter."

Love's hands tightened on the controls. Every sentence started with "In my last unit." Every observation carried implicit criticism. He was right, technically. And that made it worse.

The radio crackled. "Wolfpack Actual, this is Overwatch. Weather update for your sector. Clear skies continuing. Enjoy the milk run."

"Copy, Overwatch," Love responded, grateful for any interruption.

They completed their patrol in professional silence. Green managed systems without his usual chatter. Ford said nothing beyond required responses.

As they approached FOB Oteren, Love felt an exhaustion that had nothing to do with flying. Four hours of perfect procedure, optimal performance, and zero cohesion.

"Tower, *Jack* on approach," she called.

"*Jack*, cleared for pad seven. Welcome home."

Home. Love set them down with practiced ease, engines spooling down. Before the rotors stopped, Torres was already making notes on his datapad.

"Good flight," he said. "I'll write up some recommendations for procedural improvements. Once we implement proper standards, this crew could be really efficient. In my last unit—"

"Torres, what rank am I wearing?" Love interrupted, her frustration reaching a boiling point.

"Ah, lieutenant, ma'am," Torres replied.

"That's right, Petty Officer. I could be wrong, but do I report to *you* and implement *your* procedures, or how does this work?" she asked.

His facial expressions finally registered that he'd overstepped. "I report to you, ma'am. You are the flight leader," he replied.

"That's right. If you have a suggestion for how to improve something, I'm all ears. But I expect you to show some respect for the rank I hold. As to everyone else, debrief at 1400. I'll see everyone there. Dismissed." Love walked past Torres and headed down the hangar to clear her head.

As her crew dispersed, Love wondered how many more flights like this one they could endure. It wasn't that Torres was wrong to make suggestions. He had followed every procedure and finished every task. But he'd made everyone feel like a stranger in their own bird.
****

A Week Later

The shutdown checklist had never felt longer. Love moved through each item mechanically, while Torres typed rapidly on his datapad, occasionally making small disapproving sounds. Ford's tool work had taken on an aggressive quality as his annoyance with Torres grew—wrenches cranked with unnecessary force, panels slammed rather than closed.

And it wasn't just *their* crew that Torres was beginning to grate on. His interactions with the maintenance team and the other Osprey crews in the hangar were getting him noticed in all the wrong ways.

"Fascinating operational dynamics," Torres muttered, apparently to himself but loud enough to carry. "So many opportunities for optimization."

Green finished his postflight inspection and immediately moved to the far side of the Osprey, creating physical distance. Other crews in the hangar had noticed the tension—conversations had quieted, and glances were exchanged. Chief Rawlins paused his work on a nearby bird, watching with the instincts of a senior NCO who smelled trouble brewing.

Across the hangar, Torres had wandered over to where Senior Spacer Joe Franks was working on the *Daisy*'s gun mount. Love watched from the corner of her eye as Torres leaned over Franks's shoulder, pointing at something on the control panel.

"That convergence setting," Torres said, loud enough for half the hangar to hear. "It's completely out of regulation. Manual clearly states nine hundred meters for atmospheric conditions."

Franks looked up, confused. "But Chief Diaz likes it set at seven-fifty. Says it works better for—"

"Regulations are regulations," Torres interrupted, his tone brooking no argument. "I outrank you, Spacer. You want me to report you for noncompliance? Or are you going to fix it?"

Franks glanced around nervously, clearly torn between Torres's rank and his own crew chief's preferences. "I… I guess I should fix it?"

"Smart choice," Torres said, already moving on to inspect something else. "Check your ammunition logs while you're at it. Probably all kinds of discrepancies there too."

Franks reluctantly began adjusting the settings, his movements hesitant. Love was about to intervene when Petty Officer First Class Diaz emerged from beneath the *Daisy*, wiping his hands on a rag.

"Franks, what the hell are you doing to my gun specs?" Diaz's voice carried across the hangar.

"I was…Torres said the regulations—"

"Torres?" Diaz's face darkened. "Since when does Torres run maintenance on the *Daisy*?"

"He outranks me, Chief," Franks said miserably. "Said he'd report me if I didn't change it to regulation standard."

Diaz's jaw worked as he processed this. Without another word to Franks, he stalked across the hangar to where Ford was organizing tools.

"Chief, sorry to interrupt," Diaz said, his voice tight with controlled anger, "but I think you need to have a chat with your new guy, Torres, and remind him we have a chain of command he needs to learn how to respect."

Ford set down his wrench, frustration evident in every line of his body. He'd been dealing with Torres's inability to integrate for days, and now this.

"Torres!" Ford called out. "Get over here."

Love flinched. She wasn't sure if she should intervene or not, but she had a really bad feeling about this.

Torres approached with his characteristic confidence, datapad still in hand. "Yes, Chief?"

"Diaz here says you told Spacer Franks he needed to change the gun specs if he didn't want to be reported for not complying with regulations. Is that true?"

Torres's expression shifted to defensive righteousness. "Chief, when I checked the specs on the *Jack*'s Mark-7, it was out of regulation, and according to the maintenance logs, it hasn't been in regulation for most of the year. Out of curiosity, I asked Franks if he could show me the specs on his Osprey, *Daisy*. It was even worse, Chief. Hell, the logs on everything from maintenance to ammo to you name it are chock-full of mistakes. It's shoddy work, Chief—"

"Shoddy work?" Diaz's voice rose dangerously. "You showed up a week ago and look at you—peacocking around the shuttle bay like you're God's gift to the Fleet!"

"Peacocking?" Torres's face flushed. "The *Daisy* shouldn't be flying with the kind of maintenance logs you've clearly been fudging. Hell, if this squadron had a maintenance chief worth half a lick, he'd fail half the transports for piss-poor maintenance!" Torres gestured wildly at the *Daisy* and the other Ospreys in the bay.

Diaz lost it. He stepped forward, shouting directly into Torres's face, their noses inches apart. Torres bowed up, his head accidentally bumping Diaz as he closed the gap and misjudged the distance, getting right back in Diaz's face to shout his response.

Diaz stepped back at the contact, then threw a punch.

The blow caught Torres on the jaw, but the stocky gunner barely flinched, his thick neck absorbing the impact. Ford saw Torres cock back his own fist and tried to step between them, but his timing was off. Torres's punch, meant for Diaz, caught Ford on the side of the head instead.

Ford went down hard, more from surprise than the force of the blow. Love found herself frozen from the shock of the interaction, at least for a moment.

"Stand down!" Chief Rawlins's bellow shook the hangar walls. "Freeze, Torres! Don't move another muscle! Diaz, shut your piehole before I shove a boot down it!"

By now, Ford had scrambled to his feet, his hand going to his head. Love had recovered enough to go check on him. Ford seemed like he was ready to return the favor to Torres, but Rawlins was already laying into Torres with a verbal barrage that could strip paint.

Rawlins turned to Ford. "You OK, Chief?"

"Yeah, Senior," Ford managed, though his head was ringing.

"Get to medical, have them check you out. Then report to my office." Rawlins's eyes were cold steel as he turned back to Diaz and Torres. "You two. My office. *Now*."

Love was mortified—one of her crewmen had just assaulted another NCO, and the entire maintenance bay had witnessed it.

"Senior Chief—" she began.

"Ma'am, I know you want to jump into this," Rawlins interrupted respectfully but firmly, "and there will be a time for it. But this is an NCO issue I need to deal with before the CO gets involved."

Love wanted to take charge, but Rawlins was right. He was the squadron's senior NCO, and this was his domain. "OK, Senior Chief. But someone's getting papers. I'm not going to stand for fighting like this."

"Understood, ma'am," Rawlins acknowledged, then turned to the two offenders. "Move. Both of you."

As Rawlins marched Diaz and Torres toward his office, the entire maintenance bay could hear him beginning his tirade before they even reached the door. "You think this is how professionals handle disagreements? You think throwing punches in *my* hangar is acceptable?"

The office door slammed shut, but Rawlins's voice carried through the walls. Love had never heard the senior chief this angry, and she found herself grateful she'd let him handle it first. The dressing-down that followed was legendary—phrases like "absolute disgrace to the uniform" and "wouldn't trust you to maintain a bicycle" echoed through the hangar.

Love shivered involuntarily. She'd have her turn with Torres later, but right now, Rawlins was doing a thorough job of making both men wish they'd never been born.

****

Love waited outside medical, pacing the corridor as she tried to process what had just happened. The sound of Rawlins's voice still carried faintly from across the compound, though the words were no longer distinguishable.

The medical bay door opened and Ford emerged, holding an ice pack to the side of his head. Green was with him, having waited as well.

"Clean bill of health?" Love asked.

"Just a nice bruise," Ford said, wincing slightly. "Doc says Torres packs a punch."

"This is a disaster," Love said quietly. "My gunner just started a brawl in the maintenance bay. In front of everyone."

"To be fair, he was trying to hit Diaz," Ford offered, then grimaced. "Not that it makes it better."

They moved to a quiet alcove away from the main corridor. Love leaned against the wall, suddenly exhausted.

"Ma'am," Green said, his voice carrying that same worn quality she'd been hearing for days, "we need to talk about this. Really talk about it."

"I know," Love said. "Torres just—"

"It's not just about Torres," Green interrupted, surprising her with his directness. "With respect, ma'am, this has been building since he arrived. We've all been dancing around the real problem."

Ford shifted uncomfortably. "Green—"

"No, Chief. Someone needs to say it." Green turned to Love. "You've been managing this like we're grieving civilians, not military professionals. Torres is out there alienating everyone because no one's given him proper guidance or boundaries. He's trying too hard because he's scared, and we've given him every reason to be."

The words stung, but Love couldn't deny their truth. "You're right," she admitted. "I've been hiding behind grief instead of leading. I let you all drift because it was easier than having hard conversations."

"He's got the whole squadron turned against him now," Ford said, setting down the ice pack. "Diaz is respected. Torres questioning his maintenance logs, calling them shoddy in front of everyone… that's not just insulting Diaz. That's insulting every crew chief in the bay."

"Williams is gone," Green said, gentler now. "We honored him. We grieved him. But Torres doesn't know how to be part of a crew because no one's taught him how *this* crew works, how *this* squadron works."

Love felt the weight of her failures settling on her shoulders. "I should have integrated him properly. Should have set boundaries. Should have led instead of just… existing."

"So, what do we do now?" Ford asked. "After this mess, half the squadron won't work with him."

Love straightened, feeling the weight of command as responsibility rather than burden. "We fix this. Starting with me actually being your lieutenant instead of—"

"Lieutenant Love." A yeoman appeared in the alcove. "Commander Granger wants to see you in his office. Immediately, ma'am."

Love's stomach dropped. "On my way."

She looked at Ford and Green. "Whatever happens next, we're going to fix this crew. We're going to integrate Torres properly, teach him how we operate, and become functional again. Because if we don't—"

"Granger will split us up," Ford finished. "And then Williams really will have died for nothing."

"Ma'am," the yeoman pressed. "The commander said immediately."

Love nodded. "Ford, Green—get some food, get some rest. Tomorrow, we start over. All of us."

She followed the yeoman down the corridor, knowing that Granger had probably heard about the fight before Rawlins even got Torres and Diaz to his office. The entire squadron had seen it. Her crew's dysfunction had just exploded into public view in the worst possible way.

As she approached Granger's office, Love could see through the window that he was already at his desk, reports spread before him, expression grim. She'd failed to lead her crew through their grief, failed to integrate Torres properly, and now that failure had resulted in a brawl that embarrassed the entire squadron.

She knocked on the door, squaring her shoulders. Whatever came next, she'd earned it. But she'd also fix it—for Williams, for her crew, and for herself.

"Enter," Granger called, his tone suggesting this was going to be a very long and unpleasant conversation.

Love stepped inside, closing the door behind her, ready to face the consequences of her leadership failures.

<h2 style="text-align:center">Chapter 19:
Wounded Eagles</h2>

Year 2098
RNS *Poseidon*
Middle Reach
Sector 8

Sato entered Lee's ready room. She carried a data tablet, its screen illuminated with schematics of the RNS *Polaris*.

"Captain," she said, offering a quick salute before taking her customary position in front of his desk. "The *Polaris* repairs are proceeding ahead of schedule. The Primord engineers from the *Ek* have been instrumental in restoring the primary power couplings, amongst other issues they're working on at the moment."

Lee leaned back in his chair. "Specifics?"

"Hull integrity restored to eighty-two percent. Weapons systems at sixty-three percent capacity and climbing. Their engineers implemented an innovative bypass for the damaged targeting array." Sato scrolled through her report. "The Primords' familiarity with gravitational displacement technology proved invaluable when realigning the damaged sensor grid."

"Estimated time until full combat readiness?"

"Eight hours, sir. That's hours sooner than our initial projection."

Those Primord engineers are damn impressive, Lee thought.

His desk console beeped. Lee glanced down at the notification. "Incoming transmission from Captain Dharek. Should be good." The tone in his voice suggested sarcasm, which was very much intended.

"Should I step out, sir?" Sato asked.

"No. Stay."

Lee tapped the console and Dharek's image materialized on the screen and hovered above Lee's desk. The Primord captain's eyes narrowed when he spotted Sato.

"Captain Lee," Dharek said. "I had expected a private audience."

Lee remained impassive. "Lieutenant Commander Sato is my XO. Anything you need to discuss can be said in her presence."

Behind Dharek, the sparse decor of his private office aboard the *Ek* was visible. There, a metal desk sat empty except for a data terminal casting a green glow. Three model warships lined a shelf to one side, and a holomap was mounted on the back wall, where it cycled between star systems, pausing every so often on what were presumably contested sectors. Most striking was a display case containing what looked like bones. Long, curved specimens suspended in an amber-colored material. They weren't human or Primord in origin; whatever creature they'd belonged to was something entirely foreign to Lee.

"Very well." Dharek straightened. "I wish to formally address the tactical decisions made during our most recent engagement."

"Go ahead."

"The positioning of my fleet was… very good." Dharek's words came out sharp. "We placed Republic vessels in a secondary defensive posture, far removed from the primary engagement zone."

Lee folded his hands on the desk. "To keep us out of the fight, and for reasons I don't understand."

"I positioned all ships according to their tactical strengths and—"

"You positioned my vessels behind your battleships," Lee cut Dharek off. "I understand. Just not when you're in need. You tell us to hold? We're operating on a joint mission to gather intelligence, not to see who's better at combat."

"The *Ek* alone has twice the firepower of three Republic corvettes combined."

"Understood." *How many times do I need to say that?* "Yet you had us sitting in reserve while the *Polaris* nearly got destroyed and you yourselves were in tactical trouble."

"And the patrol formation was designed to—"

"To what? Showcase Primord vessels while keeping Republic ships from the first return fire?" Lee's voice rose in pitch. "My crews are combat veterans with many major engagements against Zodark forces. This would have ended sooner had you used my forces."

Dharek grimaced. "We have destroyed more Zodark battleships than your entire Middle Reach squadron has… combined."

Sato shifted her weight but remained silent.

Lee remained still, his expression unchanged. "Captain Dharek, Captain Roberts—"

"And that is why I messaged you as well."

Lee let out a breath. "OK, go on…"

"I do not need Captain Roberts to tell me what I already know." Dharek leaned in. "Basic military doctrine places your strongest assets at the point of greatest tactical advantage. Our ships should have been at the forefront, not yours."

"That's not what I was arguing. Listen—"

The Primord captain raised his palm, the ridges along his jawline becoming more pronounced, and Lee fell silent. "I have received a direct communication from Captain Roberts at FOB Bulwark. He has informed me that Captain Mensah of the RNS *Idaho* will be assuming command of our combined task force."

Lee kept his face neutral, though he'd been waiting for this.

"The *Idaho* will be accompanied by the RNS *Oceanus*, RNS *Thunder*, and RNS *Argo*, along with four electronic warfare frigates," Dharek continued. "They are expected to arrive within twenty-four hours."

"Given what we encountered, the additional firepower will be welcome."

Dharek squinted. "I am to assume the position of second-in-command. My vessels will remain under my direct authority, but Captain Mensah will coordinate overall strategy." There was a slight hesitation before he spoke again. "I find the timing of this command restructuring…peculiar. Almost immediately following our engagement and the disagreement regarding tactical deployment."

Lee tilted his head. He couldn't believe Dharek would even think of such a thing. "If you're suggesting I had something to do with this decision, you're mistaken. It would have been discussed among both Republic and Primord admirals. Command decisions at that level don't happen based on a single officer's recommendation."

"Do they not?" Dharek's voice carried an edge. "Your relationship with Captain Roberts is well documented. A private communication from you would carry significant weight."

Well documented? Lee thought. *What's he talking about?*

Before Lee could respond, Sato chimed in. "With respect, Captain Dharek, Commander Lee has consistently advocated for greater integration of Primord tactical doctrine in our operations. He specifically highlighted your vessels' superior firepower in his after-action reports."

"Lieutenant Commander"—Dharek's gaze shifted to Sato—"your loyalty to your commanding officer is admirable but unnecessary. The evidence speaks for itself."

"Captain," Lee said, "I understand your frustration. Command transfers are difficult, especially mid-deployment. But this is about responding to an escalating threat. The engagement we just survived suggests Zodark activity in this sector is significantly higher than intelligence predicted, along with atypical anomalies. The reinforcements and command restructuring reflect that reality."

Dharek's expression remained skeptical. "A convenient explanation."

"It's the truth," Lee replied. "And frankly, Captain, we have more important concerns than bruised egos. The Zodarks are implementing new counterdetection measures; plus we're in search of a Zodark base in this sector."

Dharek studied Lee for a long moment before his posture subtly shifted. "Perhaps. Regardless, I am now tasked with preparing my vessels for Captain Mensah's arrival. Captain Roberts was quite specific about the protocols to be observed."

"What's our operational directive until the reinforcements arrive?" Lee asked.

"We are to maintain current position and proceed at reduced speed," Dharek replied. "Captain Roberts emphasized the importance of preserving our combat capability. We will continue passive scanning of the region but avoid any engagement unless directly threatened."

He straightened in his chair. "Upon the *Idaho*'s arrival, I will formally transfer task force command to Captain Mensah as directed. Until then, we will maintain standard patrol operations with heightened alert status."

Lee nodded. "Understood. We'll coordinate sensor coverage to maintain maximum situational awareness."

"I have transmitted the relevant tactical data to your navigation officer," Dharek said. "Dharek out."

The transmission ended, leaving Lee and Sato in silence.

"Well," Sato said after a moment, "that was pleasant."

Lee sighed. "He thinks I engineered his replacement."

"That would never even cross my mind. You two disagree and butt heads like fighting bulls, which I find a little entertaining, but you both could lead this battle group and do so very well. Just gotta keep your egos out of it, in my opinion."

"True." Lee stood and moved to the small viewport, staring out at the stars. "But I guess, thinking about it, I can understand why he might think so. From his perspective, we just had a major disagreement about command protocols, and suddenly he's being sidelined."

"Not sidelined," Sato pointed out. "Second-in-command of an expanded task force is hardly a demotion."

"To a Primord? It might feel that way." Lee turned back to face her. "Their military culture places enormous emphasis on individual command. Being subordinated to a Republic officer after previously having equal standing…it's a significant loss of face."

Sato leaned against the edge of his desk. "Permission to speak freely, sir?"

"Always."

"This reminds me of something that happened during my time at the Academy." She paused, collecting her thoughts. "I was part of a joint training exercise. Republic cadets paired with Republic officers. We were supposed to be learning integrated command structures."

"Let me guess. It didn't go smoothly?"

"That's an understatement." A trace of a smile crossed her face. "Two of the commanding officers nearly came to blows over tactical priorities. Neither would yield, both convinced their approach was superior. The exercise collapsed completely. It was like…two immature kids fighting over who gets to control the candy or not. It embarrassed the Academy, and the officers in question."

"What happened?"

"A third officer—who'd been quietly observing—gathered us all and said something I've never forgotten. She said: 'Pride creates barriers where none existed. When those barriers become more important than the mission, everyone loses.'"

"Wise words."

"The thing is," Sato continued, "I watched those two officers make fools of themselves because neither could step back and see the larger picture. Their rivalry consumed them until it was all they could see. I'm assuming they had a long rivalry before that day, but nonetheless…" Her expression grew serious. "I'm worried the same thing is happening between you and Dharek."

"You think I'm letting pride dictate my decisions?"

"I think both of you are skilled commanders who respect each other's capabilities more than either will admit," Sato replied. "But this constant positioning for tactical superiority is creating a rift that the Zodarks will exploit if given the chance."

Lee was silent for a moment. "So, what's your advice, XO?"

For a moment, Sato blushed. "Usually, you're the one giving me personal advice. It's odd being on the other end of this. Regardless, here's what I think. When Captain Mensah arrives, be the bridge, not the barrier. Dharek's pride is wounded. He needs to see that you respect his position, even as the command structure changes."

"And how exactly do I do that?"

"By acknowledging his expertise publicly. By ensuring his tactical insights are incorporated into mission planning. By treating him as a valued equal, not a subordinate."

Lee nodded slowly. "You're right."

"Don't walk into that trap, sir," Sato said. "I've seen what happens when capable officers let pride override reason. It never ends well. For anyone."

As she turned to leave, Lee called after her. "Sato?"

She paused at the door.

"Thank you."

She nodded and left the ready room.

Lee returned to the viewport. Twenty-four hours until the *Idaho* arrived with Captain Mensah and a new command structure. Twenty-four hours to prepare his crew—and himself—for the transition.

The stars beyond the viewport seemed cold and distant. Somewhere out there, the Zodarks were planning their next move, implementing new technologies, preparing for something significant…and perhaps an outpost floated somewhere in this sector's expanse.

Caught between Dharek's wounded pride and the incoming command change, Lee felt the weight of responsibility more acutely than ever. Twenty-four hours until *Idaho* arrived, shortly after which the Republic and Primord leadership would speak about the planned assault on a potential hidden Zodark base. The mission was difficult enough without the politics.

Still, Sato was right. They needed to work together. The Zodarks wouldn't care about their squabbles. They'd just keep killing, keep subjugating the rest of the galaxy.

And Lee had no intention of letting that happen. Not on his watch.

Chapter 20:
Efficiencies

Year 2098
FOB Oteren
Planet Intus

Love arrived at 0730 hours to find the briefing room back in its original configuration. Four weeks had passed since the incident that had nearly torn the squadron apart. The chairs were arranged normally, the mission board displayed standard information, and there was a tentative peace that felt fragile but real.

Torres sat at the far end of the table, dark circles under his eyes a testament to his thirty days of extra duty that had just ended yesterday. His usual datapad was nowhere in sight—four weeks of punishment detail scrubbing decks and cleaning latrines from 1800 to 0200 had beaten some of the swagger out of him. The bread and water diet hadn't helped either; he'd lost at least fifteen pounds.

Diaz entered with his crew, still moving stiffly from his own punishment routine. Fifteen days hadn't been as bad as thirty, but the lost month's pay hurt them both. Worse, Love knew from squadron scuttlebutt that the incident had likely cost Diaz his next promotion board. He nodded curtly to Ford—they'd made their peace—but his jaw tightened when he glanced at Torres.

"Morning, everyone," Love began, noting how the room's dynamics had shifted. Torres no longer sat isolated but wasn't quite integrated either. Ford had taken to sitting one chair closer each week, a gradual thaw. "Standard patrol routes today, but first, Green has an announcement."

Green stood, a hint of his old energy returning. "Right, so MWR just posted about some new squadron competitions they're starting up—trying to boost morale, bring some fun to Intus." He pulled up the announcement on the main screen. "They've got relay races, tug-of-war, and…a boxing tournament."

The room perked up at that.

"Each squadron nominates one boxer," Green continued. "Thursday night fights, up to nine rounds. Win six fights, you advance to the championship. And here's the kicker—if our boxer wins the whole thing, the entire squadron gets a five-day pass and a victory bash."

"Define 'victory bash,'" someone asked.

Green grinned. "Kegs of real beer shipped from Earth. At least six beers per person. Surf and turf dinner—twelve-ounce filet, eight-ounce lobster tail. Plus, dinner with the Fleet's commanding admiral and general."

Low whistles filled the room. After months of standard rations and "near beers," the prospect of real beer and actual steak was like paradise.

"So," Green said, glancing at Ford and then at Torres, "Senior Chief Rawlins and Chief Ford both think we should nominate Torres."

The room went quiet. Diaz raised an eyebrow but kept his mouth shut, though Love could see the effort it took.

Torres looked up, genuine surprise on his face. "Me?"

Ford actually smiled—Love realized it might have been the first time he'd directed one at Torres. "Torres, you may be a pain in the butt, but damn, you throw one hell of a punch. I think all might be forgiven if you manage to deliver a kegger party for the squadron and a five-day pass to get drunk and not care about the world for a little while."

A few chuckles rippled through the room. The bruise on Ford's jaw had taken two weeks to fully fade, becoming something of a squadron legend.

Diaz surprised everyone by speaking up. "Yeah, we could make some money off this, Torres." He managed a crooked grin. "Betting pools are legal for MWR events. Might make back some of that month's pay we both lost."

Love watched the moment carefully. Green had found exactly the right opportunity—something that channeled Torres's physicality and competitiveness while offering the squadron a reason to rally behind him.

Torres looked around the room, then turned to Love. "What do you think, ma'am?"

The question caught her off guard. Four weeks ago, Torres would have just agreed, eager to prove himself. The humility in his voice now showed growth.

"I think if you want to win some hearts and minds, Torres, this is a good way to do it," she answered honestly.

"Plus," someone called out, "after thirty days of bread and water, you're probably hungry enough to fight a bear for that steak dinner."

There was more laughter. The atmosphere was lighter than it had been in over a month.

"What do you think, Torres?" Green pressed. "Can I tell Commander Granger we have our guy?"

Torres looked around the room again—at Diaz managing a supportive nod, at Ford's genuinely encouraging expression, at crews that had spent four weeks watching him pay for his mistakes without complaint.

"Yeah," Torres said finally, a ghost of his old confidence returning. "Why not."

The room erupted in approval. Someone slapped Torres on the back. Another started calculating betting odds. Even Hayes's crew at the next table looked interested.

Love caught Green's eye and nodded approvingly. He'd found a path forward—not by erasing the past or forcing integration, but by giving Torres a way to earn his place through something the whole squadron could unite behind.

As the briefing broke up and crews headed to their birds, Love noticed Ford fall into step beside Torres, already discussing training routines. It wasn't forgiveness yet, but it was a beginning.
****

As the briefing broke up and crews headed to their birds, Granger moved from the shadows where he'd been observing.

"Lieutenant Love, a word."

Love paused at the door as her crew filed out—Ford and Torres now walking together, discussing training routines, and Green trailing behind with a satisfied expression. When the door closed, Granger's countenance was thoughtful rather than stern.

"So," he said, settling against the briefing table. "Torres. Think he might have learned his lesson?"

Love considered the question carefully. "He's finally stopped comparing everything to his last unit, so that's progress. Thirty days of extra duty and bread and water has a way of adjusting attitudes."

Granger sighed heavily, rubbing his temples. "I had hoped to keep this whole episode to ourselves and try to work it out internally, but I got a message from the Wing King, Captain Bowser, about an IG complaint. Something about shoddy maintenance, dangerous aircraft flying, and crew chiefs fudging their maintenance logs."

Love's stomach dropped, and she groaned audibly. Those were the exact words Torres had used before the punches had started flying. "Sir, I'm sorry. It has to be Torres. I can't believe that little"—she caught herself—"that he filed an IG complaint."

Granger shook his head dismissively, clearly frustrated. "Lieutenant, this is both your fault for failing to integrate your replacement into your crew and my fault for having failed to teach you how to deal with a problem child like Torres when one appears."

Love started to respond, but Granger held up a hand to stop her.

"Listen, Torres is clearly acting out for a reason. The question both you and I failed to ask is why. I reached out to his last command to inquire about him, and I learned something that might help explain what's going on."

This caught Love by surprise. She hadn't considered something deeper might be happening with Torres until Granger had suggested it. "Sir?"

"Torres lost his whole crew a few months before he transferred," Granger explained, the announcement hitting Love like a physical blow.

"How?" was all she managed to say.

"Appendicitis, of all things." Granger saw the confusion on her face and continued. "He had appendicitis and required surgery. He was off flight status for a week. A replacement fresh from training took his place. His crew went out on a mission, similar to the one where we lost Williams, and didn't come home. Their bird took a hit from a Zodark missile and blew apart—there were no survivors. He probably blames himself for their deaths or feels like he should have been with them."

Love felt the pieces clicking into place: the obsessive efficiency reports, the constant improvements, and the desperate need to fix everything… "That… explains a lot. I had no idea."

"Yeah, well, he's still a pain in the rear. I've got to deal with this IG nonsense now," Granger replied, his frustration evident. "Look, Lieutenant. I think having Torres represent the squadron in the MWR boxing match is a good idea. It's a good way to try and reintegrate him into the squadron. But here's the deal—if you can't find a way to make it work with him as part of your flight crew—"

"I can make it work, sir," Love interjected firmly.

"Can you?" Granger's eyes narrowed. "This business of going around the chain of command to file an IG complaint without giving me or Senior Chief a chance to address it chaps my hide pretty bad. It puts a sour taste in my mouth, and now I've got the Wing King breathing down my neck about it."

"I'm sorry about that, sir. I don't know what to say." Love paused, thinking. "I'll talk to him. Try to figure something out. Maybe he needs some counseling or someone to talk to about the loss of his crew."

"Maybe. Whatever it is, I need you to fix it. You've got another milk run today. Show me you guys can function as a proper team and let's take it from there. Copy?"

"Roger that, sir. I'll make it happen," Love assured him, meaning every word.

She turned to leave, but Granger's voice stopped her. "Love? Understanding why someone's difficult doesn't excuse their behavior. But it does help us figure out how to fix it. Use that information wisely."

"Yes, sir."

As Love headed for the flight line, her mind was already working through this new information. Torres wasn't just a problem—he was a wounded soldier trying to prevent another tragedy. Now she had to figure out how to help him heal while keeping her crew together.
****

Following Morning
0500 Hours

The hangar was dark at 0500 hours. Only emergency lighting cast long shadows between the Ospreys. Love waited inside the *Jack*, checking her watch as footsteps approached on the tarmac outside. She'd sent messages to each of her crew: "0500, the *Jack*, come alone."

A couple of months back, Love had made a special trip for the head cook, Master Chief Blaise, a former Michelin-starred chef before he got drafted. His unique skill set had afforded him a starting rank of chief petty officer right out the gate, and he'd quickly risen to become the wing's master chef.

One day in the galley, Love had overheard him in a bit of a panic at the realization that they were not going to be able to acquire the ingredients he needed for the wing commander's surprise fiftieth birthday party.

When she'd asked him what he needed, Blaise had told her he'd found a source, but it was located in a Primord city way outside their wing's area of operation.

"If I could make it happen," she'd said with a smile, "could I call in a favor for a special dinner or something down the road?"

"I'd be in your debt," he'd answered with a grin. "Name what you want, and if it's within my powers, I'll deliver."

Twelve hours later, she'd found a reason to visit the location he needed and snuck Blaise aboard the *Jack* with the help of Williams and Ford. They'd all agreed they would call in their marker when their squadron finally received orders off Intus.

After her meeting with Granger, Love had thought about what needed to be done with Torres and how to remake her crew into a functional, mission-worthy team the squadron could count on. That was when it had dawned on her—it was time to call in her favor with Master Chef Blaise and ask for some donuts.

When she'd told Blaise what she'd needed and why, he had told her to show up the next day at 0400, and not a minute later. "If the others find out I made a dozen gourmet donuts and didn't save any for them, well…don't put me in that position, ma'am. I'll just consider this a favor and you can save your marker for a real, unique meal you can't get in the galley. It sounds like your crew and this Torres kid could use a little something special.

She'd agreed and told him what she wanted: four Boston cream donuts, four apple fritters, and four bear claws.

As though secretly meeting a drug dealer in the dark of night, Love had slipped into the galley at 0355 hours. Blaise had been there, with a box of delicious-smelling donuts. With the goods in hand, she had quickly slipped through the maintenance bay before anyone showed up and placed the baked goodies in the *Jack*.

After she'd grabbed everyone their favorite coffees, the meeting was set.

At 0500 hours, her crew began to arrive. Ford came first, climbing the ramp with a yawn. "OK, boss, I'm here, bright and early as requested."

Green followed moments later, and Torres brought up the rear. They all looked curious but wary as Love closed the rear hatch, sealing them inside their bird.

"Sorry about the early hour, but I have a surprise that I think will help make it worth your while," Love said, producing a carrier with four coffees—each one exactly how they liked it.

Green accepted his with another yawn. "Ma'am, I could have grabbed this myself. What's so important you dragged us out of bed an hour early?"

"Oh, nothing special," Love replied coyly, reaching for a grease-stained towel covering a box. "Just found these."

She pulled away the towel with a flourish.

Ford's eyes went wide. "Oh my… say it isn't so, ma'am. Tell me that's not a box of donuts you just so happened to find."

"Donuts?" Torres exclaimed, genuine surprise replacing his usual guarded expression. "How? What kind?"

Love smiled, opening the box to reveal the treasures inside. "Let's see… Boston cream, apple fritters, and bear claws. Four of each."

She handed them out, watching as battle-hardened soldiers turned into kids at Christmas. The smell of fresh pastry and glaze filled the Osprey's crew compartment.

"These are from Blaise," Ford said after his first bite, reverence in his voice. "Nobody else on this rock can make a bear claw like this."

Love nodded. "Called in a favor from a few months back. Williams was in on it—when we helped Blaise get some ingredients for the wing commander's birthday party."

The mention of Williams created a moment of silence, but not the painful kind…more like acknowledgment of a shared memory.

"I called this meeting because I feel we've all gotten off on the wrong foot," Love began, settling onto a crate across from them. "Torres, when you showed up that first day, you seemed eager to be here. But looking back on it, I'm not sure any of us were ready."

Ford raised an eyebrow. Green gave her a quizzical look. Torres stared at his Boston cream like it held answers.

"When you arrived, we didn't get a chance to talk much before you jumped into Mr. Efficiency mode—"

"I was wrong, ma'am," Torres interrupted, his cheeks flushing. "You're right. I knew I was being assigned to your crew because you'd lost someone, but what I didn't share with you or the others was the reason why *I* was here… the reason why I was a replacement."

Ford and Green set their donuts down, giving Torres their full attention for perhaps the first time since he'd arrived.

"I transferred to your squadron because I couldn't stay in mine anymore. I couldn't start over with them. I needed a fresh break, a fresh start." Torres's voice wavered. "I lost someone too—I lost my crew."

The cockiness crumbled completely as tears began streaming down his face. "A month before I came here, our bird, Badger Two-Seven… they died. All of them. All except me."

"What happened?" Ford asked gently, barely above a whisper.

"I… I don't even fully know. I wasn't with them—I should have been with them." Torres's voice cracked. "I could have saved them. They could be alive right now if I had been there. If I had done my job…but I wasn't there."

"Don't think that, Torres," Green countered. "It's not your fault. It's war. Things happen. People die."

Torres shook his head violently. "No, not like this. You don't understand." He accepted a tissue from Love with shaking hands. "I was supposed to be with them. I woke up that morning before our flight with a terrible pain in my side. I told my flight lead I needed to stop by sickbay. They said I had appendicitis and that I needed emergency surgery before it burst."

His voice grew distant, lost in the memory. "I barely had time to tell anyone before they knocked me out. The last thing I remember was Lieutenant Yamoto telling me not to worry. He said it was routine surgery, and he'd check on me when they got back."

Torres took several shuddering breaths. "When I woke up, I asked if Yamoto had stopped by. That's when I learned they didn't make it."

The crew compartment felt smaller, more intimate, as Torres continued. "We'd been flying resupply missions around Kepler-442.

There weren't many details—nothing left but debris. Their Osprey was ambushed during a supply run. Everyone was killed."

Fresh tears ran down his face. "I never got to say goodbye. We had breakfast together that morning. Washington was razzing me about my stomachache, telling me I ate too much cheesecake the night before…I didn't even get to let him know what happened to me. They were just gone."

Love saw Ford discreetly wipe away a tear, his tough exterior cracking.

"Thank you, Torres, for sharing this with us," Green said, relief washing over his face. "I think we all got off on the wrong foot because none of us knew the other was suffering like this. Thank you, Lieutenant Love, for having us meet like this. We needed this."

"Yeah, thank you, Lieutenant. I'm sorry about the mess I've made," Torres said. "I wish I could start over. I'd do it all over again and reset."

Ford stood, wiping his hands on his coveralls before extending one to Torres. "We can do that. I'm Chief Brian Ford. Welcome to the *Jack*."

Torres gripped the offered hand like a lifeline.

In that moment, Love knew they were going to make it. They were a team; they just hadn't known it until now.

"OK, people. Time for us to go earn our pay," Love announced, feeling lighter than she had in weeks. "Let's finish off these donuts before anyone else finds out we have them and get over to the briefing room. We've got another recon run today. Let's show everyone we're ready to be a team."

As they gathered their trash and prepared to leave, Love felt something she hadn't experienced in months—genuine optimism. The weight of command felt manageable again.

Yeah, she thought, watching her crew exit together instead of separately, *we're going to make it.*

Year 2098
FTL Travel
RNS *Leahy*

The RNS *Leahy*'s tactical briefing center stretched forty meters across the ship's central deck. Its bulkheads were lined with displays and tactical holos. Captain Saho Nobunaga stood at the raised platform's center, surrounded by officers settling into their seats. Company commanders filled the front rows, while platoon leaders and specialist attachments occupied the remaining space.

Coop sat three rows back with the other TASC specialists: Bear, Sawyer, Ortiz, and others. His palms were damp against his datapad, his heart beating a little faster than he'd ever admit, especially to Bear. It was his first real operation, where there'd be no simulation and no safety net.

Around him sat the 1-504th "Red Devils" leadership. The battalion commander reviewed notes at the front table. Four company commanders flanked him while their executive officers checked their datapads. Behind them, platoon leaders and senior NCOs filled two additional rows.

"Ladies and gentlemen," Nobunaga began, activating the central screen. A holographic rendering of Nightfall Moon materialized above the platform, rotating slowly. "In less than twenty-four hours, we execute Operation Blindside."

Coop's stomach tightened. *Twenty-four hours*. He wiped his palms on his fatigues.

The hologram zoomed in on a cluster of structures nestled between rocky outcroppings near the moon's equator. Antenna arrays stretched toward the sky.

"We've received new intelligence from recent Primord probes in that sector," Nobunaga continued. "The Zodarks have a small squadron of ships orbiting the moon. Nothing we can't handle. Some freighters, two frigates, and a cruiser. Our target is the Zodark communication facility located here."

Red markers appeared on the display, highlighting the installation's key areas.

"Intelligence confirms a significant military presence at the structure's perimeter," Nobunaga continued. "We believe this to be an installation with standard security protocols. There are approximately two hundred personnel who work inside, mostly researchers with limited combat training."

Nobunaga's hand swept through the hologram, marking three orbiting objects blinking in sequence.

"Communications infrastructure is our primary target. Three orbital relay satellites here, here, and here. There's one main transmission array at the facility's northern quadrant, and four secondary arrays distributed throughout the complex."

Coop studied the satellite positions, looking at potential targeting solutions. For a moment, it overrode the butterflies fluttering all too fast in his gut.

"The rest of the brigade will be deployed in supporting operations throughout the AO. Alpha through Delta companies will hit the primary objective, while the remaining elements of the 3rd Brigade will establish defensive perimeters, secure extraction routes, and neutralize outlying Zodark positions to prevent reinforcement."

The display shifted, showing the broader operational area with color-coded sectors assigned to different units.

"Each battlespace element has been assigned specific targets to maintain operational tempo within our twelve-hour window."

Nobunaga detailed the specific operational assignments. First battalion would concentrate on the primary communications complex. The remaining battalions would simultaneously neutralize defensive perimeters and blocking positions surrounding the facility. Forward Operating Base Farside would serve as the logistical hub for sustained operations if needed.

"Alpha Company," Nobunaga's eyes found the battalion commander, "will target the primary transmission array in the northern quadrant of the main facility. Alpha Company's mission involves neutralizing the most critical components of the Zodark communications network."

Coop leaned forward. This was his piece of the puzzle.

A new section of the hologram highlighted a raised rocky outcropping approximately two hundred meters from the main array.

"TASC elements will establish observation posts offering optimal sightlines to both objectives and potential enemy approach vectors. From these positions, you'll coordinate precision strikes against hardened components and enemy forces."

The battalion commander turned slightly, catching Coop's eye for a moment before returning his attention to Nobunaga.

"Standard operating procedure requires TASC specialists to maintain their observation posts throughout the operation, providing continuous fire support coordination while infantry elements secure immediate areas."

Sweat gathered at the base of Coop's neck. He'd trained for this and been through hundreds of simulations. But simulations didn't shoot back with live rounds.

Nobunaga stepped closer to the hologram, his voice dropping a bit.

"The Zodark communication system relies on encrypted channels through their satellite network. Standard jamming would be detected immediately and trigger automated distress protocols."

The display showed the three satellites in their geosynchronous positions, creating a triangulation network maintaining constant coverage.

"Instead, we'll deploy EMP munitions against those three specific orbital satellites simultaneously. This will appear as a random solar flare impact. Ground-based communications arrays will be targeted with precision kinetic strikes three seconds later."

Coop made notes on his datapad. Timing would be critical. The whole operation hinged on perfect coordination between space and ground elements.

"The electromagnetic pulse detonations must occur within a zero-point-three-second window to maintain the solar flare illusion," Nobunaga continued. "Any variance beyond that threshold risks triggering Zodark emergency protocols."

A colonel in the front row raised his hand. "What's our contingency if the EMP strikes fail to neutralize all satellite coverage?"

"Immediate transition to Plan Bravo—direct kinetic strikes against remaining satellites, followed by accelerated ground assault timelines. We lose the element of surprise but maintain mission viability."

Nobunaga turned his attention to the TASC section.

"Fire support coordinators, you'll immediately begin calling missions while assault elements secure target perimeters. Your coordination will be the difference between success and casualties."

The briefing room went quiet, and Coop suddenly felt a heavy-as-hell weight settle on him, more so than anything he'd experienced thus far in his life.

Questions followed for another twenty minutes. They went over ammunition loads, medical evacuation procedures, and communication protocols—the mundane details that kept soldiers alive when plans met reality.

As the formal briefing concluded, officers began filing out in small groups. Coop gathered his notes, checking his chronometer.

Twenty-three hours and twenty-two minutes until insertion.

"Cooper."

He turned. Nobunaga approached, having stepped down from the platform.

"Yes, sir?"

"Walk with me."

They moved toward a quiet corner of the briefing room as the last officers departed. Nobunaga's expression was impassive, but his eyes held something that might have been concern.

"I want to be clear about your role," Nobunaga said. "Your job, your *only* job, is to coordinate all air and fire support for Alpha Company. You're responsible for ensuring our two hundred and sixty soldiers get the precision strikes they need, when they need them."

Coop nodded, his throat tight.

"While physically positioned with Lieutenant Gill's platoon, you're the TASC controller for our entire company. That means you're the critical link between us and every orbital asset, gunship, and artillery piece supporting this operation."

The captain stepped closer, lowering his voice.

"You coordinate all fire support elements. You maintain positive control of all supporting fires. You stay with your platoon, under Lieutenant Gill. You maintain your position, you follow protocols."

"Understood, sir. Stick to my role. Support the mission."

"Exactly." Nobunaga checked his own chronometer. "Get some rest, Cooper. Tomorrow you'll discover what you're really made of."

They were cliché words, but they worked. Coop's breathing steadied. He pulled his shoulders back, stuck his chest out, and held his chin high. He'd prove what he was made of to Nobunaga, to the Red Devils, to the 82nd, to the Navy, to the Republic, to all of humanity…and most of all, to his dad.

The captain walked toward the exit, leaving Coop alone in the briefing room. The holographic display had shut down, and he stared at the empty space where Nightfall Moon had rotated moments before. In less than a day, he'd be standing on that rocky and forested surface, calling in strikes that could save or doom his fellow soldiers.

His hands had stopped sweating. The butterflies remained, but they'd settled into a tight knot of determination.

It was time to prove himself.

Chapter 22:
Into Nightfall's Embrace

Year 2098
Rass Moon PTX-419
Nightfall
RNS *Leahy*

The Republic battle group erupted into normal space and out of FTL behind PTX-379, a gas giant of a planet. It provided them immediate sensor coverage from the target moon, PTX-419, Nightfall. The RNS *Leahy*'s artificial gravity compensated for the transition. Coop's stomach tightened with pre-mission tension. This was it. They were here.

Two *Ryan*-class battleships led the formation. The RNS *Brewster* and RNS *Wilson*. Nearby floated four heavy cruisers including the *Marathon* and *Thermopylae*. Surrounding them were four frigates, four EW frigates, and four corvettes. The division's four orbital assault carriers, including the RNS *Leahy*, formed the core of the transport fleet, carrying troops from the 82nd Orbital Assault Division. Five additional support vessels carried vehicles and heavy equipment.

Near the center of the formation was his RNS *Leahy*, the orbital assault carrier named for Fleet Admiral William Leahy. The man was the first US five-star admiral to serve as Chief of Naval Operations; later, he served as the Chairman of the Joint Chiefs of Staff during World War II. The incredibly large vessel transported Coop's unit along with its complement of dropships, starfighters, and bombers. There were two gunships as well. Completing the battle group were two medical vessels, four supply freighters, and two fuel tankers. They had everything needed for an operation far from Republic space.

The EW frigates spread out to tactical positions. Their specialized arrays were sweeping for Zodark signals while maintaining strict emissions control. Their electronic warfare suites operated passively, cataloging enemy frequencies while remaining undetectable themselves.

Coop stood in the *Leahy*'s ready room with the other members of Alpha Company, Bravo Company, Delta Company, and Charlie

Company, along with the 9th STS and other designated companies in the brigade, performing final equipment checks as the fleet established its approach vector.

Across the fleet, similar preparations were underway as the entire 82nd Division prepared for their coordinated assault of five Zodark facilities simultaneously. Then 1st Brigade would strike the weapons facility, 2nd Brigade would hit the command headquarters, 3rd Brigade would take the communications relay, 4th Brigade would neutralize the logistics hub, and Task Force Scalpel would target the smaller defense monitoring outpost.

Coop reviewed his mission parameters one final time. Alpha Company would target the primary transmission array in the northern quadrant of the main facility. His observation post, which was a raised rocky outcropping approximately two hundred meters from the main array, would provide optimal sightlines to both the objective and potential enemy approach vectors. From there, he'd coordinate all fire support for the company's two hundred sixty soldiers.

"How's that targeting relay looking?" Coop asked, glancing over at Bear, who was hunched over his own equipment case.

Anything to get his mind off his nerves, thought Coop.

Bear snapped the final component into place. "Clean as a virgin's conscience. You worry too much."

"That's not even a saying," Sawyer muttered. She was running diagnostics on her portable sensor array, fingers working across the interface.

"It is now." Bear's massive shoulders shrugged beneath his tactical harness. "You know what they say about the 82nd—we make crap up as we go and somehow still win wars."

Coop allowed himself a thin smile, pushing down the butterflies in his stomach. "Just make sure that relay doesn't glitch when we're calling in ordnance. I'd rather not have kinetic rounds landing on our position because someone forgot to calibrate the azimuth settings."

"One time," Bear protested, pointing a thick finger at Coop. "*One time* in simulation, and you never let it go." He laughed and winked. "Of course. All will go as planned, Coop. All of it. You got my promise."

"I'll hold you to that." Coop sealed his equipment case with a sharp click. "Sawyer, how's our atmospheric compensation looking?"

Sawyer didn't look up from her work. "Already programmed in the compensators. Ran three simulations with the latest atmospheric data. We're good for ninety-eight point seven percent accuracy, which is better than standard parameters."

"That remaining one point three percent keeps me up at night," Coop said.

"That's why you're good at this," Sawyer replied, finally meeting his eyes. "The day you stop worrying about that one point three percent is the day I request a transfer."

The intercom crackled. "All assault teams, prepare for deployment briefing. T-minus twenty-two minutes to approach vector."

Coop nodded, mentally reviewing the operation timeline. The fleet would maintain position behind the planet for exactly twenty-seven minutes, allowing final alignment of all ships. Then they would begin their approach to Nightfall, using the planet's bulk as a shield until the final attack vector.

The EW frigates would deploy in a wedge formation, each vessel's electronic warfare suite generating signal masks. They'd broadcast falsified solar radiation patterns while simultaneously deploying adaptive frequency jammers tuned to Zodark detection systems. Specialized algorithms would analyze any enemy radar sweeps in microseconds, then respond with tailored countermeasures mimicking normal background radiation. Additionally, they'd capture, analyze, and decrypt enemy transmissions, providing real-time intelligence to the strike force. The corvettes would maintain close-range antimissile defense while the capital ships preserved their defensive electronic signatures until the moment strike operations began.

"You know what I miss about Earth drops?" Bear asked, breaking the momentary silence as they gathered their gear.

"What?" said Sawyer.

"The birds," Bear replied. Something about dropping through clouds and seeing birds. Don't know why." He hefted his pack. "I guess spending so much time in all this space stuff... feels too... sterile."

Coop hadn't expected that from Bear. "Never took you for a poet."

"I contain multitudes, Cooper." Bear tapped his chest. "Deep, philosophical multitudes."

"And bullcrap," Sawyer added. "Don't forget the bullcrap."

Bear grinned. "Oh, yes, I speak bullcrap about ninety percent of the time. Thanks for the reminder."

Coop chuckled. Sarcasm ran deep with this small trio of friends. The three of them looked at one another and shared an actual laugh, the kind that only comes before the most serious moments, when laughter is both inappropriate and absolutely necessary.

Coop checked his chronometer. Twenty minutes until they'd begin their approach. Twenty minutes of relative safety before they'd hurtle toward a moon controlled by humanity's most dangerous enemy, with nothing but training, technology, and each other to rely on.

The warning klaxon sounded, pulling everyone into action. The fleet had begun its carefully calculated approach. He grabbed his gear and joined the stream of soldiers moving toward the launch bay.

The Osprey's interior was cramped with equipment and the sixty-three soldiers of the second platoon who'd accompany him to the surface. Coop found his assigned seat next to the tactical console, where he'd monitor the initial strikes during descent.

As they approached Nightfall, the EW frigates would execute a three-phase electronic deception plan. Phase one: passive emissions collection, already underway. Phase two: active sensor spoofing, generating false returns that would obscure the fleet's approach vector while projecting phantom signatures elsewhere in the system. Phase three: targeted jamming against specific Zodark frequencies the moment operations began. Additionally, the gas giant's magnetosphere would mask their approach, its radiation belt providing natural interference that the EW specialists could amplify. The fleet trajectory was calculated to maintain planetary alignment between their approach and the Zodark sensor grid for maximum concealment.

"Six minutes to emergence from planetary shadow," announced the pilot over the intercom. "All personnel secure for potential evasive maneuvers."

Coop strapped himself in. As Tactical Air and Space Control specialist, he'd be the critical link between ground forces and the orbiting strike craft, artillery platforms, and naval gunfire support. Lives depended on his ability to translate battlefield needs into precise coordinates for air support, orbital kinetic strikes, and artillery fire missions.

Captain Nobunaga's words from yesterday's briefing echoed in his mind: "Your job—your only job—is to coordinate all air and fire support for Alpha Company. You're the critical link between us and every orbital asset, gunship, and artillery piece supporting this operation." The captain had been clear about expecting discipline, not heroics.

The Osprey shuddered the moment *Leahy*'s gigantic bay doors opened. Coop gripped his harness tighter, centering himself.

"Emerging from planetary shadow in thirty seconds," announced the officer over the shipwide comms. "All strike packages armed and tracking."

Nobunaga's final reminder anchored Coop as the operation transitioned into its active phase. He wasn't here to save the day single-handedly. He was a specialist with a specific role in a precisely coordinated military operation.

The tactical display in the Osprey showed the fleet's position relative to Nightfall Moon. As they emerged from behind the gas giant, immediate electronic warfare measures activated, flooding all standard communication frequencies with white noise to mask the more precise targeting operations.

"EMP packages away," reported the pilot.

On the tactical screen, specialized missiles streaked toward the three Zodark communication satellites. They detonated simultaneously, unleashing electromagnetic pulses that would appear as natural solar phenomena on Zodark sensors—but would effectively neutralize all off-moon communications.

"Satellite network down," confirmed the pilot. "Proceeding with ground array targeting."

Orion fighters and Raider bombers launched from the *Leahy*'s bays, flying toward the moon's surface. Their targets: the main transmission facility in the equatorial region, the massive relay station in the southern hemisphere, and uplink centers positioned strategically around Nightfall's circumference. Each installation formed a critical node in the Zodarks' interstellar communications network, with dozens of secondary arrays and subterranean data processing centers distributed across the moon's rugged terrain. The primary complex alone housed four major transmission arrays, each one responsible for coordinating different sectors of Zodark space traffic throughout the Rass system.

"First wave deployment in sixty seconds," announced the Osprey pilot. "Prepare for atmospheric insertion."

Across from Coop, Gill checked his assault rifle. "Once we're groundside, we establish the OP and begin immediate targeting of priority objectives. You're attached to my platoon, but your targeting authority supersedes tactical movement. Clear?"

"Yes, sir," Coop replied, checking his targeting equipment for the umpteenth time.

He wondered what Bear and Sawyer were doing now. No doubt in their own Ospreys, preparing for their specialized roles in the operation. He hoped they were focused, ready. The mission needed everyone performing at their best. Most of all, those two needed to stay alive. If not for their benefit, for his sanity.

The Osprey, call sign *Rhino*, flew from the *Leahy*'s launch bay, joined by eleven other identical craft carrying elements of Alpha, Bravo, Charlie and Delta Companies. The Ospreys, along with other troop transports, would return to *Leahy* and pick up additional platoons for drops.

The *Rhino* descended toward the moon's surface. Through the viewports, Coop caught his first glimpse of Nightfall—stark rocky terrain under a dark sky.

In less than ten minutes since fleet emergence, the Republic forces had achieved complete communications blackout and started pounding the small squadron of ships orbiting the moon. Now began the ground phase, with tactical elements moving directly to their objectives to collect information from, and eventually to neutralize, communication complexes throughout the moon before Zodark reinforcements could respond.

"Thirty seconds to touchdown," called the pilot. "Welcome to Nightfall."

The Osprey banked sharply, compensating for atmospheric turbulence as they descended through layers of dark, roiling clouds that seemed to swallow the transport whole. Lightning flickered in the distance, illuminating the storm front in brief, electric bursts. The display showed the first wave of kinetic strikes hitting the ground-based communication arrays far below. Perfect timing. The operation was proceeding exactly as planned.

Through a brief break in the cloud cover, Coop caught a glimpse of something unexpected—metallic shapes glinting in the pale sunlight, moving in formation like a flock of birds. Upon further observation, those were some type of bird species. For a split second, they reminded him of Bear. Then the clouds closed in again, and the shapes disappeared.

The Osprey shuddered when it punched through the lower cloud layer, just as the rain suddenly stopped, the storm moving away.

He thought of his great-great-grandfather's journal, tucked safely in his quarters aboard the *Leahy*. Presley Paul Cooper had flown countless missions during World War II, probably through weather just as nasty as this, facing dangers Coop could barely imagine with technology that seemed primitive by today's standards. Yet the principles remained the same: precision, teamwork, and the courage to execute when it mattered most.

The Osprey's landing gear extended with a mechanical whine as they broke through the bottom of the cloud layer, the surface of Nightfall finally visible below. Coop took his focus away from the tactical display and prepared to disembark. His role would transition now from observer to active participant, coordinating air support from the ground.

"Touchdown in three… two… one…"

Year 2098
FOB Bulwark
Sector 7

Three separate intelligence reports lay spread across the narrow table in Pilot Ready Room C. The RNS *Idaho* had left FOB Bulwark several hours ago, en route to Middle Reach, Sector 8. According to the mission timeline, they'd rendezvous with a joint task force—Republic and Prim vessels operating together—in nineteen hours.

Lieutenant Tim Hastings studied the reports, highlighting another discrepancy between enemy ship classifications, noting the conflicting estimates of Zodark strength in the target sector. It was standard intelligence variance, but worth documenting. Everything was worth documenting.

Several datapads lay before him, each displaying different intelligence reports in holographic detail. His Osprey, *Borrowed Time*, was prepped and ready in the hangar bay, waiting for whatever transport missions the joint task force would require.

The ready room reflected standard Republic Navy economical design. Gunmetal gray bulkheads were lined with secured storage lockers, each labeled with pilot designations. Six workstations featured built-in displays and hardened data ports, their surfaces worn smooth by countless briefings and mission planning sessions. Harsh, bright light glared from overhead panels. The air recycling system maintained a constant low whisper.

Despite its shortcomings, Hastings preferred the ready room's quiet. Here, he could study intelligence reports without interruption, verify mission parameters against historical data, and prepare for every possible outcome. A certain Intus operation—his third op way back when—had taught him that overpreparation was the only defense against brutal intelligence failures.

The room's hatch cycled open. His copilot, Lieutenant Amanda Day, stepped through, carrying a datapad. Her flight suit bore the creases of someone who'd been sitting in cramped cockpit seats, and her dark hair was pulled back in the regulation style that never quite stayed perfect after wearing a flight helmet.

"Afternoon, Hastings," she said, settling at the workstation beside his. "Mind if I review yesterday's mission logs here? The other ready rooms are occupied."

"Go ahead," Hastings replied without looking up from his reports. "Quiet in here."

Out of the corner of his eye, he watched Day activate her display and begin pulling up flight data from their recent supply runs between ships at FOB Bulwark.

"You've been spending a lot of time in here lately," she observed, glancing at his intelligence holos. "That's the third different assessment of the same operational area."

"Intel discrepancies," Hastings said. "Better to know about them now than during the mission."

Day worked quietly for several minutes, occasionally glancing at Hastings' multiple displays. It was usually peaceful in here, and Hastings liked solitude above all else. Quiet was more than bliss to him, if that was possible. In his line of work, calm rarely came, so he took it in as best he could whenever it presented itself. But Day shattered that peace, that brief five minutes of respite he'd managed to carve out from the constant worry always plaguing him.

"You know," Day said eventually, looking up from her flight logs, "I was reviewing the task force composition for tomorrow's rendezvous. Interesting mix of ships."

Hastings glanced up from his reports. "Joint operations usually are."

"Captain Mensah will be taking command from Primord Captain Dharek once we arrive." Day scrolled through her datapad. "Should be interesting to see how she handles coordinating Republic and Prim forces."

"Mensah's thorough. She's coordinated joint task forces between allied races many times." Hastings returned his attention to the intelligence reports, hoping the conversation would die right there.

"I noticed the *Poseidon* is part of the group. Captain Ripley Lee's ship."

Hastings's stylus froze over his datapad. The name hit him hard and heavy, but he kept his expression neutral. It wasn't because he disliked Lee. They'd been close friends in a past life, and it brought up good memories and experiences he wished he could go back to and live through again.

"Lee," he said quietly.

"You know him, I heard."

"Affirmative. We were in the same Academy class."

Day leaned back in her chair, studying his profile with new interest. "Lee's got quite the reputation now—innovative tactics, not afraid to face the enemy head on, took over a ship that'd lost its captain and XO in a battle, and single-handedly kept that crew together while saving that vessel during ship-to-ship combat."

Hastings raised his eyebrows. "You heard all that, huh? Single-handedly saved that ship?" He chuckled. "I bet Lee would love hearing that praise. And the captain that died on his watch was Captain James Oldendorf. One of the—"

"Best captains ever to live," Day finished. "I've heard that countless times."

"And countless times it's true."

Day nodded. "You think Lee's as good as Oldendorf was? I mean, he learned under the man and all."

Hastings set down his stylus. "People change."

"That's a cryptic response."

"Lee was always willing to push the envelope back at the Academy," Hastings replied. "Taking risks that other pilots wouldn't attempt. He was all about confidence in his instincts and split-second decision making. Captain Oldendorf was different. You know…more experienced, more patient with his ship, his tactics, and his crew." He paused, gathering his thoughts. "I've been studying Lee's recent tactics, and they're aggressive. He thinks outside the box, but it's not always the best approach. It worries me. One day, there'll be too many enemies on the other side of that box for him to handle, and thinking differently won't be enough to save his people or his ship."

"I don't necessarily think that thinking outside the box is a bad thing. So far, it's been a success for Lee," Day said.

Hastings gathered one of his datapads, scrolling through intelligence estimates without really reading them. "It's a bad thing when overconfidence leads to mistakes."

"But his record suggests otherwise, doesn't it? From what I've read, Lee's known for being extremely careful with his people. Successful operations, minimal losses, you know?"

"That's now," Hastings said. "Maybe he learned something."

Day set down her datapad, giving Hastings her full attention. "Look, I've been your copilot for almost a year. You don't just study intel reports like this for fun. You've seen the downside of that confidence firsthand, haven't you?"

Hastings was quiet for a long moment, staring at the holographic displays without seeing them. "There was an operation…on Intus. Lee wasn't there, of course, but the mindset was the same. Confidence over caution, instincts over intelligence, trusting gut feelings when the data said otherwise."

"What happened at Intus?" Day asked, her voice gentler now.

Since he'd run this memory a million times through his head, it came out all monotone and automatic. "Sixty-four soldiers deployed. Thirteen came home. Bad intelligence, poor tactical planning, people making split-second decisions based on confidence instead of facts."

Hastings continued, "I put those soldiers on the ground. I followed orders, trusted the intelligence, and when everything went to hell, I got out everyone I could. Not many, but…" He shook his head. "Actually, I don't want to talk about it. I mean, good people didn't come home because someone thought they knew better than the facts. Because people took calculated risks that turned out to be suicide runs, including myself. In my mind, thinking outside of the box comes with terrible consequences."

Day was silent for a moment, clearly processing this. "And you think Lee still operates that way? Outside the box?"

"I don't know how Lee operates these days," Hastings said. "Just stuff I've read, and all I really know is how he used to think. Quick decisions, trust your gut, adapt on the fly—it works until it doesn't."

Day leaned forward. "Hastings, Intus sounds like it was a command-level failure. Bad intelligence from the top down, not pilot error. But you're carrying this like it was your fault."

He nodded. "I was the one who should have questioned the intelligence. I should have seen the signs, should have refused to deploy into an obvious trap."

"What signs?" Day pressed. "If the intelligence was faulty at the source, how could you have known?"

Hastings gathered his three datapads displaying the intel reports into a neat stack. "That's exactly the point. There's always something…some detail that doesn't add up. That's why I cross-reference everything now. That's why I verify every piece of data."

"But what happens when you're in the middle of an operation and the intel turns out to be wrong anyway?" Day asked. "Are you going to freeze up trying to reconcile the reports, or are you going to trust your training and fly?"

"I don't freeze up," Hastings said, standing abruptly. "I assess the situation and respond appropriately."

Day remained seated. "There's a difference between being careful and being paralyzed by fear. I've flown with you. You're a good pilot, but sometimes I watch you second-guess decisions that should be automatic."

Hastings felt heat rise in his cheeks. Day cleared her throat. "I apologize, Lieutenant. Didn't mean to bring up painful memories, or question your methods. I just... I worry about you sometimes."

"It's fine," Hastings replied, though his tone suggested otherwise.

She was right, and that made it worse. It was painful. But Hastings believed it brought him wisdom. Vital wisdom. Better to be cautiously prepared and competent than confident and out of the box.

He gathered his materials and moved toward the hatch. "Tomorrow we'll rendezvous with the task force. Lee can handle his ship however he wants. Captain Mensah can run her operations however she sees fit. But when soldiers climb into my transport, they're getting a pilot who learned from his mistakes."

The hatch cycled open, and Hastings stepped into the corridor. Behind him, he could hear Day settling back into her chair. He didn't like making her feel uncomfortable, but sometimes discomfort got pilots to think, to really consider what's important as an Osprey pilot—keeping soldiers safe.

Walking through *Idaho*'s corridors, Hastings couldn't shake the conversation. Didn't Day understand that every soldier who climbed into a transport was someone's son or daughter, someone with a family waiting for them to come home? He owed them more than reckless confidence and split-second gambles.

Hastings reached his quarters and sealed the hatch behind him. On his small desk sat a framed photo from the Academy. Four young pilots celebrating their graduation. Himself, Jack Hannigan, Naomi Love, and Ripley Willis Lee.

They were four friends who'd thought they'd conquer the galaxy together. Now Jack was dead, killed in action years ago. Naomi was stationed somewhere. And Ripley… well, he had become everything Hastings used to admire and now feared.

His terminal displayed the task force roster. He saw multiple Republic vessels, several Primord ships, and then, there it was: RNS *Poseidon*, Captain R. W. Lee, Commanding. Hastings stared at the entry for a long moment.

He picked up the Academy photo, running his thumb over the glass. Four young faces, full of confidence and dreams of glory. Somehow, Hastings had become everything they used to mock—the overcautious pilot, the one who never took risks.

But caution kept people breathing, and overconfidence buried them. And he swore to himself, for the sake of those he transported, that he'd go to the grave with that mindset, hoping that grave would be long, long into the future, when he was an old man with memories of saving thousands of troops he'd carried to and from battle.

Chapter 24:
Wake of Salvation

Year 2098
RNS *Poseidon*
Middle Reach
Sector 8

Poseidon's main viewscreen showed a breathtaking yet dangerous vista. Crystalline ice formations spread across space, glittering like scattered diamonds. The asteroid ice belt extended beyond visual range. Frozen giants and razor-sharp fragments rotated slowly in the weak gravity of a distant star. Some chunks were the size of small moons, while others were no larger than shuttlecraft. And all of them were deadly at the right speed.

Lee sat on the bridge, studying the sensor readouts. *Polaris*, now practically born anew, operated at nearly full capacity. The Primord engineers had repaired the battle damage at a surprising pace. *Their advanced techniques accomplished in hours what would have taken Republic yards days*, Lee mused. At least that was one positive outcome of this collaboration, albeit one that seemed more forced the longer he dealt with the Prims.

Yes, at first, they had worked well together. Now, every decision, every word, seemed challenged; Dharek's scrutiny was on full display at every turn. Lately, though, the Primord captain seemed to lower his guard a bit, acting as he had when they'd first worked together—like a team player, attentive and relaxed.

"Maintain heading and reduce speed to one-quarter," Lee ordered. "Keep distance between Republic vessels at minimum one thousand meters."

"Aye, Captain," Reynolds responded.

The RNS *Idaho* had arrived hours ahead of schedule. The *Ryan*-class battleship dwarfed Lee's *Poseidon*, and Captain Mensah had wasted no time initiating the formal command transfer protocols.

The handover had proceeded well. Captain Dharek's battle group altered formation to accommodate the newcomers. Dharek executed each step without a misstep. His professionalism was impeccable despite the circumstances.

Behind the *Idaho* came the cruiser RNS *Argo* under Captain Liza Horn. Her ship slid into position easily. Lee had known Horn since the New Eden campaigns. They'd shared countless meals in officer lounges during R&R, dissecting battles and swapping stories over whatever passed for coffee in whichever building they found themselves. Other cruisers, RNS *Thunder* and RNS *Oceanus*, had followed, assuming their designated positions in the expanded formation.

Shortly thereafter, Captain Mensah reorganized the fleet. The Primord battleships now formed the vanguard, their heavy armor and firepower positioned to absorb initial contact. The Republic cruisers formed a supporting echelon, while the smaller vessels were arranged in defensive clusters. Four Republic EW frigates took point position, operating far ahead of the main formation.

Their emissions, thermal trails, and IFF signals, all artificially generated by the four EW frigates leading them in, were spoofing any potential Zodark sensors into believing they weren't there. The specialized vessels projected false electromagnetic echoes that scattered sensor returns, while their baffle systems absorbed and redirected thermal emissions. Advanced arrays generated white noise across multiple frequency bands. They created digital phantoms masking the task force's true position. Meanwhile, sophisticated scramblers altered the subspace signatures of their drive systems. This rendered the small armada virtually invisible to conventional detection methods unless sensors were literally pointed right at them.

Lee was pulled from his thoughts by his electronic warfare officer, Lieutenant Jacob Witkowski. "Captain, I'm detecting unusual interference patterns across our sensor grid. It could be natural radiation from the asteroid field, but the frequencies are oddly consistent."

"Keep monitoring it, Witkowski. Let me know if it develops into anything concerning," Lee replied. "Rodriguez, transmit that data to the *Idaho*."

"Aye, sir."

A sudden shout from the sensor officer, Lieutenant Baldry, filled the bridge. "Contact! Bearing one-four-four, range three hundred meters!"

Collision alerts blared. A huge ice meteor emerged from sensor shadows, its edges shining in the starlight as it rotated directly into their path.

"Evasive maneuvers," Lee ordered. "Full reverse thrusters."

The *Poseidon* shuddered as its engines strained against momentum. The ice formation loomed larger on the viewscreen, its surface reflecting the ship's running lights in a myriad of colors.

"Impact in fifteen seconds," Reynolds said, punching commands on his interface.

"We can't clear it in time," Sato reported, her holographic display hovering above her chair's armrest, her eyes scrutinizing the data.

A Primord vessel, *Kulente*, streaked across their bow, executing a spiral maneuver between the approaching ice shards. The ship slowly spun on its axis, its thrusters firing in an orchestrated sequence.

"What are they doing?" Rhom asked.

The *Kulente*'s wake created a localized disturbance in the surrounding space. The ship's engines were generating a controlled gravitational pulse rippling outward, creating a corridor of clear space.

"They're using their gravitational wake to pull us clear," Sato said. "Ingenious."

And no need to blast that massive ice boulder, which would have created a whole mess of problems, Lee thought.

The *Poseidon* shook again as it was also caught in the *Kulente*'s gravitational wake. Sliding sideways relative to its original course, the ice formation passed by the *Poseidon* with mere meters to spare. On the viewscreen, the *Kulente* completed its spiral, engines flaring as it stabilized on a new heading.

"EWO, what's the status on our jamming capabilities if we need them?" Lee asked, turning to Witkowski.

"All systems primed, sir," Witkowski responded, eyes squarely on his console. "I've adjusted our countermeasures to account for the ice field's electromagnetic interference. We can deploy full-spectrum jamming within three seconds if needed. Along with the EW frigates, we'll be nothing but space dust to the Zodark sensors."

Lee patched into Engineering. "Mac, damage report."

"Minor hull stress on deck four, section three alpha and deck seven, section two alpha," reported MacGregor. "Nothing critical.

We're clear, sir." There was a pause. "Cap, that maneuver the *Kulente* pulled? Absolutely beautiful. Their gravitational dampening system must be generations ahead of ours. Executing a roll like that with ships our size—it's practically rewriting the engineering textbooks. I'd give my left arm just to see how their thrust vectoring interface handles that kind of stress load."

"I'll see what I can get for you, Mac," said Lee.

He exhaled slowly. "Rodriguez, send our thanks to *Kulente*."

"Aye, Captain."

The Primord ship escaped gracefully. Like MacGregor had mentioned, the *Kulente* had executed an unbelievable spiral maneuver through the ice field, all to use its gravitational wake to pull the *Poseidon* clear of danger. The move had been quick, the decision made right away, and performed without issue, beautifully, even—and completely outside Republic naval doctrine.

"Damage control teams, stand down," Lee ordered. "Resume standard search pattern."

"Aye, sir," Reynolds said.

In a way, Dharek was right. They needed to study and learn, and heck, adopt the Primords' superior navigation protocols through fields of moon-sized ice rocks. Lee knew they should, but couldn't bring himself to admit it out loud.

But why? he wondered. Simple. Pride. Stubbornness. A refusal to concede that perhaps Dharek had a point. Still, it wasn't up to him, especially now that Mensah was in charge, and Dharek second to her.

"Captain," Sato said. "That's the third near-collision in six hours. Perhaps we should consider—"

"I'm aware of the situation, XO," Lee cut her off. "Reynolds, plot us a wider berth around the larger formations."

"Aye, sir."

Damn impressive, Lee said to himself. *These Primords, including Dharek, are experts in asteroid field navigation, no doubt about it.*

Their ships moved like water through the ice, while Republic vessels plowed forward like battering rams, relying on brute force and thick armor rather than finesse.

"Sir," Baldry called from sensors, "long-range sensors are picking up unusual readings at bearing one-eight-one mark four-three. Information is coming from our frigates."

"Define unusual, Ensign."

"Multiple contacts, sir. Faint power signatures embedded within a particularly dense cluster of asteroids approximately thirteen thousand kilometers ahead. Captain Mensah's received the data as well."

That could be the base we're looking for.

Lee moved to the tactical station, studying the readouts over Rhom's shoulder.

"Could be natural radiation from mineral deposits," Rhom said. "But the pattern is… structured. Consistent with artificial power sources operating in low-emission mode."

"Zodark technology?" Lee asked.

"Consistent with their signature, yes, sir. The readings match what we've seen from their stealth outposts in Sectors 2 and 3."

Lee straightened and headed back to his seat. "This could be what we're looking for."

Before he could issue orders, the communication system activated with the distinctive priority tone reserved for fleet command. Captain Mensah's voice filled the bridge.

"All ships, all ships, this is Captain Mensah aboard the RNS *Idaho*. All captains, report to your ready rooms for classified briefing. Senior staff authorization only."

"XO, you have the conn," Lee said, standing. "Maintain current position and continue monitoring those energy signatures. No independent action until further notice."

"Aye, Captain," Sato replied, moving to the command chair. "Lieutenant Rhom, keep me updated on those readings."

Lee walked the short distance to his ready room. The door slid shut behind him. The room's holographic conference system activated automatically as he sat at the table. One by one, the other fleet captains materialized as secure connections were established.

Captain Mensah appeared first. Then Captain Bayes of the *Polaris* shimmered into view, followed by the imposing figure of Primord Captain Dharek. Captain Horn of the *Argo* was next, completing the guest list.

"Ladies, gentlemen," Mensah began. "I'll be brief. Our EW frigates have completed their analysis of the energy signatures you've all been tracking. The situation is not what it initially appeared to be."

She gestured, and a tactical display appeared above the table's center. "What we're detecting are not Zodark vessels at all. These are small devices, perfectly distributed throughout the asteroid field, embedded in the asteroid cores themselves. They're generating artificial energy signatures designed to mimic Zodark vessel emissions."

Captain Bayes leaned forward, leaning on his elbows. "Decoys?"

"Sophisticated ones," Mensah confirmed. "The power signatures are being artificially modulated to match what we'd expect from Zodark ships operating in low-emission mode. The readings are erratic: appearing, disappearing, then reappearing in different locations. These devices are designed to create the illusion of a mobile fleet."

Captain Horn frowned. "Have we found the purpose, exactly?"

"That's what we need to determine," Mensah replied. "Someone went to considerable trouble to make us believe there's a Zodark presence right around every corner in this sector. The question is whether we're being distracted from something else, or if this is preparation for an actual ambush."

Dharek's expression darkened. "Long-range sensors detected enormous gravitational distortions forming at our entry point to this sector."

"Confirmed," Mensah said. "The decoy operation appears to be part of a larger strategy. While we've been focused on these phantom signatures, real Zodark forces may have been positioning themselves to cut off escape routes. That's a theory. It means, keep your eyes open."

Lee felt the pieces clicking together. "So, the energy signatures are a potential fake base. All of it was designed to hold our attention while they moved into position."

"Potential is a strong word. It's not potential, because we're also finding *that* base signature very real, but we're *thinking* the Zodarks are moving into actual positions to coordinate an ambushed attack," Mensah said. "They're spoofing, while we're spoofing, so we don't know if that's being spoofed as well, because from our own EW frigates, we know no Zodark has detected us. So, we're not facing an immediate combat situation, but we are looking at a potential trap here. Captain Dharek, your navigation expertise through asteroid fields will be crucial for our potentially quick extraction from this sector if needed. I commend you and *Kulente* for the help you gifted the *Poseidon*. You saved their asses. And we'll be implementing the tactic into fleet maneuvers. Impressive. Nonetheless, what we're facing if these escape vectors are indeed watched and marked by Zodarks is a tactical engagement with severe disadvantage unless we act decisively. Continue silent running protocols. We'll proceed with extreme caution and maintain readiness for immediate combat operations. This mission is too critical to jeopardize through hasty action or delayed response."

"My ships can lead," Dharek acknowledged. "The ice formations are treacherous even under normal circumstances, but we are masters at this."

"Granted. You'll take point with your battle group," Mensah replied. "I'm positioning the EW frigates directly behind your squadron—close enough to maintain our electronic deception envelope, while benefiting from your navigational wake. Those frigates are our eyes and our cloak." Her gaze swept across the assembled officers. "Captain Lee, maintain tactical readiness. While these signatures are decoys, there could be real threats guarding the perimeter, and we need to be aware if they converge on us. Captain Bayes, coordinate with our EW frigates for continued monitoring. Captain Horn, prepare for rapid movement when we identify our exit strategy."

The holographic projections faded as the conference ended. Lee returned to the bridge, where Sato immediately vacated the command chair.

"Status report, XO?"

"Those energy signatures are still fluctuating," Sato replied. "And, Captain, long-range sensors confirm significant gravitational anomalies at our jump points."

"Send data to Captain Mensah immediately," Lee said. "We may need to prepare to extract from this sector right away, and under hostile conditions."

Lee stared at the tactical display. Pride was a luxury the dead couldn't afford, and he'd been holding on to his for too long where Dharek was concerned. The Primords' navigational prowess through this asteroid field was generations ahead, and that maneuver the

Kulente had pulled to save *Poseidon* proved it beyond any flimsy argument he might conjure. Mensah had seen it immediately, acknowledged it openly, and incorporated it—exactly what a fleet commander should do. No ego. No hesitation. Just the calm assessment of available assets against present threats. If they suddenly needed to extract from this ice-laden killing ground with their ships intact, it would take every advantage they could muster: Republic and Primord alike. The Zodarks had outsmarted them once by predicting their behavior. Lee wouldn't give them the satisfaction of doing it twice.

Chapter 25:
Truth Behind the Feed

Year 2098
RNS *Poseidon*
Middle Reach
Sector 8

The Zodarks might be keeping tabs and encroaching on our exit points in this sector, Lee thought. *If so, where are they? Where's this big fleet of Zodark scum?*

"Captain, I'm detecting something on our long-range sensors," Rhom reported, eyes fixed on his tactical display. "Multiple Zodark reinforcement fleets, supply convoys, and staging areas throughout the sector."

Lee leaned forward in his command chair. It had to be yet another spoof, but he couldn't ignore everything. "Show me the tactical overview."

"Sir, sensors are indicating three separate Zodark battle groups converging on our position from different vectors. Additionally, I'm reading significant supply convoy movements and what appears to be a major staging operation at coordinates two-seven-eight mark five."

"Time to intercept?" Lee asked, studying the main tactical projection.

"The lead battle group will be in weapons range in forty-three minutes, sir. But, Captain…" Rhom paused, frowning at his readings. "Something's odd about these patterns."

"Explain."

"Zodark fleet movements typically show tactical variance based on local conditions, but these formations are maintaining textbook deployment patterns. Perfect spacing, ideal approach vectors, optimal supply chain logistics."

Sato chimed in from her chair. "Captain, I'm seeing the same anomaly. These movements match Zodark doctrine in our database exactly, but they're too perfect. No commander executes operations this precisely."

"This is a spoof," Lee said.

"It's possible," Rhom conceded. "But, sir, the intelligence feeds are also showing Republic and Primord fleet movements that don't match our actual positions. According to these readings, we have reinforcement fleets that don't exist and supply lines that were never established."

Lee's brow furrowed. "That's impossible. These feeds should be based on actual sensor data."

"Confirmed, sir. The intelligence is showing us with twice our actual fleet strength, and indicating Primord forces in sectors where no Primord ships are deployed." Rhom's attention locked on his sensor display as data streams reconfigured. "Wait. Analyzing the data patterns… the intelligence feeds are executing predetermined scenarios rather than responding to actual fleet movements. They're operating on simulation protocols."

"Simulation?" Lee stood, moving to the tactical station.

"Yes, sir. It appears to be running war game scenarios rather than tracking real fleet movements."

Sato studied her own display. "Captain, I'm detecting similar false intelligence appearing across all tactical frequencies. The system is broadcasting fake data on all military bands."

"So, we're seeing phantom fleets, nonexistent supply lines, and fabricated staging areas?" Lee asked.

"Appears so, sir," Rhom confirmed. "The Zodarks must have found a way to crack the Primord or Republic communication signals and intercept message traffic."

A burst of static erupted from the communications console, followed by Lieutenant Rodriguez's voice. "Sir, I think we're being jammed. We've lost contact with the *Polaris*, *Scimitar*, and *Bolt*. Ah crap, we've lost contact with everyone. All Republic and Primord ships, comms offline."

Before Lee could respond, Rodriguez called out, "Captain, I'm receiving sensor data that indicate subtantial Zodark reinforcements have arrived in-sector. Three full battle groups plus supply elements."

"What the hell?" Lee pushed himself up from his chair. "Rhom, confirm those readings."

Maybe it's not a spoof? Maybe they wanted us to think it's a spoof, and it never was.

"Captain, sensors show overwhelming Zodark superiority in this sector," Rhom said. "Intelligence feeds indicate we're outnumbered five to one, with additional reinforcements still arriving."

Rodriguez tapped on her interface, punching in commands. "Communications systems compromised. Working to isolate the interference."

"Get me those comms back, Lieutenant," Lee ordered. The holographic projection showed a tactical nightmare—massive Zodark fleets surrounding their position, with Republic and Primord forces scattered and outnumbered.

"Sir," Rhom said, "Fleet Command is recommending immediate withdrawal. The tactical situation appears hopeless."

Rodriguez looked up from her station. "Captain, I've got comms back online. I'm receiving emergency transmissions from the *Bolt* and *Horizon*. They're reporting the same strategic intelligence. Considerable Zodark superiority and recommendations to withdraw."

Lee's mind raced as he processed the implications. If the strategic intelligence was accurate, they were walking into a massacre. But something felt wrong about the perfect positioning and overwhelming numbers. "Reynolds, bring us to coordinates eight-three mark two."

"Aye, Captain," Reynolds acknowledged, inputting the new course at his station.

Lee asked, "Are we getting anything from Mensah?"

"Nothing yet, sir," Rodriguez replied.

"Rodriguez, emergency channel to Captain Dharek. I need to know if he's receiving the same intel."

"Channel open, sir."

"Captain Dharek, what's your tactical situation? Are you getting the same sensor readings indicating massive Zodark reinforcements?"

The viewscreen came to life, showing Dharek's face, his expression grim. "Captain Lee, our sensors indicate catastrophic enemy superiority in this sector. My tactical officers are recommending immediate withdrawal."

"Understood. We're seeing the same intelligence feeds," Lee said. "But something doesn't feel right about these readings."

"The situation appears clear," Dharek replied. "We're facing overwhelming odds with no possibility of success. We have been tricked."

"If the intelligence is accurate, yes. But I'm questioning the authenticity of these feeds," Lee said.

Dharek's eyes narrowed. "Spoof deception."

Two words that pretty much meant the same thing.

"I'm beginning to think so. The strategic patterns are too perfect, too overwhelming."

The viewscreen suddenly split, with Captain Mensah's image appearing alongside Dharek's.

"*Idaho* to all vessels. Priority override." Mensah's voice was firm. "Disregard all sensor feeds immediately. I say again, disregard all current sensor data."

Lee and Dharek both turned their attention to her.

"Captain Mensah, the sensors indicate—" Lee began.

"I'm aware, Captain," she interrupted. "We've completed analysis on that data. They've broadcast spoofed signals, designed to manipulate our decision-making. Lieutenant Commander Konkly confirms these are sophisticated false readings on all standard military frequencies."

"This is fake?" Dharek asked.

"Affirmative," Mensah responded. "The system is generating fabricated signals designed to trigger specific responses, like primarily withdrawal or tactical errors. The readings remain consistent regardless of our actual movements or tactical changes, confirming they're preprogrammed rather than based on real strategic conditions."

"So, the excessive Zodark reinforcements—" Lee said.

"Another deception," Mensah finished.

"Baldry, recalibrate our sensors," Lee said. "Filter out any intelligence that shows perfect tactical scenarios. Let's see what the real strategic situation is. Sato, cross-reference with our actual sensor data."

"I appreciate that coordination, Lee," Mensah said.

Silence filled the bridge as Baldry displayed comparative data showing the fabricated readings versus their actual sensor data. The overwhelming Zodark superiority disappeared, replaced by a much more manageable tactical situation.

"These readings are completely artificial," Lee said, pointing to the false data. "No strategic situation develops this perfectly or this catastrophically."

Dharek and Mensah studied the data comparison. "The deception was designed to force us into tactical errors," Dharek observed. "Either premature withdrawal or desperate attacks."

Lee nodded. "Exactly. Make us think we're either facing impossible odds or that we have overwhelming superiority. And then provoking us to quickly leave the area."

"Captain," Sato said, gesturing to a specific asteroid in the ice field, "I'm detecting unusual energy emissions from that formation at coordinates three-five-one mark two-two. The false spoofed signals are emanating from there, somewhere in that asteroid."

Mensah looked up. "Send me that data as well."

"This explains why our readings showed such overwhelming enemy superiority," Dharek said. "They wanted us to withdraw without engaging."

Lee nodded. "My thoughts exactly."

"Lee," Mensah said, "take the *Poseidon* and neutralize that ice asteroid housing the spoofing signals. We can't allow it to continue broadcasting false data."

"Aye, Captain."

Mensah continued, "And, Captain Dharek, you will maintain position and provide overwatch."

"Yes, Captain," Dharek replied.

The transmission ended, and Lee faced his bridge crew. "Reynolds, set course for that asteroid. Coordinates three-five-one mark two-two. Full thrust."

"Aye, Captain. Course laid in."

"Rhom, prepare a full tactical scan of the asteroid. I want to know exactly what we're dealing with."

"On it, sir."

The *Poseidon* moved through the ice field. Reynolds hunched forward at the helm, sweat beading along his hairline despite the bridge's cool temperature. The Type-002 Altairian-Human hybrid cruiser, a thousand-ton beast tamed by experience and instinct, responded well to his touch.

Through the forward viewports, ice formations drifted past, some close enough that Lee could make out the crystalline patterns etched across their ancient surfaces. Starlight fractured through the translucent monuments, sending out prismatic shadows across the bridge. A particularly large formation rotated slowly to starboard, its edges glinting.

"Adjusting heading three degrees port," Reynolds muttered, more to himself than anyone else. The deck whirred beneath them as maneuvering thrusters fired in controlled bursts, nudging the *Poseidon* between two ice giants with barely fifty meters of clearance on either side.

Sato released a breath as they cleared the passage. The target coordinates grew closer on the navigation display.

"Tactical scan complete," Rhom reported. "Confirming presence of a Zodark emission array embedded in the asteroid's core. Structure appears to be automated, no life signs detected."

"Weapons status?" Lee asked. "Trident-V variable-yield nuclear warhead loaded?"

"Missile tube four prepped and ready. Nuclear warhead armed and locked on target."

"Target the array's power core," Lee ordered. "I want that thing obliterated."

"Target locked," Rhom confirmed. "Firing solution calculated."

"Reynolds, bring us to firing position, then execute Williamson turn to clear the blast radius."

"Aye, sir. Approaching optimal firing position in thirty seconds."

The bridge crew worked as one, each officer focused on their tasks. Minutes earlier, Lee could taste the anxiety in the recycled air; now it had formed into something solid. Shoulders squared, voices steady, the shift from feeling betrayed to being determined to win.

"In position, Captain," Reynolds reported.

Poseidon's weapons locked on to the asteroid.

"Fire missile," Lee said.

"Missile away," Rhom announced as the ship shuddered slightly with the launch. "Impact in twenty seconds."

On the tactical display, a brilliant point of light streaked toward the asteroid.

"Executing evasive maneuvers," Reynolds called out, banking the massive cruiser away from the target.

"Fifteen seconds to impact." Rhom counted down. "Ten seconds... five... four... three... two... one..."

The viewscreen dimmed as a blinding flash erupted where the asteroid had been. The *Poseidon* rocked just a little as the shock wave passed through the ice field, sending fragments scattering in all directions.

Through the fading brilliance, the enormous rock split apart like a cosmic egg hatching and letting loose a furious hell. Fissures of molten orange cracked across its surface before the entire structure heaved outward, disintegrating into thousands of chunks. The larger pieces tumbled away from the epicenter.

Reynolds's evasive maneuvers placed them at the perfect distance—close enough to witness the devastation, but beyond the shotputs of debris.

"Direct hit." Rhom examined his readouts. "Ghosting array completely destroyed."

It was now time to set course to find and destroy that outpost, and like everything Lee had experienced during this war, it would require sacrifice and skill in equal measure. Fortunately, the *Poseidon* and the Republic fleet had both in abundance. And, Lee had to admit, so did the Primords.

Chapter 26:
When Technologies Dance

Year 2098
RNS *Poseidon*
Middle Reach
Sector 8

Four hours after the destruction of the ice asteroid, Lee glared out the bridge's main viewport, watching the fleet move deeper into the ice field. The Republic ships had adopted what Mensah called the Diamondback formation—a staggered, multilayered defensive pattern with the *Ek* at point, flanked by the *Vora* and the *Sulvaar*. The rest of the fleet stretched behind in a diamond shape, the EW frigates toward the front, each vessel positioned to provide overlapping fields of fire while maintaining maximum sensor coverage.

Mensah ordered this formation specifically for ice field navigation after speaking with Dharek and his staff. The Diamondback allowed quick pivots if ambushed. While the staggered positioning prevented any single impact from cascading through multiple ships, it was a formation developed during Lee's time as tactical officer on the *Kentucky*.

The formation also kept some of the Primord vessels and larger Republic ships at the diamond's outer edges.

"Captain." Sato's voice came through his comm. "The war room is prepared for the strategy briefing."

"On my way," Lee said. He stood from the command chair and turned to his EWO, Lieutenant Witkowski. "Lieutenant, you have the conn. Maintain current position and alert me to any changes in the sensor readings."

"Aye, sir. I have the conn," Witkowski acknowledged, moving to the captain's chair.

Lee nodded to the bridge crew before stepping into the corridor. "You have the bridge, Lieutenant Witkowski."

Striding through the passageway, Lee nodded to crew members who snapped to attention as he passed. In a way, destroying the ghosting array had lifted a weight from the crew's collective shoulders, but Lee knew the real challenge still lay ahead.

The war room doors slid open, revealing a circular chamber dominated by a massive holotable that occupied the center. Tiered seating surrounding it like a small amphitheater, although there'd only be four people in here today, including Lee. All around, the walls were lined with tactical displays.

The holoscreens blinked to life with Primord faces, particularly Captain Dharek's. Another screen flickered, revealing Captain Mensah from the RNS *Idaho*, along with all other captains in the task force. Lee's staff was there as well. Sato stood beside the holotable, and Rhom reviewed data on his pad.

Mensah kept her eyes forward. "Let's get started."

The holotable illuminated, displaying a map of the ice field sector.

"Hours ago, we neutralized a Zodark ghosting array designed to create false sensor readings," Mensah said. "This confirms our suspicion that the Zodarks have established a significant presence in this sector."

Mensah continued. "Our mission remains unchanged: locate and neutralize the Zodark outpost that's coordinating specific operations, negating alliance offensive and defensive capabilities across many sectors.

"The ghosting array was merely a defensive measure," Mensah said. "Based on the energy requirements to power that array, we're looking at a substantial installation—the forward operating base—and we're thinking it's nearby."

Mensah nodded to her tactical action officer, Lieutenant Paul Simons, who activated a simulation on the holotable.

"Strategy one, ladies and gentlemen. Conventional energy signature triangulation with drones deployed in a grid pattern," TAO Simons said. Tiny points of light spread across the holographic ice field. "We'll deploy dozens of drones equipped with enhanced sensor packages. They'll create a detection net spanning approximately forty thousand cubic kilometers."

Lee nodded at the all-too-human approach. "We can program the drones to focus on specific energy signatures associated with Zodark propulsion and life support systems."

"If I may add, sir," Simons continued, "we can modify the drones to emit false signatures of their own. Make them appear as ice fragments to Zodark sensors."

"Affirmative, Lieutenant," Mensah said. "We'll also want to program in randomized search patterns to avoid creating an obvious grid the enemy might detect."

When Dharek's jaw clicked with subtle disagreement, Lee did his best to ignore it, to push it down to fume over later. The Primord captain leaned forward, his pupils reflecting the holographic display.

"This approach assumes the Zodarks have not masked their energy signatures after detecting us in the sector during our engagement with their battleships," Dharek said. "Yes, we are on spoof signatures now, and they do not know where we are. But, after seeing their ghosting technology, I would not underestimate their ability to hide. Especially since they know we are here."

Lee's fingers tapped once on the table before he stilled them. "That's why we're exploring multiple strategies."

Simons cleared his throat. "If I may present strategy two, Captains."

Mensah gestured for him to proceed, and the holotable shifted to display a different simulation.

"Thermal mapping enhanced with Primord crystallography techniques," Simons said. The hologram showed heat signatures flowing through the ice field like rivers of fire. "Even with perfect energy masking, the Zodarks can't hide their thermal footprint completely. Not in an environment this cold."

To Lee, the strategy made sense, but it relied heavily on Primord technology—technology he didn't fully understand or trust. And the Republic didn't have full control over it.

"The Primord fleet carries specialized thermal imaging arrays that can detect temperature variations as small as one one-hundredth of a degree," Simons said. "If we combine them with their crystallography techniques, we can identify artificial structures by the way they affect ice formation patterns around them."

When she referenced these Primord technological advantages, Lee shifted uncomfortably in his chair before he consciously stilled himself.

Captain Mensah cleared her throat. "Lieutenant Simons, what is the accuracy rate of the Primord crystallography techniques?"

Simons opened his mouth to respond, but Dharek spoke first. "Your teams have found efficacy to ninety-eight point seven percent accuracy in controlled tests." His tone was definitely defensive.

Mensah's face steeled. "I'm not questioning the technology, Captain Dharek. I'm questioning its applicability in this specific environment against an enemy known for adaptability."

"How reliable is this crystallography technique in field conditions?" Captain Bayes of the *Polaris* asked.

"Extremely reliable, sir," Simons replied. "The Primords have used it to locate their own outposts lost in ice fields similar to this one. Captain Dharek has provided extensive data on previous successful operations."

On one of the screens, Captain Liza Horn bent forward in her seat, elbows on the table. "We could combine both approaches. Use our drones for the wide-area sweep and let the Primords do their crystallographic analysis for the detail work on anything that looks promising." She gestured at the holo hovering above the table. "I mean, why not? Gets us the best of both worlds without wastin' time. Set it up in parallel, boom—done." She straightened slightly. "Technically straightforward to implement, minimal delay to operations."

"A hybrid approach does maximize our chances of success while minimizing resource expenditure." Mensah faced Dharek. "Captain Dharek, how quickly can your vessels deploy these crystallography sensors?"

"We can begin immediately," Dharek replied. "And—"

Mensah raised her index finger at the Primord, cutting the man off. Dharek couldn't hide his dismay as his lower lip curled.

"My apologies, Captain." Mensah pressed a button. The ice field rotated slowly in the projection coming off the table, highlighted sections pulsing with data markers. "There's another approach we haven't considered. Gravitational analysis to detect mass inconsistencies."

The hologram shifted to display gravitational wave patterns flowing through the ice field like invisible currents.

"Ice has a specific density," Mensah continued. "Any artificial structure—especially one housing Zodark troops and equipment—will create gravitational anomalies we can detect with properly calibrated sensors." Mensah manipulated the display, highlighting several regions. "By deploying gravitational wave detectors at these coordinates, we can create a map of mass distribution throughout the sector."

She tapped a command into the console, and the simulation began running and showing waves propagating through the ice field and reflecting off hidden structures.

"The beauty of this approach is its passive nature. The Zodarks can mask energy signatures and thermal emissions, but they can't hide their mass. Physics doesn't allow it."

Bayes raised a hand, busy typing on a datapad with his other. "Captain, if I may?"

Mensah nodded at Bayes. "Go ahead. What's your take?"

"Ma'am, I've run the numbers on the gravitational analysis approach." Bayes punched a few commands on his pad, sending his data to the main holo. "It's solid—rock solid—but if we integrate the Primord crystalline sensors, we boost our detection rates by forty-nine percent, maybe more." He motioned at the projection. "Their tech picks up the subtle distortions we might miss. Complementary systems, Captain. Two eyes are better than one, especially when you're lookin' for something this hard to spot."

The simulation clearly showed the combined approach outperforming Mensah's pure Republic method. She studied the data, processing the undeniable technical superiority.

"The Primord sensors can detect subtle variations in crystal formation that our gravitational sensors might miss," Bayes said. "Especially in regions where natural gravitational anomalies might throw us off. Those ice fields get tricky. Lotta background noise to sort through. Their tech cuts right through that garbage, Captain. No offense to our systems, but it's like having a specialized set of eyes exactly for this kinda hunt."

"I see." Mensah looked around. "That's… a significant improvement."

Captain Dharek rose from his seat, walking closer to the cam projecting him on a holo in the war room, his face now dominating one of the screens. "If I may present another strategy, Captains?"

Mensah motioned for him to proceed.

"Many of the Zodark ships have a subtle inefficiency when using their propulsion engines," Dharek explained. "While it does not help us to track the ships during faster-than-light travel, when they are advancing at slower speeds, a small amount of chemical waste is released into space."

Lee leaned forward. "Why are we just now hearing about this?" he asked.

Dharek sighed. "Well, the Zodarks have been in the process of changing over their propulsion engines to newer models that are more efficient and do not have this problem, so in the future, this will be irrelevant information. However, for now, many of their older ships still have these drives. These pollution markers persist for years, even in extreme cold," he continued. "Primord ships can detect these molecular signatures at concentrations as low as three parts per billion, and we have adapted methods to trace how long ago the substances were left behind. I am sending specs over to you now, Captain Mensah."

Bayes seemed very excited. "I believe if we integrate all four approaches—our drone grid, thermal mapping, gravitational analysis, and Primord pollution detection—we'll create a multilayered detection net the Zodarks can't possibly evade."

Lee had to give credit where it was due. "Captain Dharek, your people developed quite the advantage. If your sensors can be calibrated to our systems, we might actually find this outpost fairly soon."

"The calibration is straightforward," Dharek replied. "My science officer can work with your science officers to integrate our detection protocols."

Bayes smiled. "The numbers don't lie. Even if the Zodarks have upgraded some of their propulsion engines, the combined approach still outperforms any single-technology solution. It's redundancy at its finest."

Mensah's image pixelated slightly. "And who controls the data interpretation? These sensors are processing information our systems weren't designed to handle."

"Why don't we route the data through the *Poseidon*?" Lee requested. "I've worked with Captain Dharek and his people before, and our teams have established some level of working relationship already. All Primord sensor data will route through Republic verification systems, and this way, nothing gets confirmed without dual-system authentication."

Mensah seemed to consider this, her jaw working slightly as she processed the information. "I want updates and reports on detection methodology effectiveness, Captain Lee… if you find the chemical markers we're looking for. If these sensors start providing questionable results, I expect immediate reversion to Republic-only detection protocols."

"Understood, Captain," Lee replied. "We'll maintain complete operational sovereignty."

Mensah's eyes flicked between Lee and the Primord captain. "Very well. We'll go with this… for now."

The meeting continued with further technical details, ending with Mensah authorizing minimal Primord sensor modifications to some of the Republic ships' arrays—a small but significant concession. As Dharek blinked off the display and the others vanished too, Lee's staff also filing out, Mensah's voice remained.

"A moment, Captain Lee. Secure communication."

Lee tapped his comm once the war room had completely emptied. "Secure line established."

"That was quite a performance in there. When did you become such an advocate for Primord methodology?"

"I'm an advocate for mission success," Lee replied carefully. "It's what I've learned from you, actually. Now, their detection capabilities offer tactical advantages we'd be unwise to ignore."

"Indeed. I'm glad you're with us, Lee. Mensah out."

The transmission cut before Lee could respond.

The ice field would hide many secrets, but with Republic and Primord technologies working in concert, those secrets would come to the surface, and as he calculated, quite swiftly.

Chapter 27:
Ice Highways to Hell

Year 2098
RNS *Poseidon*
Middle Reach
Sector 8

The *Poseidon* hung in the middle of the fleet, engines barely breathing to keep them off thermal scans. Beyond the viewport, large ice crystals caught the distant sunlight, shattering it into colors no one aboard had names for, while smaller fragments drifted between them like luminous fog.

In the far distance, almost lost against the darkness of space, a dwarf planet hung like a dim star. Its thin, icy rings were barely visible from their position nearly two million kilometers away. The fleet would reach scanning range within four hours if they maintained course. The planet was a potential hiding spot for a base, an outpost. Its gravity well and radiation patterns would mask ships and installations from all but the most precise scans.

"Drones are all out," Baldry said, not looking up from his console. "No hiccups so far."

Lee nodded, watching as the map built itself on the main screen. The little blue drone dots spread outward, creating a massive detection net. Their ships glowed green. The Primords' vessels pulsed amber at the edges with *Ek* in the front.

"Grav-wave detectors are up and running," said Ensign Baldry at the sensor station. "Ice patterns are weirdly consistent for something that looks like a drunk god's sculpture garden. These Primord sensors, though—they make our equipment look like toys."

Lee wandered over to the sensor feeds. "Keep watching those patterns, Ensign. Anything twitches, I want to know."

"You'll be the first, Captain."

Lee made his usual circuit around the bridge, checking readings. They'd spend hours and hours hunting this Zodark outpost, with four different detection systems running. If those bastards were out there— and every instinct told him they were—they'd find them…eventually.

For a moment, Lee felt Captain Oldendorf's presence beside him, almost heard the gruff voice of his mentor: "Patience in the hunt isn't weakness, son. It's wisdom. The enemy always shows themselves eventually; your job isn't to charge in guns blazing, but to be absolutely ready when that moment comes, and to recognize the difference between the target and the shadow it casts. Half of warfare is knowing when to strike. The other half is knowing where."

An hour in, Sato made her way to Lee, squinting at her datapad. She'd been speaking with Captain Mensah and the captain of the Primord ship, *Simsu*, sorting through thermal data.

"Captain," she said. "Got something in Sector 8, 14-Lambda. Temperature's doing things natural ice doesn't do."

Lee leaned over, studying what looked like heat ripples flowing through the ice—like someone had dropped hot stones in cold water and filmed the results. The computer had outlined the patterns in red.

"Might be nothing," Lee muttered. "The Primords backing this up with their readings?"

"Dharek's on it now." Sato tucked a strand of hair behind her ear. "Says there are microfractures in the ice, like something's been heating up and cooling down repeatedly."

"How old?"

"Two weeks, give or take. According to them, anyway."

"Lieutenant Rhom, redirect drone cluster five to coordinates two-eight-six mark five," Lee ordered, rubbing his stubble absently. "Priority scan pattern Bravo."

"Aye, Captain. Repositioning drone cluster five," Rhom responded.

Per Admiral Mensah's operational directive, the *Poseidon* had been assigned primary drone reconnaissance responsibilities, while Captain Dharek's vessels handled data analysis and fleet-wide information dissemination. The *Poseidon* was a fast and nimble cruiser. It made more sense to have them managing the reconnaissance work while their allies handled everything else. The structure had taken some getting used to, but it was showing signs of its effectiveness as they implemented it. Each team operated under explicit protocols established in Operation Order 2098-Delta-4, maintaining the clear command structure essential for coordinated fleet operations.

"Three minutes till they're in position," Rhom said.

Lee turned back to Sato, who was still frowning at her datapad. "Talk to me. What are we looking at?"

"Too regular," she said, finally looking up. "Natural ice doesn't pulse like this. Someone's running equipment out there. Probably a reactor cycling down to avoid detection."

"Forward this data to Captain Dharek's team."

Ensign Baldry from the sensor station waved his arms as he spoke excitedly. "Captain! We've been monitoring the grav analysis coming in from those recon drones. It's showing something I need you to see. I'm forwarding it to your screen now."

The viewscreen lit up with data that might as well have been abstract art to anyone but Baldry. It was blue everywhere except for three red patches pulsing like sore thumbs.

"I'm looking at it now, Ensign Baldry. If I'm reading this right, something's messing with the mass readings?" Lee asked.

"Bingo," Baldry replied. "But check this out." Keys clicked through the communication link as he overlaid Sato's heat map. "See that? The big gravity hiccup lines up perfectly with Sato's hot spot. Two different detection systems just pointed at the same damn thing. That ain't ice, Cap. That's something with weight that's putting off heat."

Lee hunched forward. "Coincidence?"

"Less than point oh-four percent chance. Something's there, and it ain't small."

"How big are we talking?"

"Ballpark?" Baldry replied. "Five hundred meters long, maybe two hundred wide. Buried deep too—fifty meters under the ice, minimum."

"Classic outpost dimensions," Rhom chimed in. "Perfect size for a forward observation post or a supply dump."

Lee nodded. "Sato, get the Primords on the line. I want their sensors to confirm."

"Already connecting."

Dharek's face filled the bridge display. "We have found evidence of Zodark pollution." His hand moved offscreen, and suddenly their displays filled with rotating molecules highlighted in yellow. "It is more concentrated as we near the anomaly. Info already sent to Mensah."

"How fresh?" Lee asked.

"Some less than three days old," said Dharek. "But we have evidence that they have been coming this direction for over eight months."

"That's right when sectors started reporting Zodark activity," Lee replied.

"Precisely," Dharek said. The screen shifted to show glowing trails spreading outward. "Most telling is this pattern. The residue follows exact lines. Patrol routes."

"They're running security sweeps," Rhom said. "Standard perimeter defense."

"This isn't some hidey-hole," Lee agreed. "They've moved in for good."

As they inched closer to whatever was lurking under the ice, and as Lee's team and the Primords sent vital information throughout the ships in the task force, Captain Mensah ordered comm silence except for tight-beam transmissions between ships.

Lee frowned, leaning over the tactical console beside Rhom. "Something doesn't fit. If this is their outpost, where's the security? The sensor arrays? Anything this important should be wrapped in defenses, even out this far."

"Maybe they trust their hiding spot," Rhom said. "That ghosting tech we ran into was pretty effective."

Lee shook his head. "No commander worth their salt relies just on being invisible—not for something this big."

Sato approached, arms crossed. "What if they want us to find it?"

Lee's eyebrows shot up. "Go on."

"What if we're not seeing the outpost?" Sato jabbed at the map. "What if this is bait? They love that game. Flash something shiny over here while the real base sits somewhere else entirely."

Lee chewed his lip, eyes on the main viewscreen. The ice field stretched on like a maze, perfect for anyone playing hide-and-seek.

"Run another scan," Lee decided. "Wider. Different frequencies. If they're trying to make us look left, let's see what's on the right."

"I'm on it, Captain," Baldry said at the sensors station.

Lee strode over to Baldry's console. "What you got? Radiation? Subspace hiccups? Anything that doesn't fit?"

"Nothing yet," Baldry said, eyes glued to his interface. "Digging deeper now."

The breakthrough came from left field. The Primords, with their obsession with ice crystals, found it first.

"Captain," Baldry called out, face animated. "The Primords sent something. Look at this ice." The main screen filled with microscopic images of ice crystals that looked… wrong. Too perfect.

"Dharek thinks they're markers," Baldry continued. "Like road signs, but invisible unless you know what to look for."

"They've turned the ice field into a damn map," Lee said. "Hidden in plain sight."

Mac's voice crackled through. "If these are road signs, Cap, they've gotta lead somewhere. I'm running the patterns to see where they point."

"How long, Mac?"

"Ten minutes? These patterns are a mess, but there's definitely a system."

Lee nodded, turning to Sato. "Get the Primords working with Mac. They speak the same language."

"Aye, sir. Connecting them," Sato replied.

The holographic display shimmered to life above the tactical station. Layers of sensor data built upon one another. Thermal imaging rendered in reds and blues, gravitational analytics in pulsing greens, crystallographic patterns in sharp white lines. Officers stared up at it, necks craned, as the representation slowly rotated, showing hidden corridors and suspect shadows mere visual observation would never detect.

"The chemical traces follow these hidden paths," Sato said, tracing lines. "But look. They all terminate here."

Ensign Baldry spoke up. "It's not a network, Captain. It's a transit route. These aren't highways zigzagging through the ice field. They're arterial paths all leading in one direction."

"Toward that dwarf planet," Lee said, eyes narrowing as he studied the pattern.

Rhom stabbed his finger at a spot where multiple paths converged. "Everything leads here. Right in the nastiest part of the field, by the dwarf planet."

"Where most would never look first," Lee said. "Hiding their command center in the worst possible terrain. Difficult for the Zodarks to get in and out, so they most likely think it'd be difficult for anyone else."

"Interesting, and smart," Rhom agreed. "Make your home where no one wants to visit."

Dharek's voice cut through. "Our vessels have completed the crystalline analysis. These are definitely Zodark markings. They match patterns from their bases in the Rass system."

"How fresh are they?" Lee asked.

"They're still using it," Dharek replied. "Last traffic about two days ago."

"Captain," Baldry called out. "I'm getting strange readings from our long-range scans of that dwarf planet."

"Define strange."

"The composition analysis of the rings doesn't match our database."

"The rings," Lee said thoughtfully. "What if they're not natural? Or not entirely natural?"

"Sir," Rhom cut in. "Those 'highways' through the ice? If we extend their trajectory…" He manipulated the display. "They all point to the dark side of that planet."

Lee turned to Rhom. "How many eyes do we have over there?"

"Barely any," he admitted. "Ice is too thick for decent signals. Two drones circling the edges, nothing inside."

"Get four more in there," Lee ordered. "I want to see what we're dealing with."

Rhom hesitated. "Sir, visuals won't penetrate that ice."

"Then use sound," Lee shot back. "Acoustic imaging. Sound travels through ice. If something's in there, we'll hear it."

The bridge went quiet as everyone watched the final analysis compile. The main screen lit up with what looked like a gigantic shadow buried in the densest part of the ice field. Not scattered blips anymore but something deliberately built. And most importantly, behind the dwarf planet.

Scale markers popped up, and Lee felt his stomach drop. Two kilometers across. Corridors shooting out like spider legs. Parts of it seemed to melt into the ice itself, using the natural formations as both disguise and support. They couldn't actually see it—just the shadow it cast across their sensors.

"Could be sensor ghosts," Lee said, sitting at his captain's chair. "Ice plays tricks."

"Not this time," Baldry replied with certainty. "Four different detection methods all seeing the same thing? That's no ghost, Captain.

"Sir, sensors confirm major installation at coordinates one-seven-four-four-five-nine-two, dark side of the dwarf planet. It's there all right, but… it's not what any of us thought."

Chapter 26:
Borrowed Time and Faded Dreams

Year 2098
RNS *Idaho*
Middle Reach
Sector 8

Osprey pilot Lieutenant Tim Hastings slouched at the back of the briefing room aboard the RNS *Idaho*. There, he counted ceiling tiles while Commander Bevens droned on about tactical formations. The holographic battle plans hovered in the center of the room in front of attentive pilots. Hastings understood the drill. Pay just enough attention to catch the critical details, while letting the rest wash over him like white noise.

The thing was, he paid attention to every detail that mattered. Every single one. He couldn't afford not to.

"…strategic breakthrough in Sector 8…" Bevens's voice lingered on. "Captain Lee and the Primords located a significant Zodark installation embedded within an ice asteroid."

Hastings looked at the rotating hologram. The asteroid field was a navigational quagmire if ever he'd seen one. Chunks of ice, ranging from car-sized to small-moon dimensions, all spun in nutty patterns.

Perfect, he thought. *Just what an Osprey pilot needs. At least the intel looks solid this time. Multiple confirmations. Not like what happened on Intus.*

"Captain Mensah assumes tactical command," Beven continued, manipulating the hologram to show the planned merger of the battle groups. "The fleet will establish a combat corridor for the Ospreys and Army teams."

Hastings scrolled through his datapad, checking maintenance reports he'd already memorized twice. The Osprey's port stabilizer had been flagged for a minor fluctuation. It wasn't anything critical, but it was worth monitoring. Everything was worth monitoring—every bolt, every system, anything with the potential to go wrong.

"Any questions about the drop procedure?" Bevens asked.

Lieutenant Konoski raised his hand. "Sir, what's our…"

Hastings missed the last of Konoski's words as he mumbled under his breath, way low for anyone to hear. "Intel confidence level?"

Or at least he thought no one had heard.

Lieutenant Amanda Day shot him a glance from the seat beside him. Her eyes narrowed a bit, but Hastings pretended not to notice.

She knows about my horrible stint at Intus, he couldn't help but think. *They all do.*

"Lieutenant Hastings," Bevens called out. "Perhaps you'd like to share your thoughts on the combat corridor approach?"

Hastings straightened in his chair. "Standard belly-drop procedure, sir. Seal the cockpit, depressurize the troop bay, green-light the jumpers. We maintain position while the battlesuits deploy, then execute evasive maneuvers to avoid becoming targets."

Bevens nodded. "And the ice field variables?"

"Compensate for gravitational eddies caused by the larger masses, watch for reflective sensor ghosts, and maintain minimum safe distance from all surfaces due to potential micrometeorite clouds kicked up by recent impacts." Hastings recited the protocols from memory, his tone flat but precise. "And confirm all intelligence updates before final approach."

Bevens paused, studying him. "That's… thorough, Lieutenant."

"Sir, with respect, intelligence accuracy can mean the difference…" He didn't finish the sentence. Everyone knew what he meant.

"Good to know you were paying attention, Lieutenant." Bevens turned back to the hologram. "As Lieutenant Hastings so eloquently summarized, this is a standard operation in nonstandard conditions."

The briefing concluded with the usual warnings about Zodark capabilities and the importance of maintaining communication discipline. Hastings remained seated as the other pilots filed out, discussing formation tactics and kill-zone parameters with animated gestures.

Day lingered beside him. "The intel's solid, Hastings."

"Yeah," Hastings replied, not looking up from his datapad. *That's what they said during my third drop at Intus.* It still haunted him.

Through the years, some pilots had told him it wasn't his fault. Yet he was the pilot. It was his bird, his responsibility. He finally looked at her. "We'll be double-checking everything."

She nodded slowly and joined the others, leaving Hastings alone with the fading hologram. He finally stood and stretched his back until it popped. The sound resounded off the walls in the empty briefing room.

A while ago on Intus, bad intel had reported that Hasting's landing zone was secure, and it had turned out to be a trap. Fifty-one soldiers were dead because he'd trusted the intelligence reports and flown straight into a kill box.

Hastings had followed orders perfectly and done everything by the book. Then he'd watched good people die for it. He'd attempted to tell himself it was a mistake and it wasn't his fault, but it held him back and propelled him forward at the same time. To say he'd been cautious since then was an understatement. He was by the book, and even better than by the book at almost every drop. His eyes and ears were peeled, and his crew was better trained than anyone. No risks. No negligence. Everything was about going in and out and getting the job done. But playing it safe meant he might not be in a position to truly save lives when it mattered most—and he knew it.

Hastings walked down the corridor to the hangar, like he had so many times before. One boot against the deck plates, and then the other. Officers passed him, their conversations fading in and out of his awareness.

"…heard Captain Lee's doing a fine job with… and he's…"

"…Primords are saying they can track Zodarks out here via…"

Hastings tuned them out. Rumors before combat were as reliable as jumpspace navigation without coordinates, likely to lead you somewhere, but rarely where you wanted to go.

The hangar bay doors opened. Inside, maintenance crews swarmed over the Ospreys, running final checks.

Jumpsuit soldiers clustered near their assigned transports, checking equipment and exchanging the forced bravado that preceded every drop.

Hastings spotted his Osprey. Tail number AT-70A-42, nicknamed "Borrowed Time" by its previous pilot. He'd never bothered to change it. The name seemed appropriate enough. Every mission since that op on Intus had felt like borrowed time.

"Hastings!" Commander Bobby Beck's voice boomed across the hangar bay. The burly officer walked toward him with the enthusiasm of a man half his age and twice his sense. "There's my most reliable pilot."

Most reliable. That was what they called him now. Not the best. Not the bravest. The most reliable. The one who never took risks. Hastings suppressed a sigh. "Commander."

"Ready to push those Zodark bastards back where they belong?" asked Beck. He slapped Hastings on the shoulder. "Yes, you are."

"Just get me accurate intelligence and I'll deliver them safely."

"That's what I like about you, Hastings. Steady as a rock." Beck lowered his voice. "This one's important. Lee's found something big out there. Captain Mensah wants our most dependable pilots, and that means you."

Dependable, thought Hastings. *Another word for "plays it safe."*

Hastings nodded. "I'll get it done, sir."

"I know you will. Look at recent reports when you board *Borrowed Time*, understood?"

"Understood, sir. I'll verify them against primary sources."

"Could get messy out there," said Beck.

"Not if the intel's good." Hastings glanced toward his Osprey, where Day was conducting preflight checks. "Better get to it."

Beck nodded and moved on to the next pilot while Hastings made his way to the Osprey. It was just another mission—another chance to keep everyone alive by not taking any chances.

The hangar reverberated with the shouts of crew chiefs and the hiss of systems being tested. Four AT-70As stood in formation, their loading ramps down, waiting to swallow soldiers for delivery to the battlefield. Or rather, starfield.

Army troops filed into the transports in orderly lines. Their boots clanged on the floor with each step. Some soldiers clearly prayed, touching their fingers to what would be their forehead on their helmets, then on their chest armor, followed by each plated shoulder, forming the ancient gesture of faith. Others checked weapons for probably the tenth time. Veterans stared at nothing, no doubt lost in memories of previous drops.

Hastings walked up *Borrowed Time*'s ramp, watching the soldiers strap themselves in. There were sixty-four faces in the back. He prayed he'd get them where they needed before any of them perished, and he prayed none would perish, especially with him in the cockpit.

His gunners, Specialist Lillard and Corporal Gonzalez, were at their stations, running through their precombat checklists. Hastings acknowledged them with a quick nod before pulling out his own checklist to verify their work.

"Ready to kick some Zodark ass today, Lieutenant?" A private grinned up at him through a visor. Hope showed itself in the man's eyes.

Hastings nodded curtly and continued his inspection. The soldier's smile faded as Hastings brushed past him and entered the cockpit.

The array of controls welcomed him like an old friend. It was the only relationship he maintained these days. Hastings went through the Osprey's start-up sequence, but instead of being on autopilot, he again manually verified each system against his checklist. Port stabilizer: checked. Navigation systems: double-checked. Communication arrays: verified against backup protocols.

If anything, Intus had taught him that perfection wasn't enough. You had to be better than perfect.

New Eden—the name itself had promised so much. Hastings remembered his awe during that first deployment, and the conviction he'd held that they were fighting for humanity's future. It was the reason he'd gone to the Academy—a place where simulator sessions with a woman named Naomi Love had been the highlight of his life. That woman had always pushed him to be better, to fly smarter. They'd spent countless hours in those metal boxes, competing for the highest scores, arguing over tactics. Hastings wondered how she was doing now. Last he'd heard, she was on Intus still, flying campaigns there.

And Lee… Hastings allowed himself a small smile for the first time in a long time. Ripley Willis Lee had been the quiet one in their group. Well, kind of—he'd turn quiet a lot, always watching, always thinking three steps ahead. Chess with him probably would have been a nightmare. Now the guy commanded his own battle group. Not surprising, really. Lee had always been destined for command.

Wouldn't it be something to hear Lee's voice on the comms today? *Unlikely*, he realized. Battle group commanders didn't waste time talking to transport pilots, especially transport pilots with one of the worst Intus missions on their record.

Hastings shook his head. *Get over it...*

He couldn't. Never would.

Hastings completed the preflight sequence. Responsibility pressed down on him like a ship's gravity after too long in zero-g. Sixty-four lives depended on him getting everything right.

On his monitor's cabin feed, more Army troopers boarded his Osprey.

The last soldier boarded, and the loadmaster signaled for the ramp to close. The hydraulics whined as the bay sealed, trapping them all in the metal coffin that would deliver them to the battlefield.

Hastings settled deeper into the pilot's seat as his copilot, Lieutenant Day, slid in beside him. He looked down at a small photo tucked into his console. The image was of four friends at the Academy—himself, Jack Hannigan, Naomi Love, and Ripley Willis Lee—young and ready to save humanity. That was before Intus—before he'd learned that good intentions and perfect flying weren't enough.

He touched the photo before he tucked it away into a side compartment. Hastings put on his helmet and announced. "AT-70A, the *Borrowed Time*, Aquila Two, ready for deployment."

"Roger that, *Borrowed Time*," the mission control officer responded. "You are cleared for launch sequence. Await final authorization."

Hastings pulled up the intelligence reports one more time, cross-referencing them with the tactical updates. Everything looked solid with multiple confirmations.

"Initiating launch sequence," Hastings said, seeing twenty minutes until launch on the ship's dashboard.

"Hurry up and wait," he muttered in a low voice.

The phrase captured the military reality, where personnel often rushed to prepare or get somewhere only to then sit idle waiting for the next step or order.

At the moment, the Osprey whirred beneath Hastings's hands, responsive and ready. At least the machine was predictable. At least when he did everything perfectly, the machine responded perfectly.

If only everything was that predictable.

Chapter 28:
The Moment Before Thunder

Year 2098
RNS *Poseidon*
Middle Reach
Sector 8

It'd been many hours now, and the search for their target using both Primord and Earther strategies was paying off. In front of Lee, the holographic projection showed their formation—the mixed fleet of Republic and Primord vessels arranged in the Diamondback formation.

Following Task Force Commander Mensah's tactical directive, they'd maintained the formation throughout their approach. The *Idaho* was now taking point position from Ek with the *Poseidon* serving as the sensor coordination vessel.

Hours earlier, they'd sent the data they'd found to Captain Mensah on the *Idaho*. Her team confirmed what Lee's staff and the Primords found. Captain Mensah had quickly processed the intelligence and authorized the continued approach, directing Lee to maintain tactical oversight of the sensor deployment while her ship coordinated the overall fleet movements.

On the way toward the dwarf planet, the ships' navigational computers had already cataloged the celestial body as DP-3327 in their tactical displays, the standard designation for an uncharted dwarf planet in this quadrant. And quickly, they increased speed and flew dead ahead toward DP-3327, its icy rings growing more distinct with each passing hour.

"Captain, sensors confirm DP-3327 at bearing zero-zero-zero, range two-five-zero thousand kilometers," Reynolds reported from the nav station. "Estimated thirty minutes until optimal scanning range."

Could the outpost actually be behind this planet? In a moment, Lee would most likely know.

Lee frowned. "Magnify."

The holographic display shifted, showing a rust-colored dwarf planet with deep fissures across its frozen surface. Ice-covered land spread out over its northern hemisphere. A colossal crater dominated one pole, its edges smooth, while wispy tendrils of atmosphere clung to portions of the equatorial region. A white ring surrounded the planet, and in all truth, it was difficult to spot with the naked eye through the ice field, especially because it very much matched the hues of the frozen asteroids floating all around.

Baldry typed on his console, eyes narrowing as new data streamed in. He took a sharp breath, then looked up at Lee. "Sir, there's no outpost on the planet. Nothing. Not a thing." He pointed to the sensor readings. "But like we suspected, these readings suggest there's something behind it."

There really isn't an easy path to navigate this system from the other side of the planet, Lee thought.

"Sir," Baldry said, "the massive ring system appears to be creating substantial electromagnetic dead zones."

"How so?" asked Lee.

"Like a mountain casting a radio shadow, the dense ring structure is scattering any sensor sweeps, creating natural blind spots," Baldry explained.

It's ingenious, Lee mused. *It would be perfect cover.*

The comm panel chimed with an incoming priority transmission from the *Idaho*.

"Captain," Rodriguez announced, "Captain Mensah is transmitting new tactical orders for the entire task force."

Mensah's voice came through clearly. "All vessels, this is *Idaho*. Based on sensor analysis, we're implementing a modified approach. The ring system creates an electromagnetic shadow zone that will mask our approach. We'll position the task force along the ring's interference corridor rather than risk navigation through the debris field itself. All vessels maintain formation at twelve thousand kilometers from the ring's outer perimeter. This corridor provides maximum electromagnetic interference while ensuring safe navigation clearance from ring debris."

"Acknowledge *Idaho*," Lee said. "Awaiting specific course vectors."

"*Poseidon*, maintain sensor coordination as planned. I'm transmitting new approach vectors now. The electromagnetic interference from charged particles in the ring, combined with gravitational lensing effects and natural radar scatter from ice fragments, should mask our energy signatures quite well."

"Understood, Captain Mensah," Lee responded. "Ensign Baldry, what's your assessment of the ring's interference potential?"

Baldry leaned forward. "The ring system is complex, sir. The ice fragments are charged particles creating continuous electromagnetic interference. Combined with the gravitational effects from the ring's mass distribution, we're looking at multiple overlapping interference types that would significantly degrade enemy sensor effectiveness."

The tactical display beeped with an incoming formation update from the *Idaho*. The holographic projection shifted, showing the current Diamondback formation transitioning to a new configuration, ships arranged in a single column stretching along the ring's electromagnetic shadow corridor.

"New tactical orders from Captain Mensah," announced Lieutenant Rhom from the tactical station. "All vessels ordered to transition to Line Ahead formation. The *Idaho* will maintain point with EW frigates maintaining flanking positions along the shadow zone."

"Lieutenant Rodriguez, continue communication blackout as per Captain Mensah's orders," Lee instructed. "Lieutenant Reynolds, implement Captain Mensah's new approach vector. Position us in the electromagnetic shadow zone cast by the ring system. Execute Line Ahead formation transition as ordered by task force command."

"Aye, Captain. Line Ahead formation, plotting course along the ring's sensor shadow corridor," Reynolds responded.

On the tactical display, the electronic warfare frigates took flanking positions. Their specialized ECM suites projected a carefully modulated interference field designed to blend with the natural electromagnetic chaos created by the ring system. Lieutenant Witkowski monitored the coordination from his station.

"EW frigates report full-spectrum jamming active on passive channels, sir," Witkowski said. "They're using the ring's natural interference as cover for our artificial emissions. Captain Mensah's tactical plan has them cycling frequencies to match the ring's electromagnetic patterns. Between their jammers and this electromagnetic shadow zone, we're effectively invisible."

Sato tapped on her holo. "The Primords might object to this approach."

They object to everything, Lee thought. "Captain Mensah approved this maneuver personally, and the *Idaho* is coordinating our sensor operations on this portion of the operation."

Outside the viewports, the ring system stretched ahead. No word came from any Primord captain, even Dharek, who'd been awkwardly quiet.

They must be observing, making sure nothing hostile springs at the Primord and Republic fleet, thought Lee.

For the next hour, the fleet moved along the electromagnetic shadow corridor. The bridge crew worked well with one another, and from the communication broadcast between all ships, everyone was in sync, each focused on their station. Still, tension built in Lee's shoulders. The anticipation before potential combat was always there, no matter how many engagements he'd commanded.

"Sensors are reading enormous electromagnetic interference from the ring system," Baldry reported. "The charged particles and ice fragments are creating exactly the kind of sensor scatter Captain Mensah predicted. And I'm getting better readings on what's on the far side of the planet, sir. The outpost is most likely twenty-eight thousand kilometers out."

"Forward that data to the *Idaho* immediately," Lee ordered. "Lieutenant Reynolds, maintain course as Captain Mensah directed. We'll continue using the ring system's electromagnetic shadow to mask our approach."

"Aye, sir. Thirty more minutes until we reach the position Captain Mensah designated for optimal sensor coverage."

Lee looked over the tactical display. Hours of careful maneuvering had brought them to this point.

His mind flashed back to the mission briefing from earlier that day. The holographic war room aboard the *Idaho* had connected all task force commanders, with Captain Mensah presiding over the assembled captains on screen. After reviewing the initial drone reconnaissance, Mensah had laid out the operation.

Mensah's image was replaced by a tactical display showing the ice asteroid and surrounding space. "We'll implement a four-phase operation," she had explained. "First, we neutralize their defensive capabilities and establish space superiority. Second, we disable key systems to prevent data destruction and escape. Third, once the area is secure, we'll deploy Army Special Forces via Osprey transports to extract intelligence. Fourth, once extracted, we neutralize the base."

Back to the present, the combined scans from Republic and Primord technology gave a final confirmation of what Baldry found—a Zodark outpost nestled in the shadow of the dwarf planet DP-3327, perhaps nestled in an ice asteroid, where all signs pointed. If they continued on the current trajectory through the electromagnetic shadow zone as Captain Mensah had directed, they'd emerge in optimal sensor position for the task force.

"Captain," Sato said, "we should recommend to Captain Mensah that the fleet prepare for combat operations."

Lee nodded. "Lieutenant Rodriguez, send coded burst transmission to the *Idaho*. Request permission from Captain Mensah to transition the task force to combat readiness."

Rodriguez nodded. "Transmission sent, sir." After a beat, she continued, "Captain Mensah acknowledges. Fleet-wide combat stations ordered in five minutes."

The comm panel on Lee's chair vibrated. He tapped it and a small holo projected off his chair's armrest. There, Dharek's stern face stared back at him.

"Captain Lee," the Primord commander said, his voice lower than usual. "My sensor specialist is detecting anomalous energy fluctuations within the electromagnetic interference zone. They do not match known Zodark signatures, but they are… concerning."

"Can you send the data to Ensign Baldry?" Lee asked.

Dharek nodded once. "It is done. I suggest heightened vigilance as we navigate this shadow corridor."

"Agreed," Lee said. "Thank you, Captain. I'll ensure this is forwarded to Captain Mensah immediately."

A flicker of surprise crossed Dharek's features before he masked it. "We share the same objective," he said simply and cut the transmission.

"Captain, I've got something," said Ensign Baldry.

"Go ahead, Ensign."

"Sir, I'm seeing some weird interference patterns. Power fluctuations across the array that don't match any calibrated baselines. Something out there is causing feedback loops in the ring's electromagnetic field."

"Elaborate," Lee directed.

"The gravitational lensing effects from the ring system are bending our sensor beams," Baldry explained. "The charged particles are creating microsurges every time we sweep Sector 43. The electromagnetic scatter is reflecting our own energy signatures back at us with almost perfect coherence. It's overloading the signal processors. I can compensate by recalibrating the input buffers, but this ain't normal environmental feedback. These patterns are too precise, too regular. The ring's natural interference is being artificially enhanced. I'm having to divert auxiliary power to the sensor cooling systems just to maintain baseline function.

"Sir, the Primord data confirms it. The crystalline structures in this planet's ring have been artificially modified to act as a distributed sensor array. It's... it's brilliant, actually."

"Are we being scanned?" Lee asked.

"Hard to tell," Baldry replied. "But if I were a betting man, I'd say we tripped some kind of silent alarm the moment we entered this electromagnetic shadow zone."

"Let's operate as if we did trip an alarm," said Lee. "Rodriguez, contact Captain Mensah immediately and inform her of this development."

After a brief exchange with Captain Mensah's command staff, Rodriguez reported back.

"Captain Mensah orders immediate implementation of EMCON Bravo protocols. The electronic warfare frigates are repositioning to provide maximum coverage. She's designated us as primary sensor platform while she coordinates countermeasures."

Lee nodded. On the tactical display, the specialized EW frigates slid into positions around the task force, their electromagnetic warfare suites deploying a protective umbrella of signal-distorting energy fields.

"Rodriguez, acknowledge and confirm our compliance with EMCON Bravo." He waited for her nod of confirmation before continuing to address his own crew. "All stations transition to Condition Whisper immediately. Reduce power signatures by forty percent and maintain strict comm discipline. Weapons to standby, but emissions locked down. Lieutenant Witkowski, coordinate with the EW frigates."

"Aye, Captain," Witkowski responded from his electronic warfare station. "EW frigates are amplifying the ring system's natural electromagnetic chaos. Their systems are sophisticated enough to blend our signatures with the gravitational distortions and charged particle interference. The Zodarks will see exactly what they expect to see… natural electromagnetic noise from the ring system."

"Sir," Rhom said from Tactical, "slowing might make us more noticeable if the ring's crystalline structures are indeed acting as sensor nodes."

"Noted, Lieutenant," Lee said, "but if we've already been detected, I'd rather follow Captain Mensah's directive to reach optimal strike position rather than be caught midtransit. Rodriguez, contact Dharek again."

Dharek showed on the screen. "You have reviewed our findings."

"Yes. We believe the ring system has been used as a sensor net disguised as natural electromagnetic interference. Captain Mensah has ordered implementation of EMCON Bravo. We're adjusting our approach accordingly."

Dharek dipped his head. "We received the communication. We have also adjusted our sensor harmonics to blend with the ring's gravitational and electromagnetic effects. It may reduce our detection profile."

"Good," Lee said. "Can your ships transmit those configurations to our vessels? I'll coordinate with the electronic warfare frigates to integrate these into their countermeasures."

"It will be done," Dharek replied. "Though your systems may not fully integrate the parameters."

"We'll adapt what we can," Lee promised. "*Poseidon* out."

Over the next several minutes, engineering teams across the Republic vessels worked to implement the Primord modifications.

"Captain," Witkowski reported, "the EW frigates have successfully integrated the Primord harmonics into their jamming patterns. They report that the combination of natural ring interference—electromagnetic scatter, gravitational lensing, and charged particle disruption—and our artificial masking has increased effectiveness by sixty-two percent. They're using the ring's gravitational field distortions to bend any active scans around our formation. Between their systems and the electromagnetic shadow zone's natural scatter properties, we're nearly invisible."

"Acknowledged," Lee said. "Forward that data to the *Idaho*."

As they moved along the ring system's electromagnetic shadow corridor, Lee stood from his chair, moving closer to the tactical display. "Rodriguez, connect me to Captain Mensah." After a brief pause, he continued, "Captain, the *Poseidon* is approaching optimal sensor position. Request permission to transition the fleet to weapons readiness."

After a moment, Rodriguez nodded. "Captain Mensah approves. Fleet-wide transition to weapons readiness authorized. The EW frigates will maintain masking operations."

Dharek's voice came over the task force tactical link. "Primord vessels acknowledge. We will resume Diamondback formation upon exit from the electromagnetic shadow zone as directed by the task force commander."

Lee exchanged a glance with Sato. That was the first time Dharek had voluntarily accepted a Republic tactical decision without argument, or that usual annoyed tone in his voice.

"Acknowledge Primord compliance," Lee responded. "*Poseidon* will maintain sensor coordination position as ordered."

As they reached the optimal position and prepared to emerge with clear sensor coverage, Lee expected to see the outpost just as their sensors had indicated. Instead, the tactical display erupted with new contacts.

"Captain," Rhom shouted. "Three Zodark battleships, bearing zero-four-one, range eighteen thousand kilometers."

"Why didn't our drones see these?" Lee asked.

Baldry replied, "The Zodarks appear to be using the planet's magnetic field to create a sensor shadow zone themselves. The battleships were likely stationed in that shadow during our initial drone sweeps."

Witkowski added from his EWO console, "The drones would have had to penetrate much deeper into the system to detect those signatures, Captain. At that range, they would have been detected immediately. The EW frigates' analysis suggests these vessels are also employing masking technology. They're only visible to us now because we're at an optimal angle relative to the planet's magnetic field lines."

Nonetheless, the tactical display revealed exactly what they had suspected: a massive Zodark outpost nestled within an enormous ice asteroid, approximately eighteen thousand kilometers ahead. Around it, three Zodark battleships maintained patrol patterns, along with two frigates.

"Contact," Rhom whispered. "They don't appear to have detected us."

Lee's heart rate quickened. "Witkowski, status on our electronic signature?"

Lieutenant Witkowski worked across his EWO console. "Full-spectrum emissions control active, Captain. We're running dark. Thermal baffles at maximum. Their standard sweeps are still being scattered by the ring's electromagnetic interference and gravitational effects. The EW frigates are continuing to use the shadow zone's natural properties to hide the entire task force. Even their active scans are being bent around us by gravitational lensing."

Lee nodded, studying the tactical display. The enemy vessels continued their patrol routes, oblivious to the ships now stalking them through the darkness. He could almost taste the opportunity.

"Maintain emissions control," Lee ordered quietly, as if the Zodarks might hear him through the vacuum of space. "Lieutenant Reynolds, continue present course as per Captain Mensah's approach vector."

"Aye, sir," Reynolds responded as he guided *Poseidon* forward.

The bridge turned quiet, except for the occasional whispered status report.

"Captain," Rodriguez whispered, "Dharek is requesting a tight-beam communication."

Lee nodded, and Dharek's face appeared on a small screen at his station.

"Captain Mensah's approach is… unexpectedly effective," Dharek admitted, his voice low. "The modified harmonics combined with the ring's natural interference have exceeded expectations. We are completely invisible to their standard detection grid."

"Keep it that way," Lee replied. "Maintain present course. I'll forward this data to Captain Mensah for final attack coordination once we're within optimal strike range. The *Idaho* will signal when to transition to combat posture."

Dharek nodded once and cut the transmission.

Minutes stretched into an hour as the combined fleet crept closer to the unsuspecting Zodark outpost. The tension on the bridge grew and grew, or at least it felt that way to Lee.

"Eleven thousand kilometers and closing," Reynolds reported.

"Additional contacts," Baldry announced suddenly. "Four more Zodark vessels emerging from behind the ice structure housing the outpost."

Four more enemy ships joined the patrol pattern, still showing no signs of alarm.

"Nine ships total," Sato said in a hushed voice.

"Captain," Witkowski said, "they're deploying sensor buoys. Expanded detection grid coming online in approximately three minutes."

"Can we neutralize them?" Lee asked.

Witkowski shook his head. "Not without giving away our position. However, the EW frigates are adjusting their ECM profile to use the ring's interference patterns to mask our signatures from the new sensor grid. They're targeting the buoys' specific frequency ranges and using the electromagnetic scatter from charged particles to spoof the return signals."

Lee studied the tactical display. The deployment pattern of the sensor buoys would create a web that would be difficult to navigate undetected. For the enemy, the more sensors, the better.

"Lieutenant Reynolds, follow Captain Mensah's updated course vectors." Lee checked his tactical display showing new orders from the *Idaho*. "Thread us between sectors two and three in their grid. The *Idaho* has identified a blind spot in their projected coverage."

"Aye, Captain. Adjusting course."

Captain Mensah's voice came over the tactical channel: "All vessels, maintain present heading. Continue to use the gravitational distortions and particle interference to mask your approach."

"Eight thousand kilometers," Reynolds reported.

"Witkowski, status?" Lee asked.

"Still seemingly undetected, sir. EW frigates are performing brilliantly. Our actual signatures are being hidden behind the natural electromagnetic chaos. The Primord harmonics are enhancing the deception."

Lee held back a smile. "Maintain course and speed as directed by task force command."

"Seven thousand kilometers."

On the main holo in telescopic view, Lee could now make out individual structures within the Zodark outpost: massive weapon emplacements, communication arrays, and what appeared to be a shipyard.

"This isn't just an outpost," Lee realized. "It's a forward operating base. Look at those facilities. They're staging for something big. Rodriguez, make sure all this visual data gets to Captain Mensah immediately. She'll need this for final combat planning."

"Six thousand kilometers. Optimal weapons range in three minutes," Reynolds reported.

"Transmitting targeting data to Captain Mensah now," Lee informed the bridge crew. "Rodriguez, transmit our sensor readings to the *Idaho*. Captain Mensah will coordinate the attack timing across all vessels."

Rodriguez spoke, "Captain, *Horizon* reports their weapons systems are experiencing power fluctuations. They're troubleshooting now."

Lee frowned. A single malfunction could give away their position. "Tell them to stabilize immediately or power down completely. Forward this issue to Captain Mensah and the EW frigates for contingency planning."

"Fifty-five hundred kilometers," Rhom reported. "Targeting solutions locked. All vessels report ready and awaiting Captain Mensah's order."

The moment of truth approached. The main holodisplay showed the *Idaho* transmitting final strike coordinates to all vessels in the task force.

"Five thousand kilometers."

"*Idaho* signals final weapons check," Rodriguez reported. "Captain Mensah orders all vessels to prepare to fire on her mark."

"Captain!" Witkowski's voice was louder than normal. "Navigation deflector overload on *Horizon*! They're pushing through a dense debris cluster and their deflector just spiked to maximum output!"

Lee's blood ran cold. "How close are they to enemy sensors?"

"Too close," Baldry said, monitoring the tactical feed. "There's a Zodark sensor buoy less than two kilometers from their position. That energy discharge lit them up like a flare. A Zodark patrol ship is altering course. They must've detected the deflector surge. Sending priority alert to Captain Mensah."

The main viewscreen showed one of the enemy vessels breaking formation, turning toward *Horizon*'s position and beginning an active scan pattern.

"Sir," Witkowski said, his voice tight with tension, "they're scanning directly at the *Horizon*'s last known position. Active targeting systems just came online across their patrol fleet. The *Idaho* is signaling fleet-wide combat alert."

Chapter 29:
Clearing the Path

Year 2098
RNS *Poseidon*
Middle Reach
Sector 8

The stars hung like bright dots against the void, silent and waiting. The Zodarks didn't wait and headed for the *Horizon*, two enemy battleships and two frigates.

Captain Mensah's tone came through *Poseidon*'s bridge. "All vessels, this is *Idaho*. Weapons free. Primary targets as assigned."

"*Poseidon* targeting assigned vessel. Weapon systems online," Lee responded.

The tactical display highlighted their primary target: a Zodark battleship. On screen, the EW frigates shifted from concealment to active jamming. They flooded Zodark sensors with overwhelming electronic noise while the Republic ships prepared to fire.

"Target locked," Rhom reported. "All weapons stations report ready."

"Fire," Lee ordered.

The *Poseidon* shuddered as its six twin-barreled twenty-four-inch magrail gun turrets discharged in sequence, followed by the twelve triple-barreled turbo laser turrets. At just over three thousand kilometers, the energy weapons would reach first, followed by the kinetic rounds. Across the viewscreen, the entire Republic-Primord fleet started the apocalypse. Firepower lit up space.

The Zodark vessels, caught off guard by the sudden attack, absorbed the first devastating volley with catastrophic results. The battleship targeted by *Poseidon* took direct hits from the turbo laser barrage first, the energy beams slicing through outer armor plating in brilliant flashes. Shortly after, seven magrail rounds punched through the laser-weakened hull sections. The kinetic impacts caused the ship's compromised structure to fracture along its seams. The armor plates, already damaged by the energy weapons, peeled away like petals from a deadly metal flower. The devastating one-two punch left subsystems exposed, causing bright blue energy cascades as power conduits overloaded throughout the crippled vessel.

"Hits confirmed," Rhom announced. "Target's propulsion systems critically damaged. They've lost power to their port quadrant. Weapons capacity reduced by sixty percent."

Across the tactical display, similar success reports flooded in. The RNS *Thunder*'s opening barrage had sheared off an entire weapons array from their target. The RNS *Oceanus* and RNS *Argo* had coordinated their attack on another Zodark battleship. The enemy vessel's central command module crumpled inward from the concentrated fire, its bridge collapsing like a crushed aluminum can.

"The frigates are performing beautifully, sir," Sato reported. "RNS *Bolt* and RNS *Cobalt* are systematically targeting enemy sensor arrays."

Lee nodded, watching as the EW frigates executed a perfect deployment pattern, each one focusing on a specific frequency band to maximize disruption. "What about my corvettes? Tell me they're faring well."

"RNS *Polaris*, *Scimitar* and *Horizon* are conducting high-speed attack runs on the enemy's flank," Sato reported. "They're using their maneuverability to target the Zodark frigates' weapon hardpoints. *Polaris* just disabled the main battery on a Zodark escort."

The initial advantage of surprise couldn't last forever. Lee knew this better than anyone. The Zodark vessels, though damaged, began organizing a coordinated defense, and in Lee's mind with unbelievable speed.

"Captain," Baldry said, "detecting power surges from the outpost. They're activating defensive batteries embedded in the ice asteroid."

On the TAM, dozens of new weapon signatures appeared. Hidden gun emplacements placed throughout the asteroid's surface came online.

"Evasive maneuvers!" Lee ordered as the first volley of return fire streaked across space toward them—a mix of laser beams and missiles.

The *Poseidon* banked hard to starboard. The massive *Kraken*-class heavy cruiser responded like a whale rather than a dolphin. The tactical display showed the distance counter tick down. The enemy missiles would reach them in seventeen seconds.

"Activate point-defense grid. Launch countermeasures," Lee commanded.

The *Poseidon*'s sixty 30mm quad-barrel point-defense guns roared to life. They spit out high-explosive fragmentation rounds. The proximity fuses detonated in clouds of shrapnel, creating a defensive screen around the ship. Simultaneously, the ship's four vertical launch systems unleashed a wave of missile interceptors, streaking out to meet the incoming threats.

Despite their defenses, several impacts rocked the ship. The deck lurched beneath Lee's feet as a Zodark laser found its mark, burning into the outer armor plating.

"Minor damage to decks one and two," Sato reported. "Automated repair systems engaging. Hull integrity at ninety-three percent. Hangar deck and storage having some issues."

Across the fleet, the Zodarks' counterattack found other targets. The RNS *Oceanus* took multiple hits to its command tower and propulsion section.

"*Oceanus* is reporting damage to their bridge systems and main drive," Rodriguez relayed. "Captain Kim is implementing emergency containment protocols. They're losing maneuverability and shifting to secondary command."

Captain Mensah's voice came through. "*Thunder* and *Argo*, provide covering fire for *Oceanus*. Lee, take command of the frigate squadron and neutralize those asteroid defenses."

"Acknowledged," Lee responded. "Lieutenant Rodriguez, signal *Bolt*, *Cobalt* and the EW frigates to form on our position. We'll implement attack pattern Echo-Three."

As the Republic vessels regrouped, a development unfolded on the TAM. The Primord battleships—*Ek*, *Kulente*, *Nyx*, *Simsu*, *Sulvaar*, and *Vora*—suddenly accelerated forward at incredible speed.

"Sir, the Primords," Rhom said. "They've been holding position in the planet's shadow. They're moving now."

The five Primord battleships executed a perfect flanking maneuver, emerging out of what appeared to be complete sensor invisibility to strike at the Zodark formation from an entirely unexpected vector.

"That's why they've been silent," Sato murmured. "They've been fighting the Zodarks for… forever. They know exactly when to spring the trap."

The Primord vessels fired and tore through the Zodark ships' defenses. Energy beams and torpedoes blasted through enemy hulls.

Lee nodded. "Impressive."

Their remaining Zodark vessels regrouped around the asteroid base, taking defensive positions and maximizing the coverage from the embedded weapon emplacements.

"Sir, *Oceanus* is in serious trouble," Rodriguez reported. "They've lost primary and secondary power. Life support is on emergency backups."

On the tactical display, the RNS *Oceanus* showed multiple hull breaches visible across its midsection. The ship's status indicators flashed critical red across all major systems.

"Captain Mensah is ordering *Oceanus* to withdraw from the combat zone and *Argo* to provide extraction support," Rodriguez continued. "She's designating *Thunder* as primary covering fire."

Lee grimaced. "What's the status of our frigate squadron?"

"RNS *Bolt* reports sixty-four percent weapons capacity remaining," Rhom replied. "RNS *Cobalt* has sustained moderate damage to its sensor array, but weapons are fully operational. The EW frigates are still maintaining electronic countermeasures, but their power reserves are dropping below forty percent."

"And the corvettes?"

"*Polaris* and *Horizon* are combat effective. *Scimitar* took a direct hit to its command module. They've shifted to auxiliary control and are maintaining seventy percent combat capability."

The tactical display updated as Captain Mensah's orders came through. Lee studied the new battle plan quickly.

"Lieutenant Rodriguez, signal *Bolt* and *Cobalt* to reposition and support *Thunder*'s covering fire for *Oceanus*. We'll take primary responsibility for neutralizing the asteroid defenses while the Primords and remaining Republic vessels create a corridor for the Ospreys."

As Lee gave the order, a massive barrage from the asteroid battery struck the *Thunder*. The energy weapons splashed harmlessly against the battleship's reinforced armor plating. The *Thunder* returned fire immediately. Its main batteries unleashed a massive volley, shattering the ice surface around the weapon emplacements. Massive chunks broke free, spinning away into space, some vaporizing into clouds of crystalline mist.

"We need to neutralize those asteroid weapons now," Lee said. "Lieutenant Rhom, concentrate all available firepower on the three primary defense clusters identified on the tactical display."

"Captain," Rodriguez said, "urgent communication from Captain Mensah."

Mensah's face showed on-screen. "Lee, we need to create a safe corridor for our Ospreys. Those asteroid defenses must be neutralized immediately. The ground team is prepped and ready for insertion. This is our only window of opportunity."

"We're working on it. Their emplacements are buried deep in the ice structure," Lee responded. "Our standard targeting sensors can't get a clean lock."

"I'm coordinating with Dharek," Mensah replied. "The Primords have identified structural weaknesses in the asteroid. Sending targeting data now."

The tactical display updated with new information, highlighting specific points across the asteroid's surface appearing unremarkable to standard Republic sensors.

"These are fault lines in the ice structure," Baldry explained, analyzing the data. "Hit these points with concentrated fire and we could trigger structural collapse around the weapon emplacements without destroying the outpost itself."

"Brilliant," Lee said. "Rodriguez, acknowledge receipt of targeting data and inform Captain Mensah we'll implement immediately. Coordinate fire pattern with the Primord vessels."

"Dharek is already positioning his ships, sir," Rodriguez reported. "He's requesting we synchronize our attack with theirs for maximum effect."

Lee nodded. "Tell him we'll be ready on his mark."

On the tactical display, the five Primord battleships moved into positions around the asteroid, presenting their broadsides to maximize weapons coverage. The *Ek* and *Kulente* positioned themselves above the asteroid's northern hemisphere. The *Nyx*, *Simsu*, and *Vora* covered the southern approach. The RNS *Poseidon*, *Thunder*, and the remaining

Republic vessels adjusted their trajectories to complement the Primord firing solution.

"All vessels in position," Rhom reported. "Republic and Primord targeting systems aligned."

"Captain Dharek signals ready," Rodriguez said.

Lee surveyed the tactical situation one final time. The *Oceanus* had managed to limp away from the main battle zone, trailing debris. The *Thunder* and *Argo* provided covering fire. Their giant weapons batteries were keeping the surviving Zodark vessels at bay. Only four enemy ships remained operational. The rest were floating husks, their hulls breached and internal systems dark.

"All weapons stations, prepare to fire on Captain Mensah's command," Lee ordered.

Seconds later, Captain Mensah's voice resonated throughout the fleet. "All vessels, fire on designated targets. Maximum yield."

The *Poseidon* shuddered as its six twin-barreled magrail guns discharged. Then Lee let loose a dozen Havoc-II missiles.

The combined barrage from all Republic and Primord vessels struck the asteroid at calculated points. For a moment, nothing happened. Then the ice structure began to fracture along invisible fault lines. Massive fissures propagated across the surface as entire sections separated from the main body. The defensive emplacements lost power as their mounting platforms drifted free from the asteroid, surrounded by clouds of crystalline ice particles glittering in the starlight. Power conduits severed as the structural integrity failed, silencing the weapons as effectively as direct hits would have.

"Eighty-seven percent of asteroid defenses neutralized," Rhom said.

"The remaining Zodark vessels are breaking formation," Sato added.

The Zodark ships, now reduced to four operational vessels, moved away from the outpost's command center, still intact within the partially collapsed asteroid. As if they saw their mistake during the chaos, leaving an opening for the Republic and Primords, they began to converge on the outpost again. It was too late, though.

"Captain Mensah is hailing all vessels," Rodriguez said.

Mensah appeared on the main holodisplay. "Well executed, Captain Lee. The path is clear. Prepare to receive new tactical directives for phase two."

"Captain," Sato reported, "the *Idaho* is launching Ospreys. Four transport shuttles departing main hangar bay."

The tactical display tracked the troop transports emerging from the *Idaho*'s launch tubes, forming up in tight formation behind the screening corvettes.

"The corvettes are moving to escort formation," Rhom noted. "*Polaris*, *Scimitar*, and *Horizon* are creating a protective envelope around the Ospreys."

"Captain Mensah is addressing all vessels," Rodriguez announced, putting the transmission on the main speakers.

"All ships, this is Captain Mensah. Phase one objectives achieved. The Primord fleet will maintain containment perimeter while our vessels provide cover for the insertion team. Ospreys are green for launch toward the primary objective."

Four Osprey transports accelerated toward the damaged asteroid base, their flight path now largely cleared of defensive fire.

"Lieutenant Rhom, designate any remaining active defenses as priority targets," Lee ordered. "Nothing touches those Ospreys."

"Aye, sir. Targeting solutions locked."

The Primord vessels moved, forming a hemisphere around the insertion corridor and blocking any potential Zodark reinforcements from interfering. The EW frigates intensified their jamming, creating a bubble of electronic hell, no doubt blinding any surviving Zodark sensors.

"Captain," Rodriguez said, "transmission from *Idaho*. Captain Mensah says: 'The infantry wins the battles, the Navy just gets them there.'"

Lee allowed himself a small smile. "Acknowledge with: 'And we'll be here to bring them home.'"

On the main viewscreen, the Ospreys continued toward their target. Their hulls shined against the backdrop of stars and the fractured ice asteroid. The battle was far from over, but the first critical objective had been achieved.

Chapter 30:
Manual Override

Year 2098
Rass Moon PTX-419
Nightfall

The tactical display showed Alpha Company's advance in real time. Blue markers crawled across Coop's holographic terrain map. Gill's platoon moved through the rocky terrain to establish their observation post. Twenty minutes in, and everything was proceeding according to plan. So far.

Another platoon from Alpha Company trekked on foot down a narrow ravine toward the northwestern quadrant of the Zodark facility. Something felt off. The terrain funneled too perfectly. A natural choke point. Crawford had positioned their long-range sensors to provide maximum coverage, but the jagged rock formations created dead zones in their surveillance.

"You seeing this, sir?" Li asked, gesturing at the display.

Coop nodded. "Yeah. Don't like it one bit."

The soldiers below carried standard-issue M85 Infantry Assault Rifles. Three-barrel beasts with magrail, blaster, and smart munition capabilities. Some carried the M90 Squad Automatic Weapon, spitting magrail projectiles at incredible rates. Others lugged the M91 Heavy Blaster, a simplified but more powerful version of the M85's top barrel.

Coop checked his Dragonfly drone feeds. The tiny reconnaissance units hovered silently above the operation zone, transmitting visual data back to the observation post. Nothing unusual on the eastern approach, but the western quadrant showed thermal anomalies that the system couldn't quite identify.

"Movement, southeastern ridge," Li called out, highlighting a section of the display. "Thermal signatures. Multiple hostiles taking positions along the high ground."

The signatures bloomed across the screen. Zodark forces deploying in textbook ambush formations. Coop leaned forward, spotting the distinctive shapes of Zodark froggers. Portable missile systems that could unleash hell in seconds. Each four-by-four tube launcher could fire sixty-four smart missiles in rapid succession. Ugly suckers.

"They're setting up—"

Before Coop could issue a warning, the first barrage hit. The platoon's master sergeant's voice blasted through the comms. "Contact, contact! Heavy fire, southeastern ridge! Multiple casualties! Requesting immediate support!"

In the background, the crack of Republic rifles mixed with the higher-pitched whine of Zodark energy weapons. Corporal Weber immediately began calculating firing solutions as Coop assessed the battle developing below. Staff Sergeant Crawford started establishing a direct link to the orbiting support elements while Technical Sergeant Li analyzed thermal patterns to identify enemy weapon emplacements.

Captain Nobunaga's voice burst through on the command channel. "Alpha-Actual to TASC. Priority targets are heavy weapons threatening our main advance. Maintain fires until we reach phase line Bravo."

"Vega, what's your visual?" Coop asked, patching into the sniper's feed positioned thirty meters above their observation post. The tactical data network was good, but nothing beat eyes on target.

"Confirm multiple hostiles, at least two platoons," Sergeant Vega replied. "They've got heavy weapons emplaced at coordinates four-four-eight-six-two-seven. Our guys are pinned down hard." She paused. "Wait. Movement at the facility. Bunker doors opening at the perimeter."

Coop made a split-second assessment. "Crawford, get me Guardian Six-Actual. Li, allocate the Reaper to my control." He typed on his interface, marking priority targets and establishing a safe corridor for air support. "Weber, I need a precision package ready— five-meter dispersal, danger close to our forces."

"Reaper Six-Four online, call sign Watchdog. Standing by for tasking," the drone operator's voice came through clear on the dedicated channel.

Coop quickly transmitted the targeting data, designating the heavy weapons position as the primary objective. "Copy targeting package," the Reaper drone pilot confirmed. "Have visual on hostile positions. ROE confirmation requested for danger-close fire mission."

"Watchdog, this is Coop," he said. "You are cleared hot. I say again, cleared hot. Neutralize targets at designated coordinates. Minimize collateral around the blue-force markers."

He watched on his display as the Reaper, circling eight kilometers away, banked sharply and accelerated toward the engagement zone. The AS-90 Reaper was a beautiful piece of machinery with sixteen multipurpose smart missiles, cluster bombs, fuel-air explosives, and dual fifty-caliber magnetic railguns. It was flying arsenal designed to rain destruction on anything unfortunate enough to be designated as a target.

"Thirty seconds to target," the Reaper pilot confirmed. "Guns hot."

A platoon's master sergeant's voice broke through: "Coop, we need that support now! ...hit bad... losing our position!" In the background, someone was yelling, organizing covering fire.

The Reaper crested the ridge and dove toward the Zodark position. Its dual rotary-mounted five-barrel gun turrets opened fire with a sound like reality itself tearing apart. At twenty-five hundred rounds per minute, the heavy-caliber ammunition turned the Zodark emplacement into a cloud of debris and bodies. Tracer rounds created what looked like solid beams of light connecting the aircraft to the ground.

The sound reached the TASC position seconds later. A thunderous, sustained roar echoed across the barren landscape.

Lieutenant Gill signaled to Coop from twenty meters ahead, where he was directing the platoon's security elements. "We need to move forward to maintain observation. Next position is prepped."

"Direct hit on target," Li confirmed, watching the thermal signatures of the enemy position wink out one by one. "Enemy weapons platform destroyed."

"Confirmed kill," Vega added from her observation post. "I count fourteen enemy KIA. Remaining forces repositioning."

Through the tactical feed, Alpha Company began to move again. Captain Nobunaga's command element advanced with the main assault force. "Alpha-Actual to TASC, good effect on target. Shifting priority to bunker complex at grid five-five-six-tree-tree-two."

Lieutenant Gill signaled for Coop's TASC team to pack up. "Two minutes to displacement, TASC. We're moving to OP-2 for better observation of the eastern approach."

Corporal Weber was calculating secondary targets for the Reaper's next pass, his systems maintaining targeting data during the transition.

"Good work," Coop said. "Keep the pressure on them."

The brief advantage lasted less than two minutes. While Alpha Company pressed forward, Coop's tactical display lit up with new threat indicators. Multiple signatures emerging from concealed positions around the facility perimeter. The Zodark defense had anticipated the air support and held their main force in reserve… or so it seemed.

"New contacts!" Crawford shouted, highlighting three separate hostile formations converging on Alpha Company's position. "Energy signatures consistent with heavy repeating blasters and antiarmor weaponry."

Coop's stomach dropped. The Zodarks had drawn them in, sacrificing their forward positions to reveal Alpha Company's strength and position. Classic military strategy, and they'd walked right into it.

"Coop, we're taking fire from all sides!" Another platoon commander's transmission came through broken and static-filled as enemy jamming systems activated. "Sergeant down. Corporal Dwyer's squad is cut off. We need immediate support!"

In the background, the distinctive whoosh-crack of Zodark mortars impacted near the transmission position. The sound brought back memories of his training exercises. Except this time, the explosions were real, and people were dying.

Li worked frantically to clear the communications channel while Coop reassessed the tactical situation. The Reaper was already banking for another pass, but its remaining ordnance wouldn't be sufficient to neutralize the multiple threat vectors. Alpha Company was caught in a cross fire between the facility's automated defense turrets and the mobile Zodark infantry units.

Corporal Weber pulled up satellite imagery to identify the source of the coordinated attack. Sweat dotted on his forehead. "Command bunker detected." Weber highlighted a reinforced position two hundred meters inside the facility perimeter. "That's their tactical operations center. They're coordinating the entire defensive network in this area from there."

Coop studied the tactical display. The Zodark ambush had caught Alpha Company in a perfect kill zone. He'd seen this before in simulations, but the real thing hit different. Real blood. Real screams cutting through the comms.

Coop's adrenaline spiked as he settled into his role as a TASC. All those months of training in the 1st Special Tactics Wing, learning to bridge the gap between the Republic Army's needs and the Republic Navy's orbital fire support capabilities, had led to this moment. His first real combat operation as part of the 9th STS.

"Weber, designate that command bunker as primary target." He marked the structure on his screen. "Crawford, get me a direct line to Reaper Six-Four. Priority override."

Weber tapped on his interface. "Target designated. Calculating optimal approach vector."

Li worked beside them. "Sir… got multiple Zodark squads converging on Alpha Company's position. They're using some kind of coordinated fire pattern I haven't seen before."

"Reaper Six-Four responding," Crawford confirmed. "Requesting specific targeting parameters."

Coop pulled up the tactical overlay, marking three distinct target zones. "Transmitting now. First run on the command bunker, second on those heavy weapons emplacements, third on the approaching reinforcements." He highlighted each in sequence. "Tell them to make it count. We're running out of options down here."

Lieutenant Gill appeared at his shoulder, face streaked with dust and sweat. "Need to move out. This position is compromised." He gestured toward the ridge behind them. "We got a change. Observation post three. Two minutes to displacement."

"Copy that." Coop turned to his team. "Pack it up. Crawford, maintain comms during transit. Li, keep that targeting data flowing. Weber, transfer active solutions to your portable."

The constant chatter of gunfire mixed with the whine of Zodark blasters. Somewhere in that mess, Alpha Company was fighting for survival.

"Movement time is two minutes," Coop ordered, shouldering his equipment. The targeting system weighed nearly forty pounds, but he'd trained with twice that. "Stay tight, stay low."

Gill nodded toward a narrow depression ahead. "We'll be exposed crossing that ravine. My security teams are in position, but it's still a risk."

"No choice," Coop replied. "Alpha Company needs our eyes."

They moved as a unit, each member carrying essential components of their targeting system. The terrain fought them every step. Sharp rocks. Loose gravel. All threatening to send them tumbling. Above, the occasional whistle of enemy fire reminded them of the stakes.

Crawford maintained a running commentary as they moved. "Reaper Six-Four is commencing attack run. ETA thirty seconds to first target."

The ravine stood ahead. Twenty meters of exposed ground with minimal cover. Gill's security team provided overwatch from elevated positions, but Coop knew they'd be vulnerable. He'd made this crossing a hundred times in training. Never with real Zodarks trying to kill him. He couldn't believe how different this was from his previous role as a pilot. As a TASC, he was right here in the thick of it, coordinating fire support from the ground instead of delivering it from the drone's sim pods.

"On my mark," Gill said, crouching at the edge. "Three, two, one… move!"

They sprinted across the open ground. Equipment bounced against their backs. The first shots kicked up dust at their feet before they'd made it halfway. Someone cursed. Probably Weber. Coop kept his eyes forward. Counted steps. Fifteen meters. Ten. Five.

A massive explosion lit up the sky behind them as the Reaper's first missile found its target. The command bunker disappeared in a fireball sending debris hundreds of meters in all directions.

"Direct hit!" Crawford shouted as they reached cover. "Reaper moving to secondary targets."

The new observation post offered a commanding view of the eastern approach. Positioned among massive boulders, it gave perfect visibility of both Zodark positions and Alpha Company's elements.

Gill's platoon established a security perimeter while Coop's team set up.

"Systems online," Crawford announced, reestablishing connections. "Guardian platforms responding."

Li deployed the targeting sensors, calibrating for the new position. "Thermal imaging restored. Multiple heat signatures at the facility's eastern entrance. They're preparing a counterattack." She highlighted several clusters on the display. "Heavy weapons moving into position here, here, and here."

Weber's systems came online. "Firing solutions recalibrated. Atmospheric variables adjusted." He turned to Coop. "Ninety-eight percent accuracy with current parameters. Reaper has eight smart missiles remaining, a few fuel-air explosive bombs, plus half its gun ammunition."

Captain Nobunaga's came to life on the comms, "Alpha-Actual to TASC. Heavy resistance at main entrance. Need fire support on grid five-eight-five-tree-four-tree to suppress enemy positions. Third platoon pinned down."

Coop studied the battlefield layout. "Copy, Alpha-Actual. Prepping fire mission." He turned to Li and Weber, feeling the weight of his TASC responsibilities. "Precision munitions on that position. Danger close. Again, five-meter safety buffer."

The battle intensified as Zodark reinforcements poured from concealed bunkers. Alpha Company's advance stalled as heavy fire pinned them in exposed positions. Through his enhanced optics, Coop watched Nobunaga directing his platoon leaders, fighting to maintain momentum against growing resistance.

"Communication breaking up," Crawford warned, adjusting frantically. "They're jamming our frequencies. Can't reach the Reaper or Guardian platforms." He switched to backups, fighting to maintain their critical links.

Weber's system flashed warnings. "Targeting network integrity compromised. Enemy jamming affecting data synchronization." He manipulated the controls on his interface, implementing countermeasures. "I can route through secondary protocols, but it'll take time."

Li's targeting system displayed similar alerts. "Targeting solution degraded. Jamming affecting our laser designation." She patched in commands quickly. "I can get us back online, but accuracy will drop to seventy percent."

Gill appeared at Coop's side, uniform torn. "Zodark forces advancing to encircle Alpha Company. Nobunaga reports they're cut off from extraction." He pointed to movement on their flank. "And we've got company approaching this position. My platoon can hold them, but not indefinitely."

Coop made his decision, drawing on the training he'd received in the 1st Special Tactics Wing. "Crawford, switch to narrowband frequency-hopping transmission. Li, we're going to manual targeting. Weber, disconnect from the network and run independent calculations." He pulled out his backup laser designator, an older model without the sophisticated electronics that could be jammed. "Sometimes the old ways work best."

The modified approach worked. Using manual methods and simplified protocols, they bypassed the Zodark jamming. The situation remained dire. With Alpha Company surrounded, Gill's platoon engaged with enemies threatening their position, communication unreliable at best.

"Got a clear signal!" Crawford announced. "Reaper Six-Four acknowledges. They're moving into position."

Weber nodded, his system stabilizing. "Targeting matrix reconfigured. I've isolated our systems from the compromised network."

Li maintained focus on her targeting systems. "Solution stable. I've identified the primary jamming source. That building there." She highlighted a structure near the facility's communications array.

Nobunaga's voice broke through the static, "Alpha-Actual to TASC. We're consolidating but can't break their encirclement. Need immediate fire support on all marked positions for extraction corridor."

Coop developed a comprehensive plan, prioritizing targets that would neutralize immediate threats and disable Zodark coordination. "Crawford, get me everything. Reaper strikes here, gunships on the communications array, artillery support for these sectors." He marked each location precisely. "Weber, I need perfect timing. Sequential detonation to create a moving wall of suppression."

Republic ordnance rained down on designated targets as Alpha Company seized the opportunity to break the encirclement. Nobunaga led his forces through the gap Coop had engineered, moving toward extraction while maintaining a disciplined fighting withdrawal.

"It's working!" Li called out, monitoring Alpha Company's progress.

Weber's system emitted a high-pitched warning. "Incoming! Multiple fast-movers from the north! Signature matches Zodark Zeek fighters. At least six, moving at treetop level."

Gill sprinted to their position. "Enemy reinforcements have breached our eastern perimeter. We're cut off from planned extraction." Explosions almost drowned out his words as Zodark mortars began walking in on their position. "We've got wounded and can't hold much longer."

Crawford's face went pale. "Reaper Six-Four is engaging the Zeeks, but…" A massive explosion lit the sky as the Republic drone disappeared from their tactical display. "We've lost our air support."

The ground shook as a mortar round impacted thirty meters away, showering them with debris. Three of Gill's soldiers went down.

Coop's screen flashed with a priority message. "Alpha-Actual to all elements. Massive enemy force approaching from south. Full Zodark battle regiment with armored support. All Republic elements, execute emergency evacuation plan Delta. I say again, implement Delta immediately."

Another explosion, closer this time, knocked out half their remaining systems. Li was thrown backward, blood streaming from her forehead. Weber frantically tried to salvage what targeting capability remained.

"Sir!" Crawford shouted over the barrage. "Nobunaga's position is being overrun! Alpha Company can't reach primary extraction!"

Through smoke and debris, Zodark troops advanced, using the rocky terrain for cover.

Gill dropped beside Coop, blood soaking his left sleeve. "One option left." He pointed to a narrow ravine cutting west. "Secondary extraction point two kilometers that way, but we'd be completely exposed for the first five hundred meters."

Weber's voice tightened. "Enemy armored vehicles approaching from north and east. Speeders, too. We're surrounded on three sides."

Crawford tried to establish communications with any available support as Li struggled to her feet despite her injury. Weber worked like a madman to maintain what systems remained operational. Gill's platoon was down to less than half strength, the wounded requiring immediate evacuation.

The decision point had arrived. Stay and fight a losing battle, or risk everything on a desperate dash across open terrain. Either way, people would die.

A thunderous explosion obliterated their eastern perimeter. Through smoke and flames, the massive silhouette of a Zodark vehicle emerged.

"Incoming!" Weber screamed.

The world erupted in blinding light.

Chapter 31:
Something from Nothing

Year 2098
Rass Moon PTX-419
Nightfall

Coop woke to Vega slapping his face. Not the gentle kind of slap either. The hard, wake-the-hell-up kind that left his cheek stinging.

"Wake up! We've got a window!" The sniper's face was blackened with soot. A makeshift bandage was wrapped around her right arm. Blood had seeped through in places, forming rusty patterns against the dirty fabric. During the evacuation, she'd obviously descended from her elevated position to join their desperate retreat.

The blinding light hadn't been death. It was salvation. Republic linebackers and bobcats, light and medium tactical vehicles, had appeared through the dense smog as they unleashed a barrage against the enemy. A Zodark vehicle erupted into flames not twenty meters from where Coop had been lying. The heat washed over him in a wave, making his skin prickle.

"Can you move?" Vega asked, reaching for Coop's tactical vest.

Coop nodded, his throat too dry for words. He pushed himself up, ignoring the sharp pain in his side. Probably a cracked rib. Maybe two. The world spun briefly before settling into focus.

"Let's move!" she said.

In the span of two hours, the remnants of Gill's platoon had established a defensive perimeter in a cave system one kilometer from their previous position. Bodies lay on improvised stretchers. Some moaning, others still. Li sat propped against a rock wall, Crawford tending to the gash on her forehead. Weber hunched over their remaining equipment, trying to salvage what he could.

Republic command had launched a counteroffensive after their extraction. The secondary extraction point had been compromised, but they'd managed to find these caves. They'd been dark for almost two hours, conserving power and staying off comms to avoid detection.

"Alpha Company?" Coop asked, his voice coming out as a rasp.

Captain Gill approached, his uniform torn and dirty, face covered with grime. "Nobunaga made it out with sixty percent of his force. They've regrouped with Bravo Company north of the facility." Gill's expression hardened. "Command says this fight isn't over. They're prioritizing us for immediate reinforcement."

Coop took a canteen from Vega and drank deeply. The lukewarm water tasted better than any beer he'd ever had. "What about the mission objectives?"

"Partially complete," Gill replied. "The infiltration team managed to upload the malware to the communications facility's subsystems during our diversionary attack, but the Zodarks' primary server farm, located deep in a nearby complex, remains operational. The malware needs both systems compromised to fully cripple their network."

"So we're not done."

"Not by a long shot."

An hour later, at 0800 hours, Coop could see the state of their makeshift command post. Their equipment had been reassembled into a functional, if jury-rigged, targeting system. Weber had somehow integrated parts from damaged components to create a functional hybrid. Coop was starting to see that the man had a gift for making something from nothing.

"We've got communications back," Crawford announced, adjusting the makeshift antenna constructed from debris and spare parts. "Battalion Command is on channel four."

Coop took the headset, wincing as he stretched his arm. "Coop here. Alpha Company TASC elements operational, limited capacity."

Captain Hogan, the Battalion fire support officer, came through on the command channel, surprisingly clear. "Glad you're still kicking. Situation has evolved. The Zodark force that ambushed you was only their forward element. We've identified their primary command center deeper in the facility. Our infiltration team managed to plant the malware in their secondary systems, but we need to neutralize their primary server farm to complete the mission."

The mission objectives scrolled across Coop's repaired tablet. A new assault, now with three full companies, targeted the heart of the Zodark installation. This was a regroup for a knockout punch.

"Your TASC team is being reassigned to coordinate fire support for the main assault," Hogan continued. "Vega's sniper skills will be critical for eliminating their forward observers. Extraction team is inbound to your position. ETA fifteen minutes. Hogan, out."

Li walked over to Coop, her forehead now properly bandaged. "Sir, we've got something." She handed him her datapad, showing thermal imagery of massive Zodark reinforcements amassing beyond the ridge line. "They're staging for a counterattack."

Coop studied the imagery. At least a battalion-strength force, with heavy armor support. "They're not giving up this facility without a fight."

"Would you?" Vega asked, checking her rifle scope for damage.

"No," Coop admitted. "But I'd be smarter about it."

Gill joined them, examining the thermal imagery. "I agree."

"Their strength is numbers," Coop added. "They'll throw everything they have at us."

"Then we'd better be ready," Gill said. "Extraction team is five minutes out. Get your gear together."

At 0841 hours, a Republic Osprey deposited Coop's team at the forward headquarters of Major Short's 12th Battalion. It sat in a natural depression reinforced with prefabricated barriers and camouflage netting.

The heart of the operation centered around a mobile command vehicle. A six-wheeled armored platform with extended communications arrays and satellite uplinks protruding from its roof.

Surrounding the command vehicle, a dozen ruggedized field terminals had been set up under lightweight canopies, each staffed by communications specialists wearing headsets. Red, blue, and green status lights blinked across their equipment as they coordinated between scattered company positions. Tactical overlays showed friendly positions and enemy concentrations from Republic surveillance drones and forward observers.

"Welcome to the real party," Short said, greeting them as they disembarked. The major was a stocky man with gray hair and gray eyes that had seen too much war. "We thought we lost you back there."

"Almost did," Coop replied, stepping off the ramp. His ribs protested with each movement.

A captain led them to a holographic display showing the entire battlespace. "The Zodarks thought they had us on the run, but they overextended. While their main force was hunting you and Alpha

Company, our special operations teams breached their southern perimeter." She highlighted yellow markers inside the facility. "The malware is already disrupting their automated defense systems and communications."

Captain Nobunaga approached, his normally immaculate uniform now battle-worn. "Good to see you made it, Coop." He nodded to the rest of the team. "Your fire support saved what was left of Alpha Company. We're reorganized and ready for the next phase."

Hogan pointed to a heavily fortified structure near the Zodark complex, about two kilometers deeper than the communications facility they had initially targeted. "That's our primary target. Their central server farm. It's connected to the communications facility we hit earlier, but better protected. Just west of the comm station we inserted the malware into. Take this out, and the malware completes its work by propagating through both systems. The entire Zodark command-and-control network for this sector goes down."

Coop studied the approach vectors. Heavy Zodark emplacements surrounded the target, including multiple anti-aircraft missile batteries that could tear apart anything that flew within their range. "Traditional air support won't work. Those defenses are too concentrated."

"That's why we need your team," Hogan replied. "You're going to coordinate something special." He nodded to a communications officer, who pulled up specs for an orbital artillery platform. "The RNS *Bennington* is moving into position. You'll be coordinating precision orbital strikes."

"How soon can we deploy?" Coop asked.

"The *Bennington* will be in optimal position in two hours," Hogan replied. "That gives you time to get your team in place and designate targets."

"What about the malware we already uploaded at the comm facility?" Li asked. "Won't destroying the server farm wipe out that work?"

"Negative," Hogan explained. "The targeting software has been designed to maintain the malware's integrity. The orbital strikes will physically damage the servers but leave just enough infrastructure intact for our code to spread throughout their entire network. It's like cutting off the head while letting the poison finish the job."

At 1017 hours, the assault began with a massive artillery barrage from Republic positions. The TASC team, now restocked with fresh equipment, advanced with Delta Company's second platoon. Vega moved ahead with a scout team, her sniper rifle picking off Zodark spotters before they could call in counterbattery fire. Each shot was followed by the crack of her high-powered rifle, a sound that had become strangely comforting to Coop.

"Target designator operational," Weber confirmed as they reached their assigned observation post overlooking the facility's main entrance. "Full connectivity with *Bennington* established."

"Four Zodark missile batteries identified," Li reported, highlighting the missile launchers on their display. "Each with full ammunition load. Thermal signatures indicate they're armed and ready to fire."

Vega's voice burst through their comms. "I've got eyes on the southeastern battery. Commander's in the open. Permission to engage?"

"Negative," Coop replied. "Those batteries are priority targets for orbital strike. Stay concealed until the bombardment begins."

Republic infantry advanced in coordinated waves, using a small woodland with thin trees for cover. The Zodark defenders responded, their automated turrets targeting any movement. Captain Nobunaga led Alpha Company's remnants along the eastern approach, his troops moving from cover to cover.

"All companies in position," Crawford reported. "Hogan requests immediate fire support on the outer defenses."

Coop marked the priority targets on his display, drawing on his TASC training to coordinate between the Republic Army forces on the ground and the Republic Navy vessel in orbit. "Crawford, get me a direct line to the *Bennington* fire control center. Weber, I need targeting solutions for all four missile batteries. Li, monitor for any Zodark reinforcements."

The orbital artillery platform acknowledged Coop's transmission. "*Bennington*-Actual to ground TASC. We have your designated targets. Ready for fire mission."

Chapter 32:
When Stars Welcome Warriors

Year 2098
Borrowed Time
Middle Reach
Sector 8

The *Borrowed Time* carved a trajectory through the starfield. Lieutenant Tim Hastings guided the Osprey transport like he always did, rather easily. Through the forward viewport, the ice asteroid loomed larger with smaller asteroids floating in front of it and along the flight path. Their big target—a crystalline mass pockmarked with the geometric structures of the Zodark FOB. Weapon emplacements dotted its surface like metallic parasites embedded in frozen flesh.

What had once been pristine ice now resembled a drunkard's attempt at sculpture. Perfect strikes from the joint Republic and Primord fleet had hammered the surface, leaving craters and fissures.

"Four minutes to deployment zone," Lieutenant Amanda Day announced from the copilot's seat. She monitored the stream of holographic data flowing across the monitors on the cockpit's dashboard. "Armor integrity at ninety-eight percent. Detecting targeting systems from remaining base defenses, operating at reduced capacity. Approximately thirteen percent functionality after the initial strikes."

Hastings barely nodded. He adjusted their approach vector with a slight tilt of his wrist. Another day, another mission. *Safe, controlled, by the book.* The familiar numbness settled over him like his sheepskin blanket when he was a kid—comfortable and expected. Three other Ospreys flanked their position, each carrying their own complement of Army Special Forces. He registered their positions on his tactical display and forced himself not to think beyond that.

The ice asteroid came into focus, and Hastings forced his breathing to steady.

"Zodark vessels continuing to converge," Day said, highlighting four enemy signatures accelerating toward their position. "ETA three minutes, thirty seconds."

"Just enough time to drop our cargo and get the hell out," Hastings remarked.

A volley from the Zodark ships lanced through space as bright streams of energy. Hastings weaved through with expertise. The *Borrowed Time* shuddered as a glancing shot caught its rear quadrant. He compensated without comment, banking hard to port and rolling beneath a second barrage.

"Armor at ninety-two percent," Day reported as she tapped across emergency systems. "Aquila Three is taking heavy fire. Multiple hits."

Aquila Three's port thruster erupted into a shower of debris. The transport began to spin, its pilot fighting desperately for control.

The comms channel crackled. "Aquila-Actual to all Aquila elements, accelerate to drop coordinates!"

"Deployment zone in ninety seconds," Day announced, redirecting auxiliary power to their forward engines. "Armor integrity holding. Temperature nominal." She glanced at Hastings, who maintained his focus on navigating the increasingly dense field of laser fire. Another near miss rocked their craft.

"Deploy countermeasures, Day."

She complied. "Deploying countermeasures."

Hastings successfully evaded a near hit. It'd become second nature after years in the cockpit.

A laser sliced past their starboard, close enough that the cockpit momentarily lit up with its reflected glow.

"That was too damn close," Day said.

Hastings didn't respond. His attention narrowed to the task at hand—keeping sixty-four soldiers alive long enough to reach the drop zone. Not for glory or some misplaced sense of patriotism, but because it was the job.

A concentrated barrage from three Zodark vessels forced Hastings into a spiraling dive beneath the main approach vector. He rolled inverted, using one of the smaller ice asteroids as cover while maintaining their inbound trajectory toward the main target.

"Sixty seconds out," Day called, monitoring their approach. "Aquila Two reports heavy resistance at the primary drop zone."

Hastings pulled out of the dive, realigning with their target coordinates.

"Thirty seconds to drop," Day said. "All systems green for deployment."

Hastings made a final course correction, lining up their approach vector with the designated coordinates. "Ten seconds. Initiating hover protocol."

Time seemed to stop for the next nine seconds.

"Deployment zone reached. Initiating drop sequence," Day announced, activating the cabin depressurization protocol. Behind the sealed cockpit door, red warning lights bathed the troop cabin as the soldiers prepared for vacuum exposure.

Hastings rolled the *Borrowed Time* into position, firing reverse thrusters to brake their forward momentum. A Zodark energy blast seared past the port side, forcing him to adjust with a sharp burst from the starboard thrusters.

"Maintaining position," he said through gritted teeth, fighting the controls as debris from nearby impacts buffeted their hull. The asteroid's rotation created a constant drift, requiring continuous microcorrections to his thruster output.

Hastings allowed himself a brief glance at the rear camera feed—the Special Forces troops were sixty-four men and women in specialized battlesuits, weapons secured and jump packs primed. Their helmets reflected the emergency lighting, faces hidden behind polarized visors.

"Ramp deploying in three… two… one…" Day's countdown ended as the rear of the ship yawned open to the void. The cabin had depressurized over the previous ninety seconds, and now the soldiers moved to the ramp edge.

"Green light! Go, go, go!" Day transmitted to the troop bay.

The soldiers launched in sequence, two per second in tight intervals. Their boot propulsion systems ignited in controlled bursts as they vectored toward the enemy FOB's surface one thousand meters below.

The deployment took forty-five seconds, which was longer than usual. Hastings fought to maintain position under increasingly heavy fire. He glanced again at the external feed, watching the troops descend in formation.

Then he saw the energy bolt.

One of the soldiers—midway through his descent—suddenly jerked sideways. The energy blast caught him center mass, and his suit immediately began venting atmosphere.

Hastings's hands tightened on the controls. The soldier tumbled away from formation, struggling to stabilize.

That's it. He's gone, Hastings realized. *There's no medic down there, no backup—just enemy fire and vacuum.*

The suit breach meant maybe three minutes of life support, if the soldier was lucky. He felt that familiar guilt rising again. *Another soldier dying because the intel was wrong, because someone missed something, because—*

"Last trooper away!" Day announced.

Hastings stared at the tactical display, watching the wounded soldier's suit signature flicker. Three seconds. Four. The Zodark targeting systems were locking on to their position, but he couldn't—

"Hastings!" Day's sharp voice cut through his paralysis. "We need to go. Now!"

He snapped back to the cockpit, his hands moving automatically to the controls.

On the tactical display, Aquila Three finally stabilized, deploying its troops despite substantial damage to its hull. The other Ospreys had completed their drops twenty seconds ago, immediately banking hard to begin their retreat.

"All units deployed," Day confirmed. "Initiating return vector."

Hastings hesitated for a split second longer, his instincts wanting to circle back, to help the dying trooper somehow. But protocol demanded immediate withdrawal.

"Time to punch out, Lieutenant," Day said.

Hastings nodded. "*Borrowed Time* to Aquila-Actual. Troops away, beginning withdrawal."

"Intel was off again," he said under his breath to Lieutenant Day. A few defensive platforms on the Zodark FOB weren't in the briefing.

Day glanced at him but didn't respond.

Hastings flew *Borrowed Time* toward the *Idaho*, the ship like a mother welcoming everyone home. For Hastings, though, it was a mom with too many responsibilities, too many kids to keep track of, and with too many responsibilities, mistakes happened, especially with important tactical information.

His hands remained tense on the controls as they climbed away from the drop zone. *That soldier—whoever he was—he's down because the intelligence missed something. Again.*

"*Argo* to all elements. We've sustained heavy damage to port-side armor plating! Maintaining defensive position." Captain Horn's voice came through the channel.

The Republic cruiser positioned itself between the troops heading toward the Zodark FOB, and the incoming Zodark vessels. Its reinforced hull absorbed punishment, and punishment meant for the smaller targets. The RNS *Argo*'s flank exploded in an eruption of metal as concentrated energy weapons fire compromised the outer armor.

"She's buying us, and everyone else, time," Day said.

Hastings executed a forty-degree roll to port, avoiding a targeting solution from the nearest Zodark vessel. He fired the starboard thrusters, pivoting the craft away from the drop zone as mission protocol dictated.

The weight of another perfect, safe mission settled on his shoulders. Perfect execution, and yet, more wounded soldiers.

As they approached the *Idaho*'s hangar bay, Hastings found himself already running through the extraction mission parameters in his head. *Next time, maybe I verify the landing zone myself instead of trusting the reports.*

The *Borrowed Time* settled into the *Idaho*'s hangar bay. Deck crews approached before the drives had fully spooled down: technical specialists with diagnostic equipment, maintenance personnel with repair apparatus, and ordnance technicians to replenish defensive systems.

"Fuel at sixty-eight percent capacity," Day reported as she executed the shutdown sequence. "Port armor compromised in sections six and seven. Starboard point-defense system showing thermal saturation in the primary emitter."

Hastings acknowledged with a nod, completing his postflight checklist. But for the first time since Intus, following protocol felt different. Heavier. Maybe he could have done it better. Maybe he could have held his position in the void at the extraction point another five seconds before every soldier jumped out of his bird, and maybe that soldier would have survived.

"What's the estimated timeline for ground force extraction?" he asked.

Day consulted the operational timeline. "One hour, maybe sooner, assuming the operation proceeds according to mission parameters."

An hour won't come soon enough, he thought. Hastings unstrapped his safety harness and stood. The transition from zero-g operations to ship gravity seemed unusually noticeable.

"I'll remain on standby status," he said. "Notify me immediately when extraction operations are green-lit."

"Yes, sir," Day replied, making a note on her checklist. "Flight Operations has confirmed we're primary for extraction duty. Same crew, same bird, per standard mission continuity protocols."

Hastings nodded. That was how it should be—the same pilots who brought them in should bring them home.

"Lieutenant Hastings." Lieutenant Day lowered her checklist. "We need to talk. Five minutes. This isn't optional."

Chapter 33:
Calling Down the Storm

Year 2098
Rass Moon PTX-419
Nightfall

Coop studied the Zodark positions through his enhanced optics. The batteries had been cleverly placed to provide converging fire zones. Their operators waited for Republic forces to commit to the attack before revealing their full firepower. Smart. Dangerous. The kind of setup that had chewed through countless Republic assaults in the past.

"*Bennington*," Coop transmitted. "Priority target follows." He designated the southeastern battery. "Requesting precision kinetic strike, grid four-four-eight-seven-eight-tree. Fire when ready."

"*Bennington* copies all. Kinetic round loaded. Firing solution computed. Stand by for impact, over."

Coop switched channels. "All elements, be advised. Orbital strike inbound, southeastern quadrant."

The Zodark battery commander never saw it coming. A tungsten round, accelerated to hypersonic velocity, punched through the atmosphere with a supersonic crack, splitting the air like thunder. It struck the battery's ammunition storage, creating a blinding explosion. Shattered trees were flung skyward, their burning remnants raining down across the battlefield. The concussion wave flattened the sparse vegetation for hundreds of meters in every direction.

"Direct hit!" Weber confirmed as the shock wave reached their position, rattling Coop and vibrating the ground beneath them. The distant crater glowed red-hot, belching a column of black smoke rising like an angry fist into Nightfall's sky. Around them, small stones and debris fell. "Target destroyed!"

The Zodarks reacted immediately. Their remaining batteries swiveled to fire blindly at potential Republic positions. Panic. Disorganization. Exactly what they needed. Coop marked each launcher in sequence, calling in strikes and reducing them to smoking craters.

"Hogan is requesting we shift fire to the main entrance," Crawford reported. "Republic forces are ready to breach."

Vega's voice cut through the comm chatter. "I've got a target of opportunity. Zodark battalion commander and his staff, exposed position on the northwest bunker. Range one thousand, two hundred meters."

Coop didn't hesitate. "Take the shot."

The crack of Vega's long-range precision rifle echoed across the battlefield. Through his optics, Coop watched the Zodark commander collapse. Three more shots followed in rapid succession, eliminating the remaining officers before they could reach cover. Clean. Professional. The kind of shooting that had made Vega's reputation as one of the best.

Coop swept his optics across the battlefield. The once orderly Zodark positions had transformed into destruction. Blue bodies lay scattered and broken where precision fire had found them. An alien crawled toward cover, leaving a trail of blood across scorched earth. Near their observation post, a dead Zodark scout lay sprawled unnaturally, half of its head missing from a defensive shot Crawford had made earlier. The beast's blood had congealed into something resembling motor oil, attracting native insects swarming over the corpse.

Coop swallowed hard, pushing down the bile moving up his throat. This wasn't like the clinical distance during his previous role as a Navy pilot. No. This was immediate, hellish, and overwhelmingly real. Death was everywhere, and he could smell it.

"All targets neutralized," Vega reported with that calm she carried herself with. "Zodark command structure compromised."

"Outstanding," Coop said. He scanned the battlefield again, watching Republic forces advance through the gaps created by the orbital strikes. "Weber, mark secondary targets along the western approach. Li, I need updated positions on all Republic elements."

"On it, sir," Weber replied, his eyes on his display. "Marking three hardened bunkers and what looks like a vehicle depot."

Li spoke up. "Alpha Company advancing on grid four-five-two-seven-eight-zero. Bravo holding position at four-four-seven-seven-eight-five. Delta moving to support from the north."

Coop nodded, processing the information. The tactical picture was coming together. With the anti-aircraft batteries neutralized, they could bring in more direct air support. "Crawford, get me a line to Phantom Squadron. Tell them we've cleared the AA defenses in the southeastern quadrant."

"Copy that," Crawford replied, adjusting his communications gear. "Patching you through now."

With the batteries eliminated, the Republic infantry surged forward. Alpha and Bravo Companies breached the outer perimeter, engaging the Zodark defenders in close-quarters combat. Delta Company established firing positions on the high ground, their heavy weapons suppressing enemy movements.

From Coop's vantage point, he noticed a new element moving into position. Two squads of C100 combat Synths advanced toward the most heavily defended Zodark position. They moved with remarkable speed through the battlefield debris. Unlike the human troops taking cover or advancing in irregular patterns, the C100s marched forward in perfect formation.

"They finally deployed them," Weber commented, motioning toward the Synths.

The C100s reached the edge of the Zodark defensive line and split into attack formations without a word exchanged between them. When the Zodark warriors emerged with their signature swords, Coop expected the machines to fall back. Instead, the C100s engaged directly, their integrated weapon systems on one arm firing with ridiculous accuracy while their articulated hands on the opposite arm caught and deflected the blades.

"Whoa," Coop muttered as a C100 took a direct hit from a sword slicing clean through its shoulder joint. The damaged Synth continued fighting without hesitation, using its remaining arm to literally tear a Zodark warrior in half with a clean shot. "Those toasters are something else."

"Terminators," Li corrected with something like admiration in her voice. "Infantry calls 'em that."

Two more C100s fell as Zodarks blasted them apart, but the remaining Synths pressed onward relentlessly, creating a breach in the Zodark line that human soldiers immediately exploited.

"Multiple Zodark vehicles deploying from the main hangar. We got speeders and heavy vehicles," Li warned, shifting her attention back to the tactical display. "Eight… no, ten moving to defensive positions."

Coop watched through his optics as the Zodark vehicles emerged from concealed bays. Fast-attack speeders, flanked by heavier armored vehicles. The kind of firepower that could hinder the Republic advance.

"We need support on those… those speeders are fast. Right now, they're standing pat, don't know why. Guess waiting for further orders? Gonna eliminate them and the heavies," Coop decided. He switched to the artillery frequency, connecting directly to the Republic Army's 120th Field Artillery Brigade positioned ninety kilometers away. "Ghost Element One-Four. Stand by for fire mission. How copy?"

"Ghost One-Four. Ready for fire mission. Send it." The artillery officer's response was immediate, eager.

"Multiple targets identified, Zodark heavy and light tactical vehicles, coordinates and image attached. Requesting fire for effect, high-explosive. Danger close to friendly forces."

"That's a good copy. Coordinates and image received. Stand by for fire mission. Ghost One-Four will commence fire for effect in thirty seconds."

Coop called Nobunaga. "Alpha-Actual, be advised. Danger-close artillery inbound. Get your people under cover."

"Copy that. Taking cover now." Nobunaga replied. "Make it count."

"Always do."

The first artillery rounds screamed in fifteen seconds later, detonating with thunderous precision among the Zodark speeders shooting at Republic forces, most likely getting ready to advance and spread out. Too late. The Zodark warriors and tactical vehicles around them vanished in blossoming flowers of fire and shrapnel. The sequential impacts created a hellscape of secondary explosions as ammunition and fuel cells ignited, sending alien bodies and mechanical parts cartwheeling through the air. Coop's position quaked with each detonation.

"Direct hits on multiple targets," Crawford confirmed, watching the destruction through their sensors. "Zodark speeder and armor contingent at sixty percent and falling."

"Confirm when destroyed," the artillery commander's voice came through. "If successful, conduct follow-on strikes to eliminate remaining targets."

Coop continued directing the artillery barrage, eliminating the Zodark heavy armor. Each precise strike weakened the enemy's defensive capability until the last of them blew to hell and back.

"All Zodark armor neutralized," Weber announced. "Artillery's effect on target is outstanding."

"Damn, sir," Crawford said with admiration. "Battalion artillery just gave us a personal shout-out on the command channel. Said your TASC fire direction is 'textbook perfect.'"

Coop allowed himself a small smile—his training in the 1st Special Tactics Wing was paying off in real combat. "Tell them thanks, but we're not done yet." He turned to Li. "What's the status on the Republic advance?"

"Alpha Company has secured the outer perimeter. Bravo is moving to support. Delta is providing covering fire from elevated positions." Li's fingers worked fast across her tablet, updating the tactical display. "Casualties are moderate but within acceptable parameters."

"Weber, I need targeting solutions on those secondary defensive positions. The ones with the heavy blaster emplacements." Coop pointed to three hardened bunkers that were still pouring fire onto the advancing Republic troops.

"On it," Weber replied, already inputting the coordinates.

"Markers updated," Li said. "Republic forces advancing on all fronts."

Coop shifted his attention back to the C100 squads he'd been monitoring. Of the thirty that had initiated the assault, only eleven remained operational. The rest lay scattered across the battlefield in various states of destruction. some still attempting to drag themselves forward despite catastrophic damage. One C100, its legs completely severed at the hip joints, continued to provide covering fire from its back, its weapon systems still functioning.

"The C100s have breached the command bunker entrance," Crawford announced.

Coop stood, mesmerized, as the remaining combat Synths formed a perfect semicircle at the bunker entrance. Three Zodarks charged from the doorway. The lead C100 stepped forward to meet them. A Zodark blade sliced clean through its chest cavity, but the Synth didn't fall. Instead, it grasped the warrior's head with its articulated hand and crushed it with a single squeeze, blue ichor spraying across its metallic chest.

The remaining C100s hurried into the bunker. Weapons fire erupted from within.

"Republic infantry teams report C100s have cleared the primary corridor," Li reported. "Human elements moving in behind them."

Coop felt a conflicted admiration for the machines. They were efficient killing platforms, yes, but there was something almost brave about their relentless advance. The way they sacrificed themselves without hesitation for the mission objective reminded him of the most dedicated human soldiers he'd heard about, like the Delta operative, Brian Royce. Fearless. Strong. For a moment, all contradictory thoughts about these toasters, these C100s, melted away.

Hours and hours into the renewed assault, the Republic forces had secured most of the Zodark facility's outer defenses. The malware, working its way through their systems, had disabled major sections of their automated defenses. Zodark infantry fought tenaciously for every corridor and room, but the momentum had decisively shifted.

"Republic engineers have breached the main server complex," Crawford said. "Special operations team is moving to secure the primary objective."

Vega had rejoined the TASC team, her sniper rifle slung across her back. "Zodark snipers eliminated along the western approach. Delta company is advancing without opposition."

"Good work," Coop said, nodding to Vega. Her uniform was torn and dirty, but her eyes were clear and focused. "Any sign of counterattack forces?"

"Nothing significant," she replied. "Mostly scattered resistance. Their coordination is breaking down."

Hogan's voice chimed in through the command channel. "All elements, be advised. We've detected Zodark forces attempting to purge their systems. We need to accelerate our timeline. TASC team, I need you to coordinate a final strike on their backup generator complex."

Li highlighted the target on their display. "Backup power facility identified. Underground structure, heavily reinforced. Standard munitions won't penetrate."

"I have something that will," Coop replied. He established connection with the *Bennington*. "Requesting magrail kinetic strike on grid four-tree-seven-niner-six-four. Target is hardened underground facility, estimated fifteen meters below surface."

"Copy. Hypervelocity penetrator authorized. Charging magrail systems. Be advised, minimum safe distance is eight hundred meters from target."

"All Republic forces," Coop broadcast. "Orbital magrail strike inbound on grid four-tree-seven-niner-six-four. Minimum safe distance eight hundred meters. I say again, clear the area immediately."

Republic forces pulled back from the target area. The tactical display showed blue markers retreating to safe positions. When the last unit confirmed they were clear, Coop gave the authorization.

"*Bennington*, all forces clear. You are cleared hot."

"Roger that. Magrail firing sequence initiated. Impact in ten seconds."

Coop instinctively braced himself, though they were well beyond the danger zone. The hair on his arms stood up as the atmosphere itself seemed to charge with electricity. Then a blinding streak of light tore through the sky. A magrail rod superheated to plasma temperatures as it punched through the atmosphere at thirty times the speed of sound.

There was a heartbeat of absolute silence after impact. Then the world exploded.

The ground beneath Coop's feet bucked like a living thing. He staggered, nearly falling as a shock wave of displaced air hammered outward from the impact zone. The sound came a split second later. Something deep. Primal. A sound like the planet itself crying out in pain. It hit Coop's chest like a roundhouse kick, making his ribs vibrate and his lungs compress.

Through Coop's tactical display, the Zodark facility simply ceased to exist. The hypervelocity round had transferred so much kinetic energy that the underground complex collapsed in on itself, creating a near-perfect circular crater two hundred meters wide. Just absolute devastation as millions of tons of earth and reinforced structure imploded. The ground around the impact rippled like water, concentric waves of soil and rock radiating outward before settling.

"Holy mother of all that's holy," Weber whispered beside Coop.

Li's screen showed temperature readings off the scale at the impact site. "The kinetic transfer superheated everything within fifty meters of impact. That's… that's not just structural damage. Everything down there has been vaporized."

Coop felt a strange mixture of awe and dread settle in his stomach. He'd called in heavy ordnance before from the sim pod's cockpit as a pilot, but nothing like this, nothing this big, nothing this… devastating in his new role as a TASC. Yes, he'd called in tungsten rounds a few times—magrail rounds—but for some reason, this one hit harder than the rest. It made him momentarily lightheaded. The screeches of the wounded carried across the battlefield, punctuated by the persistent crack of small arms fire where pockets of Zodark resistance continued. A Republic soldier stumbled past their position, his face coated in blood and soot, eyes wide with a thousand-yard stare. This was different from his previous Navy assignments watching feeds on a monitor thousands of kilometers away. Here, death had weight, substance, smell. He could taste copper in his mouth, though he wasn't wounded himself.

"*Bennington* confirms effects on target," Crawford said. "Target destroyed. Malware completion at ninety-eight percent and climbing."

"All units, this is Command," Hogan's voice bellowed over the stunned silence. "Confirm total destruction of Zodark backup systems. Orbital telemetry shows no surviving infrastructure. Well done, TASC."

Coop swallowed hard, his mouth suddenly dry. "Copy that, Command. Target neutralized."

As the dust cloud billowed upward from what had once been a hardened military installation, Coop couldn't help but think of the ancient tales of gods hurling thunderbolts from the heavens. Except this wasn't myth. This was the reality of modern warfare, where a man with a targeting system could call down devastation that would have been unimaginable even a century ago.

He shook his head subtly, focusing on the mission parameters rather than the philosophical implications. They'd accomplished their objective. The Zodark command infrastructure was crippled.

"This is Special Operations Team Leader," a new voice announced on the secure channel. "Primary objective secured. Malware upload at ninety-nine percent. Zodark systems are falling offline across the sector."

A second later, the battalion communications officer said, "All units, be advised. Primary objective secured. Malware integration complete. Full mission success confirmed."

Coop exhaled slowly, feeling the tension drain from his shoulders. They'd done it. The mission was a success. The Zodark communication network in this sector would be compromised, giving Republic forces a critical advantage in the upcoming Rass invasion. This moon was no longer a risk.

"Good work, team," he said, looking at Weber, Crawford, Li, and Vega. "Let's finish this up and get ready for extraction."

The remaining Zodark forces, cut off from their command structure and with their systems failing, began a disorganized retreat. Almost all of them fought to the last soldier. After so many hours of combat, the Republic had secured the Zodark facility.

Coop's team gathered at the forward command post as Brigadier General Mathis addressed the assembled officers. The man's face showed signs of fatigue, but his eyes were bright with victory.

"The operation is a complete success. The malware has propagated throughout the Zodark network, giving us access to their communications and defense systems across three sectors. Intelligence is already extracting critical data that will help us plan the initial phase of the Rass invasion."

Captain Hogan stood at attention next to Mathis, nodding in agreement. As the Brigade Fire Support Officer, he'd coordinated the TASC elements throughout the operation, reporting directly to the general. His work complete, Hogan caught Coop's eye and gave a subtle nod of appreciation.

Captain Nobunaga walked toward Coop. His uniform was ripped across the arm, and his forearm was covered in blood. Who knew whose blood—maybe a fellow trooper or the captain himself. "Your team saved Alpha Company twice today. We won't forget it."

"Doing what we're trained for… glad it helped, Captain," Coop replied.

"That was some of the best fire support I've ever seen," Nobunaga added. "You've got a gift for this, Cooper."

Coop shrugged. "Just applying what I've learned."

"Practiced response, but I'll take it."

Hogan turned to Coop's team. "It's true. Your element's TASC performance has been nothing short of extraordinary."

Weber, Crawford, and Li stood a little straighter at the praise. Vega merely nodded, her expression unchanged. From what Coop had observed, this seemed typical for Vega. Praise meant little to her compared to mission success.

As the briefing concluded, Coop stepped outside the command post. Light from who knew how many suns in the system brightened the area. Maybe there was one sun. Coop had forgotten to get that intel. At the moment, he didn't care. His team joined him, battered but unbowed by what they'd endured. Of all people, he wanted to see Bear. Wanted to swap war stories, but most importantly, the man made him feel calm sometimes. Just by talking, by chatting, by being around. The laughter was contagious.

Captain Hogan approached Coop's team again. "The Zodarks' entire command infrastructure in this sector has collapsed. Orders just came down from Space Command. We're to return to our ships immediately. Extraction transports inbound, ETA twenty minutes."

"We're pulling out of the system," Coop said.

"Affirmative. The entire battle group," Hogan confirmed.

This was a surgical strike mission, not an occupation. With the Zodark network compromised, the Republic fleet could monitor their activities remotely through the malware they'd planted.

"We did hit and run," Weber said.

"Hit, cripple, and gather intelligence," Hogan corrected. "The Osprey will take you directly to the ships. The *Leahy* breaks orbit at 1800 hours."

Coop looked around. Where was Bear? Sawyer? Hell, Ortiz? Still, he thought about Bear the most. Where was that guy? Probably packing things up, heading to one of the extraction points. He'd see him soon.

He turned to his team. "Pack it up. We're going home."

As they gathered their equipment, Coop took one last look at the battlefield. The smoking ruins of the Zodark facility showed exactly what they'd accomplished. The cost had been high, no doubt. Too many good soldiers wouldn't be making the return trip. But they'd struck a significant blow against the Zodarks, one that would reverberate across multiple sectors. One that would greatly help the Rass invasion.

The distant whir of approaching Ospreys grew louder. Extraction was inbound. Time to go home, or at least back to the ship that served as home for now. Coop shouldered his pack and joined his team. The mission was complete, but the war was far from over. There would be more battles, more calls for fire support, more life-and-death decisions to make.

But for now, they'd won. And sometimes, that had to be enough.

Chapter 34:
Seventeen and Counting

Year 2098
RNS *Poseidon*
Middle Reach
Sector 8

The tactical array monitor flickered as a Zodark frigate adjusted its position within the enemy formation. Lee tracked its movement with practiced eyes. It was attempting to establish a firing position directly on the Osprey's extraction corridor.

Not happening on my watch.

"Sir, Zodark frigate has adjusted course to intercept our extraction lane," Rhom reported.

Lee leaned forward in his command chair. "Time until extraction Ospreys require that vector?"

Sato checked the chronometer on her console. "Two minutes, sir. *Idaho* has launched the Ospreys to extract the teams from the base."

"Target that frigate," Lee ordered without hesitation. "Forward batteries only. We need to keep our flank coverage on the other vessels."

Rhom patched in commands on his tactical console. "Targeting solutions acquired. Magrail batteries one through four have lock. Triple-barreled turbo lasers standing by."

"Fire."

The *Poseidon*'s forward batteries discharged, the massive ship's frame vibrating as electromagnetic accelerators launched kinetic projectiles toward their target.

"Time to impact, one hundred seventeen seconds," Rhom announced, initiating the agonizing wait as the tactical display tracked the rounds hurtling through the void at thirty kilometers per second.

The bridge fell quiet, all eyes fixed on the countdown. Finally, the projectiles struck. The first two rounds compromised the Zodark vessel's outer armor layer. The third punched through with catastrophic force. The fourth penetrated deep into the power distribution grid.

"Direct hit confirmed," Rhom reported as explosions blasted along the enemy ship's hull, the two-minute journey of their rounds culminating in this incredible devastation. "Target's primary power systems critically damaged."

Lee watched the tactical display. The enemy vessel's energy signature fluctuated wildly. "Launch Havoc-II missiles, tubes one and two. Clear that extraction corridor."

"Havoc-II missiles away," Rhom confirmed.

On the main viewscreen, two bright streaks emerged from the *Poseidon*'s vertical launch systems, accelerating toward the wounded Zodark vessel. The frigate's point-defense systems attempted to respond, but with its power grid compromised, the laser countermeasures fired erratically, missing the incoming missiles entirely.

"Impact in five," Rhom counted down from his TAO station. "Four… three… two… one…"

The Havoc-II missiles struck, their armored tips penetrating deep into the vessel before detonating. The first missile ruptured the frigate's inertial dampening core, releasing a catastrophic wave of gravitational feedback through the ship's structural frame. The second missile destabilized the navigation array, creating a chain reaction that tore through the vessel's central spinal conduits, where power, data, and life support were fatally intertwined. With a sudden flare of blinding energy, the frigate's reactor containment failed completely, vaporizing the vessel in a flash that temporarily overwhelmed the viewscreen's filters.

In all truth, it went better than Lee had planned.

"Target neutralized," Rhom said, already shifting targeting priorities. "Three Zodark vessels remain operational near the FOB."

Lee nodded, satisfied. One problem down. "Keep suppressing fire on those remaining vessels. Don't let them near our extraction corridor."

"Captain," Rodriguez called from communications, "incoming tactical update from ground forces via *Idaho* STRATCOM."

Lee activated the secure holographic display at his captain's chair. "Put it through."

The CIC's battle assessment appeared, showing a detailed holographic schematic of the asteroid facility's interior. Green indicators represented Republic forces, red showed Zodark resistance, and yellow highlighted secured objectives. The display updated in real time, fed by data from tactical drones deployed by the ground forces and individual soldiers' helmet cams.

"Sitrep from ground forces," Rodriguez summarized from the encrypted feed. "Alpha—command center secure, data extraction in progress. Bravo—perimeter established. Charlie—heavy contact, requesting fire support. They've accessed the main intelligence repository and are extracting all files on Zodark fleet deployments and communication protocols."

"Casualties?" Lee asked.

"Seventeen KIA, twelve ambulatory WIA, five nonambulatory requiring priority medevac," Rodriguez replied. "Medical teams standing by aboard *Idaho* for immediate care upon extraction."

Every death weighed on him, but Lee kept his focus on the mission. Those seventeen had not died in vain.

Lieutenant Baldry approached with a secured data tablet. "Sir, preliminary SIGINT analysis from the ground team's data extraction."

Lee accepted the tablet, scanning the encoded report. His eyebrows rose slightly as he processed the information. "This confirms the Zodarks were planning to bring a substantial reinforcement fleet to this sector: at least thirty battleships and supporting elements."

"Yes, sir," Baldry confirmed. "If they'd established this as a forward operating base, they would have compromised the entire Rass invasion corridor." He paused to look at his datapad. "Ground team also reports demolition charges being placed at critical structural points throughout the facility. The primary charge is being positioned at the outpost's power core. Detonation timeline is showing T-minus forty-one minutes."

Lee nodded, calculating extraction timelines against the demolition schedule. "Inform Captain Mensah we'll maintain suppressing fire on the remaining Zodark vessels during extraction."

"Captain," Sato said, "long-range drones are tracking hostile reinforcements approaching from the outer system. ETA fifty-nine minutes."

The tactical display showed the red markers of Zodark vessels moving in formation toward their position.

"They won't arrive in time," Lee replied. "But we need to expedite extraction operations. Status of our assets?"

"The Primord vessels have taken position to cover their withdrawal vector," Sato replied. "EW frigates maintaining electronic countermeasures at maximum capacity."

Lee nodded, watching as the holographic display updated with the positions of allied vessels forming a protective screen around their escape corridor. The *Idaho*'s Ospreys had already launched, currently en route to the extraction points on the asteroid's surface. The clock was ticking.

"Sir," Rhom interjected, "ground tactical feed shows intensifying firefights near extraction points Alpha and Charlie at the outpost. Zodark security forces are mounting a coordinated counterattack."

Lee leaned forward, studying the real-time combat footage from the ice asteroid base. Republic soldiers were pinned down by heavy Zodark fire at two of the four extraction zones. The tactical situation was deteriorating rapidly.

"What's the status of our point-defense grid?" Lee asked.

"All systems operational, sir," Rhom replied. "PDGs at ninety-seven percent capacity."

Lee considered his options. Direct fire support was too risky with Republic troops in close proximity to the targets. "Shift our defensive posture. I want all point-defense systems reconfigured for precision ground support. Target Zodark positions within fifty meters of extraction points, but maintain minimum safe distance from our forces."

"Sir, that's not standard protocol for PDGs," Rhom hesitated.

"I'm aware, Lieutenant," Lee said firmly. "But those PDGs can fire with surgical precision when properly calibrated. Make it happen."

"Aye, sir. Reconfiguring targeting parameters now."

The bridge crew worked fast across control panels as they reprogrammed the ship's defensive systems for an offensive role. It wasn't textbook, but Lee had learned long ago that combat rarely followed the textbook.

"Ground force commander sends: 'Primary objectives achieved,'" Rodriguez reported. "'All intelligence data secured. Demolition charges set and timers synchronized at T-minus thirty-five minutes. All units initiating tactical withdrawal to extraction points.'"

"Acknowledged," Lee replied. "Inform ground forces that we're establishing suppressive fire corridors to extraction points Alpha and Charlie."

The main viewscreen shifted to show a tactical overlay of the asteroid facility. Green indicators representing Republic forces were converging on three extraction points while red markers showed Zodark security forces attempting to cut them off.

"Captain Mensah is signaling from the *Idaho*," Rodriguez announced.

The command channel activated, and Captain Mensah's voice filled the bridge. "All Republic vessels, this is *Idaho*. Transition to extraction phase. Maintain suppressive fire on designated targets. Primord vessels will hold containment perimeter. All ships prepare for immediate withdrawal on my mark."

"*Poseidon* acknowledges," Lee responded. "We're reconfiguring point-defense systems to provide precision fire support for extraction points Alpha and Charlie."

There was a brief pause before Mensah replied. "Unconventional, but approved. Make it count, Lee."

"Always do, ma'am," Lee said, allowing himself a small smile.

"PDG targeting solutions locked," Rhom reported. "Ready to engage on your order."

"Fire."

The *Poseidon* shuddered slightly as dozens of 30mm quad-barreled point-defense guns unleashed a barrage of high-explosive rounds toward the asteroid's surface. The projectiles streaked through space, their proximity fuses precisely calibrated.

"Impact in eight seconds," Rhom said, counting down from his console.

On the tactical display, the rounds closed on their targets. This was the dangerous part—threading the needle between providing effective fire support and avoiding friendly casualties. Lee was confident, though. Very confident.

"Ground forces report incoming fire," Rodriguez said. "They're taking cover."

The rounds impacted, detonating just above Zodark positions. The explosive fragmentation pattern created a deadly curtain of shrapnel blasting through the alien forces while sparing Republic troops.

"Direct hits on Zodark positions," Rhom confirmed. "Ground forces report enemy suppressed at extraction point Alpha."

"Maintain fire," Lee ordered. "Shift targeting priority to extraction point Charlie.

"Sir, *Idaho* reports all Ospreys will be at the asteroid in three minutes to touch down at extraction points," Rodriguez announced. "Boarding operations commencing soon."

Lee nodded. "Cease fire on extraction point Charlie."

"Aye, sir."

Lee checked the mission clock. Twenty-six minutes until demolition charges detonated. The margin for error was razor-thin.

"Keep those extraction corridors clear," he ordered. "I want those people home."

Chapter 35:
Buy Them Time

Year 2098
Rass Moon PTX-419
Nightfall

The tension was thick. Lieutenant Lincoln "Bear" Bowman and his fire support team settled into their new position just as the 1st battalion, 504th orbital assault regiment, the Red Devils, began their assault on a Zodark command center. Bravo Company was leading the assault, steadily advancing toward the fortifications protecting it.

"Flores, what's the status on our eyes? We need to see what's happening," Bear asked the team comms specialist.

"Drones up. Check your display," replied Staff Sergeant Christine Flores.

Bear grabbed for his tablet. Video feeds from the aerial drones populated several windows, giving him a bird's-eye view of the battlespace.

"Outstanding, Flores. Establish comms with *Anzac* One and Fire Support Base Falcon and provide our coordinates. Inform Red Devil elements Gun Devil Two is on station and ready for tasking," Bear relayed.

He took in the scene unfolding before them. They needed to alert the heavy cruiser in orbit and the firebase dirtside they were in position.

Dirtside, FSB Falcon provided the division with artillery and local drone support. In orbit, the RNS *Anzac*, a Republic orbital assault transport, would provide the division's orbital strike support. It was up to Bear and the other TASC units to bring the pain and crush whatever the infantry couldn't.

There are few things on the battlefield that the proper application of high explosives can't solve, thought Bear. At least, that was what the instructor at Fort Moore had said.

Checking for nearby friendlies, he saw Gun Devil One and Gun Devil Three were still on the move, relocating after their position had been burned. The Zodarks had started to zero in on the teams responsible for directing the calls for Republic close-air support.

Switching to another drone feed, Bear spotted Alpha Company, Red Devil One, moving into a tree line a few hundred meters to the right of Bravo Company, Captain Shane Walker's unit. Bear's team had been specifically tasked with supporting Walker's unit as they assaulted the command center. It had taken a few hours to maneuver the regiment around the flanks of the heavily fortified position, but they were nearly ready to begin the attack.

I can't believe I gave up flying to do this... damn you, Coop, Bear thought as he glanced up to see the rest of his team getting themselves situated. Part of him enjoyed the more direct role in supporting his Army brethren. The other part of him missed his old job. He also missed the safety of flying a drone and not having to worry about being gored by one of these blue devils.

"Understood, Falcon," Sergeant Kyle Baker said. "We'll have targets for you shortly. Out." Baker was Bear's targeting systems operator. He was a twenty-two-year-old kid—the kind that looked like he should be fixing motorcycles instead of calling air and artillery strikes. But he was solid, with steady hands and a gift for mathematics. He could multitask an artillery strike with an orbital bombardment and time it all to the beats of his favorite rock band.

"We good, Baker?" Bear called out.

"All good. We've got a battery at Falcon on standby, and I just confirmed with *Anzac* we have two turrets assigned to support our AO," Baker reported. He added, "Gunslinger Six confirmed they have a flight of four Reapers coming on station in three minutes: call signs Gunslinger Two-One and Two-Three."

"Good job, Baker," Bear said, praising his newly minted sergeant.

He turned to the rest of his team. "Gun Devil One and Three are still on the move—that means we're it for fire support until they're back on station. Sergeant Reyes, start finding targets and get 'em assigned to Falcon, *Anzac*, or Gunslinger. Flores, keep the drones moving and replacements ready, so we don't lose comms in the middle of a fight. Baker, help Reyes in finding targets and coordinating strikes with Alpha and Bravo Companies as the attack gets underway. Oh, and Sergeant Cox, deploy the perimeter drones and mines. I don't want to get surprised by a Zodark hunter team looking for us." His team set in motion as soon as the orders were given.

The sounds of battle grew as Bear watched the Zodark defenders react to the sudden presence of Republic soldiers appearing where they hadn't been expected. He zoomed in on a few locations, spotting some bunkers and fortified positions. Bear tagged the locations, sending them over to Baker and Reyes to make sure they got targeted.

"Hey, Flores, you got comms with Bravo—Red Devil Two?" Bear asked, not taking his eyes off the display.

Captain Walker's company had taken up positions roughly nine hundred meters from a row of bunkers. Bear liked Walker. The guy was cool as a cucumber under pressure. He was one of the few junior officers who genuinely listened and used his TASC support in the way it was meant to be. Bear appreciated that.

"I can if you need him," replied Staff Sergeant Flores. "His last message said Red Devil Two was holding at phase line Charlie until we give 'em a green light to proceed."

Bear smiled. He turned to Baker. "What's your read on those positions, Baker?"

"I've tagged what looks like four defensive positions, approximately nine hundred meters to RD Two's nine o'clock position. I'm labeling this Zulu One. I have three larger fortified structures of some sort approximately four hundred meters further behind Zulu One that I'm labeling Zulu Two," explained Baker. "I've also got a third set of targets with another three positions, located eleven hundred meters in front of RD Two at their two o'clock position that I've labeled Zulu Three. These are the targets you tagged for us," he said, highlighting points on a shared screen he and Reyes were using. "If you're asking for a recommendation. I'd recommend we hit 'em before we clear the area for the knuckle draggers to advance. It'd make for a hell of a crossfire if our guys wandered into it."

Sergeant Terry Reyes interjected, "Sir, I've confirmed with Falcon the grid locations for Zulu One, Two, and Three. They have a gun battery on standby and ready to commence strike on your command. I'd recommend we hit 'em with the arty and keep our air units ready for targets of—"

"Whoa, heads up, sir. I've got movement along the tree line. Eight hundred meters to the right of RD One's position," interrupted Sergeant Jesse Cox. He shifted beside his observation scope to the right of their position. "I can't make out exact troop numbers just yet, but it looks like a flanking element trying to get behind Alpha and Bravo's position. I'm labeling this as Yankee One. I am dispatching a couple of scout drones to investigate and see if we can get a better look at what we're dealing with."

Bear acknowledged the changing situation. He studied the terrain through their scout drone feeds, and cursed with a Zodark zapped one of them. He'd just hopped to a new feed when it too was zapped. "Damn it. They nicked a couple of drones. Get a few more in the air and start having 'em do some zigzagging patterns to try and keep 'em alive a little longer. We can't have 'em blinding us in the middle of a fight."

The fact that the Zodarks were zapping their drones told Bear they were preparing to do something they didn't want the Republic to see before it happened.

Bear had to admit, the Zodarks had chosen their ground well. The terrain offered natural choke points that funneled an approaching force into different kill zones. Unfortunately, the Zodarks probably had a few positions his team still hadn't found.

He sighed in frustration as another drone was zapped. "All right, people. It's showtime. Let's bring the pain and let 'em know we're here. Flores, get RD Two for me. Reyes, start working those gun bunnies to go after the Zulu targets. Cox, see if Gunslinger Two-Two can show some love to Yankee One. Contact RD One and let 'em know they've got movement along their right flank."

Time to light this place up. This was the part of job Bear loved.

"Red Devil Two, Gun Devil Two. We've spotted four defensive positions nine hundred meters to your nine o'clock we're labeling Zulu One, break," Bear relayed to Captain Walker as he sent a digital map of the location to Walker's tablet. "Four hundred meters behind 'em, we've got another trio of structures we're labeling Zulu Two. To your two o'clock position, eleven hundred meters to your front, we have another three defensive positions we're labeling Zulu Three, break. Stand by for fire missions on Zulu One, Two, and Three. How copy?"

"GD Two, good copy on last transmission. Standing by for fire mission against Zulu One, Two, and Three. Out."

Satisfied, Bear switched to his team frequency. "Baker, what's the status of those guns?"

A couple of seconds tipped by before Baker responded. "Sir, Falcon Six is requesting confirmation of the targets from you—it's danger close and he needs OIC confirmation." It was protocol to have the officer in charge of a team sign-off on danger close missions. Someone with rank had to make the call.

"Dot the i's and cross the t's," Bear muttered as he connected to the fire support base. "Falcon Six, this is Gun Devil Two-Six. Confirm Zulu targets. How copy?"

A second later the radio crackled. "Gun Devil Two-Six, Falcon Six. Standing by to confirm Zulu targets," came the calm voice of Major Ankrom, the battery commander.

Bear sent the geolocation of the targets to the major's tablet before verbally confirming them. "Falcon Six, Zulu One, grid Romeo Papa four-four-two-one dash eight-niner-one-one, three rounds HE, break. Zulu Two, grid Romeo Papa four-eight-five-five dash eight-seven-five-five, four rounds HE, twenty-five-meter airburst, break. Zulu Three, grid Romeo Papa six-four-seven-five dash five-five-six-niner, three rounds, HE, break. How copy?"

Normally he wouldn't call for an airburst, but after looking at the targets more closely, Bear had spotted very little in the way of overhead protection. Better yet, he saw several clusters of Zodark soldiers milling about. If they got the grid coordinates right, the airburst rounds would obliterate the enemy soldiers with a hail of shrapnel.

Falcon confirmed the coordinates a few moments later, passing along the familiar cadence. "Fire mission confirmed. Zulu One—three rounds HE. Zulu Two—four rounds HE, twenty-five-meter airburst. Zulu Three—three rounds HE...shot out."

"Shot out," Bear echoed. The fire support base was sixty-two kilometers to their rear—too far for Bear to hear the report of the guns firing as they hurled the 340mm projectiles through the air at blinding speeds.

Seconds ticked by as they waited for the rounds to approach.

"Zulu One—Splash," came the response from Falcon.

Bear and the others craned their heads in the sky as they heard what sounded like a train roaring through the air overhead. Bear barely registered the splash call for Zulu Two and Three as the shells screamed overhead, tearing through the air like the sound of fabric being ripped.

Bear looked in the direction of the targets. The earth around them exploded in a flash of fire. Orange, yellow and red flames burned the trees hundreds of meters from the epicenter. Thick clouds of black smoke expanded outward.

"Whoa! Look at Zulu Two!" Reyes shouted excitedly over thunderous booms.

The four airburst rounds eviscerated the trees and structures across a three-hundred-meter radius from ground zero. Bear smiled in awe as he watched the trees simply disappear from the overpressure and shrapnel from the 320mm projectile exploding overtop the area. Scores of Zodark warriors lying in wait beneath the tree cover were thrown across the forested ground like the rag dolls of a petulant child. In an instant, what might have been a hundred or more of the blue devils lying in wait simply disappeared in a mist of blue-and-red gore and bones.

Bear cursed under his breath as he watched two of the three rounds land a few hundred meters long of Zulu Three—two of the fortified positions escaped the worst of the damage. Seconds after impact, the positions came alive with blaster fire zipping across the battle space between their position and RD Two's. Captain Walker's soldiers returned fire, sending blasters and magrail fire back at the enemy.

The eleven hundred meters between Bravo Company and the remaining Zodark defenders came alive with blaster fire and magrail projectiles. Trees and anything else between the two sides wilted beneath withering fire—it was a killing field where neither side could advance.

"Holy crap! That's the first time I saw an arty round go long," Reyes commented in surprise. "Give me a minute and I'll have another fire mission hit it."

Bear listened to the net as Falcon confirmed a pair of 320s were on the way.

"Heads up, people—Reapers inbound!" Cox announced as the sounds of jet engines grew in intensity. Bear looked in the direction of where he knew they were approaching from and smiled. He'd flown the AS-90 Reapers during the Intus campaign.

He watched as the first one dove out of the sky in the direction of Zulu Three, the forested area to the right of Alpha Company. A company-sized Zodark force was attempting to flank the Republic position. If the blue bastards could close the distance and get in close, the Republic's advantage in artillery and close-air support would quickly be negated. It was Bear and his team's job to make sure that didn't happen.

As the Reaper descended through the clouds, dropping below angels fifteen, blaster fire reached into the sky from the forest below. A missile leaped emerged from the trees, then a second, then a third. The Reaper ejected flares and chaff canisters in spherical bursts, jinking to the right, then to the left with each burst of countermeasures.

A missile exploded harmlessly away from the Reaper, spoofed by the chaff. A second missile exploded closer to the Reaper as a defensive drone slammed into it. The Reaper fired, but the third missile met its mark, and it exploded.

Bear cursed the Zodarks for scoring what he felt was a lucky hit, then smiled in satisfaction as three of the four missiles exploded in the forest. One of the missiles had been struck by Zodark ground fire. He counted one secondary explosion, then two more. He couldn't tell what they'd hit, but whatever it was, it exploded.

"Ah, that was Gunslinger Two-Two they got," Cox announced. "Two-Three's wingman is going in now."

The second Reaper swooped down through the clouds, dropping below angels twenty. At fifteen thousand feet, the Zodarks began firing in earnest in its direction. The drone pilot wasted no time, unleashing a barrage of missiles at whatever ground targets its sensors had found. Bear watched as five missiles leapt from beneath its wings—racing into the forest before exploding within it. More missiles emerged from the trees into the air. This drone pilot appeared better prepared than his counterpart. He fired a series of flares and countermeasures before jinking hard to one side, then diving rapidly before the missiles could change their vectors, causing all but one of them to sail harmlessly by. The remaining missile exploded when a defensive drone slammed into it.

Bear found himself rooting for the pilot, almost reliving past occasions when he'd flown the same aircraft, doing the same kinds of missions. As the pilot leveled out somewhere around two or three thousand feet, the Reaper released a series of cluster munitions and fuel-air explosive bombs overtop the forest.

"Holy hell!" Reyes shouted to be heard over the scene that had come to resemble Armageddon.

Nearly a kilometer of trees and whatever was beneath the canopy erupted into a giant flaming fireball. Dozens and dozens of trees ignited in flame—a mini-firestorm exploded outward before contracting like a dragon drawing a breath before blowing fire outward. He watched in awe as flames consumed everything in its path. It was one thing to see this kind of destruction from the vantage point of a drone pilot. It was another thing entirely to see it at the ground level as a soldier.

For the next ten minutes, Bear's team called strike after strike, dismantling the enemy wherever they found them. The flanking element, Yankee One, had been shattered, their advance nothing but smoking craters and ruined trees.

Bear called RD Two, letting Bravo Company know it was safe to advance. He watched as the Ranger Company rushed forward, bounding from one position to the next. As a platoon rushed, another covered its advance. Pockets of resistance appeared; however, within moments they were suppressed before eventually being overwhelmed and ultimately destroyed.

Bear allowed himself the briefest moment of pride. His team executed a flawless attack, clearing the path for the ground force to advance with limited casualties. It was the kind of textbook TASC operation that would make an instructor smile.

"Lieutenant, we've got movement along the southwestern quadrant," Sergeant Cox alerted them. "Oh wow. They've got vehicles, sir. I'm showing multiple high-speed contacts—a few dozen speeders and what looks like some sort of heavy transport vehicle or tank-looking thingy."

"Wait, what the hell is a 'tank-looking thingy,' Cox?" chided Staff Sergeant Flores.

Bear ignored the comments as he swung his optics in the direction Cox had called out. Sure enough, he spotted a few dozen speeders racing toward the left flank of RD Two, Bravo Company. The Zodarks' speeders were dangerous—not because they were armored or carted major firepower but because they were quick and agile. A speeder could easily carry two to three Zodarks into battle.

While the speeders were a problem, the vehicles just behind them were a bit of a mystery. If he had to guess, they were about four meters wide and seven to eight meters long. He was about to say they were unarmed when two of the ten vehicles fired some sort of blaster bolt in the direction of Bravo Company.

Bear watched in horror as trees around Captain Walker's soldiers were blown apart. Republic soldiers were thrown to the ground from the blast waves of multiple explosions. Bear was certain soldiers on the ground would be calling for a medevac, while others would attempt to reach his unit for fire support.

"Stand by. I've got Gunslinger Two-Four angling in for an attack run on these guys," Reyes announced to Bear's relief.

Bear called Captain Walker on the comms. "RD Two, GD Two. You've got two dozen speeders approaching from your left flank and at least a dozen unknown medium-sized vehicles following in their wake. Be advised, we have AS-90 Reapers en-route to engage."

He barely heard Walker's reply as the roar of the battle hit a fever pitch. The sound of explosions, blaster fire and magrails had grown in intensity and it became hard to hear much of anything happening around them.

Bear scanned the field, brain working through the geometry of disaster. Walker's unit was seconds from being caught in a vice— enemy positions dug in ahead, a fresh wave closing in from the flank. Without immediate artillery and air support, they'd be forced to fall back or be chewed apart.

What to do, what to do? His mind raced the options, until a sound froze the blood in his veins.

"Perimeter Alert—Perimeter Alert!"

The alarm blared across the comms, warning of a breach.

How far out did they set the trip line? Bear wondered in a panic.

Sergeant Cox's voice tore through the chaos. "Contact, rear!" Blaster fire and magrail bursts erupted behind him.

Bear spun and caught sight of three blue-skinned devils vaulting from a speeder, landing in the middle of their position. One roared in savage glee, his lower hands flashing twin swords and his upper hands gripping blaster pistols.

"Baker!" Bear tried to shout a warning, but it was too late. The Zodark's blade swept down, carving from Baker's left eye to the corner of his mouth. The young trooper crumpled without a sound. Rage surged in Bear's chest. He leveled his rifle and poured fire into the alien's back. The beast staggered, then collapsed forward.

"Behind you, Lieutenant!" Reyes shouted.

Bear dove, his instincts screaming. A blade hissed through the air where he'd been a heartbeat before. Rolling onto his back, he snapped the rifle up and loosed a burst—two shots went wide. He steadied, exhaled, and fired again. The next volley struck his attacker center mass. Its eyes widened in shock, then narrowed with a predator's fury as it advanced. Bear tilted the muzzle higher and squeezed. The bolt punched through the monster's face this time, caving it in. The body toppled into him, pinning his legs beneath its weight.

A scream tore Bear's attention to the right. Staff Sergeant Flores was locked in a death grip with another Zodark. Twin swords punched into her abdomen, then crossed in a brutal scissoring motion that separated torso from hips. Bear gagged at the sight, bile rising in his throat.

Bear shoved the limp weight of the Zodark corpse off his legs, boots slipping in the gore-slicked dirt as he fought to stand.

"Die, you bastard!" Reyes shouted somewhere to his left, his blaster snapping out rapid bursts. A Zodark howled in pain.

Then a voice, low, guttural, and far too close, sent shivers down Bear's spine. "Now you die… human."

Bear twisted toward it. A towering Zodark advanced, twin swords dripping blood, its upper hands leveling a pair of blasters straight at his chest. Bear raised his weapon and squeezed the trigger—muzzle flashes strobed white-hot across his vision—then a sledgehammer blow slammed into him.

The world tilted. For a heartbeat, he was weightless, floating backward, before gravity dragged him down. He hit hard. Breath fled his lungs in a gasp, and fire bloomed through his chest and abdomen—hot, merciless, and deeper than any pain he'd ever known.

He heard bootsteps, and a shadow fell across him.

"You die now, human," the voice repeated, closer.

A kick rolled him onto his back. Tears blurred his eyes. His hand twitched—and he felt something cold and round in his hand. His fingers closed over it, and despite the agony, a slow smile formed on his face.

The Zodark loomed over him, sneering down. "Why smile, human?"

Bear's gaze locked with the alien's. He raised his right hand just enough for the Zodark to see. Understanding flickered in those predatory eyes at the recognition of the grenade clenched in Bear's fist.

"Die, you—"

The rest vanished in a thunderclap. Light and heat engulfed them both. The last thing Bear saw before darkness claimed him was that look frozen on the Zodark's face.

Chapter 36:
We Keep Flying

Year 2098
Borrowed Time
Middle Reach
Sector 8

Tim Hastings guided *Borrowed Time* through the ice asteroid field.

Twenty-six minutes until detonation, he thought. *Twenty-six minutes to extract soldiers from a Zodark base rigged to blow.*

He'd launched from the *Idaho* ten minutes earlier, following a corridor cleared by Republic and Primord vessels. The battle around them had shifted since their initial insertion. Fewer Zodark ships remained operational. Their defense systems were crippled by the combined fleet's assault.

After Day had confronted him following the last flight, her words still echoed in his mind. "Lieutenant Hastings, we know what happened at Intus. That's in the past, but you're continually carrying it with you today. It's affecting your judgment up there. I understand it's bad, but war shows the worst in everything. Now, you're one of the best Osprey pilots I've ever flown with, but second-guessing intel and freezing up when soldiers are dying… that's not you. Trust the intel, adapt when it's wrong, but don't let ghosts make decisions for living people who need us."

The conversation had been brief, direct, and exactly what he'd needed to hear. No one else dared speak to him that way, or knew how to, but somehow it had snapped everything back into perspective. It reminded him of high school basketball, when Coach Pritchard had called him out at halftime for not rebounding. That criticism had gotten in his head, driven him to fight for every loose ball until he led the team by game's end. Sometimes that was all it took: one person willing to tell you the bold truth.

"Aquila-Actual reports successful approach to point Alpha," Lieutenant Amanda Day announced from the copilot's seat. Occasional weapons fire flashed past their viewport as she continued, "Aquila Three and Four are on trajectory for Bravo and Delta."

Hastings nodded, eyes fixed on the looming ice asteroid. "And we get Charlie. The hot zone."

"Would you expect anything less, sir?" Day's attempt at humor barely masked her tension.

The tactical display showed sporadic enemy fire—nothing like the concentrated barrage they'd faced during insertion. Most Zodark defense systems had been neutralized by the fleet's bombardment, but enough remained operational to make their approach dangerous.

"Charlie-Actual, this is *Borrowed Time*," Hastings transmitted. "We're two minutes out from your position. Status report."

Static crackled before a voice responded. "*Borrowed Time*, Charlie-Actual. We're defensive, holding position at junction C-7 but taking heavy fire. We've secured an extraction point at the main breach, but you'll need to get in fast. Enemy's trying to collapse our exit route."

"Copy that, Charlie-Actual," Hastings replied, banking the Osprey sharply. "Inbound for immediate extraction. Stand by."

The massive ice formation loomed ahead. Its crystalline surface reflected the battle's flashes. The soldiers had blasted multiple breaches during their assault, and now they'd withdrawn to the largest one—a gaping wound in the asteroid's surface that served as their extraction point.

"Twenty seconds to touchdown," Hastings said. "Day, initiate combat extraction protocol. Side gunners, stand by to provide covering fire."

Sergeant Barajas's voice came through the internal comm. "Guns ready, sir. Just get us close enough."

Hastings pushed the Osprey harder than protocol recommended, diving toward the breach point, where soldiers waited behind ice formations and debris from the blast. The "extraction pad" was nothing more than a flat section of ice near the breach, exposed to enemy fire but close enough for rapid evacuation.

Through the external cams, Hastings could see soldiers maintaining position with slight thruster adjustments, laying down suppressive fire into the facility's depths. Wounded personnel lay behind blast debris, while combat medics worked frantically to stabilize them for transport.

"Taking fire!" Day reported as impact alerts flashed across the console. "Automated defense turret at two o'clock, exterior mount."

Hastings maintained position, hovering the Osprey with centimeter precision in the asteroid's minimal gravity field. "Barajas, take out that turret."

"On it, sir."

The Osprey's port-side magrail gun roared to life. Five-barrel rotation spitting tungsten penetrator rounds at the Zodark emplacement. The turret exploded in a shower of ice fragments and metal.

"Turret down," Barajas confirmed.

The soldiers began their evacuation, carrying wounded comrades and critical intelligence data. They moved in coordinated teams, using controlled bursts from their battlesuit thrusters to navigate the short distance in the minimal gravity.

The troops reached the ramp and the first ones climbed aboard while others maintained suppressive fire toward the breach entrance.

"Armor's holding," Hastings responded, but he maneuvered the craft to provide better cover for the evacuating troops. "Keep her steady."

"Thirty-four aboard," Day counted. "Thirty-five… thirty-six…"

A massive explosion rocked the asteroid, sending vibrations through the Osprey's frame. Warning lights flashed across Hastings's console.

"Charlie-Actual," Hastings called over the comm. "What's your status?"

"Last squad coming out now," came the response. "Need immediate extraction."

The final group of soldiers retreated from the breach, half carrying, half dragging their wounded.

"Forty-eight aboard," Day updated. "Forty-nine… fifty… fifty-three… fifty-five. That's everyone accounted for!"

That wasn't everyone, Hastings thought. Some hadn't made it back from the facility's depths. They'd died fighting for something they'd believed in. *And we honor that by getting their brothers and sisters out alive. Focus on who we saved, not who we couldn't.*

"Ramp closing," Hastings confirmed as he began easing the Osprey away from the breach site. "Charlie-Actual, confirm all personnel accounted for."

"Confirmed, *Borrowed Time*. Get us the hell out of here."

The Osprey's ramp sealed, pressurizing the troop compartment. Hastings executed a minimal-thrust maneuver to clear the asteroid's negligible gravity well before engaging the main drives, accelerating away from the asteroid.

"Twenty minutes to detonation," Day announced.

Hastings pushed the Osprey to maximum thrust, plotting a course back to the *Idaho*. Around them, the other extraction craft were similarly departing, each laden with soldiers from their assigned points.

"Aquila Two to all Aquila elements," he transmitted. "*Borrowed Time* has package secure, fifty-five personnel aboard. Returning to *Idaho*."

Three acknowledgments came back as the extraction squadron regrouped, forming a tight defensive formation for the return journey.

Day glanced at him as they accelerated toward the fleet. "You flew that differently."

"How so?" Hastings asked, though he knew what she meant.

"Faster. More aggressive. Like you remembered why we're out here."

He had remembered. Day's words from their conversation after the last mission had hit home. These soldiers counted on him to bring them home, not to second-guess every decision because of old ghosts, to focus on the ones who survived in order to keep them alive.

"Eighteen minutes," Day said quietly.

Hastings nodded, maintaining focus on their approach vector.

"All extraction craft, this is *Idaho* Control," came a voice through the comm. "Status report."

The Osprey pilots reported in sequence: "Aquila-Actual here. Alpha team extracted, thirty-four personnel aboard."

Hastings's stomach tightened. Thirty-four. Alpha team had deployed with sixty-four soldiers. Thirty had been lost. The math was simple and brutal. But thirty-four lived to fight another day.

He keyed his comm. "Aquila Two," Hastings said. "Fifty-five accounted for."

"Aquila Three, Bravo team secured, full extraction complete."

"Aquila Four. Team is aboard, proceeding on departure vector."

"Copy all," *Idaho* Control responded. "Be advised, demolition timer shows thirteen minutes to detonation. Expedite your return."

The *Borrowed Time* accelerated away from the asteroid along with the other Ospreys in formation.

"We've got this," he said to Day.

She nodded. "Affirmative, sir."

Hastings gave a nod in return. "We got them out. That's what matters."

The old numbness was gone, replaced by something sharper but cleaner. A purpose without the paralyzing weight of past failures.

Just hours ago, he'd been going through the motions, treating this as another routine transport mission. Fly in, drop off, pick up, fly out. Bodies in, bodies out. Flying safe, flying perfect, flying scared. Because perfect meant no one could blame him if things went wrong. Bad intel, equipment failure, command decisions, anything but pilot error.

Then Day had finally said what she'd been holding back for who knew how long. Lieutenant Day, who'd spent almost a year being the perfect copilot, being respectful, being supportive, always trying to nudge him forward without overstepping. He could see it had been eating at her, watching him make excuses while that op failure haunted every decision, until she simply couldn't stay silent anymore.

When she'd finally crossed that line today and called him out, her words had stripped away all his careful justifications. She'd forced him to own his piloting and see what the event had turned him into: a pilot so afraid of losing another transport full of troops that he'd stopped really flying at all.

These weren't cargo. They were people. People who fought in the same war. People with families, with dreams, with futures they trusted him to protect. That failed mission, that bad intel, and those he'd lost on that transport, had been running this ship long enough.

He pushed his Osprey to maximum safe velocity. Twelve minutes to detonation. The *Idaho* grew larger in the viewport, its massive hangar bay doors already cycling open to receive them.

"*Idaho* Control, Aquila Two requesting priority landing clearance," Hastings transmitted. "We've got wounded aboard."

"Aquila Two, you're cleared for immediate approach," came the response. "Medical teams standing by."

Hastings checked the time. Six minutes to detonation. The *Idaho* was already accelerating away from the asteroid, its massive engines glowing blue-white as they pushed the carrier to a safe distance.

Hastings guided the Osprey through the hangar bay opening, compensating for the carrier's acceleration. The landing was rougher than he'd have liked, but they were down. Safe.

"*Idaho* to all vessels," Captain Mensah's voice announced fleetwide. "Extraction complete. All ships clear minimum safe distance. T-minus four minutes to detonation."

Hastings completed the shutdown sequence as the wounded were transferred to waiting medical personnel. Around them, damage control teams secured the Ospreys, intelligence officers took custody of the recovered data, and medical staff attended to the injured.

"Lieutenant," Day said as they prepared to exit the cockpit, "you did… a damn good job."

Hastings paused. "So did you. Couldn't have done this without you. Or our crew back there." He motioned toward the Osprey's cabin, where Barajas and their gunner were securing their stations. "Or them," he added, looking through the viewscreen at the troops being helped from the rear compartment.

"You're remembering why we fly," Day replied.

Hastings nodded.

"So, we just keep flying," Day said.

"We keep flying," Hastings confirmed. "And we make damn sure we're the best at what we do, because they're counting on us."

They quickly made their way to the observation deck as the *Idaho* continued accelerating away from the asteroid. The ship's PA system announced: "All hands, brace for potential shock wave. Detonation in thirty seconds."

From the viewport, they watched as the timer reached zero. For a moment, nothing happened. Then a giant flash erupted from the center of the asteroid. The ice structure fractured instantly, massive chunks accelerating outward as the shock wave propagated. The three remaining Zodark vessels disappeared in the expanding cloud of overheated particles.

"Mission complete," announced the ship's commander over the PA system. "All personnel stand down from battle stations."

As the *Idaho* engaged its primary engines for the return journey, Hastings stood at the viewport. There he watched the distant debris field that had once been a Zodark outpost.

"Think we hurt them?" Day asked, coming to stand beside him. "Really hurt them, I mean."

Hastings considered the question. "Taking it out blinds them in this sector."

"You counted how many died, didn't you?" Day asked.

"Yes. Across all four teams."

Day studied his face. "You didn't use to."

"No," Hastings admitted. "I didn't."

They stood in silence for a moment, watching as the last traces of the explosion faded into the blackness of space.

"Think any of them will remember our call signs?" Day asked.

"Probably not," Hastings said. "But that's OK. They'll remember they made it home."

The *Idaho*'s massive engines pushed onward, along with the rest of the task force, all still intact. Behind them, where the Zodark outpost had stood, there remained only scattered debris drifting in the void, and one fewer threat to the people they were sworn to protect… that Hastings had sworn to protect.

Chapter 37:
In the Broken Places

Year 2098
FTL Transit
RNS *Leahy*

Coop lay motionless on his bunk aboard the *Leahy*, still in his sweat-dried uniform. Around him, the vessel whirred with the resonance of transit in the FTL bubble. It was a steady vibration that usually lulled him to sleep.

Not tonight.

His body ached with the bone-deep fatigue he realized must come directly after ground combat. Muscles knotted from tension and exertion. The ceiling above his bunk bore a small scorch mark from when Bear had once attempted to light a contraband cigar inside their quarters. It had set off the smoke suppression system, earning them both extra duty.

"You can't smoke that in here," Coop had warned him.

Bear had just grinned that wide, infectious smile of his. "Watch me."

The memory cut through Coop like a tungsten round. Bear. The name reverberated in his mind. He'd learned it three hours after boarding the *Leahy*. After this operation on the moon. After he'd looked for him and couldn't find him. Lieutenant Lincoln "Bear" Bowman was killed in action during the final push. The information had come from Captain Hogan himself, face solemn as he delivered the news.

"Lieutenant Cooper," Hogan had said, standing at rigid attention in the corridor. "Bear's TASC element was providing fire support for a Republic Army fireteam pinned down near the Zodark command center when they were flanked. They fought to the last man, giving the soldiers time to complete their objective and extract."

Coop had simply nodded, unable to form words as the captain continued with the clinical details of a death that was anything but clinical.

At the moment, the ship's lighting dimmed automatically to transition to night cycle. Coop's journal lay untouched beside him. The leather-bound book felt impossibly heavy tonight, as though the weight of the day's losses had seeped into its pages. Bear was gone. The man who'd welcomed him to the Jolly Rogers with arms wide open. Not literally. Figuratively. The mess hall would never again fill with his booming laughter.

"To the Jolly Rogers," Bear had toasted once, "where we fly fast, fight hard, and somehow make it back for breakfast."

According to the soldiers who'd witnessed his final stand, Bear had lived up to his call sign. When Zodark forces breached his position, he'd emptied his sidearm into the first wave before resorting to hand-to-hand combat. A sergeant described watching Bear physically lift a Zodark warrior and bodyslam the creature. Bear had then charged another advancing enemy, armed with nothing but a combat knife.

The last Zodark had engaged Bear in close quarters. Both had fallen in that desperate struggle, the Zodark with Bear's knife buried to the hilt in its throat, and Bear with a cauterized wound through his chest.

You don't mess with Bear. That phrase had become something of a mantra among the Jolly Rogers whenever someone pulled off something seemingly impossible. Now it echoed in Coop's head with hollow reverence. *You don't mess with Bear.*

The knot in Coop's throat tightened.

A soft knock on his quarters' hatch preceded Sawyer's entrance. Her eyes were rimmed with red, her uniform still bearing the dust of Nightfall's surface. She'd been crying, although she'd clearly tried to hide it. Sawyer stood at parade rest, a formality she'd never once observed with Coop before. She gestured toward the corridor with a tilt of her head.

"They're… they're letting us see him," she said, voice cracking slightly. "Not him. His casket."

Coop nodded and hopped off the bunk. His boots felt like they were filled with lead as he stood.

The ship's morgue lay three decks below, a sterile compartment that had been expanded to accommodate the day's losses. Row upon row of metallic caskets lined the space. Each draped with the Republic's flag. The sight hit Coop hard, almost like an icy spike through his solar plexus.

Captain Saho Nobunaga, Alpha Company Commander of the 1-504th "Red Devils," stood by one of the caskets. He nodded at Coop and Sawyer but said nothing.

Bear's casket stood in the second row, his name displayed on a small digital readout embedded in the unit. The technology inside the casket would preserve his body perfectly for the journey home, wherever home was. Coop didn't even know where they were going. Didn't care. It'd been told to him many times, but right now, only fog clouded his mind.

"Colorado," Sawyer said suddenly. "He was from some tiny town in Colorado. Said his dad ran the only bar in a fifty-mile radius."

"He never told me that," Coop said.

"He told me once." She cleared her throat. "Said he was going to go back there someday, take over the bar, name it the Jolly Roger in honor of the squadron."

"I think… yeah… he mentioned that." And he did. Coop wasn't just making that up. He remembered.

While Coop stood with his head bowed, memories of Bear cascaded through his mind. The time Bear had smuggled an actual live chicken aboard the RNS *Gallipoli* to win a bet, claiming afterward that he simply "wanted fresh eggs." His habit of dropping to do push-ups midsentence whenever he felt the conversation was getting too serious. The one time he'd stepped between Coop and a drunken Army Special Forces soldier who'd made fun of drone pilots being assigned to easy roles.

"You touch my boy Coop here," Bear had said, chest puffed out like a rooster, "and I'll fold you into a pretzel so tight your own mother won't recognize you."

The soldier had backed down. They always did when Bear stepped up.

Bear had been the glue of the squadron, seemingly universally beloved despite—or perhaps because of—his constant skirting of regulations. When Coop had first joined the Jolly Rogers, still carrying the stigma of his failed military life, butting heads with everyone, his beef with just about every drone pilot in his squadron on New Eden, and subsequent transfer, Bear had been the first to treat him as just another pilot rather than damaged goods. He'd dragged Coop to the squad's unofficial gatherings, pushed him to join their poker games even though Coop was trying to ease up on cards, refused to let him isolate himself when the shadows grew too long.

"Isolation is for monks and prisoners," Bear had told him once, physically hauling Coop from his bunk. "And last I checked, you ain't taken no vows and you ain't committed no crimes. Yet."

Sawyer placed a hand on Bear's casket, and on the Republic emblem embossed into the metal. At the moment, the flag's colors seemed vibrant against the brushed titanium of the casket. In death, Bear had received the respect often denied to him in life due to his irreverent approach to just about everything. His service record would show his final act of heroism, but it couldn't capture the man who'd named his datapad "Honeypot" and won the heart of Coop. Something Coop thought would be impossible.

"He told me one time he challenged a drone pilot named Ninja to an eating contest," Sawyer said, her voice barely above a whisper.

Coop nodded. "I was there. Somehow they got, and ate, pounds and pounds of mystery meat from the mess. Bear won by a full pound."

"Bear said he threw it all up in Ninja's locker."

Coop snorted, doing his best to withhold his laughter, his tears. "Said it was an accident."

"It wasn't?"

"No," Coop said. "It wasn't."

He quickly lost his smile. Nothing felt right. Not right now. The universe had tilted on its axis, and Coop was struggling to find his footing in this new, Bear-less reality.

Coop finally turned away from the casket, unable to reconcile that Bear was within, the larger-than-life figure who'd walked all muscles, all bulk, a freak of a man, through this ship's corridors.

Sawyer walked alongside Coop as they left the morgue, their footsteps echoing in the quiet corridor. The *Leahy* felt different now, as though the ship itself mourned its fallen.

"You OK?" Sawyer asked as they reached the lift.

Coop shrugged. "You?"

"Negative." She punched the button for their deck. "But I'm asking about you."

"I'm fine."

"Bullcrap."

The lift doors closed, sealing them in momentary privacy. Coop leaned against the wall, suddenly exhausted. "What do you want me to say, Sawyer? That I feel like someone ripped out my insides? That I keep expecting him to jump out from around a corner and yell 'gotcha'?"

"Yeah," she said simply. "That's exactly what I want you to say. Because that's how I feel too."

Life would never be the same. There would be no more impromptu performances of ancient rock songs with Bear using spoons as drumsticks. No more late-night philosophical discussions where Bear, surprisingly well read despite his cultivated image as a bruiser and a strangely well-oiled machine when it came to inspiring others like a motivational speaker, would quote Aurelius and Hemingway with equal ease.

"The world breaks everyone," Bear had quoted once, after a particularly brutal mission, "and afterward, many are stronger at the broken places."

The lift doors opened, and they stepped out into the corridor.

"I need some time," Coop said.

Sawyer squeezed her own arm. "I know. We all do."

Back in his quarters, Coop finally reached for his journal. The leather was warm in his hands, worn smooth by generations of Coopers who had read this diary, read Presley Paul Cooper's fears, his hopes. He flipped through the pages until he found his great-great-grandfather's entries from World War II, written in faded blue ink that had somehow survived longer than a century.

The entry was dated June 7, 1944: "Buried Thompson today. And Mitchell. Collins, too. Good men all. The living owe it to those who no longer speak to tell their stories. In remembering them, they achieve a kind of immortality. Their sacrifice becomes meaningful not just in what it achieved, but in how it changes those who remain."

How many times had his ancestor faced this same hollow feeling? How many friends had he watched die in the skies over Europe?

The knot in Coop's throat remained, the grief still raw and pulsing, but alongside it grew something else. A determination that Bear's story would not end here in the confines of a casket. As long as

Coop drew breath, Bear would live on in the stories he told, in the way he approached life, in the laughter he wouldn't allow to die.

For the first time, Coop opened to a blank page in Presley Paul Cooper's journal and began to write: "Today I lost a friend named Bear. Not his real name, of course. Lincoln Bowman was his government name, but nobody called him that. He was Bear because he was built like one, fought like one, and sometimes, when he thought nobody was looking, showed the gentle heart of one too."

The words came slowly at first, then faster. Much faster.

Chapter 40:
Cherry Blossoms and Chili Mac

Year 2098
Deck Five – Atrium
RNS *Poseidon*
En Route to Stavros Naval Shipyard in Kita

The artificial sunlight in the *Poseidon*'s arboretum cast dappled shadows through the cherry blossoms. Lee sat at a small metal table, watching the light play across the surface as he unpacked his lunch. The environmental systems hummed quietly in the background, maintaining the perfect spring day that never changed in this small pocket of Earth recreated among the stars.

Lee removed his standard-issue MRE. It was a Menu #12, the coveted "Chili Mac" with jalapeño cheese spread, crackers, and a side of mixed fruit. Across from him, Sato carefully unwrapped her bento box. There sat perfectly arranged onigiri, pickled vegetables, and grilled mackerel.

"You never eat the ship's food," Lee observed, tearing open his cheese packet.

Sato shrugged. "I prefer to prepare my own when possible. The replicators never get the rice right."

They were in FTL, heading back to Kita Shipyard for repairs. Life was returning to normal, whatever that meant these days. The loss of the Army soldiers at the outpost during their operation sat heavy on Lee's shoulders. He did his best to push it to the back of his mind, hide it from his heart if he could. One of these days, it'd catch up to him. He didn't want to be there when it did, but of course, he would be.

What a silly thing to think.

"Dharek surprised me," Lee said, stirring his chili mac. "I didn't expect him to adapt so quickly to Mensah's command structure."

Sato nodded, her chopsticks hovering over her bento. "His navigation through those ice fields was remarkable. Even Reynolds was impressed, and you know how he feels about other navigators. He scrutinizes them like crazy."

"That's putting it mildly," Lee said before he took a bite. "Remember Dharek's navigational suggestion to mask our approach? I thought Reynolds was going to have an aneurysm."

"Yet it worked perfectly," Sato said.

Lee pulled up a tactical report on his datapad, scanning the damage statistics. "We got off light. Minor hull breaches on the port side, thermal stress on two point-defense emitters. Nothing the yard can't fix up quickly."

"The Army troops performed admirably," Sato said. "Extracting that intelligence and setting those charges was textbook."

Lee nodded, his expression darkening slightly. "Opening this corridor for the Rass invasion is significant. Now we just wait for the brass to pull the trigger."

"Have you noticed," Sato said carefully, setting down her chopsticks, "how often the Altairians position our forces at the front of engagements?"

Lee raised an eyebrow. "You gonna use that cannon fodder argument again?"

"I didn't say that. But the pattern is becoming difficult to ignore."

Lee leaned back in his chair. "We're good at it, Noriko. Humans have superior tactical adaptability in combat situations. It makes us naturally suited for vanguard operations."

"There's a bitter irony there," Sato replied. "Our brutal history of warfare prepared us for this… interstellar conflict."

"Our major contribution to the alliance," Lee said. "Not advanced technology or spiritual wisdom, but the hard-earned expertise that comes from millennia of conflict. I mean, look at our recent mission. Human Special Forces accomplished what Primord commandos wouldn't dare attempt."

"That doesn't make it easier to send them into harm's way."

"No, it doesn't." Lee set down his fork. "I memorize every name, you know. Every casualty from operations under my command. Or, I should say, I do my best to."

"I write to their families," Sato said. "Personal notes, not the form letters. Even when protocol doesn't require it."

The artificial breeze rustled through the cherry blossoms above them. For a moment, they sat in silence.

"How's your… who is it… your best friend back at home?" Lee asked finally, changing the subject. "Still sending you those civilian job listings?"

A small smile touched Sato's lips. "Every month like clockwork. Last week it was a research position at Tokyo University. Before that, a corporate executive role at Mitsubishi Orbital. She'll find whatever and send it to me."

"She's persistent."

"She worries," Sato replied. "She's the only family I have left. Or, I should say, what I call family."

Lee nodded, understanding in his eyes. Sato's parents had died long ago.

"What about you?" Sato asked. "Any word from your family?"

Lee's expression grew somber. "My sister sent a message a while back. Dad had a minor stroke."

"I'm sorry, Ripley. Is he all right?"

"Stubborn as ever. Refusing advanced medical treatment, relying on the community's traditional healing practices instead." Lee's voice carried an edge of frustration. "If he'd just go to a proper hospital…"

"Have you considered requesting emergency leave?" Sato asked.

Lee shook his head. "My presence would only cause greater distress. The shunning is still in effect." He attempted a smile, but it fell quickly. "I'm fighting to protect a family that won't acknowledge me, defending Earth for a community that rejected me for choosing this path—same old story, same old drama."

Sato crunched down on a pickled daikon. "We have a situation brewing in Engineering. The reactor specialists and propulsion team are at each other's throats again."

"Resource allocation?" asked Lee.

"And maintenance schedules. Wiggins wants exclusive access to Bay Two for reactor component testing. Kemp insists his propulsion team needs the same space for thruster calibrations." Lee caught the slight tightening around Sato's eyes. "I'm organizing a joint training exercise…simulated cascading system failures."

"Forced collaboration," Lee nodded appreciatively. "Smart."

A maintenance Synth walked past their table. It pruned dead leaves from a neighboring tree. Lee kept his eyes on Sato as she outlined her idea of a solution within the simulation she'd create, her expression animated. She liked doing this, and in truth, she'd handled the situation exactly as he would have, maybe better. He scraped the bottom of his chili mac container.

"That's good work," he said when she'd finished. "So, when's the last time you took a full rest cycle?"

Sato blinked. "I've been monitoring repairs during my off-hours."

"That's not what I asked."

She hesitated. "Honestly, I don't know when I took some time off other than to sleep here and there. Ten minutes here, five minutes there—but I'm fine, Captain."

"Even Noriko Sato needs good sleep occasionally. I mean, when we're not in battle, of course."

"There are certain responsibilities I find…difficult to delegate. Particularly during our most recent mission parameters."

Lee nodded. He understood the feeling all too well. "You're an exceptional XO, Noriko. The best I've served with. But you're not a synthetic."

"Thank you, sir."

"Ever think about your next steps?" Lee asked. "Career-wise."

Sato was quiet for a moment. "I'd like my own command someday," she admitted. "Though I'm satisfied with my current position."

"You'll get there," Lee said. "Still have a few things to overcome before you're ready, but you'll get there."

"Such as?" Sato's eyes narrowed slightly.

Lee chuckled. "You already know," he replied.

She nodded, the acknowledgment passing silently between them. They both knew the unspoken truth. Part of him didn't want to lose her as his XO, no matter how deserving she was of promotion. It was the coach's dilemma. Pride in seeing your best assistant ready to lead their own team, mixed with reluctance to see them go.

Lee scraped the last of the jalapeño cheese spread onto a cracker. He remembered his own early command days, and the mistakes that had shaped him. He remembered Captain James

Oldendorf's always reassuring words, and his constant help. The man had essentially shaped Lee into the captain he'd become, which was what he wished to do with Sato. Though he couldn't say if he'd done an entirely good enough job. The woman was truly a natural anyway. Not much slipped by her; she caught just about everything.

"I hope I've been someone you've learned from," he said to her.

Sato nodded. "I've observed different command styles throughout the fleet. Captain Mensah maintains distance from her crew. She's professional but remote. Captain Bayes is more personable and builds individual connections. Captain Roberts, well… he's a jerk half the time but ultimately well meaning, and he gets to the point. You…" She paused, considering her words. "You balance all approaches. Formal when necessary, approachable when beneficial, blunt when needed. To say I've been lucky under your command, well, that's an understatement."

"Different situations call for different tactics," Lee said. "Same with people. And… thank you. It means a lot."

They fell quiet for a moment. Lee watched the artificial breeze stir the cherry blossoms above them. Pink petals drifted down, landing on their table.

"The *Scimitar* will need a captain when Captain English retires next year," Lee said finally. "It's a good ship. Solid crew."

Sato looked into his eyes. "You trying to get rid of me, sir?"

"Just the opposite," Lee admitted. "But holding you back would be selfish. The fleet needs good commanders."

"I appreciate your guidance," Sato said. "But I'm not in a rush. There's still much I can learn here."

The ship's intercom chimed softly. "Attention, all personnel. Preparing for exit from FTL in forty-five minutes. Department heads report status to the bridge."

Lee checked his chronometer and sighed. "Back to reality."

He gathered the remains of his MRE, folding the packaging. Sato reassembled her bento box, each component returning to its designated place. The arboretum's lighting shifted subtly, the bright afternoon giving way to early-evening hues.

"Stavros Naval Shipyard has the best Primord engineers I've ever seen," Lee said, standing. "Their attention to detail is almost obsessive. Last time we docked there, they discovered a microscopic fracture in our port stabilizer that our diagnostics missed completely."

"Agreed, sir."

They walked toward the arboretum exit.

"These moments always end too quickly," he said. "Just when conversations get meaningful, duty calls."

Sato grinned. "The nature of our profession. Brief periods of reflection punctuating the constant demands of command."

The cherry blossoms continued their dance in the breeze behind them as the doors slid open, revealing the corridor beyond. Lee took a deep breath, mentally shifting from Ripley back into Captain Lee as they headed toward the bridge and whatever challenges awaited them at Stavros.

Chapter 38:
Mahogany of War Plans

Year 2098
Republic Liaison Wing, Skjarnhold Command
Valdrakar, Primordia
Kita System

Admiral Bailey studied the holographic display of the Middle Reach sector. The battle simulation replayed itself in miniature above the conference table. The Zodark installation inside the ice asteroid disintegrated in a brilliant flash, scattering debris across the projection field. He tapped his stylus against the polished mahogany, nodding with quiet satisfaction.

He checked the table, giving it a double take. *We're in Primord territory*, he thought. *Where would they get mahogany?* Regardless of whatever type of wood it was, it looked identical to mahogany.

"Remarkable execution," Bailey said, looking up at the assembled officers sitting around the briefing room's table. "One of the cleanest joint operations I've seen in this war."

Admiral Dhorsar, the Primord fleet commander, inclined his head. "The coordination between our forces was…efficient."

Bailey caught the hesitation. After several years working alongside Earthers, the Primords were still getting used to admitting humans could coordinate worth a damn. He didn't blame them. Hundreds of years of war against the Zodarks had made them cautious about everything.

"Captain Mensah integrated command protocols seamlessly," Bailey replied, scrolling through the after-action report on his datapad. "Minimal communication lag between Republic and Primord vessels."

Admiral Bjork Stavanger, seated across from Bailey, tapped his finger against the table. One tap. Two taps. Done. Bailey couldn't figure out if that was a tic the man didn't know about or a cue to the rest of those in the room that he was about to speak.

"The Republic's magrail technology proved decisive," Stavanger said. "I cannot ignore such a truth. I am continually impressed by your kinetic weaponry. Our energy weapons would have required three times the engagement window to achieve similar results."

Bailey nodded. "And your navigation systems got our ships through that ice field without a scratch. Saved the *Poseidon* too on one occasion. Wouldn't have mattered how good our guns were if we'd been picking ice chunks out of our hull breaches."

The door slid open. Captain Roberts of the RNS *Australia* entered, followed by Commander Ripley Lee. The man who'd been commanding one of the few Altairian-Human hybrid ships in the fleet and was doing a damn good job of it, too.

Lee took a seat at the far end of the table without drawing attention. Roberts, by contrast, made his presence known immediately.

"Sorry for the delay, Admiral," Roberts said, dropping his tactical pad on the table with a clatter. "The comms array on the *Australia* decided to take a vacation right when I needed to transmit the final damage assessments."

Bailey waved away the apology. "You're here now. We were just discussing the operation's success."

"Success is an understatement," Roberts said, grinning. "We kicked their asses six ways from Sunday."

Captain Dharek, who had entered behind Lee, took his position standing near the Primord admirals. His expression remained numb—neutral, at best—but Bailey had spent enough time with Primords to recognize the subtle signs of pride in his posture.

"The Republic transports performed admirably and the RASs… what do you call them? Performed beyond expectations," Dharek said. "They secured the intelligence cache intact, despite the destruct protocols, despite a minimal amount of time to do so."

"Yes. Correct. It's indeed RAS or RASs. Republic Army Soldiers." Bailey turned to the holographic display again, expanding the view to show the outpost assault phase. Tiny figures representing Republic troops moved through the installation's corridors fast. Most would call it textbook. Bailey knew it was the result of years of professional training, the honing of tactics by the Republic Army that had turned them into the efficient warriors they were.

"Also, the chain of command transition went well," Bailey said. "Captain Mensah assumed tactical control without disrupting ongoing operations." He glanced at Dharek. "Your willingness to integrate your battle group under her command made that possible."

In truth, Bailey had been concerned about the handover. He'd also heard Dharek had some issues but got his butt in gear in good time. No matter how the Primord captain took it, he relinquished authority somewhat easily, especially to humans they'd only recently stopped viewing as primitive upstarts.

"The mission objective superseded protocol considerations," Dharek replied.

Roberts laughed. "That's diplomatic Primord for 'I did what needed doing.'"

Admiral Stavanger's expression tightened slightly. "Captain Dharek recognized the tactical advantage of unified command. It was the logical decision."

Bailey watched Lee from the corner of his eye. The commander sat quietly, absorbing the conversation without contributing. In all truth, the man sitting across from him, Commander Ripley Lee, should be in command of a bigger task force, even at this point in his career. The young man was brilliant, taught by one of the best—Captain James Oldendorf. But, at the same time, he should keep Lee at arm's length from a bigger task force to let him learn, let him master his current post before he moved him onto the next. Experience trumped talent in many cases, and Lee was still building experience.

Give him time, Bailey thought. *He'll get there. Heck, he'll probably take my position one day.*

"The intelligence recovered from the installation has already yielded results," Admiral Dhorsar said, changing the subject. "Which brings us to our next campaign."

The holographic display shifted, showing a new star system.

"Rass," Dhorsar continued. "This is primarily going to be fought by us Primords and you humans. The Altairians, Tully, and Gallentines will not be participating."

Bailey raised an eyebrow. "Political considerations?"

"Resource allocation," Stavanger corrected.

Dhorsar nodded. "As you know, the Zodarks still control two of our colonies. One of them is the planet Rass. It was the first colony the Zodarks seized from us more than three hundred years ago. It is a Zodark world at this point. Our latest intelligence indicates that the

Zodarks and the Orbots have turned it into an industrial center and a major military outpost. They have turned the Primord civilians on Rass… my people… into slaves.”

The holographic display zoomed in, showing multiple Zodark installations scattered across the planet’s surface. Bailey studied the defensive grid. A starbase orbited the planet. Ground-based cannons covered approach vectors. A substantial fleet floated in high orbit.

“Expect fierce resistance for this world,” Dhorsar said. “I have developed an approach that could minimize our casualties.”

With a gesture, he manipulated the tactical display. The hologram transformed, revealing an assault strategy with color-coded insertion corridors and phased deployment zones glowing against the planet’s topographical features.

Roberts’s brow furrowed. “And if their defensive screen proves impenetrable?”

Several of the officers nodded. A few transports carrying more than seven thousand soldiers had been lost during the invasion of Intus when that Orbot battleship and its Zodark escort had materialized amid the vulnerable transport formation. Those Republic vessels, packed with soldiers preparing for planetfall, had been helpless against the sudden onslaught.

Bailey remembered the after-action reports. Thousands of lives had been lost in minutes. Those were the kind of casualty figures keeping admirals awake at night.

“As at Intus, there will be two fleets,” Stavanger explained. “The first fleet will jump into the system and move to secure the stargate. Then they will engage the enemy fleet over the planet Rass. Once it has been cleared, the second fleet, consisting of the transports, will jump through the stargate and then head to the planet.”

“Phased approach,” Bailey said. “Sensible.”

“We are embarking on a mission that has never been attempted before,” Dhorsar added. “To actually capture an enemy starbase, control it, and make it ours. If all goes according to plan, we will take over the facility and learn a lot more about our adversaries.”

“My fleet will provide the majority of the vessels for this operation,” Stavanger said. “Admiral Bailey, we request that you commit a majority of your ships to the initial assault.”

The Republic Navy was stretched thin with ongoing repairs. But with a continued surge in ship manufacturing, it was steadily beginning to catch up with the demands of the alliance. They were also receiving more of the Altairian-Human hybrid ships from the Altairian shipyards. Frigates, heavy cruisers, and even some of the battle cruisers were starting to arrive in large numbers. The battleships were still years off, but everything else was finally moving at a good pace. However, the strategic value of Rass couldn't be overstated despite the strain it was placing on the Republic. Bailey would lend all he could to this invasion, as was the plan from the get-go.

"I believe this battle will go differently than Intus," Bailey said finally. "We've learned from our mistakes. The Zodarks won't catch us with our pants down again."

He tapped his datapad, bringing up the Republic fleet disposition. "I'm positive I can commit my forces as previously discussed."

"Good. I like your Earther words: 'a deal's a deal,'" Stavanger replied.

Bailey dipped his head. "A man is only as good as his word. Your word is your honor, and your honor is your worth."

Roberts cleared his throat. "With respect, Admiral Bailey, we should discuss contingencies. If the Zodarks detect our approach and bring in reinforcements—"

"They will not," Dharek interrupted. "The intelligence from the ice asteroid facility included Zodark patrol schedules. We know their blind spots now."

That explains the Primords' confidence, Bailey thought. *Hopefully not overconfidence.* "When do you propose to launch this operation?"

"We've been discussing this invasion for a while now, and with the Republic's continued contribution and commitment, we'll start the operation in four months," Stavanger replied. "Our shipyards are completing final modifications to the assault vessels now."

Bailey glanced at Lee again, noting the commander's intense focus on the holographic display. He was already analyzing approach vectors, Bailey guessed, planning how he'd tackle the Zodark defenses if given the chance.

"Very well," Bailey said. "I'll issue the necessary orders. The Republic stands ready to support the liberation of Rass."

As the meeting continued into technical details, Bailey found himself thinking about the broader implications. Earthers entering this war started because of Zodark aggression. Those three-eyed blue beasts didn't realize who they'd just messed with. As his grandpa used to say, "Don't poke a sleeping bear unless you're ready for the claws."

Now they were taking the fight to yet another Zodark-controlled territory, liberating yet another Primord world the Zodarks had held for centuries.

Progress, he thought. *Slow and bloody, but progress nonetheless.*

Chapter 39:
Bracketed and Bloodied

Late 2098
RNS *Poseidon*
Valdrakar, Primordia
Kita System

Months of recon patrols along the contested borders of Middle Reach in Sector 8 had left Captain Ripley Willis Lee and his crew aboard the RNS *Poseidon* battle-hardened but weary. The endless cat-and-mouse games with Zodark scout ships wore on everyone. Deep-space surveillance missions stretched nerves thin. The constant threat of ambush made sleep a luxury few could afford.

When they returned to Kita for some much-needed R&R, Lee could practically feel the collective sigh of relief that swept through his ship's corridors.

"Captain," Lieutenant Commander Sato had said as they docked, "the crew's earned this."

Lee nodded, watching his officers file off the bridge with their shoulders finally relaxing. "Make sure they get it, Noriko. Full rotation. Everyone gets dirt time."

The time at Kita had been exactly what his crew needed. Shore leave meant real food instead of synthesized rations, and beds in a private room all to yourself. For Lee himself, the luxury of uninterrupted sleep without the constant whir of the reactor or the ping of sensor alerts was priceless.

But even during the downtime, he'd known something big was brewing.

The intelligence they had gathered during those months of patrol work had been forwarded up the chain: detailed scans of Zodark fleet movements, defensive positions mapped to the meter, and supply routes, tracked and catalogued. The battles he'd fought, the ice asteroid base they'd overtaken and destroyed, all of it had helped pave the way for what was coming.

It was on the final day of R&R that the orders arrived, sealed and marked with the highest security classifications. Lee had stared at

the mission parameters in his quarters, a cup of real coffee growing
cold in his hand.

The Rass campaign.

He'd read the briefing twice before the full weight of it hit him.
Their reconnaissance work had provided crucial intelligence for what
would become one of the most ambitious joint operations the Republic
had ever attempted. The *Poseidon*, along with a massive Primord fleet
and Task Force Rass under Admiral Fran McKee's tactical command,
would spearhead the assault on the heavily fortified Zodark positions
orbiting the planet Rass.

"Sir?" Sato had knocked on his door that evening. "The crew's
asking questions about recall orders."

"Tell them to enjoy their last night planetside," Lee had said.
"Tomorrow, we'll brief everyone on our role in the coming Rass
campaign."

On their way to the staging area, the *Poseidon*'s crew had
thrown themselves into intensive training exercises. Lee walked the
corridors during the third day out, watching his people prepare.

In the electronic warfare section, Lieutenant Jacob Witkowski
ran his teams through constant drills on the latest jamming protocols
and countermeasures developed to aid their own efforts in overcoming
a recent improvement in Zodark jamming. "Again," Witkowski called
out to his technicians. "The Zodarks adapt fast. We need to be faster."

"Witkowski," Lee said, stopping by his station. "How we
looking?"

"Ready as we'll ever be, sir. The jamming packages should give
us an edge. For a while, anyway."

Lee nodded. The battle ahead would test every system aboard
their vessel. Their ability to disrupt Zodark communications and
targeting systems could mean the difference between victory and
catastrophe.

At the nav console, Lieutenant Reynolds plotted and replotted
their approach vectors. At the TAO station, Lieutenant Rhom studied
tactical formations until Lee ordered him to get some rest. The whole
ship hummed with nervous energy as Lee and Sato drilled the crew
hard until it was time to form up with the fleet and prepare to invade
their second star system and liberate one more planet from the clutches
of the Zodark Empire.

****

RNS *Poseidon*
Stargate 352-NHW

The approach to the stargate had been both magnificent and terrifying. The massive fleet of Primord vessels led the way through the stargate in precisely timed waves. Lee watched from the *Poseidon*'s bridge as group after group of alien warships disappeared into the shimmering portal.

"Wow. Look at the size of this fleet," Baldry whispered from his sensor station.

"Maintain comm discipline," Sato said.

Each departure was marked by the characteristic distortion of space-time that made Lee's stomach clench involuntarily. The waiting was the worst part, knowing that each passing minute meant the first wave of Primord forces would have to face the full fury of whatever defenses lay on the other side.

"Flash traffic from the *George Washington*," Rodriguez reported. "This is Admiral McKee. Task Force Rass, prepare for gate transit."

The *Poseidon* held position within a formation of sixteen Republic warships. They were among the first wave that would jump. Like their Primord allies, they were precisely spaced, ready for battle the moment they exited the other side if it came to it.

"All stations report ready," Sato said.

"Very well. Reynolds, take us in," Lee ordered.

The stargate activated ahead of them. Its center filled with that liquid shimmer that always reminded Lee uncomfortably that they were diving into dark, unknown space. The *George Washington* disappeared first, followed by the other ships in sequence.

"Our turn, sir," Reynolds announced.

"Take us through," directed Lee.

The *Poseidon* and the rest of the Republic Fleet shot from the gate like a war lance hurled across time, its hull shuddering as space snapped back into alignment. Instantly, upon entering the Rass system, the bridge erupted in motion.

"Sensor active," Baldry called as the *Poseidon*'s eyes and ears came online. "Multiple contacts—whoa, we jumped into one hell of a mess. It looks like the Zodarks were waiting for us. The Primords are heavily engaged."

Lee didn't need to hear more. The main viewscreen painted it in blood and fire. Dozens of capital ships danced through debris fields, plasma beams slashing across the void. Swarms of interceptors tangled like angry insects. A massive Primord dreadnought took a direct hit to its ventral flank, venting atmosphere and flame.

"Sir, we're receiving a message from the Primord fleet commander. All Republic warships are ordered to form a battleline and prepare to push through the enemy formation."

"Acknowledged. Confirm receipt of the order!" Lee snapped. "All hands to battle stations. Rhom, target nearest Zodark vessels engaging our Primord allies—frigates or heavy cruisers only. I want quick kills that'll make a difference, not slug matches with a battleship."

"Aye, sir! Bearing zero-eight-one, Zodark frigate peeling off from the main fight—trying to flank the *Ek*," Rhom called out. "I've got a firing solution with our port-side magrails locked."

"Fire!" Lee shouted without hesitation.

The *Poseidon*'s twin-barreled twenty-four-inch magrail turrets hurled fury at the unsuspecting target. The six slugs slashed through space, closing the gap between them in seconds. The Zodark frigate didn't have time to maneuver before the first round cratered its dorsal fin; the second hit its port-side reactor housing as the four remaining slugs sailed past harmlessly. The ship buckled as the explosive charge detonated deep within. A second later, it blew apart in a brilliant flash of light.

"Confirmed kill," Rhom said, grinning in satisfaction. "The frigate's gone."

"Good shooting, Rhom! Line us up on the next one. Reynolds, hold our current vector—give our guns a clean sweep." Lee ordered, his adrenaline pumping hard as the battle continued to unfold around them.

"Holding vector. Adjusting attitude—two degrees pitch up to compensate for turret elevation," replied Reynolds calmly, cool as a cucumber despite the fury around him.

Sato moved from console to console, coordinating actions with department heads as the ship brought its full spread of weapons to bear.

Her experienced voice cut through the organized chaos. "Sir, MacGregor confirms all reactor systems nominal—power is max one hundred percent. EW stations report sand-water countermeasures active and jamming on cycling burst pattern."

"Outstanding, XO! Let's keep it that way," Lee acknowledged.

"Captain!" Baldry shouted. "Zodark heavy cruiser, dead ahead. She's hammering that Primord cruiser. Bearing zero-seven-five mark niner."

"You heard him, Rhom. Get us a targeting solution on that cruiser and let's make 'em pay!" shouted Lee excitedly. He felt his blood going now as his ship continued to maul its way through enemy vessels around them.

"Magrails ready now. I've got Havoc-IIs in VLS pods one through sixteen ready in six seconds," Rhom called out their weapon status.

Lee nodded, then tapped the armrest of his chair. He watched as the targeting overlay synced. The enemy cruiser was an older class they had encountered often, bristling with laser turrets and plasma torpedo launchers. It was a tough ship in a head-on fight, but weak on ventral shielding.

"Reynolds, adjust trajectory to skim her belly," Lee ordered. "I want our VLS pods to have line of sight as you fire."

"Course adjusted," Reynolds confirmed.

"Firing Havocs!" Rhom shouted.

Sixteen missiles screamed from the *Poseidon*'s underside, the rocket motors igniting, the guided warheads increasing speed rapidly toward their target. The Zodark cruiser's defensive weapons lit up the space around them, Havocs exploding. It tried evasive maneuvers, but it was too late. Seven of the sixteen Havoc-IIs struck home—a pair obliterated several midship batteries, while the others shredded its bridge tower and the central spine of the ship.

"I count seven hits! Looks like four secondary explosions—main power's out. It's dead in space—disabled," Rhom said, his voice grim. "No sign of escape pods launching."

"It's done. Move on and get us another target," directed Lee, a sense of urgency in his voice. "We've got to keep working through these frigates and cruisers to keep 'em off our capital ships."

The *Poseidon* continued to surge ahead, pivoting its support from Republic to Primord ships caught in one cross fire or another. They unleashed barrage after barrage of magrail slugs into Zodark frigates and corvettes as they fought to keep the torpedo-wielding ships off the backs of the larger Republic and Primord capital ships. Like the torpedo ships of a bygone era, these smaller vessels could wreak havoc against battleships and star carriers if they weren't dealt with.

"Brace for impact!" Reynolds shouted, hands gripping the helm as the *Poseidon* twisted through the incoming storm.

Five plasma torpedoes had just completed their final phase shift—igniting into roiling balls of solar fury that Republic spacers called "death comets." Lee felt the deck shudder beneath his boots as the first streaked past the starboard bow, narrowly missing. Then came the second… third… fourth—

The fifth struck home.

The detonation rocked the *Poseidon* from stem to stern. Lights flickered. Alarms wailed. Lee's fingers dug into the armrest of his command chair as a cascade of sensor alerts flooded the damage control board.

"Report!" he barked.

"Torpedo hit forward section," Sato called, voice taut. "Decks seven and eight—section one—fires reported in both. No hull breach. I repeat, *no* hull breach."

Lee exhaled sharply. Close. Too damn close. The damage board pulsed yellow across multiple compartments in the ship's bow, but nothing red. That meant structure held—barely.

"Engineering is reporting a shock wave fracture," Sato added. "Support conduits near the lower and mid gun decks. Turret one just went offline. Magrail's down."

"Damn it," Lee muttered. "That's one of our primaries. How bad, and is the fire contained?"

Sato scanned her console, fingers tapping fast. "Damage Control Nine reports deck seven fire is under control. Deck eight… partial containment only. If it spreads, it'll reach section two within minutes. Still no breach, but we're skating the edge."

She turned to weapons. "Rhom, status on your crew?"

"Stand by," he said, already keyed into a short-range link with his gunnery station. His jaw clenched as he listened, nodding once before turning toward Lee.

"It's bad, sir. We've lost three spacers. Seven more are injured. The turret itself is intact—barrels and targeting are fine. But the magazine reload shaft's jammed. Engineering Synths are en route. ETA, three mikes. We'll know more when they get eyes on it."

Lee grimaced. Three dead. Seven wounded. All to keep the guns firing. There'd be time to mourn—but not now.

"Acknowledged, Rhom. We need that turret back online. We're not out of this yet."

"Already on it," Rhom said. "My spacers know what this means. They won't let you down."

Across the battlespace, the tide had turned.

Primord capital ships drove forward in disciplined wedges, their weapon batteries tearing through Zodark formations like tungsten through glass. The *George Washington*, battle-scarred and unrelenting, unleashed a punishing broadside from its main battery. A salvo of magrail slugs speared through the flank of a Zodark battleship. For a breathless moment, the enemy vessel remained whole—then it came apart like wet paper. Secondary explosions erupted along its hull, sending fire and wreckage cascading into the void. Lights flickered, then died, as its reactors imploded. The skeletal remains of the ship fragmented into tumbling debris, vanishing into the growing graveyard of wrecked hulls.

Victory hovered at the edge of reality, so close it throbbed in their teeth like static before a storm.

Then Baldry's voice cut through the bridge like a blade.

"New contacts—hold up. Correction, *three* incoming. Um, these aren't Zodarks, sir."

Lee snapped toward him. "What? Say again?"

"The new contacts—they aren't Zodarks, sir," Baldry said, eyes locked on his console. "Emissions signature's off the charts. Hull configuration don't match any of the known Zodark vessels in the Republic or Primord ship libraries."

Sato sensed his frustration with the absence of information and was already working to find them an answer. "I got it!" she announced triumphantly. "Sir, they're Orbots—battleships to be precise. It's the same hull configuration we saw during the Intus invasion." Her tone then dropped half an octave. "All three of them are vectoring straight for us. One-eight-zero mark three. Range: two hundred and thirty-two thousand klicks. Accelerating rapidly."

Lee felt a familiar crawl of dread settle at the base of his spine. "Confirm that, Sato." The bridge fell still. A dead, weighted silence as everyone seemed to wait for Sato's response.

"Confirmed, Commander. They're Orbots, and they're coming in hot."

The main screen flared as the optical arrays rendered the advancing giants in chilling clarity. The three obsidian monsters crept into view. At least six thousand meters in length and bristling with weapons. Their matte-black hulls devoured all light, allowing nothing to glint or reflect off them. There were no running lights along any section of the ship. No heat blooms. Just a silent, cold advance.

As the ship progressed forward, more details across its exterior became visible. They saw dozens upon dozens of plasma torpedo ports glowing faintly along its midsection. These were flanked by dozens of turret housings that lined their dorsal ridges. Unfurling along both flanks of the battleship like jagged wings was a pair of flight bays—one for launching torpedo bombers while the other dispensed fighters like meteors. Altairian intelligence reports confirmed long-held beliefs about the hundreds of fighters and bombers that could be launched by these cyborg merchants of death.

"Commander," Rodriguez whispered. "The Zodark battleline is breaking. They're pulling back. It looks like they are reforming behind the Orbots."

Lee stood frozen. His fingers gripped the edge of the console as if to anchor himself to reality. The Orbot ships continued forward— deliberate, unflinching. And they weren't angling for the fleet. They looked like they were coming for *them*.

"Sir…" Reynolds said, breath catching. "Their vector. They're on direct intercept with the *Poseidon*."

A cold dread settled over Lee's spine. *My God, they really are heading right for us…*

"Well, I didn't have a trio of charging Orbot battleships on my bingo card today, but I guess there's a first time for everything," Lee joked, unsure how else to respond to what was happening. "I guess we're famous. Of all the ships in the fleet, they've chosen us."

No one laughed at his joke. They watched in abject horror as the giant ships surged forward, closing like a blade. Then they saw it, dozens, then hundreds of small objects emerging from their flight decks. It was a swarm of automated fighters spilling into space like a horde of angry hornets, their engines glowing with baleful blue fire as they raced ahead of their motherships.

"Holy crap," Sato breathed. "That's… *hundreds* of fighters."

"Flash message from Admiral McKee," announced Rodriguez.

"Pipe it through to the ship," Lee ordered. He wanted the crew to hear whatever it was she was about to announce.

"Attention, all Republic vessels. This is Admiral McKee—prepare to close with the enemy. All ships…damn the torpedoes, ahead full speed…let's kill 'em all! McKee out!"

Lee's mouth curled into a feral grin as he laughed loudly, standing as he ordered, "You heard the admiral! Ahead full speed! Rhom, fire at will—all guns, lasers, and missiles. Let's kill 'em all!"

From the Authors

Brandon and I hope you've enjoyed this book. If you'd like to preorder book four of the Battles of the Republic series, *The Rass Campaign*, and continue this action-packed military sci-fi series, please visit Amazon.

If you would like to stay up to date on new releases and receive emails about any special pricing deals we may make available, please sign up for our email distribution list. Simply go to https://www.frontlinepublishinginc.com/ and sign up.

As a bonus, if you sign up for our mailing list, you will receive a dossier for the Rise of the Republic Series. It contains artwork of the ships we've written about, as well as their pertinent stats. It will really help make the series come to life for you as you continue reading.

As independent authors, reviews are very important to us and make a huge difference to other prospective readers. If you enjoyed this book, we humbly ask you to write up a positive review on Amazon and Goodreads. We sincerely appreciate each person that takes the time to write one.

We have really valued connecting with our readers via social media, especially on our Facebook page https://www.facebook.com/RosoneandWatson/. Sometimes we ask for help from our readers as we write future books—we love to draw upon all your different areas of expertise. We also have a group of beta readers who get to look at the books before they are officially published and help us fine-tune last-minute adjustments. If you would like to be a part of this team, please go to our author website, https://www.frontlinepublishinginc.com/, and send us a message through the "Contact" tab.

Abbreviation Key

AA	Anti-aircraft
AI	Artificial Intelligence
AO	Area of Operation
ASAP	As soon as possible
BDA	Battle Damage Assessment
BP	Blood Pressure
CAS	Close-Air Support
CHU	Containerized Housing Unit
CIC	Combat Information Center
CMO	Civil-Military Operation
COMSEC	Communications Security
CPR	Cardiopulmonary Resuscitation
CPT	Captain
DZ	Drop Zone
ECCM	Electronic Counter-Countermeasures
ECM	Electronic Countermeasures
EENT	End of Evening Nautical Twilight
EMCON	Emission Control
ETA	Estimated Time of Arrival
EWO	Electronic Warfare Officer
EVA	Extra-vehicular Activity
FOB	Forward Operating Base
FSB	Fire Support Base
IFF	Identification Friend or Foe
FAE	Fuel-Air Explosives
FLIR	Forward-Looking Infrared
FTL	Faster-than-light
HUD	Heads-up Display
JAG	Judge Advocate General's Corps
JATM	Joint Advanced Tactical Missile
KIA	Killed in Action
LIDAR	Light Detection and Ranging
LT	Lieutenant
LZ	Landing Zone
MRE	Meals Ready-to-Eat
OIC	Officer in Charge

OPFOR	Opposing Forces
QRF	Quick Reaction Force
R & D	Research and Development
REDCON	Readiness Condition
RNS	Republic Naval Ship
RON	Remain Over Night
RPG	Rocket-propelled Grenade
RTB	Return to Base
SAM	Surface-to-Air Missiles
SEAD	Suppression and Destruction of Enemy Air Defenses
SIGINT	Signals Intelligence
SW	Sand and Water
UV	Ultraviolet
VTOL	Vertical Takeoff and Landing
WFJ	Wideband Frequency Jamming
XO	Executive Officer

THE END

www.ingramcontent.com/pod-product-compliance
Lightning Source LLC
Chambersburg PA
CBHW071235300726
48975CB00002B/422